The Magnificer

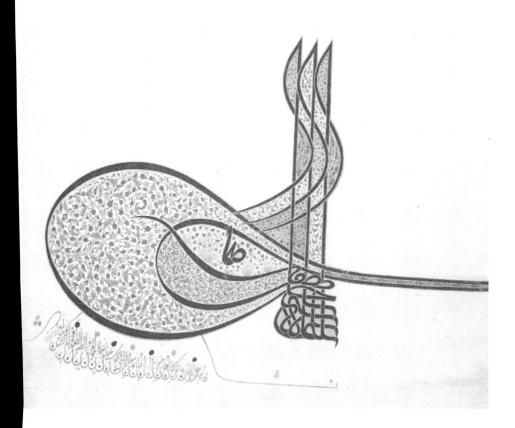

A saga in five parts based on historical characters from the Era OF Suleiman the Magnificent

Part II

IBRAHIM

An Ottoman For All Seasons

By

Alexander GarbolaS

MAGNÆ ES ET GETICI TIBI GRATIA PRONA TYRANI
SERVIT AT EX ALTO MAGNA RVINA VENIT.

ABRAHIMVS BASSA.

TE PROCERES ODERE DARESQVÆ ET REGIA CONIVX
HORVM NE PEREAS PRODITIONE CAVE.

5

TABLE OF CONTENTS

Introduction of the second volume series

Long introductions of novels are uncommon, but since this is historical novel based on real heroes, the author felt that few explanations may be appropriate.

This particular volume is freely based on the historical evidence related to the acts and days of Grand Vizier Ibrahim Pargali. Ibrahim Pargali was an intimate friend of Suleiman the Magnificent, rising from the lowest possible status of a slave to the highest posts in the Ottoman hierarchy becoming Grand Vizier, i.e. Prime Minister.

Writing novels based on the biographies of historical personalities is a difficult task, especially when they refer to a controversial personality which puzzled not only the notable posterior historians, but also several contemporary Christian and Muslims authors.

Ibrahim Pargali was unquestionably a brilliant diplomat, a capable statesman and a competent general, and the reasons that led to his execution by the Sultan are still baffling a portion of the public as his life became the subject of a history documentaries and an extremely popular in the East, Turkish TV series.

Contrary to what happens with famous people of long-past eras, his exact lineage is not known. What we know of his origin is that he was from Parga, a town that at the time was a Venetian colony; so, in principle he could be called a Venetian; however, Venice does not claim even a drop of his blood, because the Ottoman Empire was the greatest enemy of Venice at the time.

Parga is a small town that presently belongs to the Greek prefecture of Epirus, but it is close to the borders with Albania; so naturally both Greek and Albania have a right to claim Ibrahim's origin. Therefore, the author had to make a critical choice based on other facts, even though in modern times few Greeks live in Albania and even more Albanians reside in Greece.

Unquestionably, there have been many very capable Ottoman Grand Viziers from Albania; however, the author trusts Ibrahim was of Greek mentality as he carried into Constantinople three Olympian god bronze statues after the conquest of Budapest, as well as two bronze candle holders he dedicated to the cathedral of Agia Sophia, a historic temple intimately connected to the Greek nation and the Christian Orthodox religion. This is one of many similar choices the author had to make during the composition of this novel, trying to be as fair and accurate as possible in terms of lineage as in the Balkans breed still matters often leading to bloody wars and endless controversies.

Another puzzling fact about this distinguished Ottoman statesman is that during the early stages of his meteoric rise Ibrahim served as a "Hasodabashi" namely as a Chief Chamberlain, or Butler of the Sultan, a post traditionally covered at the time by a White Eunuch. One British historian claimed this is a strong indication Ibrahim was a eunuch too; however, if this was true, then it would make no sense for the Suleiman Khan to organize the most magnificent public marriage ceremony of a eunuch to his sister. It also would also dismiss other testimonies that Ibrahim had children and few less distinguished wives, possibly slaves. Therefore, the author had to discard or adopt various conflicting pieces of evidence in his novel.

Since the author believes that in historical novels evidence should not be discarded at will to glorify or degrade the heroes because it might shed the wrong light on other unfolding historic events, practically every solid evidence is incorporated in this novel, considering that exceptional personalities are per force more twisted than what common people might presume.

The present author, as explained in greater detail in the introduction of the first volume centered on the deeds of Selim I the Grim, tries hard to create a myth that encircles unquestionably fixed in time and space historical facts in a similar way as a string acts in the childish game "cat's cradle", knowing that drastically different shapes may appear using the same string and fingers depending on the skill of the player.

As the content of the future third and fourth volumes will indicate, the path that led to the atrocious crimes Suleiman committed later can be traced to similar crimes committed by his father Selim. Indeed the existing historic evidence suggests that Selim was the instigator of "peculiar" behavior that was later imitated by various Sultans almost till the end of the Osman dynasty, when a number of religious genocides were carried out for the "good" of the state.

To seek answers in the first volume the author had to travel back in time, when the hero's cruel but brilliant father, Selim the Grim, was the Sultan for eight short years. During this period narrated in the first volume, Selim had not only usurped the throne from his father Bayezid and executed his two older brothers and their children; but also two of his own children for rather obscure reasons. Similar appalling crimes occur occasionally also in modern times by so-called "disturbed personalities", as many mental disturbances are caused by childhood traumas and severe sexual aberrations. Therefore, if a biased author tries to bypass few real historic events, he may be left with several insolvable puzzles that have no convincing answers worthy of modern more sophisticated and uncompromising minds.

Fortunately, despite few isolated cases of modern world leaders, contemporary audiences and readers are more liberally oriented than in the Middle Ages and tend to adopt more scientific and refined approaches than simply the medieval assertion "It was Allah's will".

Another problematic personality that plays an important role in the present second volume is a female Ukrainian slave. The "official" narration of Suleiman's story, accepts the rumor that Hurrem was the daughter of a priest abducted by marauding Tatars, and carried to Constantinople as a virgin to be sold in a slave bazaar for the Sultan's harem. However, considering what happens to captive young women even in the "civilized" present era during "religious" or other violent wars, as the Yugoslavian crisis, the present Islamic revolt in the Middle East or WWII in the Ukraine and Germany, this is a highly unlikely scenario this suspicious author is not willing to accept even at gun point, because it would mean that humans in more than the last five centuries had been transformed from angels into raping murdering beasts.

On the contrary, it is much easier to presume that the largely dissolved or subtly transformed constitution of slavery that extends even today, leading women or young men into prostitution, worked equally efficiently in the Balkans during the Middle Ages as it presently does during several political and economic crises in this region.

Traces of our more violent past can be still discovered in the most unexpected places. For instance, a very common curse even among present era Greek Orthodox Christians in the Balkans is the despicable: "I'll f... your Virgin Mary". If such appalling concepts were so widely spread around in the Middle Ages that have reached modern times, imagine what chances had the virgin daughter of a Christian priest captured by pagan or Muslim Tatar raiders to reach Constantinople slave bazaars unmolested!

Modern nationalistic states tend to create perfect national heroes with impeccable characters to serve as idols for the ignorant masses. During this process many human faults are swept under the rug with the false notion that, if all these character "weaknesses" became widely known, the historical image would fail to perform as unifying national symbols as intended. For the present writer this may be understandable but not convincing enough to be accepted at face value. The author philosophically trusts that all world leaders are human beings as faulty as anyone else in a state of continuous evolution from inventive monkeys to benevolent divine entities operating supercomputers, spaceships, drones, or performing delicate open heart surgeries.

Therefore, the fact that someone manages to unite nations around him and perform uncommon deeds despite few character "faults" is a notable fact that makes his deeds even more remarkable historical phenomena. For instance, if we present Napoleon Bonaparte as a magnificent male specimen like the classic Apollo, Hermes or Hercules, we are distorting his image so much that if he was a foot taller, he may not have become who he was.

Napoleon was not the only great man with drawbacks. For instance, gossip says that Julius Caesar when he was young he was abducted by pirates and held hostage. When he was eventually released after the ransom was paid, he raised a naval squadron, captured the pirates and crucified them. As a measure of Caesar's lenience, on the cross he decided to "mercifully" cut their throats of his abductors to shorten their painful ordeal!

The notable historian claims he did that because when he was captured, he had promised the pirates he would return and crucify them, but obviously they didn't take him seriously enough to kill him, because he was young and young boys of superior breeding were highly praised in the courts of sovereigns as consorts.

Now several questions naturally rise. Was Caesar sexually assaulted by the pirates and how this possible event distorts his saga? Is it possible that this event may have created an emotional trauma he later affected his behavior towards every barbarian he captured in Gaul?

I will not trouble the reader with more such historic cases at this stage, as there are many such cases among the heroes within the pages of the book. Therefore, at this point the author will simply point out that many times during a war extremely violent behaviors are encountered and there has to be a reason for it deeply imbedded in human nature. For this reason the author has adopted the strategy of accepting morally compromising scenarios for most of his heroes, so no one can claim that he is idealizing the ruling class and demoting the proletariat!

Finally, it may sound like a truism, but it is a well-known historical fact that in every royal or imperial family, secrecy is forcefully enforced, and there is no reason for secrecy, if there are no secrets. On the contrary, it has become a popular motto that absolute power corrupts absolutely!

A summary of historical facts on the main heroes of the second book

1. **Selim I the Grim:** He was the son of Bayezid II and Aisha Hatun. He was born in Amasya in 1470 and he reigned from 1512 to 1520 until he died. With the help of the Janissary Corps he forced his father to abdicate because he was too benevolent, religious and peaceful. Sultan Bayezid favored as his heir his older son Ahmet, but this son lost favor with the Ottoman clergy, when he followed the heretic sect of Sufism. Immediately after the "coronation" of Sultan Selim I in 1511, on his way to Edirne his deposed father died suddenly, possibly by poisoning. Thereafter, Selim's older brothers Ahmet and Korkut were strangled together with their six children on his orders. Next Selim executed also three of his sons, keeping alive only Suleiman and his six daughters, Hatidge Sultan, Fatma Sultan, Beyhan Sultan, Shah Sultan, Hafsa Sultan, and Hâfize Sultan from two of his wives Ayşe Hatun I and Ayşe Hafsa Hatun II.

Selim was a tall and strongly built male. He was a valiant warrior, expert rider and swordsman, as well as capable archer and wrestler. He was also educated with intense interest in sciences, fine arts, and religion. When he was young, he was posted as governor of the Pontus region in the city of Trabzon. There he became known for his successful raids on horseback against the Christian Georgia.

He had simple manners, didn't seek luxury and ate in wooden plates. As a result of his diplomatic skills he managed to unite the Turcoman and Tatar tribes under his banner. Then he achieved a decisive victory against the Shah Ismail of Persia in the battle of Chaldiran in 1514, crushing the superior Persian heavy cavalry with his artillery. The victory was so extensive they say Shah Ismail never smiled again.

Subsequently, Selim attacked the second major military power in Middle East, the Mamelukes of Egypt winning several battles, conquering within a year all major cities Aleppo, Damascus, Jerusalem and Gaza. The next year 1517 he crossed the Sinai Desert in thirteen days, and crushed the Mamelukes at Giza in front of the gates of Cairo, putting an end to the Mameluke dynasties that dominated the Middle East since the Crusades.

As a result of the Egyptian conquest, Selim became the master of Mecca and Medina, extending his empire all the way to the Yemen border. This way he became the "Protector of Islam", and was awarded the religious title of "Caliph" in Constantinople by the Serif of Mecca, carrying inside Topkapi the holy relics of the Prophet where they still lie. After these conquests the entire trade of silk and spices passed in the hands of the Ottoman Empire, forcing Spain and Portugal to seek new trade routes to the Far East around the Cape of Good Hope and towards America. Gradually the occupation of all major Palestine harbors also led to the decline of Venice, Genoa, Pisa, and Florence as world powers.

Selim died suddenly in 1520 probably because of a rare skin cancer or an anthrax infection developed by his prolonged contact with the saddle. At the time he was preparing a new expedition in the West probably against Belgrade. When Selim became Sultan, the Ottoman Empire occupied an area of 2.4 million square kilometers, and when he died eight years later more than 6.0 km^2. Selim's tomb is in Istanbul inside the courtyard of his mosque built by his son Suleiman on the Fifth Hill of the New Rome, Constantinople.

2. Ayşe Hafsa Hatun: She was Suleiman's mother and favorite legal wife of Selim. She was probably a daughter of the Tatar Khan Mengli Giray of Crimea, but few historians claim she was of Greek origin as Crimea was an ancient Greek colony! Besides Suleiman, she produced three daughters, Hatidge Sultan, Fatma Sultan, and Hafsa Sultan. She had great influence on her son and she was probably the one who supplied Suleiman with concubines of her choice.

Eventually she supported Ibrahim Pasha in his quest, but after her early demise, Suleiman gradually fell entirely under the influence of Hurrem Sultan who gradually managed to create conflicts between Suleiman and his intimate friend Ibrahim. She finally died in 1534, 55 years old from an unknown cause. Today her tomb lies ruined by an earthquake in the courtyard of Sultan Selim's mosque next to his tomb. There are plans for a modern restoration of her tomb.

3. Suleiman the Magnificent: He was born in Trabzon in 1494, son of Selim the Grim and Ayşe Hafsa Hatun. He became the tenth Ottoman Sultan, ten being the holy number for Muslims.

Suleiman continued his father's conquests, firstly in the West by conquering Belgrade, occupying the strategic island of Rhodes, and finally entering Budapest twice, and unsuccessfully besieging Vienna. Later in the East, he recaptured the Persian capital of Tabriz as his father had done, and finally Baghdad and Basra. Using the Ottoman fleet and supporting the Barbary corsairs, he effectively occupied the entire northern Africa coast all the way from Egypt and the Sudan to Morocco. He also conquered Yemen, imported coffee into Europe and through Basra extended the Ottoman commerce all the way to India; but there the Ottoman fleet suffered several naval defeats in the hands of the Portuguese.

Another major setback was the unsuccessful Ottoman attempt to wrestle Malta from the Knights of Saint John Suleiman had defeated previously in Rhodes. Despite these failures during the last stages of his reign, the Ottoman Empire achieved its maximum military power in both land and sea, threatening Western Europe either by pirate raids all the way to the Spanish coast, or by major invasions into Austria, leading immense armies of more than 200000 warriors. As a result of his expeditions he succeeded in doubling the empire he inherited from his father who had also doubled his inheritance.

Besides his military conquests, Suleiman had major contributions as a lawmaker and as a prolific builder. He was very fortunate during his reign to be served by great generals and brilliant statesmen, like Ibrahim, and Sokollu Pasha, effective admirals, like Hayrettin Barbarossa, Piyale Pasha, Turgut Reis and Piri Reis, efficient administrators and tax collectors like Rüstem Pasha, and talented architects like Mimar Sinan.

Physically he was tall and slim, with a long neck and an aquiline nose. According to testimonies he was suffering from kidney disease and gout, and especially during the last years of his life, his overall state of health was weak.

His disposition was often effected by his environment, and especially by strong personalities as Ibrahim Pasha, Hurrem Sultan and Rüstem Pasha. He was religious and somewhat superstitious. He committed war crimes, executing enemy prisoners, but this kind of behavior was not uncommon during his era. He also executed many of his able and devoted associates like Ibrahim Pasha, Piri Reis, Kara Ahmet Pasha, and two of his own children, Mustafa and Bayezid because of suspicions of conspiracy.

Suleiman's death occurred during the siege of the city of Szigetvar in Hungary on 7/9/1566 possibly of a major stroke, and this news were received with great joy in the rest of the non-Muslim European Continent from the Atlantic Ocean to the Caucuses.

His tomb is in the courtyard of his mosque, Suleimaniye, on the Third Hill in Istanbul.

4. Pargali Ibrahim Pasha: He was born in 1494 and probably he was a son of a Greek fisherman from Parga, but others claim he was Albanian. For his early years nothing is certain as few claim he was a slave of a rich widow who gave him to the then Prince and heir Suleiman as a present. Others claim he was a member of the Janissary Corps, serving in Topkapi under Sultan Selim I after successfully concluding several years of education in the Seraglio School.

Initially during the reign of Sultan Selim he became chief of the falconers, and then, when Suleiman became Sultan, he served as Hasodabashi (Chambermaid) of the Sultan. Because of his numerous talents, extending from string instrument player to diplomacy and military commanding, he was quickly promoted to Pasha (General), Beylerbey (Governor) of Rumelia, Grand Vizier (Prime Minister) and Serasker (Field Marshal) of the Ottoman armies.

According to the prevailing historical evidence, he became the husband of Suleiman's sister, Hatice (Hatidge) Sultan; but there are other versions of his biography claiming he had three wives and three children. Few notable historians even claim he was a eunuch as traditionally the post of Hasodabashi was given only to White Eunuchs. Although it is very difficult to prove conclusively what he really was, many historians claim his friendship with Suleiman had also erotic dimensions, as they were practically inseparable, eating together and sleeping in adjacent rooms of the Seraglio, or in the same tent during the numerous military expeditions, facts that created considerable gossip at the time.

As a Grand Vizier, Ibrahim had important contributions in several military successes, as in the Battle of Mohacs, the Conquest of Budapest, Tabriz, and Baghdad. Despite his high position in the Ottoman hierarchy, Ibrahim was considered as an atheist by both Muslims and Christians or even worshiper of the Olympian Gods, a rather dubious claim. Nevertheless, they all agreed he was well-educated and extensively cultured; he also spoke many languages and laid the foundations of the Ottoman diplomacy by establishing the Sublime Gate, i.e. an organized ministry corresponding to an Ottoman Foreign Office. Supposedly he also transformed the Seraglio School as the first state university for competent public officials.

His sudden and enigmatic execution was most probably the result of a conspiracy, since he favored the extremely popular Prince Mustafa as Suleiman's heir, coming into conflict with Suleiman's favorite Hurrem Sultan who naturally favored one of her sons as heir of the throne. It occurred inside the Sultan's apartment on 15/3/1536 under mysterious circumstances.

Today there is a mosque on the shores of the Golden Horn on Ibrahim's name, but it is a newer construction as the old one was burned to the ground many decades ago.

5. Haseki Hurrem or Roxelana (Russian): She was born between 1502 and 1504 and died on April 15, 1558. She was the favorite wife of Suleiman the Magnificent, and mother of five sons known as Sehzade Mohamed, Sehzade Abdullah, Sehzade Selim, Sehzade Bayezid, and Sehzade Gihangir, and one daughter, Mihrimah Sultan. Three of her sons, Abdullah, Mohamed and Gihangir died prematurely of sicknesses, while Bayezid was executed by his father for treasonable behavior. She was a slave from Ukraine, but Suleiman early on became infatuated by her personality and charm and wrote for her many erotic poems in Persian.

6. Mahidevran Sultan: She was Suleiman's first legal wife (Kadin). There are many conflicting stories about her which is not surprising since there are not many details for any Sultan's consorts in the annals of Ottoman history. She is supposedly a Circassian or an Albanian slave, or possibly the daughter of a Tatar Princess wife of a Circassian Prince. She was supposedly married to Suleiman in Constantinople in January 5, 1512. If this date and ceremony are true, then Mahidevran could not be just a concubine slave, but had to have noble ancestors, as marriage of a slave to a Sultan was inconceivable. This opinion is supported by the fact Suleiman's father was also married to at least one Tatar Princess, and Tatars remained trusty allies of Suleiman throughout his reign, and by Mahidevran's proud and rebellious acts unfit for a slave.

Mahidevran was supposedly born in 1498. She bore her husband three children Sehzade Mustafa in 1515, Sehzade Ahmet in 1517 and Raziye Sultana in 1524. In 1521 two sons of Suleiman, Abdullah and Ahmet, died, and Mustafa became the oldest surviving heir.

7. Mimar Sinan: He was born in 1491 in the town of Ağırnas in Cappadocia and became the greatest architect not only of the Ottoman Empire but possibly of the entire world in terms of number of building projects. Originally he was a Christian, but was recruited in the Janissary Corps, quite possibly taking part in the sieges of Belgrade, Rhodes, Baghdad and Vienna as numerous others.

During his service in the Janissary Corps he probably impressed the Sultan with his bridge building ability and prompt delivery, which made him Chief Architect of the Empire. Sinan eventually served four Sultans, namely Selim I, Suleiman, Selim II and Murat III, completing or repairing 477 buildings among which 159 mosques, 74 schools, 38 palaces, 56 public baths and 31 Caravanserais and numerous bridges considered the most important constructions of the Ottoman Empire of that era.

From all these buildings 204 still exist among which 85 are inside Constantinople. His most important works are the mosques of Sultan Suleiman, Sehzade, Mihrimah Sultan, Hurrem Sultan, Rüstem Pasha, Sokollu Pasha, Nurbanu Sultan and finally Selim Sultan in Edirne which he considered as his masterpiece. He worked hard until 1588 when he died 97 years old from natural causes. He was buried in the courtyard of Suleiman's Mosque in Istanbul; nevertheless his work was continued by his assistants and students who built the Blue Mosque and probably the Taj Mahal too.

If a single personality can be considered today as responsible for the Magnificent Era that lasted for almost one hundred years, Mimar Sinan is the man who lived for 99 years and participated in almost every victorious military campaign of Sultan Selim and Suleiman.

Secondary nameless characters

1. Janissary Aga: The military commander of the Janissary Corps, an elite force acting on land and sea comparable to the US Marines, but with even more civil rights and duties. During the Magnificent Era members of this corps were ex-Christians mainly from the Balkans and Asia Minor who had been converted to Islam at an early age either willingly or by force. For the selection of a Janissary very strict rules were applied that allowed only gifted individuals to join.

Later on after several centuries, Muslims, mainly Turks, were allowed to join the Janissaries; but this measure quickly deteriorated the Corps to a state of civil servants, protesting more for special privileges rather than fighting as elite soldiers ready to die for their Sultan and faith.

During the nineteenth century the Janissaries became a menace, refusing to fight against the enemies, preferring instead to exert political pressures during the selection of the Grand Viziers and the Sultans. The Corps was finally dissolved with extreme cruelty by Sultan Mahmud the Second during the Greek Revolution killing many thousands by artillery shots. Up to final stage, the

Janissaries had revolted innumerous times leading to the execution of two reigning Sultans, Osman II and Selim III and many Grand Viziers and state officials.

2. Kapi Aga (Chief of the White Eunuchs): A Circassian white slave comparable to the Lord Chamberlain of the British Court in charge of the White Eunuchs Corps that served exclusively the Sultan inside the Topkapi Seraglio.

3. Kislar Aga (Chief of the Black Eunuchs): A Nubian eunuch slave in charge of the Black Eunuch Corps responsible for keeping order among the concubines in the Sultan's Harem.

4. Bostanjibashi (Head of the Mute Executioners): One of the main aides of the Sultan in charge of the secret execution service of the Sultan responsible for clandestine murders. This service was comprised by mutes who also served as gardeners of the Seraglio and normally executed their distinguished victims by strangulation using silk ropes.

5. Hasodabashi (Chief of the Imperial Valets): Another important aid of the Sultan in charge of his personal service. This page was normally a White Eunuch and among his duties were the organization of the Sultan's daily and night activities in close cooperation with the Chief Black Eunuch (Kislar Aga). In the case of Suleiman, Ibrahim despite becoming the husband of the Sultan's sister, he served also as his Hasodabashi for many years and spent innumerable nights in an adjacent room, a fact that caused many negative comments in the Ottoman court.

Dates of major historic events described in book 2

1494 Birth of Ibrahim Pasha in Parga, Rumelia
1494 Birth of Sultan Suleiman in Trabzon, Anatolia
1497 Birth of Gülfem Hatun
1500 Birth of Mahidevran Sultan
1512 Sultan Bayezid II abdicates from the Ottoman throne
1512 Selim becomes Sultan
1512 Bayezid II dies in Chorlou, Thrace
1512 Birth of Sehzade Murat, first son of Suleiman
1514 Battle of Chaldiran, Armenia
1514 Conquest of Tabriz by Sultan Selim
1515 Birth of Sehzade Mustafa son of Mahidevran Sultan
1517 Birth of Ahmet second son of Mahidevran Sultan
1520 Death of Sultan Selim I, father of Sultan Suleiman
1521 Death of Sehzade Murat, son of Gülfem Hatun
1521 Birth of Sehzade Mehmet son of Hurrem
1521 Death of Ahmet son of Mahidevran
1521 Conquest of Belgrade
1522 Birth of Mihrimah Sultan daughter of Hurrem Sultan
1522 Conquest of Rhodes
1523 Ibrahim Pasha becomes Grand Vizier
1523 Birth of Abdullah second son of Hurrem Sultan
1523 Marriage of Ibrahim and Hatidge Sultan sister of Suleiman
1524 Ibrahim Pasha travels to Egypt
1524 Birth of Selim third son of Hurrem Sultan
1525 Repression of a Janissary riot
1525 Birthday of Raziye Sultan daughter of Mahidevran Sultan

Book 2
Ibrahim

"Ask an infant with its eyes still closed and trust its words.
There are no other worlds or lives!
Everything I know is just my own experiences.
You are the one who is hallucinating!"
(Rumi)

Chapter 6
In the Gate of Felicity

'Become melting snow and wash yourself off yourself'
(Rumi)

When a man dies, no matter how powerful he has been alive, only his life comes to an end and no one else's. For all the other living souls surrounding him, life continues as if nothing much has happened. Then, after his demise, a most remarkable phenomenon occurs as the vital beats of everyone else around him accelerate in the same way as when an old, hollow tree falls and crashes on the ground and many young shoots rooting in his shadow start to grow with renewed vigor fed by the sun rays that can now reach their leaves.

Death creates an unsustainable vacuum and people around the deceased rush to fill the void, share his power and divide his fortune. The more powerful is a man the more people will try to share the power he has left behind.

The transfer of Selim's absolute authority commenced in the Ottoman Empire the very next day of his death, as besides his son Sultan Suleiman, his mother Valide Sultan Hafsa took a large portion of the ability to affect the lives of her subjects. From then on and as long her son or she were alive, she would exert absolute authority inside the Harem.

As a good housekeeper who moves to a new home, she started her era with a general housecleaning. Each of Selim's concubines who wished to be turned free, the new Sultan would let her go, providing a handsome pension on her behalf. On the other hand, if a concubine wished to get married instead, Hafsa would do her best to find an appropriate husband of high rank at the earliest opportunity. There were many noble statesmen who would be more than happy to marry a Sultan's concubine, because they were not just attractive, but most of all they were educated and able to realize the fantasies of every Ottoman to feel like a Sultan.

Finally, every concubine who was happy residing in the Eski Saray and did not wish to take the risk of a free life, she had to move to inferior rooms to make space for the newcomers the new Sultan would eventually acquire for his pleasure.

Hafsa had many bold dreams for her son, and she would do her best so that Suleiman would gradually stop sleeping in the same room with his favorite slave Ibrahim. The escapades of an immature Prince Heir should not be continued by a mighty Sultan.

To accomplish this task, every young woman around him should continuously attract the Sultan's eyes and preoccupy his mind with her affluent charms and erotic performance. Thus, from the next morning of Selim's funeral, a new wing adjacent to the Sultan's apartments was commissioned for his wives and concubines. If a mother did not understand the needs of her son, no one else could. For the time being, and until the new wing was completed, any new residents of the imperial harem that arrived as presents for the new Sultan from all the corners of the Empire would occupy the vacated rooms of the Eski Saray.

Every Pasha, Beylerbey, or state official who wished to advance in the new hierarchy had to pay handsomely to gain the favor of the new Sultan, and offering expensive presents meant he was confident enough to invest handsomely in his own future. Many of these women were not just captured slaves; they were daughters of common men who did not hesitate to send their most beautiful offspring to find happiness inside the Harem's impenetrable walls.

The opportunity was truly unique and a young girl could never again in her life get the chance to meet such a gifted young man in his prime like Suleiman Khan, when she was still an untouchable flower bud. Every true Ottoman considered the highest honor, if a daughter of his spent a single night with the Sultan, and if she was lucky enough to exploit his seed, then it would be best for everyone involved in this transaction.

Valide Sultan had the final word on every matter concerning the Sultan's harem. She decided which would be the occupant of every room in the Eski Saray, and what would be her duties. The best rooms were the ones that faced the Sea of Marmara with a southern orientation. They not only had the best view and the sun rays to stay warm during the winter months, but were also blessed by the sea breeze remaining cool during the summer. All the rest were dark and humid, a natural breeding ground for deadly illnesses.

The concubines' order in the hierarchy was directly related to their merits. Their ability to offer something special to the Sultan at night was the prime concern; but also their talents in dancing, playing music, needlework or simply remaining joyful were seriously considered. The origin of all this information was the Kislar Aga who knew everything there was to know inside the Harem that concerned an odalisque. The Black Eunuchs were his spies and he had many that gave him full reports of all occurrences; but, his ears was open for every gossip he considered as relevant for keeping order in this institution. In this way there were very seldom serious complains, as every good deed was rewarded handsomely and every disorder punished severely on the spot on his exclusive command.

The sacred mission of the Harem was to keep the Sultan happy and relaxed, so that his spirit was always elevated and equal to the monumental tasks at hand; thus, every problem related to the Harem had to be resolved before it reached the attention of the Sultan.

Another notable post in the Harem hierarchy was the Hasodabashi occupied by a Greek slave from Parga, Ibrahim. There were many rumors about him and his close relationship with the Sultan; but the rumors had to be cheap slender, as all the Hasodabashi were eunuchs, trustworthy slaves in a harem full of women eager to bear the Sultan's children.

****

When the Kislar Aga led the Russian maiden to her new room that day, a widespread murmur of complaints was heard. The girl was a true greenhorn and had never produced any moments of pleasure to the Sultan. It was common knowledge inside the Seraglio Suleiman as a Prince had not responded at all to her charms. There was even a White Eunuch who claimed that the same night Suleiman had preferred the company of a young man than cut her rosebud. Fortunately for him no one knew who he was, because spreading false rumors against Allah's Shadow was treasonous and a capital crime. It did not really matter if this rumor was the truth or not. What was uncontestable was that she had never proved her worth, while there were few other harem residents who even had given him a son and deserved a better apartment. It was sheer discrimination and gross injustice!

In the past under Selim Khan, when a newcomer arrived in the Harem, she had to stay with many other women in the same room until the Sultan noticed her in his weekly visits and asked for her services. This was considered as an act of "rendering justice", and it could often change in one night the harem status of an odalisque.

If this preference continued for a number of nights, she was considered especially gifted and acquired the lucrative title of "Ikbal" (Favorite). After this memorable occasion she had earned the right to have a room with a sea-view for as long as she could keep his undivided attention or became pregnant. It was now clear to anyone who believed in meritocracy that the special treatment of the Russian by the Kislar Aga had broken a fundamental Harem rule, and she should return immediately to the residence of the lowest rank of concubines.

However, despite the deafening noise from all the complaining odalisques, it did not require nothing more than a stern look of the Sultana the Kadin of Selim to restore order and stop the murmur. Everyone knew that from the moment Hafsa expressed plainly her views any further complain would be treated harshly. There were many possible punishments in the Harem starting from simple drudgery, as cleaning the toilet floor, to more severe, as the beating of her soles with a hard stick, or the ultimate penalty for severe cases involving definite proof of adultery, namely drowning in the Bosporus Straights inside a canvas sack.

This time the murmur in front of the Sultana stopped, but behind her back the gossip kept on growing, waiting for a new opportunity to explode reaching new heights.

****

Early this morning, Hafsa had met with the Kislar Aga to give him her last instructions for the coming night and then called the Russian for a last moment's tutoring. This night was very crucial for Hafsa's plans and no detail should be left unattended. Good luck was useful to a cause but not always enough. She knew her son better than anyone else, and he seemed very depressed coming back from Selim's funeral. In his veins run both the blood of the father the devil, and the grandfather the saint, and during the oncoming period the Ottoman Empire needed both.

For the next few months a religious war in the Christian West was the only feasible approach that could keep the ferocious Janissary corps content. Their appetite for new conquests, looting, and ravaging was an asset the Sultan could always rely upon, and going to Belgrade was a path more rewarding for marauding soldiers than getting drunk with "raki" in the Galata taverns; but Janissaries needed a competent leadership they could trust. The Viziers Piri and Ahmet Pasha were quite trustworthy under Selim, but it was still an open question how these powerful officials would behave under his younger, untested son. In her mind Suleiman had to become more of a man first before he could become a trusty military leader.

She had considerable experience with the harem ways to know well that the best way to resurrect a man of any age and give him back the illusive spirit of a conqueror was to send a pretty virgin to his bedroom. This was not a trivial task for the common man with limited income, but it was an easy assignment for a Valide Sultana, if only she could whet his appetite once. The only true problem Hafsa faced in this case was Ibrahim who was the most frequent companion of her son each night since the day they arrived in Constantinople.

Normally, there was always at least one eunuch present in the bedroom

26

of the Sultan every night attending his master for security, if for some reason he woke up and had an urgent need; but, since Suleiman's harem had come back from Edirne, Ibrahim had become the "Hasodabashi", I.e. the Sultan's bedroom keeper, expulsing every other eunuch page. It was an unacceptable break of a Sultan's Selamlik tradition and a source of constant gossip. Why should the new Sultan change his father's traditions the very first night after his father's death?

She had to find a way to keep Ibrahim preoccupied this night, and there was only one reasonable way to achieve it. She looked at her slaves surrounding her. One of them, a girl or a boy should become the bait, but she had to be careful to make the correct choice. Perhaps, the only one that could properly resolve this dilemma was the Kapi Aga who had supervised the training of Ibrahim; thus, she summoned him at once.

Unfortunately, the only reliable information he was able to provide her was that Ibrahim during his training had several intimate experiences with eunuchs in the School following Sultan Selim's instructions; but, his reactions to women had never being fully tested. Nevertheless, her own impressions from the meeting between Ibrahim and the Russian maiden had been favorable, but not conclusive. Since the only companionship Ibrahim sought was her son the Sultan, it was quite risky to apply the tender woman's touch; but, under the circumstances, it was the only available option, as the presence of the male Nubian slave had not triggered any noticeable reactions, but simply a brief comment that might well be simply a polite expression of courtesy. The Kislar Aga was unquestionably an attractive male specimen, but his skin was black, and Nubian slaves were still an expensive rarity in the slave markets.

Selim Khan while looting the Mameluke palace had not failed to bring to the Eternal City everything he considered valuable. His main goal was to appear at least as civilized as his enemies; but still the conservative Muslim aristocracy had not adopted his estimations of what was valuable and what not. In the slave bazaars only a blind man would fail to notice the differences between the two races, and the Muftis were not blind. The resemblance of any black man with the Devil was apparent; so only few very bold customers bought few of the black concubines for sale with the hope that the Ottoman blood would eventually prevail if given half a chance.

She was a woman and she was much more practical and down to earth. Selim had already brought a Nubian slave in the Harem and the Eski Saray was the ideal surroundings to test any female specimen from East and West, North or South on equal footing.

******

Among the many goods provided to all the inhabitants of the Seraglio during Selim's reign, was the great variety of available pleasures; but, this was not an exclusivity of the Imperial Court. The entire Constantinople was nothing less than an earthly paradise where every man could find what he was looking for.

For a pious Ottoman it did not make much sense to wait until he was dead to enjoy everything Allah's Paradise could offer. The pleasures of the Second Life had always been in this ancient city a subject of debate and the causes for well-founded doubts. They were something the Mufti and Ulema promised in the Sunni and Shiite mosques, or the Christian and Jewish Priests mentioned in the church; but, reasonable doubts were expressed by every experienced man who felt he should trust more tangible evidence than just elusive religious promises.

No man in the sophisticated Orient had any objections to go to a mosque and pray five times a day or even more, if there was a solemn promise this habit would be enough to secure him the promised pleasures of heavenly Paradise. However, very few had the firm conviction or the extreme foolishness to deny the earthly pleasures offered in the streets of Galata by Christian and Jewish whores or infidel dancing boys and girls for something so remote and untouchable. The few puritans who had trusted such teachings were not residing in the Seven Hill City any more. They had moved long time ago to the solitary monasteries of Syria, Cappadocia, Sinai, or Mount Athos.

Besides tea, wine, food, hash, or opium, there were also other temptations that made life worth living in the Eternal City. They were the decadent ones who set the flesh free from the control of the mind. However, the pious believers had to be patient and wait for the first night hours to enjoy them until sunrise, so that the youth and the ordinary women remained as pure and devoted to chastity as possible, locked behind ironclad doors and railed windows. These were the pleasures enjoyed by every citizen who didn't have to wake up early in the morning to go to work. They were mostly sailors, travelers, rich landlords, slave traders, and accomplished merchants, and the Galata district across the Golden Horn from Constantinople was the proper place to explore pleasures beyond the strict limits of the ordinary.

Unusual pleasures were actually the only activity on which all Muslim, Christian and Jewish opinions were in completely accordance. It was as if the continuous coexistence had infected all citizens by the incurable native disease of the satyrs and maenads who used to live on these Thracian hills in the Bacchus era long time ago. Thus, in the Galata District the teachings of Moses, Jesus and Mohamed on immortality seemed to be in limbo, as everyone enjoyed his temporary mortal existence as a true Ottoman, trying to follow closely the example of their mighty Emperor Selim Khan. He may now be dead, but his death had allowed all sorts of rumors to leak from the confines of the Marble Kiosk.

****

As the last call of the Muezzin was heard coming from the Bayezid Mosque, the Valide Sultan realized how much tension this historic day had created. It was not just the ceremonial burrier of her husband that had awakened many happy memories of days past that would never come back again. It was much more her worries about the future.

It was definitely not Ibrahim's fault, but the Suleiman's who had advanced in the ceremonial parade his favorite slave so close to him. Not too many people knew Ibrahim's face, but she most certainly did. He was the magnificently dressed slave who led the Sultan's magnificent horse all the way to the Eyup Cemetery. If this was Suleiman's way to degrade his slave or elevate Ibrahim's status she could not say, but for her it was enough of a shock to see the slave so close to her son. There was not much she could do on this matter, since this gesture could be explained in so many ways. Was it possible Ibrahim was destined to take care of the Sultan's mares instead of his harem? That would be really a shock for Ibrahim.

Just before going to sleep the Kislar Aga knocked on her door to ask if she had any last moment commands to relay at the end of the day. She had none and said so, but the Nubian slave seemed reluctant to leave her in peace.

"Are you sure?" he inquired. "Your Majesty seems more tense than usual," he added, questioning her command to depart.

Under other circumstances she wouldn't think twice to chastise him, but this was indeed a very strenuous day since daybreak.

"What do you suggest I should do?" she snapped back expecting the worst.

"If I were you, I would give me a thoroughly clear order to carry out," he boldly suggested.

"What kind of order would you like to hear?" she asked ready to explode in case he volunteered for the errand.

She actually wouldn't mind to feel the hands of an attractive young man like Ibrahim all over her that very night. It would be the proper punishment for Selim's spirit. However, the Kislar Aga promptly proved he was one step ahead of her.

"I have the perfect girl for this task. I bet my head you will be immensely pleased with her dexterity. She used to be the Mameluke Sultan's Bash Hanum favorite. She is indeed a jewel made to please the most sensitive and cultured women of Egypt."

The devious eunuch had touched a sensitive spot. How could she ever deny this girl services? Wasn't she insensitive and uncultured?

"Besides her soft hands, she also has the most seductive body in the harem."

"Is she black?" Hafsa noticed very suspicious of a possible unjustified promotion.

"She is of mixed blood," the Kislar Aga replied with the kind of embarrassed smile a slave in difficult position would display.

"Is she white?" the Valide Sultan asked.

"No! She is as black as ebony," the Kislar Aga finally admitted.

"Is that what you call mixed blood?"

"Yes! She is half Nubian half Abyssinian, the best breed for a slave, feverish passion with absolute obedience. She will bring the smile back on your lips. I promise!"

****

It was easy to see why Aslan was so impressed by this girl. She was ebony black and she was made to be adored. Allah had made her to satisfy every sinful male's infatuation.

Now she couldn't resist a question. Had Selim ever asked for her services? The Kislar Aga denied any knowledge with a node of his head, but she was sure he was lying. He had selected her in Cairo, and traveled her all the way to Constantinople.

"You should never try to lie to me about my dead husband. He is dead and I'm alive."

She didn't have to say anything more. The Kislar Aga lowered his head to show his respect for her intelligence and retreated towards the door.

"What should I do with her?" she asked as he opened the door.

"You are the Valide Sultan, so nothing is required for you do. She will do everything that needs to be done."

Hafsa had to admit the black maiden was up to the task, as none of her courtiers had removed so quickly her intricate dress and all her jewels. Facing the next obstacle of removing her corsage and the rest of her undergarments, she didn't fail to untie the strings as fast as if she was a Venetian sailor expert on knots, while Hafsa had nothing to do but admire her dexterity. She needed to relax for a while and empty her mind of all these worries that kept chasing her daily.

The burden of managing the Harem seemed superfluous compared to the importance of keeping her son focus on his mission in life. Suddenly he seemed overwhelmed by the great effort of becoming a Sultana. If she was suffering from a similar cause she couldn't say. She only needed to rest; so she lay naked on her bed to collect her last traces of energy.

The black slave seeing her milky-white flesh at such a state of weakness changed her submissive expression to that of infinite lust, licking her lips suggestively. It was such a sudden reaction and so intense her passion Hafsa felt threatened and had to react.

"Why are you looking me like this?" she inquired rather sternly, but the slave's expression didn't change at all.

In fact, instead of lowering her head as a sign of obedience as she should she reached and touched her nipple with the tips of her fingers in a very gentle way. Her gesture was so unexpected and so bold it numbed any thought of reaction. Now it became almost natural for the audacious slave to claim not just a piece, but the whole. Thus instead of retracting back away from her master, the slave kneeled and gently touched her nipple with her succulent lips, while her long skillful fingers milked her breast gently as if she was a baby.

"What are you doing there? How do you dare touching me so boldly?" she asked, but from the submissive tone her plea sounded more like an attempt for exploration of intentions than a strict order to be obeyed.

"Because this is right now what you need to relax," the slave replied and she was right.

Hafsa was simply too ashamed to admit it. However, even though her mind still refused to react, her lips uttered the magic word "peki" that meant the master was pleased with the slave's performance. It was magic word because it led to a cataclysm of passionate kisses and tender caresses that shifted the focus of the invasion from her breasts to her belly.

It was more than she could bear that strenuous night. Her tension suddenly collapsed, and she could do nothing but open the gates to the experienced attacker who could do nothing wrong. Soon she felt so happy she simply had to express her gratitude, and in such a case she felt more natural to reattribute fairly and justly than venture into the unknown. The slave's breast were within easy reach and as her lips parted expressing her ecstasy, her tongue slipped like a snake out of hibernation to announce the majestic return of the spring. Now how could she blame the slave for offering her pink rosebud for her pleasure?

****

Coming out of her trance Hafsa Sultan could do nothing but recall the enchanting sensations of her unconditional surrender. The repeated series of explosions had been too recent and too intense to be denied and too loud to be refuted or even silenced; but surprisingly the thrilling sensation she remembered most was the explosion of the courtier's passion when her tongue expressed more eloquently than ever before her immense gratitude.

Instinctively her hand extended on the night table seeking the purse she always kept to show her gratitude at daybreak for the services of the night attendant, but the hand of her courtier stopped it on the way before any contact was made with the velvet.

"Pleasure must be repaid only by pleasure," was the slave's message conveyed bluntly and surprisingly the Valide Sultan's authority was not the least offended in any way by becoming the instrument of pleasure of this impudent courtier who didn't have enough to be fully content, as she pressured her succulent flesh on her face.

Even if she was appalled by her immense sassiness, the Valide Sultan could not effectively react to the challenge as her head was most forcefully squeezed in the powerful vice of the slave's thighs; but she never considered anything else but complete submission to the slave's modest demands. Perhaps it was the narcotic effect of the heavy but exquisite scent of sandalwood, or the rhythmic motions of the slave's waist that numbed for one more time her reaction. Somehow, the beat matched her heartbeat so perfectly; but in such a state it could equally well be the other way around.

The Valide Sultan was now so dazed by the intensity of the mutual excitement she simply could not refuse to submit to the needs of tiny piece of flesh that reached from the darkness of the abyss towards the light seeking all the compassion and tenderness she was willing to provide. She was a woman and a long time had passed since anyone had asked her to prove her maternal instincts. She most gladly accepted the challenge. It was in her feminine nature to respond to an attack with submission. In fact, it was much more than that. In this Universe, it was the mission of any true woman to do her best to turn hardness into softness, and sourness into sweetness.

When the slave had her fill of bliss and slipped away to rest by her side, Hafsa Sultan had discovered that there were indeed two ways to govern the Harem. She could become as grim as Selim Khan or as humane as his father Bayezid Khan. Sooner or later she would have to choose which role fitted her needs better. At the moment the authority she had inherited allowed her the luxury to choose, but this night had shown her that despite what the Holy Books said all human beings had the tendency to bend their will for the sake of pleasure. If she was destined to become an effective ruler she simply could not forget this unwritten divine law.

****

Unexpectedly now it became also quite clear what she had to do to lure her victim into submission to her will. If Ibrahim had no experiences with women, then what he needed was an experienced woman to show him what he was missing. She only needed to find an immoral accomplice she could blindly trust.

It was a grave misfortune this gorgeous slave had black skin. Ibrahim would never consider her for anything more than a temporary pleasure toy. He was still young, but soon enough he would adapt the time tested role even Selim had adapted, for a long portion of his existence. Love affairs with men were simply treats that fitted well with his urge to conquer, the same way Turkish delights pleased his palate after smoking a pipe. However, no true man could survive for long eating only Turkish delights. Selim's meals included surely female flesh. She was simply too far away most of the time to follow exactly how Selim Khan spent his nights. This pretty girl had to be just one of the consorts he had invited to his tent to calm down his natural urges in Egypt. The two eunuchs had to be the exception rather than the rule.

This thought led her to an option she felt was an inescapable conclusion. She had to find a beautiful creature she could trust completely; but seeking an answer in a slave bazaar might not be enough for an ambitious slave like Ibrahim. With such a greedy and exceptional male a female slave might not be a permanent solution but a temporary respite. Slaves were as useful as pieces of furniture. Ibrahim's ambitions for a higher status could not be as trivial.

Just before departing the remarkable African girl had explained to her that she was attached to her daughter Hatidge, another present of Sultan Selim when he came back from Egypt. If for the life of the slave this transaction was just another chapter of her adventurous life, for Hafsa it was a revelation. Selim Khan never did anything without a purpose. He was the one who had offer the hand of their daughter to an ambitious and promising nobleman, Iskander Pasha. He was also the one who had ordered his execution after few years. He was not a man who placed great value to the lives of his male relatives.

On the other hand, Selim had shown compassion for his daughter needs now that she was a widow. The black slave was ideal for soothing the tensions the lack of a male lover generated in a young woman. She was the best witness of the Nubian slave's erotic skills. The Kislar Aga had been most competent, performing his duties with the sensitivity she needed. Did her daughter know of this temporary exchange of a very delicate piece of furniture? Even if the slave had the nerve to deny it, her logic said otherwise. The slave was as sincere as she was bold. Her daughter had given her the name "Basm-i-Allem". In Persian it meant "Jewel of the Universe".

Basmi had added with a giggle that her daughter resembled her mother so much that one could be very easily fooled under the candlelight.

Her daughter was no fool. She was also an exceedingly licentious Sultana. During the first two years her marriage had lasted she had produced two children as she had done with Selim Khan. Was she as promiscuous as her daughter?

No! She was married to Sultan Selim and had to be very careful with herself. Her daughter was simply married with a Pasha who had been punished by death for his greed for gold. By offering a slave like Basm-i-Allem as a present, Sultan Selim protected the image of his family. This was one of the essential functions of a harem, and he had made sure no rumor escaped for his daughter's weaknesses by inviting her to the Eski Saray. The next question came to her lips as naturally as the first.

"Does your mistress know where you have spent the night?"

Basm-i-Allem giggled for one more time and replied with a most delicate manner.

"My mistress guards all her jewels by her bed."

She needed nothing more to realize that Hatidge was a compassionate daughter. She had followed the funeral ceremony till the end, but she must have had mixed feelings about her father. She couldn't deny his authority to govern the Empire justly, but Hafsa Hatun was also a woman violently separated from her man. Her daughter's gesture was a clear sign she loved her mother, but kept a grudge against her father. She couldn't harm him in heavens, but she was happy to erase his memory from her mother's mind at least for a night or maybe more.

The Nubian slave was eloquent once more. She had to leave, but the Valide Sultan could summon her every night she had any difficult in sleeping. She couldn't but be happy to hear this piece of news. Many aging widows sought oblivion or amnesty inside the illusive paradises of opium seeds or cannabis leaves. The succulent lips of this exquisite African flower were a much safer and inspiring alternative. She only had to decide if her lips were the gate of Paradise or her tongue the alluring snake. How happy she could be if there was a way this Nubian slave could wipe her memory of Ibrahim!

****

It was midday when Hafsa managed to disperse the last drops of bliss Basm-i-Allem had left behind. She took several deep breaths to diffuse the heavy scent of sandalwood from her nostrils, and then she licked her lips to discern if her taste was still haunting her; but she had been kissed so many times before her voluptuous dark figure disappeared through the door that she had no trace left to be ashamed for her debauchery. Fortunately, the Holy Quran never said a word against a widow seeking comfort so soon after her husband's death in the embrace of a woman.

Now that she was more sober she could plainly see that a female slave was just a feeble substitute for a man like Selim. It was a trace better than those ebony penises she had come across one time while searching the trunk of a concubine she suspected of stealing a ring of hers. The odalisque had stolen nothing. The ring was simply misplaced; but when she inquired about this incriminating presence, the naughty concubine had vaguely but sincerely replied that Selim Khan was fighting in the Holy Lands, and no one knew how long his absence would last.

She could punish the slave's insolence, but it would be grossly unfair. There were many similar trunks in the harem and she had searched only one. Back then she was not the Valide Sultan and she had not the rights to start such an extensive search that would prove nothing but that she was not among the majority. Being a member of a minority made everyone feel like the degenerate freak in the Harem.

With a naughty smile she asked the Kislar Aga about what the rest of the odalisques did to quench their thirst, but even he was too embarrassed to give a detailed reply. She had to forget the incident as Selim took his time on the way back. A man absent was as good as dead, was the moral lesson. She had been a morning widow for many years without knowing it.

The very thought woke up her body from the lethargic emotional state of a frustrated wife and recent widow. Instinctively she turned around to see if any of the eunuchs who surrounded eager to relay her first commands of the day could read in her eyes her sinful thoughts. Long time ago, she had overheard a eunuch boasting that he could smell the different scent a woman emitted when she was excited, as if he had the sensitive nose of a bloodhound. Now all she saw were frozen faces empty of emotions.

This was the last she needed. Eunuchs had never become a permanent solution for any woman. Men were from the very beginning of creation an anomaly. Castrating them made them matters much worse. The problem was not related to their moody penises, but to their unreliable minds. Their minds were not as practical as that of a woman's. She simply had to squeeze hers hard enough to find an adequate solution. Her only problem that very moment was that the eunuchs were not the inspiration the widow of Selim needed. His absence was still strong and the caresses of Basm-i-Allem offered just an illusion of true ecstasy. Only a desperate woman would seek joy in the hands of another woman no matter how expedient she might be.

She dismissed the eunuchs. She would remain in bed because she was not feeling well enough to rise and exert her commanding authority.

****

It took her many hours of contemplation alone in bed to find the Ariadne's thread out of the Labyrinth of very devious thoughts.

The solution she had found was indeed ideal for all concerned and this perfection was possibly its only flaw. Her motherly worries would finally find their redemption, and most important of all, this way she could take revenge for the myriads of nights she had stayed awake waiting for Selim to summon her to his bed. Now that she was a widow, no one could blame her for using a slave to combat her loneliness, and no one would dare to question the wisdom of her preference to a younger man. Who should she choose to be respectable, the Seih-Ul-Islam?

The Holy Quran suggested for a widow to be patient for a reasonable time after her husband's death before she should let another man enter her body. However, it did not specify exactly what this reasonable period was. This was unquestionably an extraordinary occasion. Anyway her involvement would be just for a single night and nothing more than that, an instantaneous weakness, a motherly sacrifice and a momentary sin. Even Allah the Beneficiary forgave a single sin, if it was not repeated to become a habit. After all, it would be for the glory of Allah and the salvation of His Shadow from the unacceptable immorality of Sodom and Gomorrah.

The only one who would get hurt, if he ever found out the truth was her son; but, she was quite sure Suleiman would never dare to raise this dubious point. After all, he had also succumbed to the same immoral temptation; however, she was sure her son would never find out. The possibility that something would escape from the lips of her Kislar Aga was remote. He had been her trusted associate for several years, and many times when she had sent him to spy on Selim, he came back with tears in his eyes reporting that the heartless Sultan was once more locked in his bedroom with his pages. Kislar Aga was her most trusted servant and he would be the last man in the Harem to betray her trust.

She felt now that same anger coming back to torture her. Even the eunuchs pitied her lonely state and it was all Selim's doing; but, this night the cosmic forces would fill the emptiness of her heart now that Selim's terror existed no more.

She turned abruptly to face the mirror and carefully inspected the reflected image. Her feminine coquetry pushed her to make a pirouette to view her face from its best angle, face to face, and then assume many poses to measure the effect of her body. It was quite difficult to be objective with her flesh, but what she saw was unquestionably very pleasing. Her hair was shining from the laurel oil she used after each steam bath, and fell like a cascade on her shoulders. Her Tatar nose, slim and proud, made her stand out from all the other concubines in the Harem cursed by fat and curved Turkoman noses. Her son had inherited the color of her eyes, but her nose was absent from his complexion. It was one more victory of Selim's blood.

She closed her lips as if she tried to kiss through the mirror an invisible lover. Her lips were one of the features that were clearly superior, and her son had inherited both her lips and her delicate chin. She was quite sure that Ibrahim had sensed the similarities and would feel as comfortable with her as he was with her son; but in her case, face to face, she could also add the decisive advantage of a low cleavage that made her irresistible for any young man of Ibrahim's age and licentious disposition. Males had deeply implanted in their brains the divine images of their feeding mothers.

Now it was time for her to get dressed in absolute privacy and be ready the moment an Aga would bring Ibrahim along. This solemn thought created the first doubts. Was it ever possible Ibrahim might refuse her offer and try to leave to conclude the night with a man? It wasn't only fear that could make him hesitate, but also the embarrassment of confronting an older, experienced woman.

She was certain she was capable to drive away the fear of eminent danger from his mind, but she also had to convince his body to follow her lead. This was one more fault of the male sex. For any woman if the mind was attracted, then the flesh would surely follow, but men were clearly less developed creatures; so a woman had to tempt both the spirit and the flesh, as if they were two separate entities. Perhaps this was what had given the dubious idea of the Holy Spirit to the indiscriminately lustful Byzantine bishops.

She took off her finely laced undergarments and touched her velvety breasts. They were still almost as firm as when Selim touched them for the first time, only considerably fuller. Could she make Ibrahim happy enough in her embrace that night?

For a sophisticated noble woman like her every detail had its purpose. Satisfied with what she saw, she turned around quickly enough to catch the Kislar Aga's eyes still fixed on her back. After last night he had become so bold he had failed to knock on her door for permission to enter. His cheeks had now a faint shade of pink caused by shame as he tried to correct his indiscretion; but, her smile assured him he had nothing to fear. She was now certain her back was attractive too, if this was Ibrahim's secret affliction.

Now that she had finished the inspection, her mind was freer to wander unrestrained in the fertile lands of lust, where a single seed of desire could multiply a thousand times. She needed this surge of desires to combat the state of hibernation Selim had imposed on her sensations; but perhaps it was not just the death of Selim that had affected such a drastic change. Maybe more important was Ibrahim's role in the Seraglio as a Hasodabashi that had caused so many strict traditions to change. Having a true man in the Harem had the effect of a landslide. On a steep slope a single rock could be removed or added and then the entire mountainside could tumble down. Human beings were so strangely connected to each other that the violation of a single rule could cause the reexamination of an entire old tradition.

Few special men were indeed like drastic catalysts of changes and Ibrahim was one of them. Just few days ago she would never have thought that tonight she would entertain the incredible thought of taking a male slave as her lover. Women were too unpredictable beings for comfort!

She remembered a quite implausible story she heard in the Harem few years ago. Ibrahim was supposedly the slave of a widow in Manisa who made him a present to Suleiman to please him, because her son the Prince liked the way he played the "oud" (large mandolin)!

This crude tale was clearly the creation of a male mind. Men were so naïve in all their lies and excuses that it was impossible to convince a woman worthy of her gender with their unsophisticated fairy tales. All the time her collocutor chatted aimlessly, she had tried hard to keep a stern face to the end and make a comment that would give credibility to the entire tale.

"I know all about this widow," she had said back then, "but do not mention it to anyone else, because our girls might get naughty ideas, if they hear a young man trained by a lusty widow has become the Odabashi of my son's harem!"

This confession was more than enough to promote this story to reach all the corners not only of the Harem but of the Eternal City; but now Allah the All-Knower was pushing reality to imitate fiction. Only the flow of the tale had been reversed and she would become the widow to claim Ibrahim back from her son.

****

Everything she had imagined was nothing but creations of the disturbed mind of a woman that had been deprived for years of a loving man. Allah never made an effort to affect reality. It is simply one more coincidence among so many others which fools the simpleminded into seeking for a logical explanation for every event. All these coincidences are to be expected as long people keep on living on a sphere that forces many paths to intersect naturally, if they are long enough. And if life follows a spiral, then it is not surprising that any given affair can be repeated many times in the future with very few notable alterations.

****

Now, what was left for Hafsa Sultan was to choose the best possible dress. It should look like nothing else he had seen her wearing before. Back then she was the Kadin of a Sultan and the proud mother of a Prince, so she had to look majestic, untouchable and dignified. Now the slave would never suspect the Valide Sultan's appearance was just a show and underneath her sumptuous brocade was bear naked to save time!

She still remembered how deeply she was offended when Ibrahim suggested she was just another slave in Selim's harem. It was another misconception common men made, presuming that a Sultan's mother was nothing more than a slave who had changed many masters before being admitted into the Seraglio. Of course, the Ayin tradition demanded that every slave who reached the Sultan's bedroom would be a virgin; but how could anyone be absolute certain that a sensual girl had not utilized her delicate lips to improve the conditions of her captivity?

Men were so weak and a woman's body so versatile, if she had the right instincts namely the instinct of survival. This was the reason why she didn't pay too much attention to the Kislar Aga's assurances that all his odalisques had been thoroughly tested. Most of the girls were so attractive that they would have tempted a saint not a lusty Nubian who was audacious enough to try to seduce her with his despicable show of manliness inside the women's hammam. He was a devious man and he was probably trying to turn Selim's Birinci Kadin into his obedient whore, but she was not sure she could find such a competent assistant to her plans. In the Harem she had discovered that it was a much better policy to use people instead of exterminating them.

Selim was notoriously suspicious, and the last thing he wished to hear was that his Kislar Aga had tried to seduce his favorite Kadin. He would surely execute the villain, but since there were no witnesses to the event, her status would surely deteriorate and even her son's life might be in danger.

She was still puzzled by this incredible event, and the eunuch's explanation that he was following Selim's orders to keep his harem free from complains was not thoroughly satisfying. Everyone knew that in the past, many Roman Emperors had been assassinated by their wives' lovers.

Life was simply too complicated in an Ottoman Seraglio where the Ayin had gone to extremes to assure the Empire of the best possible Heir and Sultan, and to be safe one should take into account all factors. Even a dog could betray the content of a licentious mind, so to put a dam to all this frustration, strict rules had to be applied to make sure the system didn't go out of control as it did during the damned Romans. This simple suggestion was so convincing most women in the Harem had accepted this hypocritical role without complaint, and tried to live their lives to the best of their abilities by taking advantage of every available opportunity to bypass the dam that separated the genders as effectively as the walls of Eski Saray from the Janissary barracks.

Now, in the few remaining hours she had to convince a young man she was still young too and fully capable to discover a new purpose in life besides raising a Prince Heir to the throne of Osman. She felt her heartbeat rise thrilled with excitement; but for her scheme to succeed, it was necessary to retain her coolness. Everything had to appear natural, a momentary weakness induced by his attraction with no preparation or premeditation; otherwise, the slave might feel threaten by a devious conspiracy meant to harm him. They had to be alone without the presence of a witness, who could later open his mouth under pressure, or even torture.

Ibrahim had to sit next to her, so that after the initial and formal exchange of views about the news of Eternal City, she could make a casual and innocent looking bodily contact to encourage him. For instance, she could ask Ibrahim to teach her how to play the "oud". Then, it would be natural for him to touch her hand and place it on the correct keys of the strings. If she pretended she didn't know anything about an oud, he would most certainly lay his musical organ between her legs. It was the critical moment and she had to blush shyly even if she had to keep her breath. If he was as bright as he seemed, by then he should have grasped the allegoric message.

Her next devious step would be to make a request for him to play a special song to sooth her troubled heart. If he was a true descendent of Ulysses, he would choose a love song to seduce her as a siren. Even if she couldn't understand the words, it would be easy to guess the context from the tune. Love songs in the Mediterranean were so alike it seemed all men had the same complains or inspirations from their mates.

Then, it would be the proper time for her to ask for a translation. She had heard many stories about the Ionian singers who wondered in the narrow streets trying to seduce young girls and widows with their love songs. This would be also the right moment for her to blush once more and even shed a tear for her unbearable solitude. She would then confess she was so alone and desperate she would give her heart to the first courageous troubadour who wasn't scared to offer a Valide Sultan some comfort for her loneliness.

However, all these preparations would be unnecessary, if she had judged this immodest young man correctly. She had felt by instinct Ibrahim was such a passionate lover that if he was tempted to lay only a hand on her, he would be incapable of slipping away from her bed until sunrise. Allah would have given up on humans the day a frustrated widow of her experience could not seduce a young man like Ibrahim.

****

If Allah has a peculiarity, is that He wishes mortals to be simple and predictable in their desires; thus, He never tolerates their efforts to exceed Him in canning or in wisdom. That is why, even if He doesn't really care of the consequences of an intricate plan, He does whatever He can for it to fail. Nothing can escape Him, because He is the Knower of All the Great Secrets of this World and the next.

****

Hafsa had just started getting dressed when she noticed few drops of blood as they left her body and landed on the rug. She was suddenly so depressed by the event, she started sobbing so hard her servant thought she was in great pain. She would never find out if this was the wish of Allah the Protector of Honor, or an act caused by Selim's spirit everlasting presence, but it was plain that some supernatural force didn't wish her to find happiness. Her plan was a perfect baby, but it had died at birth.

It took her some time before she could think straight once more. This sudden intervention of some benign spirit had made her lose every contact with reality. However, soon enough she became once again the powerful Valide Sultan from the land of the Tatars, and the eternal mother who had to fight hard against all odds for the happiness of her only son.

Her basic plan was sound. Simply the hero had to change. If the experienced woman that would seduce the young man to his demise was unavailable this night, she should find a younger girl to tempt him using other feminine charms. Fortunately, there were still few dependable choices in Selim's Harem, and she did not waste any time to find the right one. She was a combination of youth and experience. She was also as licentious as she as Basm-i-Allem had hinted, and she agreed as any caring mother she was the best judge of characters of all her three daughters.

Now there was not a moment to lose. The Kislar Aga had to be summoned to guide the Russian girl to her destination in the Seraglio, and then seek and fetch Ibrahim, while she had to visit the apartments of the Ottoman Princesses. Sultan Suleiman might initially raise few objections, but the time was too short for her to be concerned with similar minor obstacles that might arise in the distant future. If the human chemistry was right, no obstacle could block the path to completion, and then the consent of a Sultan could be secured to reinstate the Osmanli honor.

****

Ibrahim was mildly surprised when the overly excited Kislar Aga entered his room, inviting him to follow him. It was already getting dark and the prospect of wandering through the labyrinth of Seraglio corridors reminded him his past experience with Selim. He was not overly worried this time. He presumed that the mighty Sultana had many other means to use, if she wished him dead.

40

Potent poisons were always available and a cook could be easily bribed to add into his food or tea a deadly additional ingredient like a poisoned mushroom.

Soon enough he was able to extinguish completely his fears as he was informed Hafsa was asking him to come and bring his oud to the Eski Saray. The invitation this time was also expressed in more friendly terms, but this piece of news did not warranty security by itself. Flies are caught with honey, not vinegar. He was already clean, dressed, perfumed and ready to visit Suleiman when the Aga arrived; so, it didn't take him much time to arrive in front of the Eski Saray Gate in a carriage.

This time Hafsa was waiting in the reception room. She was sitting on a comfortable chair made of dark walnut wood decorated with shining pieces of mother-of-pearl surrounded by purple embroidered pillows. Next to her on a sofa of similarly luxurious style sat a girl Ibrahim had never seen before. Her face was hidden behind a transparent veil in a light shade of peach-flower red. Under the veil she wore a silken dress one shade darker, ornamented with floral golden thread designs made of white pearls. Her breasts were covered by a delicate pink lace that rose high enough to cover sufficiently her slender aristocratic neck. Her hair was pitch-black and her skin had the dark tint of the Orient. Her eyes rising above the veil were like moon reflections on two abysmal lakes. Her eyelids were dyed deep purple like a pack of clouds masking a winter sunset.

The first thought that came into his mind was that he had seen these pitch-black eyes before, but with the excitement he could not pinpoint the exact moment; however, she didn't also remain unmoved by his hesitant entrance. The interest of her eyes betrayed her sinful thoughts, but even more suggestive were the ripples of her dress that gave away the instinctive crossing of her legs, as if she instinctively tried to protect herself from the imaginary threat of a raping raider busting in her Tatar tent.

Ibrahim's mind calmly registered all her bodily reactions, but with his limited experience with harem women he found hard to draw the right conclusions. Anyway, the girl was too attractive and authoritative to permit a slave the orderly processing of all the available stimuli. On the other hand, the Sultana graciously announced she was very pleased with his prompt visit and her wide smile was much more explicit than her words; however, there was something in the air that Ibrahim couldn't yet firmly grasp.

Hafsa sensing his growing insecurity quickly made the introductions. This young and very pretty girl was the Princess Hatidge, one of her three daughters with Selim. It was right then when Ibrahim recalled where he had seen these eyes. She had the dark eyes of her grim father, but somehow one could discern the softness of a woman hidden right behind them.

For the time being Hafsa continued undisturbed her rather boring social chatter, while Hatidge remained silent, immobile, and reserved. She had heard a lot of praises from his brother about Ibrahim's brilliant performance in the Seraglio School, but it was quite clear this was not the sole subject of discussion in the Harem about him.

Ibrahim could easily read in her eyes that whatever she had heard about him had made her interest grow in bounds, and she was now curious to discover how much of it truth or fiction was. Unquestionably listening to a woman's subtle insinuations was a vast improvement over obeying a man's firm commands.

He knew well enough that according to the custom all the Princesses who had some of Osman's blood in their veins would have to marry eventually high officials of the Empire, or offered as brides to sovereigns of neighbor states to promote military alliances. The only reservation for such a union was that the bridegroom should not be a Turk to avoid creating another Turkish family with blood connections to the Ottoman throne.

Ibrahim was not this kind of threat for the House of Osman, but the office he held as an imperial falconer was usually the threshold for a brilliant career. Nevertheless, apart from all these customs, Hafsa's initiative was bold and much further advanced than the strict rules he had to learn about Harem's traditions would permit. No male should be caught in the same room with a Princess and this indiscretion should remain a secret. This was in fact the favor the Sultana asked him next with a funny conspiratorial tone.

Ibrahim was perplexed by this unexpected development, as within a few days he had become Hafsa's trustee. This was not the first time that absolute power had swept him off his feet raising him like a whirlwind to heavens; so he reassured Hafsa Hatun bluntly he was ready to cooperate, as he had sworn to keep the secrets of Selim's family as if they were his own.

Hafsa realized the slave had seen through her devious plan and tried his best to be accommodating, being too smart for his own good. However, it was now too late to change the pleasant attitude of a welcoming hostess, even though Ibrahim's attention had now another focus. On the other hand, Hatidge's impression of Ibrahim's presence was positive. Every moment his head turned to face Hafsa, the Princess examined him intensely; but, when he tried to oppose her eyes, she would rush to lower her head, avoiding direct confrontation.

Ibrahim could never hope to be victorious to this silly eye game, as the girl was much more experienced in evasions and she was always the first to react. This was a quite new sensation for him, as up to now men's eyes were more sincere and relentlessly focused on their point of interest, and thus it was very easy for him to accept or refuse their invitation. However, now everything was much more complex and subtle. When your enemy retreats without a fight, you cannot decide if he is simply terrified of your armament, or if he tries to lead you into a trap. It was the first time he had to play the role of an attacker and his experience in this role was very limited. Up to now defending his integrity and self-respect was his constant concern.

****

Before this evening started, Hafsa was worried Ibrahim's behavior might be negative or at least unreliable. She knew well from personal experience that many men who had affairs with other men, would cease to care or be attracted by women, even if this seemed quite incomprehensible to her. It was a fact no one could deny and one of the reasons she had chosen Princess Hatidge, a widow, as bait since she combined youth with experience. Fortunately, Ibrahim was an exception and his eyes seem to steer constantly in the Princess' direction.

Ottoman men never ceased to fascinate her with their dubious choices; but surprisingly her plan was progressing on track. The first contact was successful, and she shouldn't try to rush things. The fish had noticed the bait, and it was just a matter of time before it was going to bite hard on the hook. Now every unnecessary move might scare it away and make it run back into its hideout. The only danger that still existed was Suleiman who theoretically had the authority to spoil this developing love affair; however, right now her son was facing a similar trap with the Russian maiden as bait and he had even less chances of escaping than his slave. If Hatidge was just a lusty widow with two children, the Russian was a well-trained seducer.

The Kislar Aga had never been so reassuring about any sold meat he had ever provided to Selim's harem. Most men had peculiar urges. When they were young, they yearned for experiences, but when they grew older, they went mad for purity. Selim was a determined warrior and in all his military expeditions experienced women or slaves was his most common choice of a consort, and this was a most comforting thought for a legal wife.

Her son Suleiman was also no exception. His two first Kadin, despite their elegance, training and beauty, had eventually ceased to excite him. This was the true reason Ibrahim had been such an attractive alternative. However, hosting a professional enchantress in the Harem was a risky task. This kind of woman could affect the entire harem's disposition. If she resided within the same walls, her licentious behavior could infect like plague all the occupants, as every girl who sought success any way possible would try to imitate the ways of the trained professional. This was the reason the Russian resided isolated in her own room, not unjust favoritism; but she simply could not reveal Kislar Aga's reasoning to anyone.

****

Now that her intricate plan was in operation, Ibrahim had to stay in her chambers for as long as it was required past midnight; so, she asked him to play a song from his country, while the servants would serve some tantalizing "meze" for a late light supper. She was quite correct in her planning, as Ibrahim started indeed with a mesmerizing love song. When he finished, Hafsa asked him for the meaning of the verses. He tried his best to translate them directly into Turkish, but for the strict Muslim ethics they sounded so exceedingly bold and suggestive that both women started laughing off their embarrassment, and he was quick to follow.

The ice between them was melting away, and no one knew how this

43

night might eventually turn out. Hafsa simply would not know how her daughter would react if Ibrahim suddenly decided to leave. The invitation was so sudden, she simply did not have enough time to plan that far ahead and prepare Hatidge for such an adverse contingency.

For the Princess the offer to meet Ibrahim and possibly marry him should sound reasonably convenient. It would be a chance to get away once more from the strict tradition and the restrictions of the Eski Saray and come in touch with the world of freedom that extended outside its walls for the noble women of her class. She was quite familiar with this state of affairs. She was the widow of Iskander Beg, a nobleman from Albania who had been executed by Selim for incompetence and financial scandals. For a rich young widow there was no worse fate than residing in the Eski Saray surrounded by the younger concubines of her brother without the freedom to invite a man to her quarters.

Her only reservations she expressed had to do with the virtues of the groom. Ottoman Princesses in the past were not always fortunate and happy with their marriage. Many times they were given as prizes to foreigners to secure the support of a vassal state and often enough the groom was much older to avoid the danger of a childbirth. Sometimes they were even paired with eunuchs with crushed testicles as a reward for their services to the state; but, Hatidge would not accept any such compromises and would fight hard to win a fully functional young man. Hatidge was sincere enough to confess she was gradually getting bored even of Basmi and her African tricks she was too ashamed even to describe to her mother.

However, now that she had met Ibrahim face to face, the lukewarm acceptance of her mother's proposal had turned into an emotional crisis of intense impatience she expressed by crisscrossing her legs. It was a clear sign she was not attracted by the prospects of the groom for a quick accession to the higher offices of the Empire, but by something much more primitive. Anyway every Pasha who married a Princess was well provided with a very handsome dowry. This slave's unique charm was his blond hair and his green eyes, and this attraction was stronger than what she could withstand. It was the natural tendency for a race to mix its blood with another, the primordial reason that had started all the wars between East and West, Greece and Troy, or Romans and Barbarians. It was the instinct that pushed a light race to mate with a dark, black hair to mix with blond and black eyes to wash away their darkness within the deep green of evergreens, or the royal blue of the seas.

The Roman utopia of clean blood and racism that had led other dynasties to deterioration and degeneration wasn't going to affect the Ottomans. The last two centuries they had already assimilate almost all the nations in Anatolia and it was now the time to do the same in the Balkans. This much her mother could read in her daughter's eyes.

Hatidge was no virgin any more, as every Ottoman Princess should be before her first marriage; but, this short fault was an unimportant issue compared to her elevated social status. Ibrahim didn't look like any other traditional Muslim official she had ever met. His eyes could not stop exploring her assets as if she was the slave and he a very demanding buyer. Soon enough she was determined to demolish such illusions. The moment Hafsa made up her mind, his fate was sealed one way or another. After all he was a slave of her brother trained to obey the superior will of an Osmanli.

If not tonight but soon enough, she was going to test his obedience too. Until the moment she saw him for the first time, the raw material of her fantasies was collected from the neighborhood, as the Janissary barracks were visible from her window over the western low walls of the Eski Saray. In fact, every day she had more than 2000 sweaty images of very manly warriors exercising half-naked under the sun to choose from. During the summer months she could even smell traces of their sweat as the sun in the Eternal City during the summer was scorching, evaporating even the last drops of male decency. It was mostly during the summer when few Janissaries went crazy with lust, pulled down their pants, and exposed their hard genitals in the direction of the Eski Saray to demonstrate their contempt for the Osmanli. No one had ever complained for the spectacle.

Anyway, it would be a useless gesture as long as Selim Khan was alive. The excuse was more than obvious. From such a distance no one could discern if on the Saray windows a eunuch, a concubine, a slave or a Princess was watching. Anyway exposing genitals to the enemy, cursing, beating drums or blowing long horns had been military maneuvers Sultan Selim utilized against his enemies with great success. Was it ever possible for an Osmanli widow to complain and disrupt this proud military tradition?

Did Ibrahim know of her secret affliction? Sneaking in and out of the Eski Saray someone could have described him this rather common event. As he boosted that he also belonged to this notorious army corps, he looked at her in a very peculiar way. She didn't know the reason, but he simply could not face up to his eyes and had to lower her glance and her pride.

Nevertheless, she had to admit that as a male specimen Ibrahim was as exceptional as the very best Janissary guards, and her mother had been very keen to choose him over any other nobleman. His sole drawback was his title as Hasodabashi; but, her mother had assured her earlier he was no damned eunuch.

She trusted fully her mother, as Hafsa Hatun knew most of the Seraglio secrets. Her Kislar Aga was indeed very nosy and the least discrete eunuch. He had made a habit to burst at night without knocking not only in the concubines' bedroom halls, but also in the Princesses' quarters just to catch them red-handed and demand a bribe. No Princess could do anything about it, as the Kislar Aga had assured them it was one of Selim's orders to know anything unusual that went on behind closed doors. The only distinction the Aga made in favor of the Princesses' was he didn't impose any punishments for any naughty acts we witnessed. He simply reported what he saw to his grim master.

In her case, Selim had been very appreciative for her discretion. When he came back from Egypt, he brought her many jewels and exquisite fabrics to make her more dashing and attractive to a man's eyes; but, he also gave her as a present one of the Nubian concubines of his vanquished opponent he left hanging to rot from a Cairo gate, a different kind of testimony of his impeccable justice. This attractive slave was the best antidote to her affliction compatible with the demands of the Ayin.

Of course in the Eski Saray there were strict rules as in every Muslim harem, and the Eunuchs tried their best to keep away everything as suggestive as a cucumber or an eggplant. All vegetables and fruits had to be sliced before any salad could pass the inspection point in the harem entrance. Even candlesticks were replaced by oil lamps to protect the innocence of the girls; but all these nasty efforts were in vain, as it was quite impossible to prevent two women from comforting their loneliness the moment the last candle flame was extinguished. If a man's body was forbidden to enter the Harem, a woman's flesh was the next available substitute.

Now that the first Black Kislar Aga was appointed, gradually more eunuchs of the old guard were replaced with Nubians. This Kislar Aga had also relaxed the most ridiculous old rules that served no other purpose but to increase tensions unnecessarily. Now he was the most popular eunuch in the Harem and also the most trusted. He simply could not squeak, because receiving bribes had become a capital offense under Selim. If her father was eager to cut the neck of a Grand Vizier, what chance a black slave may have?

But tonight everything was different, the young Princess's mind was free of all the past men, and able to test her feelings in front of another man who was not her brother or a eunuch, and his heavy jasmine scent in her nostrils was potent enough to taste it. This new experience was fascinating and she was trying to soak up all the details her mind could hold to have plenty to talk about and gossip with Basmi. She was more than certain it would be very hard that night to sleep with only her silken pillows to relieve her anxiety; but in her age, the expectation was half the satisfaction. Despite Hafsa's very brief descriptions of Ibrahim's virtues, by now she was certain that before long his fleshy lips would travel on her skin, and these long fingers of an expert oud player would extend to excite all the chords of her secret weaknesses, putting an end to a long interval of isolation and seclusion behind the bars and ironclad gates of the Harem.

****

Allah in his infinite wisdom had made this world so that dreams were free to roam much further than the mind could ever reach on its own. Dreams were the mighty oxen that pulled ahead the heavy load of the entire humanity towards the future. Princess Hatidge did not know that yet, but that night her dreams would be invaded by something much gentler than a bold man yearning for her flesh but perhaps equally mesmerizing; a blond baby hungry for her milk.

******

Ibrahim quickly realized from the seductive climate of his present visit that Hafsa Sultan had decided the Princess was to be sacrificed for the sake of her only son. He didn't really mind this exchange, as he knew that in his case a wedding could mean for him at least the office of a Pasha or a Governor of prosperous island like Samos or Chios as a wedding present, or possibly an even more desirable "Beylerbeylik", the office of an entire region like the Balkan Peninsula, Syria, Egypt or Anatolia. This would be the next step to his final destination, the control of the entire Empire. If the Ottoman had their Red Apple, he had his own dreams that even Allah the Knower of the Secret Dreams could not guess.

The only way he could make his dreams come true was to keep Suleiman under his spell for as long as possible; but, this juicy fruit lying on top of the silken pillows and examining stealthily behind her veil all his manly virtues was a most intriguing offer. He had to taste it, even if he had to become her husband. It was not just the fear that if he refused, this open flower was bound to find another bee to steal its nectar and his antagonist would automatically become a sworn foe. It was this sinful woman herself that had triggered his desires with her eye games and sneaky glances.

He could read in her eyes that she was begging him to take her in his arms and treat her as a slave despite of being an Ottoman Princess. Initially, the very first thought popping in his mind was to push her to the point of begging a "raya" to make her happy; but, his mood for revenge did not last long. Soon the heavy scent of her flesh mixed with spices and opium from far away islands in the Indian Ocean reached his nostrils and numbed all his other senses, putting on hold all his vengeful plans for a night of thorough ravishing.

Perhaps her lips that opened to let out a pink tongue eager to wet her dried lips were all the signs he needed to change plans. After all he was civilized. There was no way he would dare rape such an exquisite creature that wanted to be united with him even more than he craved to conquer her. He closed his eyes and took a deep breath. His fate was sealed. From now on he would be a desperate addict of her scent. He will fill his lungs and never have enough; however, his brain was made in such a way that it would never be content pleasing just one sense. It was quick to react and raise many more questions. How would the soft skin of her breasts taste when she came out of a steaming hammam? From far away it seemed it was smooth like Bursa silk and tried hard to contain her overflowing sensuality. Would she be a gentle lover or another Tatar rapist, an Amazon who used men only for their pleasure or proliferation? Now that he was young, he didn't mind either way; but, was he going to be young forever?

It was the first time he was able to examine a woman's body as close and as calmly since the day he was also merchandise in the slave market; but, back then his only concern was his immediate survival that dictated his interest. He was a slave, and to survive unharmed he had to adapt his preferences to the demands of the male buyers.

When he was still training in the Seraglio School, he was fed up watching the most handsome Janissaries and slaves exercise their muscles next to him, as if the only goal of every male was to make his flesh tough, eager to break out of the prison of the skin like an immense penis. For him this was just a small portion of any man's aim in life, namely expand your bodily limits. To be balanced, a man had to expand his mind too as far as it could go. However, even when men had succeeded in their conquering plans, it was just a temporary victory, as muscle always had to retreat to rest and recover from the excruciating tension.

The seductive promise of the female flesh was easy to comprehend. He could still pursue his foolish dreams of glory and conquest; but later, when it was time to seek eternity, he would have to come to terms with the female superiority, surrender and become her slave for the rest of his life. This night he had to find ways to resist this irresistible attraction, and he found a refuge in the image of the Russian girl.

Her body was stressed like steel and highly trained by dancing. She had the tension of the male muscles and the moves of an athlete, without the rich and suggestive curves of female fertility. Making love to her would be as testing and tiresome as keeping afloat in an angry sea. Only an experienced sailor could ever hope to reach port safely.

The body of the Princess from what he could discern under the soft silk and the delicate laces was something different. It was soft like velvet, grown up in the affluence of the Ottoman court. It had the charm of a calm sea that welcomes you into her bosom and lets you swim and feel her every ripple for as long as your heart desired. Being the son of a fisherman, he was never afraid of the angry seas. He simply had to be patient and wait for the right moment to cast his fishing nets; however, life was an immense ocean that could never be fully crossed under calm weather. There would always be violent storms and tempests, and a good sailor was the one who knew how to trim his sails according to the demands of the oncoming weather.

****

Sultana's voice put a pause to his sinful daydreaming. Several hours had passed pleasantly and it was now time for the Princess to retire to her quarters. Feminine beauty was a sensitive commodity and sleep was the only period it could flourish, repairing the scars of the endless fight with Time. Anyway, their first acquaintance should not last too long; otherwise, the mystique of Eros would suffer. They had an entire life to cultivate their relationship and trim it the way that pleased both of them most. She had done her duty and realizing each other's needs, had brought them close enough to touch. Now it was strictly up to them to let this brief acquaintance flourish to their heart desires; but, such decisions took time and had to be taken with cool mind, not in the spur of the moment, since marriage was a mystery that should last a lifetime, not just a blazing wedding night.

Ibrahim agreed and added that at least for him such a happy marriage would be no mystery. The enchanting promises that lay hidden in the first eye contact were going to last forever. He was as usual short and subjective, without really revealing what he had in mind; but, this time Selim the Grim was not his opponent demanding his unconditional surrender, but two highly attractive females that negotiated gracious peace terms giggling.

As far as he could tell, both women knew exactly what he had in mind, so they were able to plan their next move accordingly. The young woman got up exactly the moment the muezzin's voice came in through the windows. She hesitated for a moment, as if she really wanted to continue this visit for as long as possible; but she wasn't ready to disobey the will of a Valide Sultana, her all-caring mother.

She made a deep bow before her superiority and kissed the tip of her fingers as if Hafsa was just a stranger and not her creator. She gave him a last chance to look deep at her bosom and turned to depart, but she was so excited that a laced handkerchief slipped through her fingers and Ibrahim tried to grasp it in midair. She was quicker and grabbed it first, but he boldly grasped her hand instead. She tried briefly to free herself, fighting like a wild animal to escape the trap; but, soon she changed her mind and left her hand at his disposal.

Ibrahim now kneeled before her and kissed the palm of her delicate hand, as he had seen young men do back in the shores of the Ionian Sea. In this case, soon enough it became obvious Ottoman women were not ready for similar expressions of extreme liberties of western culture.

Hatidge blushed behind the veil and Hafsa's eyes shone in anger. According to the Seraglio protocol, any bodily contact between a Princess and her groom-to-be was strictly forbidden before the marriage ceremony. Only eye contact was permissible. The whole relation should progress first a long way into the imaginary world, and then proceed into the vulgar reality of procreation. They had to let the imagination sweep away all the imperfections and faults from the idealistic form of their relation, so that every sensory perception was pure and morally flawless.

Hafsa's initial plan was to make them both dream of the final union, but the youth had moved one step ahead of her and grabbed reality. According to her initial planning, the seduction should start from the singing of the song to the first contact, but it was her hand that Ibrahim should touch at the very end of this process. She was now disgusted with the weakness of her body that couldn't wait for a few more hours. Maybe she might have better luck next time. At the moment, she had to wait to see how the Russian had progressed with her son and hope for the best. As long as she controlled the Harem, she could always exert her authority and give herself a second chance for fulfillment.

Ibrahim's impudence was actually a welcomed surprise. This slave knew the way to overwrite all the rules on the Seraglio and remain unpunished, so she had to remain calm and patient. She knew well the destiny of all men who moved further than the tolerance of their era permitted was bleak. Traditions were the limits a man should never cross, if he wished to age safely as long as his health permitted.

****

It was late afternoon when Suleiman returned from the Eyup cemetery. He was physically exhausted and mentally depressed. More than a week had already passed since the day he was notified Sultan Selim had died. It wasn't so much that he had missed his father's presence. As far as he could remember, the last few months when they were under the same roof were actually an exception rather than the rule.

It didn't make much sense for a Sultan to be attached to his sons, because many times in the past sons have tried to dethrone their father just to become Sultans few years earlier. Even Mehmet Fatih had been one of such ungrateful sons; but, the pleasures and the power of a Sultan were such that they made even an angel to wonder why he should not behave like a devil. Angels simply sang in heavens, while devils imposed their will on all weaklings.

Despite of all the precautions and the security measures there would always be many scoundrels who would not hesitate to help a usurper to overthrow a weak Sultan. For instance, the Janissaries were always ready to welcome any change of the reigning Sultan and receive a prize in silver just for expressing obedience to a new sovereign. Thus, a Sultan had only one way to keep the universal order in balance, cut without hesitation the heads of every conspirator he could uncover. Perfect stability was the will of Allah in a universe that constantly evolved, and he had created an Ottoman Sultan to accomplish this monumental task.

Yes! Finally after so many years of terror and doubt, now he was very proud that Selim Khan was his father. He was the best teacher about how a Padisah should behave and treat his enemies. He was now less concerned about the significance of any human life that could end suddenly by a stroke of bad luck. Even a common stumble of his horse could humble the most powerful regent as if he was a worthless servant. It was what common folks called the hand of Allah, while others described it as the Kismet. What was the use of all these years his father had spent fighting, conquering, and faithfully keeping all Allah's Commandments, if death could come so unexpectedly, paying no attention to a man's dreams and ambitions or even his worth?

Before Selim's inglorious demise, he hadn't spent a minute thinking about his departure, but now that death had knocked on his door, he felt like a lighted candle in a violent storm. A Rumi's rime came back into his memory from long time ago, when his father was still alive and he was seducing Ibrahim reciting love poems composed by another man for similar purpose:

When you are with them without me,

50

You are all alone.
When you are alone next to me,
You are with everyone

Perhaps it would be best for him to follow the advice of the poet. Thus, arriving at the Seraglio, he sent a page to summon his favorite. He was certain that Ibrahim could find a way to change his disposition for the better with few jokes or songs; but, the servant came back alone reporting Ibrahim had been invited earlier to the Eski Saray by his mother.

For a moment, he contemplated the option of going there to join them, but soon he concluded she shouldn't see them together. Anyway this second invitation was a good sign which possibly meant his slave was doing his best to calm down her anxieties for their "improper" relation. Eventually Hafsa had to accept that for a Sultan no relation that pleased him should be considered as improper.

He had already decided he should go to sleep early, when the Kislar Aga appeared at the doorstep. He was a slim, tall man of impressive appearance. He had a black skin that shone like a well-polished ebony statue. When he became Sultan, he had decided to keep him in his place after he heard the recommendations of his mother. Slaves very manly like him were useful in a Sultan's harem to keep free of depression all the concubines that lost favor; his attractive body was delicious food for concubine imagination. Hafsa had warned him that only if he was planning to exhaust his harem personally, he should fire him and search for a replacement; so, he kept him without a second thought.

The Kislar Aga came now closer and keeping his face down he asked humbly:

"If Your Majesty so wishes, I, your most worthless servant, would like to remind You that many days have passed since the day the presents for Your coronation arrived. If there is no particular reason for Your Eminence to offend them all and spoil their eagerness to please, it would be most appropriate to welcome them as the imperial tradition rightfully prescribes."

Suleiman didn't wish to carry out any social obligations this specific evening, but an effective Kislar Aga had every right to remind him of every issue that had something to do with sexual activity. He had earned this right with considerable effort from Selim, offering him for few years advices and services, guessing with the increased sensitivity of his ambiguous sex what he should say and where to stop. Anyway, a young Sultan should not fail in his role as an imperial stud, when an entire nation has laid its hopes on his vitality.

The Nubian slave was basically right and Suleiman was too feebleminded to offer tonight any serious resistance to his suggestion. From the moment Suleiman had claimed the sword of Osman, he had also accepted by oath all the obligations that went along with his position. Everything now had to proceed according to the ceremonial order prescribed in great detail for the occasion, and the Kislar was too happy to recite his obligations.

51

Firstly, he had to visit the hammam, and then pass from the ointment and the perfuming process. He finally had to end his journey in the dressing and the turban room that had multiple mirrors to examine the overall result from all sides.

After the steam bath cleansing process, it didn't take much time under the care and supervision of so many skillful hands and experienced eyes to get ready even though the Aga had at least one crucial detail to improve at each stage of this enterprise, up to the rings of his little fingers that had to match the color of his turban. Thus, Suleiman worn in an amazingly short time white undergarments, a purple shirt with dark blue trousers, a silken "salvar", and a yellow brocade kaftan weaved and embroidered with golden threads in Bursa and red rubies from distant India.

On his head a light green turban was put and in the middle of his forehead the cloth was held together by a large golden broach in the shape of a phoenix. This mythical bird had a body shaped by small rubies and turquoise and wings made of peacock feathers that opened like a fan high above the turban. In his waist there was a golden thread band, holding a small knife tuck inside its coils. It had a hilt made of crystal, a Persian spoil of his father that now was the right time for him to wear, and a mirror-like inscription Malik-al-Muluk, (Master of the Kingdom) that could be read the same both ways in Arabic. Finally, the White Eunuchs help him put on his boots made of camel leather colored like a ripe maraschino cherry.

He was so very pleased by what he finally saw in the mirror that all his anxieties disappeared. Now, he was full of confidence and ready to face his lusty new slaves that waited patiently for his undivided attention; but, suddenly he froze on his step as the Aga let a terrible scream that made everyone present jump on his feet. The Aga quickly fell on his knees and asked humbly for forgiveness for his terrible mistake. He had almost forgotten to put some red dust on the cheeks and a bit of henna on his lips to reach the perfection masculine he was aiming for.

****

The first visit of a new Sultan to his harem was a momentous occasion expected anxiously by all its inhabitants. It was a fact a slave could not ignore unpunished. It wouldn't be only a sign of disrespect for her master, but also the proof she was entirely unscrupulous or ignorant of her duties in this life. The conquest of the world demanded leaders who had unbending determination and would not falter in front of any obstacle during the harsh military expeditions. The Harem Paradise was Allah's just reward, awaiting a victorious Sultan on his return.

In the Christian barbaric West, they believed that behind every successful man there was a wise woman, and they tried to follow closely this recipe; but in the Orient, carrying along the wisdom of many millenniums of civilization, they could see much further than the nose of the hypocritical western Christianity.

If a man was truly of great stature, then behind him there was plenty of space where many attractive women, men, boys, or even eunuchs could be hidden, if they were slim enough.

What was a worthy prize awaiting a world leader who undertook all the dangers and the hazards of global conquests, if he was to enjoy the same privileges of his lowest subjects, a single and aging female consort of questionable attraction? Democratic equality could only lead to mediocrity. Anyway women were always abundant, and frequent wars were constantly creating a need for more and better men and a social problem that had somehow to be addressed convincingly. Perhaps the Ottoman solution seemed inhuman to other less ambitious nations and religions, but for Islam, which was becoming again a blooming flower, this generous choice was wise and just, and only an incurable hypocrite could deny the demands of reality.

Of course, the main reason for all these preparations in the Harem didn't have purely patriotic roots; it was much more related to pure feminine ambition. Every attractive and virtuous girl that could arouse the interest of Suleiman should have a chance to bring into this world a child with his blood. These few special moments of happiness she offered would be most generously rewarded by an entire life of comfort and splendor without any worry about the future. And if she were lucky enough to give him a son, then reality would exceed her wildest dreams.

However, Suleiman's harem hadn't started its existence that very night. There were already several women that had inspired feverish passion and there were several children from his recent past as a Prince Heir that supported this fact. Among them first in his heart and attention was the dashing Gülbahar Mahidevran who had given him the first in line Heir, Mustafa and then a second boy to prove her devotion and constant desire.

Mahidevran had noble Tatar blood in her veins more than Suleiman had, and she knew how to keep his interest alive with her demands, even now when her main duty was raising two of his two sons. She would also be present in the reception of the Sultan and everyone was sure she would fight hard to keep her place in the hierarchy not only for herself but also for her two boys. There could be no question about her determination. The rumors claimed she was already pregnant for a third time.

****

The preservation of a Sultan's sexual interest as any other man's was never an easy task for a Kislar Aga. It required a constant effort because any day could bring unexpectedly a new event that could change the balance of power. This distraction might be a fresh group of concubines graduating from the School, "the fresh meat" as they were called. They had as their main weapon the pureness and the innocence of youth, a priceless commodity; but many times something much more trivial and common might suffice. A revealing dress, a sparkling jewel, a mesmerizing perfume, or a different hairdressing style could catch the eye of the young Sultan for a single moment, or even a simple gesture as ordinary as a promising tremble of her hips or an imperceptible ripple of her breasts during a dance might put his heart on fire.

In this entirely magical process the role of Kislar Aga was extremely critical and influential. He had the power to keep a concubine unnoticed by sending her to do some other menial work whenever the Sultan was planning to visit his harem, or promote her by shown her few tricks he knew from past experiences that could excite the Sultan's interest. However, even a simple servant could acquire knowledge of an intimate erotic secret simply by spying his master, and this information could be worth many gold coins in the Harem's market; thus, it was everything but boring the life of an odalisque in the Harem. Under the surface of leisure, tranquility and isolation there was considerable intrigue, preparation and excitement that could keep everybody's interest alive and focused, from the crack of dawn, when the favorite of the previous night returned to show-off all the presents she had gain with her efforts, until the next evening, when a new cycle of preparations and anxiety was bound to start the moment the Kislar Aga announced the Sultan was in the proper mood.

Nevertheless, this night, although no one could predict the final outcome off-hand, the events would change irrevocably the flow of Ottoman History. And every wise man who understood how human History was written, knew well that its pages are so light and flexible that a single breath of wind could turn a new page at every moment.

****

When the Russian maiden entered the Imperial Harem quarters in the Eski Saray for the first time few years back, she felt entirely lost. The many other maidens who had arrived there from all the corners of the world seemed older and much more experienced for the kind of life she was about to start. She had only been instructed what to avoid that could offend her master, but very few pointers were given about what course she should pursue to enslave his heart. She was a Christian and could only rely on her instincts and her past experiences.

Christian or Jewish maidens had already a bad reputation in the Eternal City. All the oriental dancers, tavern waitresses and prostitutes were Christians and she was hardly any different. If this was the effect of Maria Magdalene or Salome on their minds, no pious Muslim woman could say with absolute confidence; but, most odalisques didn't even care to fathom another woman's motives. What they yearned to discover was the success or the failure of their actions.

Perhaps the words of the Kislar Aga at the entrance had inspired this behavior. The future counted always much more than the past, he had wisely warned them; but the warning was also a promise for a better future. Her past was known in some detail to him. The tavern she had been working didn't allow the privilege of keeping too many secrets. To absolutely sure what he was buying, he had paid to watch her full presentation, but surprisingly he didn't exploit her that much. He had left her a bit of her dignity and she appreciated a man who was not so eager to collect all of his money worth.

When they left her place of employment for good, he was much more talkative. He explained to her that if she was bright and ambitious enough, there was no limit to what she could achieve in the Harem. She only had to be patient and obedient. He also warned her that during the first few months she would need a lot of training. He considered her a gem, but even gems had to be cut, honed, and polished to reveal their true brilliance.

It was strange, but she felt he was in love with her at first sight; otherwise, how could she explain he spent so much time kissing, caressing and tasting her as if she was a holy icon. It was an intense experience she never had before, but she had arrived just few months ago and an immense city had to contain many surprises. He also had promised her that he would keep a secret where he had discovered her and claim he bought her from the Avret Bazaar like most of the other female slaves.

The Sultan was from the very beginning of her training the sole subject of discussion and the naval of the entire harem world. The other young slaves had focused all their efforts in extracting information from his few previous favorites; but the veterans had most wisely kept their mouths shut even tighter than a sphinx. Deeply disappointed the new odalisques had turned their attention to the Eunuchs who seemed more willing to exchange knowledge for a favor; but soon realized these creeps could easily fool them and exchange their gold or favors for ambiguity or even plain lies or exaggerations.

On the contrary, the Kislar Aga had been sincere with her. She had to be patient and hope that this young, inexperienced Sultan would be easy prey for her array of weapons.

Many months passed since then, and she still had not met her next object of seduction yet, because he was living in another city; but her dreams were somehow full of his intriguing image. The Kislar Aga had explained to her that her future master was a very licentious individual; thus if a woman was wise enough to diagnose his weaknesses, she could use him and become rich just from his expensive presents.

The Aga claimed her best asset was her well-trained body reminiscent of a boy. Sultan Selim was a warrior before anything else. He was also very selective. He was clearly an uncommon man because he didn't seem to appreciate overwhelming curves and overflowing flesh that was so popular in the Eternal City. This was probably the reason he kept slims eunuchs by his bed, and rarely visited his harem where most women grew gradually fatter from good living. Sooner or later he was going to dismiss the entire lot, except perhaps his Birinci Kadin, Mahidevran Sultan, who was slim and light on her feet like a "peik". She shouldn't worry about any distant resemblance, because her body was still much better than hers. She had gone through four births after all, while she was still a virgin in terms of deliveries.

For a moment she thought he was flattering her, but soon realized he was just fooling around offending her Christian beliefs. It all became clear when he said she was actually much more of a virgin than Holy Mary, because she had one child while she had none.

The Aga was not always in such good spirits thought. Sometimes he was trying deliberately to hurt her, but at least he had told her the truth about Sultan Selim and his son. If Sultan Selim hadn't be involved into so many military expeditions, he would still be alive making her his new Birinci Kadin; but, few Turkish men paid more attention to their horses than to their women, and life had strange ways to punish all excesses. Perhaps her becoming an oriental dancer in Galata was her punishment for her excesses. Perhaps, if during her strive to survive, she hadn't please her captors so much, they wouldn't have considered her as the proper merchandise for a bordello.

This was the reason Selim Khan had been unexpectedly a small disappointment. He was simply too old to realize her adolescence dreams. Perhaps his son would be different. The Kislar Aga had sensed he was going to be more prolific, and this was a piece of good news after few years of deprivation.

He had warned her in advance Suleiman was slim and fragile and not as manly as his father. He also had a beard, not a long Tatar mustache. He was also too attached to his Birinci Kadin, Mahidevran Sultan, as well as his cute and witty falconer. No man was perfect, the Aga concluded. It was up to the perfect woman to turn him into a world conqueror. If she failed, the Aga was planning to resale her to the tavern; but, if she succeeded, he made her swore she would never say no to his demands.

She sympathized with Aga's problems. In the past she had entertained few eunuchs. Now that she was living in the Harem she was surprised to find out how many they truly were. It was a disgrace. These people were the result of one more dubious concept men had, "Deep inside all concubines were whores, so a Sultan's honor had to be protected from manly men by impotent servants."

After many months locked inside the Harem she had realized how insane this idea was. At this age she was so sensitive she could be turned on by a breath of wind that would tickle her ear. With her mind full of sinful thoughts, to remain pure she had to have constantly an Aga by her side to watch her every step; however, it was relatively easy for any concubine to seduce any of her guardians. The Kislar Aga in some sense was like a baby that needed his mother's milk, soft kisses and tender caresses to be happy.

He had made sure she understood his needs from the very first time he invited her into his bedroom for the first lesson. He told her back then that every man, despite the superficial similarities that were only skin deep, was different and needed a patient woman with creative imagination to find what exactly his life was missing to be fulfilling. For few men even a word at the right time was enough to ignite their passion. For other men a woman had to search much deeper to find what exactly triggered their imagination and pleasure. It was simply a matter of patience and of determination to succeed in her mission; but the rewards would be worthwhile.

The relationship between a tutor and a student was something like marriage; so, the first step was to build up their trust. This requirement meant she should not take advantage of all the secrets she learned from her partner to dominate their relationship.

He was unquestionably a very difficult man to decipher, and becoming Kislar Aga had made him even more complicated. The Kislar Aga had many associates among pages, servants, Janissaries, or eunuchs. He simply had to ask a favor and then pay the price they required in full. Having all sorts of people within the Seraglio walls, made every person behave singularly. Everyone wanted to satisfy his superiors, but having to obey a moody man like Sultan Selim affected everyone's behavior down the line of command.

Now that Selim was dead, the condition had not improved much, because no one knew exactly what the new Sultan needed to be content. All that was known was that he feared his father and adored his mother. His influential lover, Ibrahim had to be a more complicated creature, but for a capable female the best and fastest way to judge a male was to make love to him even just once.

****

Contrary to people's behavior that felt safer forming hordes, Allah believed most of all in the power of uniqueness, and He was determined to make the dreams of only one woman come true despite all her sins. Perhaps, Allah didn't consider making men happy a sin.

****

Every young girl had to pass without complain a thorough examination by the Eski Saray doctor, and then stay for a long time under the hot steam of the hammam to clean off her skin the last remains of their previous life. Then, it was the proper time for the Black Eunuchs to take command and cover every last bit of their bodies with the proper ointments and waxes to make their skin soft, smooth, hairless and spray then with flower oils to make it as fragrant as a baby's.

Finally, the dressers had to make the final adjustments to the clothes each odalisque had chosen that would fit better the color of their hair, eyes, and complexion. However, most of all a woman's dress reflected her character and her solution to the vital problem, namely what kind of woman would excite the fantasies of the Sultan and force him to respond to Mother Nature's call. It was a most critical question, because they all had one chance to erase the divine image of Mahidevran from his memory even momentarily. Despite being pregnant Mahidevran was still in control of her man as she already had two sons with the Sultan and a chance for a third.

To achieve the almost impossible task to dethrone Mahidevran from their master's heart, most of the younger girls had chosen to look innocent and romantic to match the Sultan's disposition, as according to the prevailing rumor, he was an inspired poet and a sensitive soul. On the contrary, no maiden had chosen to be bold and explicit betting their future on the hope the Sultan might be bored by now of long seduction periods and delicate social maneuvering.

Finally, the hairdressers arrived to fix their hair, as every single hair should be at its proper place according to the general strategic plan. Their individual strategies many times called for the hair to stand up like a turban to make the face look slimmer, leaving the ears and the necks exposed to passionate kisses.

For others the choice was their hair to be hanging low to cover like a velvet curtain their wholesome breasts and exposed backs, one more veil to be removed before their beauty could be fully revealed to a young man's hungry eyes. There were also a few radical ones who would rather cut their hair short like boys to exploit a different source of the Sultan's desire and passion according to the prevailing rumors. Seeing the existing affluence of choices one conclusion was truly uncontestable. The Sultan was destined to find something new to arouse his interest, every time he wished to seek inspiration in the plethora of services offered by his affluent Harem.

****

Seeing the doctor and the Kislar Aga come closer, the Russian maiden only momentarily grew worried. She was an older purchase and she had been examined few years back. Was she going to be exempted from tonight's performance? Was it possible Valide Sultan had changed her mind despite her assurances to give her a second chance?

In this unstable world anything might happen depending on the circumstances and a woman's ability to manipulate the existing possibilities. This was her mother's last moment's advice, selling her to the Tatar slave traders during a wretched winter of extremely poor crops, when even the richest boyars had no reason to celebrate God's blessing. She had been her best teacher at the time. Her mother was also the one who had realized there was no future in Ukraine for a young girl with her talents. She was not exceedingly beautiful to become the whore of a boyar. She only had an unbending resolution to succeed in her life.

In a troubled era when the exploitation of women was the rule, the only decent road to success for a woman was through her husband. It was an inescapable conclusion, since men had become too important1 through fighting wars, and now fortunes were made not through hard work, but by raiding for slaves and indiscriminant looting of your enemy lands.

Everything could change in a young woman's life in a single moment. A pious Prince might see her in a church or on the street after school, and a barbarian raider could ambush her as she came back home from the fields or the

58

river bank where she washed clothes. A rape was the lesser evil, death the worst alternative, and a life of servitude the near optimum average.

Her mother had played safe and taught her all she knew how to enslave any possible master. She claimed the ideal career for any woman these violent days was to follow the steps of the Roman Empress Theodora. When this exceptional maiden was young, she had all the fun in the world, becoming an accomplished dancer in a Galata tavern, and then, when she yearned for a drastic change of living, she was lucky enough to meet and seduce a simpleminded Roman Emperor, Justinian.

It was a well-known story in Ukraine a country that had the Roman Empire as a model, and the last proof she needed to be convinced that unscrupulous women could do just about anything, if they were beautiful and devious enough and married a man with a weak character.

However, to be a successful teacher, first of all a mother had to be realistic. Her daughter was no smashing beauty. She even lacked the overflowing femininity violent men of the military profession craved for to smother their violent instincts.

Her mother had always been straightforward in all her teachings. When dealing with your children, truth is always better than lies, and lies better than truth when dealing with everyone else. If she remained in Ukraine, her fate was sealed. Sooner or later a more violent gang of Tatars was bound to knock on their door and steal her. Even if somehow she remained untouched, the local boyars would turn her into an obedient serf like her mother. Boyars employed professional soldiers to do their fighting and soldiers demanded a pleasant respite between raids. How could a serf refuse to obey a boyar or his soldiers? It was one small step further down the stairs of society for such a consort to become a prostitute when the warriors were away.

Her mother was well aware of this decline because she had followed this path herself. Then, when she aged, a bit more an old Christian priest bought her to help him in his quest to civilize the hordes and show them the divine power of abstinence.

This was not the fate her mother had envisioned for her precious daughter the only present the pious boyar had left her. In the South there was a much more civilized empire than either the Tatars or the Huns. There they treated women and slaves with more respect and people progressed according to their merits. It was a local custom that brought the best out every human being, and so the Ottoman Empire prospered and serfs would rather become Ottomans than serve the boyars in the entire Balkan Peninsula.

Unquestionably, she was well proportioned and properly dressed with her fiery red hair drawn higher by a ribbon or under a hat to reveal her exquisite neck she could easily pass for a very cute boy. Perhaps, this was one of the reasons the Tatar slave traders paid her a very good price for her, as they were world renown for their indiscriminant raping customs towards all genders; but they may also have appreciated her pearl white skin lighter than any other boyar offspring, legal or bastard.

She still remembered her mother's eyes as she left for the greatest adventure of her life. She was standing all alone in front of the front yard of the locanda with her eyes wet. Her mother had warned her. Don't trust crying eyes. You'll never know if the tears are shed out of compassion or envy.

In her case her mother had made-up a good story to cover her tracks. The Tatars had grabbed her pretty daughter. They had spared the mother because she was too old to fetch a good price down South. It was an old popular tale, nobody sober in the village would believe. The Tatars had raped her but spared her life because after the treatment they received, they would surely come back another day for more.

Her mother was blond, but she was redheaded unlike her mother. She must have had some Tatar blood that also turned her eyes from blue to chestnut color, but her mother denied it and there was no eye witness, just poisoned tongue gossipers claiming there were too many raiders visiting the priest's house to get her blessing. The priest's wife understood the true meaning of Jesus teachings, "do to others what you would like them to do to you."

This much she believed too; but, she also had realized early on that an unscrupulous mind could find all sorts of excuses for its deeds. All that mattered in life was not the application of dubious moral principles but the survival of the fittest. However, sometimes even wise rules like this failed badly because of bad luck. They preached often that the blessings of the God were not enough. The believers had to act too; but even then success was not certain. When everything else failed, any pious believer had to be lucky too to prosper.

****

The doctor and the Kislar Aga bypassed her. They knew well she was a virgin and didn't want to waste their time with so many other unfamiliar girls available. They knew it because they were the ones who made her so and had been well rewarded by Hafsa for their expertise.

All these preparations were indeed a waste of time. No one would dare to offer a used woman to the Sultan as a present. It was another case of unrealistic hypocrisy among many others in the Harem. How could a virgin satisfy an experienced man? A widow had much better chances, but a professional whore could top any amateur any time any place.

If pleasure was the only consideration in Suleiman's mind, the Kislar Aga had warned her that one of the Sultan's Kadin was truly gorgeous. To challenge them would not be easy. She simply had to do her best and offer her imperial lover something he had never experienced before in his life, an erotic technique or a trick she knew extremely well.

****

The carriages left the candidates at the entrance of the Sultan's Selamlik.

Within this gathering of women that buzzed like a swarm of bees over spring flowers, Mahidevran, Gülfem, and all the other older odalisques of the Sultan's past were standing still and perplexed, wearing all his presents from the past times he had found pleasure in their bosoms. Standing still in their heavy brocade dresses they resembled miraculous Byzantine icons covered by old offerings waiting patiently the faithful Sultan to return and kiss them, so that they could perform one more miracle rewarding his devotion; but now, it seemed the old church might remain empty, as younger flesh shone much more brilliantly than any other precious jewel.

Thus, they remained where they stood motionless and unable to repel this invasion of youth, trying to criticize every defect they could find to reassure themselves that every other woman should be excluded from Sultan's bed this special night; but deep inside their hearts fear had already grown roots that possibly from now on very seldom the Sultan would seek refuge in their arms. It was certainly not their fault. It was Allah's will who always wants the young to have the best chance when new life must grow and conquer Earth.

The Kislar Aga first gave a last advice to all the women about how humbly they should behave in the presence of the Sultan and then retired unnoticed to the room of the Russian for a last minute briefing. Hafsa's orders were plain and simple. He should make absolutely sure this night she had to be the one to captivate Suleiman's preference.

Kislar Aga's remarks to the Russian were much more encouraging. Despite her beauty Mahidevran was essentially a housewife the Sultan summoned whenever it pleased him. It was a formal arrangement without thrills. Mahidevran after her third pregnancy would be as exciting as a Muezzin who climbed a minaret regularly and announced Allah was great.

This time the Sultan could not evade the crucial test. He would be assaulted in front of an entire harem and the Black Eunuchs, so he simply could not bypass her challenge without losing face. She simply had to be aggressive enough and push him to a corner where no escape was possible. He had to prove he was a man. If he was indeed a stallion, he had to prove it to a mare.

****

Now at last all the girls were ready to spend the most critical night of their lives. The moon was already high up in the skies and all the oil lamps were lit inside the Harem. Silently they all took their right places along the sides of the long corridor, the "Altin Yolu", the Golden Path. This was the corridor that connected the female visitors' preparation quarters to the Sultan's wing, the Selamlik. It was named so because of the golden coins every new Sultan threw to all his odalisques without exception the first time he visited the renewed Harem occupants.

Suleiman as soon as he was informed that everything was ready for the ceremony didn't try to delay his entrance, as it was customary to show who was the master of the Harem, but preferred to proceed to the conclusion of this ordeal, since he was already tired and depressed. His mood was not up to the requirements of the occasion and all he was hopping for was that he could fulfill his obligations without giving any further cause for gossip.

In his mind the idea of choosing a Kadin as his night consort was slowly gaining ground. Both knew him well since he was in his teens, and she would never misinterpret his bad mood as their fault. Perhaps it would also sound good to the general public, if it became known that the young Sultan was faithful to his old preferences, and didn't rush at every occasion to find something new, behaving like a horny rooster.

If someone didn't have a bright new idea, keeping traditions was always a good choice. Anyway there would always be another chance to honor his new acquisitions, when he was in the right mood for something different and challenging. He had already confided his choice to the Kislar Aga and his faint smile could mean nothing else but his agreement.

"If this is the final wish of my Master, no slave may have an objection. We all should follow the wish of Allah, blessed be His name to all eternity," the Aga murmured obediently.

Upon the entrance of the Sultan in the Harem quarters absolute silence spread throughout the lively gathering. It was not just the deep respect for the Emperor that kept all the mouths shut, but also the intense curiosity of every new concubine to examine closer the man who from now on would have the right to demand absolute obedience to his every wish no matter how strange, novel, or perverted might sound in her ears. He was the one who held inside the Harem all the authorities of the judge, the punisher, or even the executioner, if the offence was serious enough, without asking for anyone else's permission. But this night no girl was terrorized by his awesome power, because in every mind the hope that tomorrow morning she would be the master of the Master of the Universe was firmly established.

Every young girl had heard stories that the Sultans were growing fat from eating and drinking and doing nothing; but, this was an obvious and malicious lie. As they were now able to examine methodically the young Sultan, they could find no vices, but only virtues. Even the rumor that he was showing his preference to men had to be nothing more than a vicious slander, as they could plainly see his eyes searching to discover what tantalizing secrets lay hidden under each veil. This luxuriously dressed slim man who walked among them like a lion among a herd of gazelles with his gray eyes and noble stature was much more than they could have hope for in their boldest dreams. And now they could not wait much longer to surrender their being to his caresses, even if he was not the mighty Sultan, but an insignificant page. They had suddenly discovered that when a woman was in love, happiness and slavery were the two different faces of the same coin, namely complete dependence on the chosen man's will.

Suleiman was also amazed and caught his eyes staring aimlessly at the surrounding beauty as the gold coins slipped purposelessly through his fingers. He could never have imagined such beauty could emerge out of a woman's womb. In front of his eyes lay every possible shade of skin, hair and eyes. All sorts of adorable bodies, few slim and slender, but also others corpulent and shapely, but all of them firm, flexible and youthful were there waiting for his choice in quantities and proportions that could please even the most demanding customer of the Constantinople slave market. If he could, he would have been delighted to invite them all to his bedroom; but, he knew such an exuberant greed would kill even the mightiest Janissary.

Reaching the parade's end, his eyes met with the fiery and familiar glance of Mahidevran. She was the picture of sincere devotion, but now inside of him greed had displaced any other feeling; so, he bypassed her impatient to experience what was the next activity in store prepared by the Kislar Aga for his pleasure, and sat comfortably on his throne.

His throne was wide and comfortable and full of multicolored pillows, as if it was a couch. It was made of sandalwood and surrounded from three sides with low rails. Its scent filled the entire reception hall anytime the air temperature was raised high enough. Perhaps on this very throne his father had mated with his mother to conceive him. At last, the crafty eunuch was right. A state of euphoria was taking hold of his mood, pushing the sadness and the pessimism of death into a dark corner with all these startling women surrounding him.

In Allah's universe only a young woman could ever put Death to shame.

****

The Ayin tradition required that every girl passed right in front of him, kneeled and presented the best she had to offer, and when the procession was finally over, he had counted at least fifty new faces among which he would have to make tonight's choice.

Now it was time for him to relax and enjoy the best pleasures life had to offer to all his senses. Soon the rugs around him were full of trays and plates with different kinds of food and the atmosphere had relaxed most of its previous tension. The music that came from the orchestra hidden in the next room helped also to give a festive note to this ceremony.

Suleiman felt now the gravity of the moment, since this was a unique moment in his life and he had to try to make it truly memorable.

The music started playing a lively tune and few of the girls who had just finished eating got up and danced. Their happy mood was highly contagious and pretty soon the one after the other they got up and joined the others, as none wished to stay behind and look lifeless or depressed for her fate. Tonight their future would be decided and they had to show the most enjoyable side of their character, as eating was clearly not the best they could do in such a momentous occasion.

All the songs were joyful and optimistic reminding Suleiman of the early years he had spent in Trabzon. They were warlike dances, and the fast pace of the music thrilled the female dancers to imitate the movements of the mountaineer warriors of that region. Soon the room was full of sweeping hair flowing in the air like the battle banners of the Spahis and the Janissaries, of arms that rouse like angry snakes and wholesome breasts that vibrated like ripples on a lake when rain started falling.

Suleiman now could not contain any more his urge to turn around and inspect all these determined warriors, fighting passionately to gain his praise; but, every time a face attracted his attention, another one would jump out from the crowd to steal his attention, and every time a body looked divine, another would spring out to expose its superiority. Their dance was not restricted to just an effort for his visual and audible enchantment, as with every move they made a new and unrepeatable mixture of scents was born filling the air with its invisible tracks.

The temptation to reach out and grab this whirling flesh to satisfy the last two remaining senses was so strong that Suleiman had to combat hard the primal urge to get up and join their dervish-like dancing retaining his imperial dignity. However, the rhythm now kept going faster and faster as the music approached a crescendo, and the girls, swept away by the fever of competition for beauty and grace, soon approached their limits of endurance; however, no one dared to quit and destroy the thrill of the moment, disappointing their master with their limited fortitude. Then, suddenly the music stopped cold, and all the dancers fell breathless on the rug like puppets that had their pulling strings severed by an invisible scimitar. And there they lay, trying feverishly to catch their breaths with their bodies covered with tiny drops of sweat that penetrated the delicate fabrics, exposing everything their girlish modesty had tried so hard to conceal under the ethereal waves of silk dresses. They looked right now as excited as if they had just made love, and were trying to regain their composure for a new round of debauchery.

Suleiman felt for the first time that night his body to revolt, trying to escape from the prison of his clothes. He felt the urge to shade away all his garments and roll among the women on the rug and measure the ultimate limit of his manhood vitality. This was the first time in his life he realized what the true meaning of becoming an Ottoman Sultan was. He owned such an immense amount of pleasure his entire life could pass without ever facing the end of his good fortune. A Sultan's reality far exceeded the boldest human dreams.

****

Without any announcement, obeying a secret command, the discrete sound of softer music was heard coming from the next room once more and Suleiman instinctively froze on the throne. This time the tune was slow and rhythmic as if invisible hands beat gently the surface of a drum, while a funeral procession was parading.

Gradually the drum was followed by a violin and then a flute. Next, an "oud" and a clarinet joined the melancholic melody. It was a motive no one had ever heard before, arriving in the Topkapi Seraglio from the distant steppes of Samarqand. These were the saddening notes of a race so disappointed by the infertility of Mother Earth, it had decided to change its destiny and traveled far to conquer and occupy foreign, fertile lands.

Suleiman now saw inside his mind rising from oblivion old forgotten memories, as every sound stirred deeply the annals of his past. Perhaps, these were the lost memories of his great grandfathers Ertogul, Osman, and Orhan who had left the motherland steppes to seek fame and fortune, and now were given life once more resurrected by the manmade miracle of music.

Kislar Aga had returned now in the hall as stealthily as he had departed just to give a single silent order. The servants, as if they had knowledge of a secret plan, put out all the lamps in the perimeter walls. The Aga was knowledgeable enough to see that for a Sultan making love should feel like enjoying food. For his Majesty it was not enough if the ingredients were pure and tasty, the proportions ideal and cooked to perfection; the serving should also be outstanding.

By now the only lamps alight were the glass candles of the heavy, wrought iron chandelier hanging from the roof in the middle of the expanse; but, the eyes quickly adjusted to the glooming light and focused on the dim silhouette that slowly materialized at the reception hall's entrance. Its shape was unclear, as it still lingered in darkness, approaching carefully like a skillful predator, sneaking on its unsuspected victim. Only when it reached the center of the room under the candlelight, Suleiman was able to discern clearly what kind of creature he was up against. Her face was covered entirely by a Venetian mask made of black porcelain that had two eye-openings surrounded by tiny precious stones that glittered in the dusk.

Her neck was naked covered only by a golden band, resembling the necklaces the slaves wore in the galleys; but this particular band had a different purpose. It was used to hold by golden threads delicate veils in all the Iris colors from the vivid yellow of a ripe crocus to the brilliant magenta of a blossoming violet that concealed her body. However, with every move she made as her arms and legs followed the rhythm, the naked milky-white flesh found ways to escape the silken prison and declare audaciously its vulgar independence.

The beat of the music gradually became more euphoric, resembling the rhythm of a trotting horse. These were the sounds of the horses' hooves commencing the long journey of the race to the West. The dancer expeditiously complied with the change of rhythm, pulling with rigor off the collar the green and cyan veils covering her shoulders.

She was now right under the chandelier and the room lighted up from the reflections of her white, shining skin; but, she was alert and skillful to cover back whatever she had left open for inspection by spinning around her veils like a mad whirling dervish. Everyone thought she would keep on teasing her master's eyes for long, but it soon became clear that the aim of her mesmerizing dance was to revive history, not to tax his patience. She stopped her spinning and approached the Sultan, following the rhythm with the motion of her hips, and with a graceful motion left the first two veils by his feet. However, her gesture was left unnoticed, since his glance was now focused on the spatial orbit traced by the sapphire stone fixed in her rippling navel.

Kislar Aga was the first to realize from the intensity of Sultan's look that the beauty pageant was essentially over. The Sultan had found his favorite female companion for the night, his new "Haseki" (favorite). It had to be a unanimous decision, because without a sound the room was gradually deserted. Only Mahidevran hesitated for a while, but the austere face of the Aga convinced her it was not the right time to fight for the legal rights of a Kadin. She was his legal wife, but having a harem was a sacred right of every Ottoman Sultan.

In her mind a single thought was dominant. She was still legally married to a Sultan and her son Mustafa was still young and vulnerable. Mustafa needed her protection in the difficult days to come. Her new opponent was just a pretty dancer who simply knew how to shake her butt like a cheap Galata whore. Her legal husband was a Sultan and had every right to invite a dancer to his table like any tavern customer in high spirits. Then, if the dancer was capable to stir his flesh in such profound way to be irresistible, the best way out for everyone involved would be to let the Sultan use the slave anyway that pleased him and put an end to this momentary fascination once and for all. A whore could not challenge the divine superiority of the Shadow of Allah and remain unpunished.

Now in the dusk, only the white of the Aga's eyes was visible from all the entire volume of his presence. His duty was to remain there until the very end, making sure everything was going as planned. The music was still accelerating its beat inside the empty hall. It was the Sultan's ancestors that now were galloping on the Anatolia highlands, conquering the one after the other all the Roman cities, Sevasteia, Konia, Caesarea, Laodicea, Nikea, Nicomedia and Bursa.

The girl with a firm hand ripped-off the blue and the violet veil covering her chest and shamelessly two firm breasts lighted up the room with their impeccable but temporary, milky-white immobility; but, it was one more illusion, since her dancing movement of her hips sent gentle ripples on their surface that captivated his eyes leading them to the very source of human existence that challenged every man to try his luck, if he felt well-prepared for the task.

As the music now gained both volume and tension, Suleiman witnessed the glorious fall of Adrianople and Salonika as the girl fell twice flat on the rug as abruptly as if she was struck down by lightning; but, soon she rose up again and started dancing all around him with renewed vigor like a Maenad in rage. Seeing her gradually closing the diameter of her circles, he felt besieged as if he was the Roman Emperor, and his anxiety grew as he felt in his heart the thunder of her twin guns that shook intermittently as her hips shook violently from left to right. All these firmly determined gestures were far beyond her mental control, as she also looked bewitched by the sound of music.

Collecting all of his willpower, he tried to resist the pressure of her savage, primitive assault; but, it was in vain as her firm flesh took command over his weak spirit.

The girl pulled now two more veils off her back, the yellow and the orange, revealing with a single stroke both her shapely buttocks. From then on, she didn't try to keep anything hidden, but turned her back, so he could examine better both her firm assets, rising more audaciously than the Cilician Gates challenging every world conqueror from Alexander the Great to Selim the Grim to pierce them. However, she was rather merciful and did not linger for too long, showing him that his pleasure was not her ultimate goal. Instead, she turned around, so that his eyes would always look at something new, avoiding the boredom of repetition at all costs. Moreover, that moment they were many shades of darkness that could attract his gaze on her sweating flesh, as men's eyes were always ready to explore dark voids. She seemed to know her trade well, forcing his eyes to follow closely her every move.

The success of her plan demanded that his eyes were focused on the smooth muscles of her belly and the sapphire reflecting the light of the chandelier had enslave his attention inside the slit of her belly button. He had to notice by every possible means that her waist was thin, her pelvis wide, and her stomach flexible enough to give him many healthy sons without ever losing its elasticity or its attraction.

Suleiman in a state of trance stared back at the eye of Allah. He was incapable of moving hypnotized by the spell of her mesmerizing wavy movements of her belly. He was now ready to surrender his will to her every wish, if it meant she would be willing to put an end to this torture. This was the state of mind she was waiting for, and as all of a sudden the music stopped, the girl froze stiff in front of him. The only veil she kept now on was the red one hanging between her breasts and opened thighs, covering the bold nakedness of her puberty.

Sultan simply couldn't stand the suspense any longer; so, he reached boldly and pulled it off. The girl followed the motion of the cloth and fell down on the carpet, hiding on the floor a tiny but critical portion of her nudity, but exposing her back side. She was now surrendering ready to accept her conqueror as obediently as the Seven Hill Roman Metropolis had welcomed his illustrious great grandfather to go through her battered gates.

Suleiman desired her vibrant flesh so much that he felt uncomfortable, as her face rested hidden between his legs as closely as if she was monitoring the extent of his excitement. To find some relief he touched her chin and raised her head gently, so he could also see her eyes. He next tried to combat his embarrassment with a few common words.

"What's your name?" he inquired with a trembling voice.

The girl looked him straight in the eye, opened her lips and with a harsh voice full of the tension of her previous effort she whispered softly:

"I feel like a present a child didn't desire and left it idle in the closet,
And now I must beg the wind to whisper to the Sultan of my heart
That without his presence near me, I'm nothing more than
A lonely nightingale, singing in the night in search of a mate for life"

Her words found their way to his ears rhyming like a poem captivating his brain as magically as a siren's song. He felt bold enough to pull away her mask. A teardrop fell from the corner of her sapphire-eyes, capturing for a fleeting moment the glow of the Venetian chandelier. The sadness of her looks became suddenly a burden he could not bear. It was not the first time he had seen these eyes and instantly he remembered everything, as their brilliance pierced the fog of his memory. She was the neglected present of his mother!

During the many months that passed since then, the growing pressure of the woman's saps had put great strain on her soft skin. It was apparent that she was passing quickly through adolescence to maturity, and her scent carefully hidden among the fragrance of rose petals she had spread all over her skin an hour ago could now enter his nostrils, increasing even further the extent of his sensations.

Suleiman reached to the girl's neck and with a deliberate and forceful move broke the ring around it and the sad memories of slavery that went along with it. The girl remained motionless waiting for his next decisive move, and he was quick to bend and touch her belly with his lips as if he was trying to steal the sapphire stone. His beard tickled her and she could not help but laughing filling the hall with the transparent crystal of its sound.

****

If a human being with his feeble mental capacity is audacious enough to make the dubious claim that he understands the wills of such a powerful and complicated entity, it was right then the Allah the All-Wise chose to make him the eternal slave of her womb. However, as his thirsty lips tasted the extent of her primal excitement, the eternal goddess of love Aphrodite guided wisely her hands to find among the labyrinth of oriental garments the source of his male superiority. It was a gesture destined to be remembered forever for the intensity of its fortitude that demonstrated beyond any doubt the voracity of their mutual primal attraction.

The divine presence of the most powerful goddess of all slowly extended its realm to the entire reception hall with the subtleness of the escaping vapors of an expensive perfume bottle left open by mistake. It even reached through the delicate openings of the mashrabiya screen at the most distant dark corner of the room where the Kislar Aga still lurked in total silence, waiting patiently to take into account accurately all the events of this monumental night.

He had to make a complete report to his employer, and he was very conscientious of all the delicate duties of his important official post. This must

68

have been the reason for his persistence to observe every detail, even those who would never dare to report and offend the impeccable decency of a Valide Sultan early next morning.

****

Ibrahim was pensive leaving the Valide's apartments; but, for the first time in his life he was truly happy in the Eternal City. The presence of the Princess had made him forget all his worries; but, now in the darkness of the night outside the Eski Saray, the cold air chilled shortly all his excitement. He was once again a slave whose duty was to serve his master.

Now it was rather late and the Sultan might still be awake, waiting eagerly for his arrival. Perhaps his luck would hold, and by the time he reached Topkapi, the Sultan would be fast asleep.

He wouldn't have any problem entering his room, and it would be a nice surprise to feel his presence in the middle of his sleep; but, tonight Ibrahim was feeling strangely. He could still recall Hatidge's eyes and his lips still tasted her heavy perfume. Her essence had dissipated any desire that he might have to seek the company of his master or any other man.

Within few days this was the second time he had come face to face with a beautiful young woman inside the Eski Saray, and the second night he would have to spend dreaming. His blood was now galloping fast under the powerful beating of his heart. Maybe he was in love, but there was no one he could trust to explain him the meaning of the word. He only knew that from the moment he became intimate with a woman in Manisa, his flesh yearned for nothing else.

It was a dramatic change because in the Seraglio School his entire sensuality had been focused on the male gender. Back then for him love was simply the submission to a stronger, irresistible force; but recently, he had discovered love could take another more delicate form that had nothing to do with an unconditional surrender to a superior opponent. It was mostly a friendly game, where eyes first gave out freely generous promises of eternal happiness, then hands tried to reach further than ever before, bending the opponent's will to resist your desires. Finally, the bargaining continued until a conditional surrender was reached the moment each gender gladly agreed that it would be to its advantage to satisfy all the demands of the opponent.

It was a mesmerizing game where no one lost and everyone gained; a game where participation was infinitely more exciting than the ultimate conclusion of sheer exhaustion. These playful experiences were much closer to his delicate idiosyncrasy, as he was convinced that a gentle caress and a tender kiss were much more convincing arguments to achieve total obedience than mortal threats or intimidating sharp blades.

He thought of Suleiman, his habits, his vices, and his character. If he could ever explain to him these ideas, perhaps he would be willing to test them with him just once. By now he had arrived at the Imperial Gate and the Janissaries guards recognized him and let him through smiling under their long mustaches fashioned like the deceased Sultan mimicking the Mongols.

This kind of moustache was for him a strong reminder of Sultan Selim and their brief encounter. Was it possible to relive these moments now that Selim was dead in the hands of a manly Janissary? Perhaps he could attempt it in the past, but now it was almost impossible. These raping brutes had recognized his face. If such a disgracing act ever came out into the open, he would lose every chance to advance to a higher position, as it was his dream from the very beginning. How could he ever command a Janissary as a Pasha to advance valiantly to his death?

To have a decent chance to become a leader of men, he had to be better conqueror than any of them. He had to reach the Red Apple Tree they could never reach. He had to marry this juicy widow, Suleiman's sister as soon as possible. He also had to impregnate her to prove he was not a eunuch as everyone thought especially now when the Sultan had made him his intimate Hasodabashi. It was that simple and that complicated.

Women were as competitive as men and possibly more envious, if they felt an extraordinary man was within their grasp. If for a man a beautiful woman was another flower he had to visit to smell her scent, for a woman an exceptional man that came across was much more. He was the future father of their children.

It was difficult to say when exactly he reached this novel explanation. Was it when he came face to face with the expression of divine by Mahidevran's flesh, or when he realized the cause for his dramatic emotional change was the Devil's influence on the Russian dancer?

Tonight Hatidge had captured his undivided attention. It was the third time in a row a woman had such a profound effect on his life. Was he a problematic personality, because he found in another person's erotic disposition the true source of euphoria?

He had to admit that right now his mind was full of Hatidge's sensuous image; but, what would happen if she was not readily available? The answer was almost apparent. He would seek comfort in the arms of another female image, the hard flesh of the Russian maiden Hafsa Sultan was preparing for her one and only son. And if this image had deteriorated, if she ever became pregnant by the mighty Sultan the same way the divine flesh of Mahidevran was soon to be deformed by her widely rumored pregnancy, then her two audacious courtiers could be summoned to lead him surely to the desirable state of nirvana.

But what would happen if in a faraway place in the Balkans he was surrounded only by handsome Janissaries with long mustaches? It was very difficult to decide; but, tonight he didn't have to make any risky choice. Thanks to Allah and Hafsa Sultan, his mind was mesmerized by the young widow, Princess Hatidge. By becoming a widow, Hatidge had become his angel savior dispersing every devil with a long moustache that would dare to appear and tempt him with his vigor. He was finally sane and safe, free from every threat that had terrorized him in the past.

By now, he was already facing the entrance to the Sultan apartments. It was guarded by the Solaks of his personal guard as always, but this time they were most unwilling to allow his entrance. This memorable night his master didn't need his company too, and the only logical explanation consistent with his emotions Ibrahim could find was it had to be a mesmerizing woman the cause of this unexpected development.

His pride was somewhat tinted, but no deeper than a scratch thanks to Hatidge Sultan. Tonight he didn't feel like chatting, and he would rather spend his bedtime hours alone dreaming of Selim's daughter. Anyway, it was natural for a Sultan to spend some time with his wives every once in a while. He didn't know if his master's consort might be Mahidevran, Gülfem, or even the Russian dancer. Since the moment Suleiman had become a Sultan, his enriched harem offered him a much greater number of choices than ever before.

Essentially this was a very unfair development for both his Kadin, but they should have expected it. Sultans were born to be greedy and seek conquest after conquest to quench their egoism. Flesh had very little memory anyway. This was why brains were so important. Gülfem was very timid, while Mahidevran Sultan too authoritarian. She was made to become the mightier Sultan of a Sultan, or the jealous Shadow of Allah's Shadow. One issue had been now confirmed. Life was becoming very complicated the moment the Sultan's harem had come back to Constantinople residing in the Eski Saray.

There was only one easy way to unravel the present enigma. Pay a visit to the present ruler of the Harem and make the proper inquiries.

****

The Sultan tried passionately to pull her closer, but the slave kept him decisively at a distance for as long as possible. Her stance increased considerably his unbending desire for conquest, but she was determined to resist his efforts unless she got the answer she required. He felt her lips by his ear and heard her conditions to surrender.

"Are you really sure you desire only me tonight?"

Such a question coming from the lips of a concubine was an insult to his impeccable authority, but the hazy condition of his mind was unable to clarify similar subtle discrepancies. The physical attraction was so strong that no resistance could be raised by his troubled brain. Under the pressure, he managed with great difficulty to find a few words that made sense.

"Will you ever forgive me for this long delay," he uttered and gradually her stiffness withered away.

These were like the magic words that opened the gates of the treasure cave in the old oriental fairy tale. Gently she let his passion enter her sweaty body. It was apparent she was well prepared for such a development, and she was ready to help him overcome all the obstacles he was bound to face as she pulled him even closer. Soon a whisper escaped from her lips together with a deep breath.

Up to that moment, he had tried hard to resist the building tension, but now his heart could not take it anymore and galloped in his chest. The tide that kept rising for some time broke now through all the feeble sand barriers his mind could raise in a seemingly unending sequence of tidal waves. He felt like transcending to previously unreachable heights, as she violently moved her body to enjoy greedily his every shiver.

Finally, his mind was at last rested and content. It seemed as if he had reached the end of all his journeys. He had tried hard to reach this state in a number of previous relations, but he had failed. Only now, he could feel that he had tasted the ultimate satisfaction a man could expect to find very few times in his entire life; but he was quite mistaken as soon he saw her bursting into tears as if she was unable to contain too the exhilaration of the moment.

He was a man made of flesh, so he couldn't restrain himself from thinking he was the reason why she became so excited; but he was wrong.

****

A cataclysm of depressing thoughts came uninvited from all her previous harsh experiences, her first moments of despair, when the Tatars snatched her from her home in that frightful day until the moment when she had falsely imagined she had finally made her own the man of her dreams. She recalled the miseries of the long trip through the steppes of the Ukraine, and the long marches through the mountain passes of the Balkans up to the gates of the Eternal City. She could still feel the bitter cold of the lonely nights she spent under the shabby cover of the tents and the ripped-off blankets that could not keep her warm.

Back then she had to beg her capturers to share their bodily warmth with her under their soft bear skins, and the awful smell of their sweat, when they did their best to keep her warm with their caresses. She felt also the pain under her soles, when every sunset they stopped and made camp, and she had to cook their meals and trade temporarily her favors for some daily vital substance. At last, the will of Allah had finally ended her ordeal, and the only test she had to face was to find a master that could make all her dreams come true.

Fortunately, the Eternal City from the very first day she passed its gates seemed like a hospitable paradise she could have never enjoyed, if she had stayed in the Ukraine. This magnificent city had to become her final destination.

The first buyer was a civilized man who knew his trade and recognized the inherent limits of young maidens to please different categories of men. Young men need experienced women to excite their passion, while aged men were fascinated only by the charms of adolescence. Within a week she became the girl with the most tips because she was the most pleasant and the most skillful seducer with her dancing routines.

It had to be a good fairy who guided the second buyer to her door. She didn't know that back then, but the Kislar Aga was a very difficult man to please and most girls in Galata considered him a nuisance. He asked her to show him privately her dancing skills and she considered his preference a great compliment. Would she be happy to leave Galata and move to Eski Saray, was his next question that was not as stupid as the first one: "Was she a virgin?"

As soon as the Kislar Aga, the main supplier of woman's flesh of the Seraglio, paid gladly her price to the proprietor and covered her nakedness with the purple velvet of a cape, nothing else mattered. It was as if all her life was transformed in a moment into an unending dream.

The quality of her training in the Seraglio School for odalisques by far exceeded her highest expectations, and very soon she was able to exercise all her natural talents. The music, the dancing and the singing lessons were a most enjoyable experience, and even sewing, stitching and needlework was a graceful way to pass honorably the time among the other concubines, chatting in the Harem that did wonders for her self-respect. She felt she was at last someone important that just money couldn't buy.

Since that fateful night, when she was first asked for the first time to dance for the Selim Khan, her only fear was when someone opened unexpectedly the door of her room during the night. She was afraid the awesome Selim might demand her company, as his son seemed to be interested in other pleasures she could not provide; but, her fears soon resided.

Selim Khan might be a mighty warrior in a battlefield, but by then he was approaching fifty, and he was no match for a young maiden with her background. When days later the Kislar Aga arrived to announce the Sultan's invitation, she was only momentarily terrified; but then the Aga assured her this was going to be a secret meeting and her fears receded.

She had attracted the eye of the Sultan, and it was natural for him to invite her to add one more concubine conquest to his long list. His intention was to use her youthful flesh to boost the morale of his aging flesh. At the time she had become furious because just for a fleeting triumph the Sultan was going to put her entire future into jeopardy just to please his endless greed.

At this crucial moment a miracle happened and another woman volunteered to take her place, Gülfem, one of the heir's Kadin. She was hardly as skillful as she in dancing, but had somehow achieved the goal she was seeking.

She didn't have to think very hard to reckon what that goal was. As every other odalisque, she also wanted to steal a child from Selim Khan, and from the long smile she had on her face she might have succeeded. She had many doubts back then, but after few months no matter how hard Gülfem tried to hide it, she was gaining weight. Only she knew the exact cause of this fattening process, everyone else believed she was simply eating too much to forget Mahidevran's third pregnancy.

When they became close friends withholding no secrets, Gülfem confessed the reasons for this desperate act. Selim the only other witness to her indiscretion had departed by then.

She was greatly surprised to hear Gülfem's side of the story. She was desperate not only to get pregnant again but to have a son that looked like Selim Khan exactly as Mahidevran Sultan had accomplished. Every other similarity would raise doubts of a possible infidelity. If Allah had kept Selim alive for a few months, everything might have been different. Her new son would have a mighty protector, and he might even become the next Sultan, if Suleiman died soon.

Gülfem Sultan was speaking with such hate for her master, it was scary. She was like a lioness protecting her cubs. Suleiman and Selim were simply the tools for her to achieve her goal, namely one of her sons to become somehow a Sultan. Was it possible even her first son to be Selim's son?

Odalisques were lambs compared to a Kadin. A Kadin could even kill a child to raise her own to the throne.

****

She didn't have a child yet, but she remembered well what her mother had done for her. Life was difficult for a single mother in Ukraine. Her mother had sold her away to save her from wasting her entire life as a serf of a cruel boyar.

Her life had not been easy since then. She had to make compromises, but she didn't feel she could do anything else and this was some kind of relief. She had done the best under the circumstances. If the boyar had accepted her as a legitimate child, her life would be much easier. She would be a virgin now seeking a nobleman to get married. Reality had force her to adapt to survive and acquire knowledge in the process. Now she knew how to handle men and this was a factor to her favor.

In concubine training the only issues that gave her trouble were the languages she had to learn, Turkish, Persian and Arabic which had no connection with her native language. The discipline in the School was also very strict and every student who failed to pay the proper respect to every instruction received severe punishment. Fortunately, the rules were exactly the same for all the students no matter if they were slaves or Princesses, so the teachers very seldom insisted on enforcing their worst threats.

Now all these toils belonged to the past. The fearful Sultan was dead and his son was relaxing by her side, trying to recover from the feverish effort of her conquest. She still could not believe she was lying in bed next to the richest and most powerful man on Earth, while few months back she was sharing a bear skin of a rude Tatar raider. Now that he was undressed, the Sultan looked less impressive than the average Janissary guard; but, when she saw him sitting on his throne, she became so excited with anticipation she almost forgot the choreography. The power resting on this man's arms had to be what truly turned her on, not his physic or vigor. Suleiman may have been as eager to conquer her almost as much as a rapist, but in the process he showed enough consideration for her feelings and more tenderness than she had ever encountered in the embrace of any other man.

Anyway, most men were not asking too much from a pretty woman. They were very easily pleased. In fact, the less sophisticated men were the less they demanded. The Tatars never asked her to dance for their pleasure, but just to make them happy in exchange for some food. It was an attitude they followed with every attractive woman they grabbed. They had to make sure when she was sold, she would never refuse her master no matter how old, ugly, dirty and smelly he was. However, entering the Eternal City, her luck had miraculously changed, and in few months it became clear she was not destined to become a Galata whore but a Sultan's concubine.

The Kislar Aga had explained her it was going to be a much more difficult task. For a pretty girl like her, becoming a whore was a breeze. She wasn't the first or the last to follow this track. In the City there were literarily thousands of women willing to provide comfort to men one way or another. They had many excuses depending on the case. The married women claimed their husbands were gone for many months each year, the widows that their husbands were missing fighting the infidels, and the unmarried women that they needed money to buy clothes and jewels to attract men and to get properly married.

Prolific men were plentiful in the Eternal City as it was the crossroad of the Ottoman armies fighting often in either East or West. Galata was also a busy port between the Aegean and the Black Sea, and the Tophane armory an industrial powerhouse, where workers made good money making all sorts of armament for the Ottoman army and navy. After work, there was still some strength left for entertainment and a good salary to spend.

A hard working prostitute could become rich in few years, and then move to Venice as a rich and respected lady; however, most of these common women eventually were bought or employed by Janissaries and moved to other cities, because by working in a harbor, sooner or later they were destined to catch a deadly disease and die. Very few whores changed drastically their way of living because they were addicted to the compensations of the profession and forgot all about the drawbacks. There were not too many professions for enterprising women that combined pleasure with profit.

She was much luckier than they were. As a concubine, she had to attract a single young man for an entire life, as Hafsa Hatun had done with Selim Khan. After his demise Hafsa had become Valide Sultan and taking command of the most luxurious and exclusive whorehouse in the middle of the Eternal City, the Sultan's Harem. This was going to be her home until Suleiman ceased to invite her to his bedroom, or if he died.

Dedication to your duties was what Ayin demanded. The Kislar Aga had informed her, the young Sultan was a very delicate and complicated personality. The rumors said, he was also very demanding and licentious. To keep him interested for long she had to remain attractive time after time. In Ukraine a Tatar wouldn't mind even if she slept with the entire raiding gang. On the other hand, in Constantinople this Turk wanted her exclusively and he might kill her, if he was caught her in the same bed with even a eunuch. The Tatar wanted to fuck and sell her. The Sultan yearned to fuck and own her. To get him interested she had to become a virgin once more. She could have no objections as this was the only way to make her desirable to her owner.

The Kislar Aga appeared not as greedy as his master was. He explained she had to obey him for as long as it was going to take her to become the Sultan's Birinci Kadin. It sounded like a logical request, because no man could lay his hands on a Birinci Kadin except the Sultan, but it meant also that if she failed to achieve her triumph, she might end her life as a whore in a Kislar Aga's brothel.

She was very surprised to find out there was a clandestine one right outside the Eski Saray in an immense caravansary. With so much unfulfilled lust generated inside the Saray by all the women the Sultan failed to satisfy, it was natural for an enterprising man to try to find creative ways to prevent a sexual explosion. The simplest solution was always the best. The Eski Saray consumed a great variety of goods each day and someone had to supply them. Eunuchs were mostly responsible to carry out these tasks, but they were also guarding the gates and they were all under his command and could look the other way, when an infraction of the Ayin had to be accomplished.

However, these liberties did not apply on her, and she was never allowed to wonder in the Grand Bazaar shopping. She was a much more precious investment. She was not to be touched only to be watched. The Aga simply adored watching her dance in the privacy of his room. He claimed perfection was the child of practice.

After all these trials, she could never have imagined that taking off her clothes in front of a Sultan would be such a thrilling experience; but she was wrong. The Sultan was a sensuous man and the Kislar Aga a neutral eunuch. With every veil she pulled off uncovering parts of her body to his hungry eyes, she could feel the particular part of her body that was uncovered getting excited, as if his imperial glance was an inquisitive hand that probed thoroughly her local carnal weaknesses, and she had many as all the girls of her age. It was as if parts of her flesh needed to be exploited to the fullest for her mind to stay in balance.

The Aga had warned her in advance. She had to be careful of similar licentious trends. If she used all her ammunition during the first battle, she might be left defenseless at some point, and then this over-sensuous Sultan might look for someone else.

Perhaps, this was the reason why Mahidevran was put aside for the time being. She might have been too hot for her own good. She might be better looking than her, but a woman had to know how and when to use each weapon in her disposal. A wise woman should also be stringy with her favors rather than openhanded. She had to treat a man like a shy customer rather than a commanding master. She had to be cool rather than fiery.

Men were curious creatures. They yearned for what was untouchable. Obedient women eager to please were considered by men cheap, because they exhibited the mentality of a slave. She was a slave; so, she had to behave like a Princess. Diamonds were more precious than rubies despite being colorless because they were harder. For men hardness was the desirable virtue.

These were his wise advices and for as long as she comforted his affliction, she could count on his assistance. It was a clear sign Mahidevran had rejected his advances, so he kept his mouth closed and their relationship strictly formal. This was a grave mistake, because the Kislar Aga was not a bad ruler. He was like a pimp of a bordello. Every whore needed his advice and protection for a modest portion of her gains. His reward didn't have to be in hard cash. He was happy with just a taste of her social influence.

Being a concubine she knew that well, but Mahidevran as a Kadin could not imagine it. Her superior position had made the princess more haughty and careless. She would not allow such a "man" to touch her; but one good deed deserved another and the Kislar Aga was the most informed man in the Eski Saray.

The Aga's advices were indeed wise, professional and fair. Sometimes she was indeed too bold and acted truly as a shameless whore. Her first rape was still too vivid in her mind to resist a chance to relive it. Nevertheless, somewhat she had to contain her urge for excesses. For example, her dance especially approaching its conclusion had turned into a demonic cycle that had aroused her desires even more than her master's, as she saw that with every new move she increased his passion beyond proportion. Then, she had reached a point when she could not help but making her dance more vulgar and explicit. In reality she might have been even bolder, if there was a handsome Janissary like Ibrahim in his shoes. If Suleiman was a man, Ibrahim, the Prince of her dreams was manlier.

For some reason the Valide Sultan was playing with Ibrahim's desires. It could be a deliberate or an unconscious tease; but her gut feeling said it was deliberate. The Birinci Kadin of Selim was not a fool. It was not entirely her idea. The role the Kislar Aga had played in that occasion had ringed a bell. Hafsa Sultan was testing Ibrahim's reflexes. The fact he was captivated by her charms rather than the eunuch's meant Ibrahim was also a womanizer. Being the Kadin of Sultan Selim was a good excuse for such a dubious test.

She could sympathize with Hafsa Sultan. She had similar doubts. This was the reason why she had tried to boost Suleiman's vigor by letting her lips free to visit his source of passion. It might have been a strategic mistake and the wrong thing for a virgin to do, but she had a good excuse any concubine would easily understand. This was the second night in two years she had tried her luck with Suleiman. She was so desperate to attract him that she had felt victim of the same urges she had attempted to trigger. It was not entirely her mistake. His overall behavior had led her to a state of sheer desperation. If he had not denied her the first time, then she would have been more patient and tease instead of pleasing him.

Men were awful creatures. They were so competitive they couldn't sleep unless they surpassed the deeds of their competitors. An adventurous woman could become rich by taking advantage of this trend. They even had a motto for adventurous women like her. A whore would always be a whore; but, she was determined to become an exception to the rule. She was not after riches, she was after power. She simply could not forget she was the bustard offspring of a boyar. Her children would not have to face the kind of disgraces she had to experience in her life.

The first time Suleiman had fallen asleep inside her arms unable to utter a single word of love to her. In the end, to save the remaining few specks of decency she had snubbed the Selim Sultan's golden coin reward, and rushed to her room to hide her sorrow in the arms of her devoted teacher, the Kislar Aga. It was the worst wound her ego had to suffer since the day she entered the Harem. However, now everything had changed, and with the honest woman's sweat she had regained the right to hope that the Sultan's warm seed in her womb would be the key that would open wide the gates of a magnificent future for her and her children.

The Kislar Aga had been extremely useful for her aims. Even the monthly days of her fertility matched perfectly the night of expression of the Sultan's passion. Perhaps it was the wish of Allah the Foresighted that she was going to bear the next heir of the throne of Osman. It was not long ago since the first time and she was so frustrated she felt clearly the desire to try her luck with a true man. Inside the concubine school all her classmates were girls around her age, and the teachers much older female slaves or repulsively fat eunuchs with high pitched voices.

Hafsa Sultan had been probably informed of her past and behaved very cautiously trying to keep her always in complete isolation and only once she found herself in the presence of an attractive young man. At that earlier time, she got the impression that Hafsa was preparing her to become the slave of that nice blond young nobleman with the thrilling green eyes, but she was mistaken. Hafsa's plan was different; so, she had to be punished for showing her face to the witty stranger; but how was she supposed to know what were the intentions of a devious widow?

Fortunately, Hafsa Sultan was wise enough to let the Aga decide what the proper punishment of a concubine should be for having licentious thoughts, and he was not the kind of man who believed that such thoughts were truly a sin for any odalisque. They were her salvation; thus, he gave more food for similar thoughts in the absolute privacy of his bedroom. He taught her the most valuable lesson of all in a city where once Holy Mary was worshiped and now was prospering under the Ottoman rule, namely how a woman could please a man and remain virgin forever.

****

She turned and watched the Sultan resting by her side. He had his eyes closed still trying to recover from the whirlwind of her passionate kisses. His lips were smiling and in his face, calmness had replaced the intense tension of her superior lovemaking. In the Harem, she had heard the rumor Turks made love exactly as they struggled in battle, raging mad; but Suleiman was different. Love with him was more like giving a reward to a child that had tried his best. This thought aroused her affection, so she bent over and kissed him gently on his lips. He failed to react as he was again sound asleep from exhaustion, but now everything was different. She knew all his weaknesses and she would never again run away to her room to hide her shame.

She bent over and this time her teeth searched for his lips. The pain was enough to wake him up from his lethargy. It was the right time for him to learn that wars were not always won in a single battle. If the first time she had been wild, this time she had to tease him to death. She had to wake up the dozing conqueror in him, and the best way to do that was to resist him and struggle desperately before surrendering the price he valued most.

Thank God, Ukrainian women were very resilient and resourceful by nature. They could exhaust a horde of Tatar raiders before the night was over. They had to. Ukraine was not like the Caucuses. There were no narrow passages that could be defended and women had to be open and hospitable to all raiders, Tatar or Vikings, to survive and see another day and then another.

If Mahidevran was as proud as her black slave claimed, it had to be the result of her mountainous country, Georgia. She probably couldn't even stand to constantly submit to the will of a single man. She had to be conquered many times to become an obedient subject; but, Suleiman was probably too busy and too complicated to devote so much time to a single woman who was also so foolishly egotistical. If she was to conquer his heart, she had to outsmart every other odalisque or Kadin.

****

The news for the selection of Sultan's new favorite were quickly spread around the City of Constantine, as every concubine rushed to tell her version of the night's events to her favorite eunuch. From there the news reached the ears of the Janissary guards on the Seraglio walls who always had a piece of information worthy of exchange with the lusty eunuchs.

Thus, in few hours the news had reached every bazaar, hammam and teahouse from the hilltops down to the harbors. All versions had this common theme; the Sultan was now spending his entire day in the company of a Russian slave with mediocre looks who had stolen his heart with some secret weapon, possibly a love potion product of devious Christian sorcery.

By noon, the story had spread from the hammams of the Eternal City's to the harems of the Asian suburbs and there was where the opinions divided. All the mothers held the view that the Sultan's behavior towards the mothers of his sons was improper. He should not have any complain, since these pious Muslims had given him in such a short time three healthy sons; thus, it was unfair to put them aside and choose instead a cheap Christian dancer who knew only how to swing her hips and shake her breasts audaciously at his face. There were even few loathsome rumors claiming that besides dancing she was also comforting old men in Galata. It was a bold claim, but made a lot of sense since she was a Christian, and everyone knew Christians besides Jews were the best whores in the Balkans and the Middle East. Such a whore had to know how to please an old man and still retain for a Sultan her precious virginity.

No pious Muslim woman could ever compete with such cheap belly-dancers. The Quran ordered that slaves should be well treated, and nothing more detailed than that. Anyway, this was not the first time a Christian prostitute had mesmerized a naïve Muslim youngster. This was why the Muftis insisted that no Muslim young man should go across the Golden Horn to Galata, because he would lose his soul and possibly the hard earned content of his purse. This time the devil had slipped into the Harem and made the young and inexperienced Sultan lose his head over a professional enchantress of abysmally low morality. In any case, this was not the proper way for a just Sultan to run his harem or bestow a good example to his subjects. The entire world order would collapse, if husbands forgot their obligations to families or his legal wives for every spring chicken that passed along looking for a horny rooster.

On the contrary, the impression of these events on most unmarried women was very favorable. The struggle of the enterprising youth against the elderly establishment was always hard and every change of the old guard was bound to cause little resentment; but, true love would always be triumphant at the end, so healthy offspring can be born. For young women the recent developments were very romantic and inspiring.

However, the women's opinions carried little weight in the City from the sunrise to the sunset and could reach the ears of their husbands only during meals and at bedtime. The general consensus among men was very positive. Men needed a leader who could show to every direction that the vigor of the Ottomans remained undiminished, and every night a young and exciting girl spend in Sultan's bed meant that in a few months another child would be born. If this Russian slave was half as good as everybody claimed, then another son ready to take command of the Empire would be born. It was the will of Allah that the vigor of a nation could only be measured by the number of the newborn boys. They were the ones who could hold arms and extend the borders of the Empire against the infidels. Anything else was nothing but silly women's chatter, or remnants of decadent Roman traditions that had started declining the moment they replaced the inspiring pagan image of the divine prostitute Aphrodite with the Christian miraculous icon of a pseudo-virgin Jewish slave.

During the last years of the reign of Selim, all enemies had fled shamefully from the battlefields. The only danger that still existed was the possibility of a civil riot in the Eternal City. The first discussions among the Janissary Ortas had already started triggered by the delay of the new planned war. Up to now all the money Suleiman had spread around during his coronation were holding the spirits quite high with celebrations for all the future victories; but, there was also a lot of negative comments about the love affairs of the new Sultan that kept him preoccupied from his military duties with bodily exhausting erotic escapades.

It was precisely during one of these festivities when a drunken Janissary joking about this erotic affair, provided an alternative connotation to the phrase "We will meet again at the Red Apple Tree", and then disappeared in the thin air, waiting for the entire event to be forgotten. However, the entire incident soon became the laughing stock of the City and the Russian girl became the Red Apple Tree of the young Sultan.

Valide Sultan was as usually the quickest to find out what the subject of gossip in the City bazaars was from the fleshy lips of her eunuchs. Undoubtedly her elaborate plan for her son to fall in love with the pretty Russian was a smashing success, and in few months everything would turn out all right; but, now something had to be done to turn around the adverse popular opinion.

Many times before in the City similar trifles had triggered violent riots. In peace times it was difficult to find constructive ways to dissipate the exceedingly aggressive spirit of the Janissary Corps. War against the infidels was the best way to resolve internal struggles, as it had been proven time and time again.

Hafsa called her scriber and dictated a letter to her son, expressing all her worries and she concluded that he needed a quick victory to establish his authority as a Sultan; but before saying the last word, she communicated few of the jokes that circulated around the teahouses and reached her ears. She estimated that few vulgar words were only needed to shake her son out of the nonchalance attitude and extreme optimism that characterizes men in love with women of such inferior breeding.

****

When Hafsa's letter reached Suleiman, he was isolated once more in his suite, listening to Russian love songs from the mesmerizing lips of his beloved concubine that had never failed to please him. He was indeed most pleasantly surprised, when he found out that a concubine could be interested in his poetry.

It was a rare virtue he did not expect from someone coming from the barbaric North. Usually the women from the steppes were daughters of farmers or shepherds, and their only desirable characteristics were their white complexion and blue eyes; but, she was much more than that. She knew how to read and write, and she had intellect and a captivating personality too.

Her hair was dark red and her delicate features reminded him of Roman statues. She also seemed to have a positive and dynamic personality, but at the same time she was as refined and educated as the best slaves imported from the West. However, her seductive dance had proven beyond any doubt she could also become earthly and sensuous as any woman from the East, if she believed this was his wish.

This woman was like the City and he was her Ottoman conqueror in every sense of the word. She knew how to resist him, increasing beyond any measure his desire, and then when he thought he had no more strength left, surrender completely and treat him as magnificently as a Sultan should be treated.

Every woman was different in that respect. According to Ibrahim it all had to do with the way she had lost her virginity. All women kept deep in their hearts the details of their original sin, and if they had a chance, they tried their best to relive these singular moments.

Indeed Mahidevran Sultan had been different than this slave. They were both very young at the time. She was too impatient, while he was too shy. Their love making was condemned to follow the same pattern according to his wise Hasodabashi. However, the expedite letter from his mother was enough to spoil his early morning high spirits after a steamy night of debauchery. If he believed Hafsa's words, then he should worry each time a drunkard dared to criticize the resolve of his Sultan and Padishah. Nevertheless, the most annoying issue in her letter was that she was very accurate in all her observations.

It was most certainly true the last few weeks he had done nothing more but slip under the covers with his new favorite, testing her complete obedience to his absolute authority, while neglecting the affairs of the Empire and especially the urgent preparations for the war against Hungary.

Angrily he threw away the letter on the floor and walked to the window trying to find a good way out of the disturbing reality. The Russian maiden seeing him upset, picked up the letter, read it, and soon her laughter reverberated in every corner of the room. Surprised by the noise, he turned around to see what was happening, but the girl kept on laughing so hard he could not help but follow her example, even though he did not know the true reason for this expression of vivacity.

When her laughter finally subsided, she told her master she was truly flattered that in a few days she had become the dream of the entire Ottoman Empire the same way the Romans worshiped Virgin Mary. If this was indeed the case, maybe her master should seek a competent Italian painter to paint a naked portrait of her bust to inspire the Janissary Corps in battle, offering them another reason to fight to the death.

It was another tease to make him lose his jealous mind, and before he had time to react, she inquired holding up her naked breasts, if he really liked her red apples so much that he was willing to forget his Belgrade siege to taste them as Adam has done for Eve in Paradise. Her suggestion was a bit too bold for an Osmanli Sultan, but her offer was much more than any young man could resist under the circumstances.

It was really remarkable how quickly she had learned in the Seraglio School how to use her body to lift the spirits of a frustrated man and her pointed joke calmed down all his anxieties. It had to be Ibrahim's influence on the Odalisque School curriculum that made all the difference.

His Hasodabashi had a mysterious way to convey his ideas to the eunuchs no one could copy. Now he was more than ever eager to demolish the Belgrade Walls with his heavy artillery and push through the Iron Gates of Danube, as it was the plan he had drawn with Piri Pasha. However, he did not get the chance to respond to her suggestion as a White Eunuch came in announcing that the Hasodabashi was waiting to be admitted is his quarters.

This was not the first occasion in several days that Ibrahim had tried to see him, but each time he was too busy to see anyone. However, this time Suleiman felt a strong need to see Ibrahim and asked the girl to disappear into the adjacent Hasodabashi bedroom, leaving the two men alone.

Ibrahim did not waste any time to come in, and seeing the bed untidy he realized Suleiman was not alone. The rosebud perfume that was still lingering in the air gave him a clue about the name of his company, but the Sultan somewhat embarrassed by his presence handed him the letter and asked for his expert suggestion for a good way out of the jam.

The slave read carefully every line. It was in complete agreement with the rumors he had also overheard already in the corridors. Her perfume had materialized his fears and now it was clear his master and friend had met the woman of his dreams and become her slave too.

The prospect of spending his life as a slave of a slave turned into dust all his self-esteem. His first reaction was to keep clear from this entire affair and leave his master find his way out of this mess; but he soon reversed his mind. If this new affliction created any problems, it was to his advantage to solve them.

Whatever Suleiman might be doing today, he was the one who saved his life in the bazaar and protected him in the Seraglio from the designs of his terrible father.

The Russian girl was just a minor obstacle in his path, and he would be unworthy of any higher destiny, if he could not overcome her alluring influence. After all, this promiscuous girl was exploiting the Sultan's sensual nature to increase her influence in a way very similar to what he had done in numerous occasions. With a background like hers, it was natural for her to try to give her battle in the field she knew best, seduction.

He could still easily recall the Russian maiden's excited face, and imagined her naked in the arms of an equally fervent Sultan. It seemed ridiculous, but his emotions were so confused he did not know for which partner of the two he felt more jealously. He was perplexed, and facing Suleiman he had to make an effort just to smile and look happy and calm. It was a natural reaction for anyone facing an overwhelmingly powerful opponent to try to appease him. If he was a dog, he should have wiggled his tail by now. Now as a man he was upset by this turn of events; but, seeing him smiling, Suleiman thought he had found a solution and anxiously asked him for an explanation, as a smile was much more difficult for him to explain than an angry face.

Any human mind was capable of finding a solution to a logical problem, if it had enough time to analyze it; but brilliancy was the ability to analyze the existing relevant facts in the shortest time by surmounting or bypassing every irrelevant obstacle. Suleiman could surely find the proper solution on his own, but now he was visibly upset and by the time he could see clearly the way out, other problems might surface and confuse his judgment even further. A great leader like Alexander was able to solve an unexpected problem in the fastest way possible, cutting each knot in two with his sword.

Ibrahim took a bow to gain extra time and play out his master's weakness. The Sultan would not understand if all these gestures were a sign of respect or simply an acting performance. Displaying absolute obedience was for Ibrahim the most advantageous approach.

"My Sultan and Divine Master, if you resembled your grandfather Bayezid the Saint, a prayer to Allah would surely provide the best way out. On the other hand, if you were made like your mighty father, Selim Khan, then you would simply try to find the Janissary who insulted your Imperial Majesty and cut his head off, and if you took after your mother, you would start urgently another war unprepared. However, you are Suleiman Khan, Padishah and Shah-in-Shah and only you know exactly what you must do, while I am just a humble page who always tries to serve his Master best any way he can."

His loquacity increased further Sultan's impatience.

"It would be enough of a service simply to tell me what you, my trusted slave, will do in my place."

Ibrahim sensed his anxiety and tried to emphasize his superiority.

"If I were a Sultan and had as much authority as Your Magnificence, it would be rather easy to resolve this trifle matter. I would simply summon the Aga of the Janissary and give him a purse as a reward for this joker who has entertained the City in strenuous times. When this man is found, I would ask the Aga to send him next in a secret mission as a spy to find out how many Hungarians guard the walls of Belgrade. Then, every Janissary would know which the true Red Apple Tree is for an Osmanli Sultan. If he comes back alive, then I would make him a Pasha, because every Sultan needs to have competent and witty men at his service; but, if he died this would mean he was good only as a buffoon and Allah had punished him justly for doubting the determination of His Shadow."

Suleiman was so pleased when he heard Ibrahim's proposal that he rushed with open arms and embraced him. He had strong guilty feelings for his sudden love affair with the Russian, and wished to prove to him that his intimate desires were not seriously affected. Initially he was afraid that perhaps Ibrahim might become jealous for his new love and lose his devotion, but this wise advice had clearly shown that for Ibrahim nothing had changed. Perhaps later he should find some free time and explain to his intimate friend what a joyful, witty and thoroughly pleasing girl like her meant for him, and as a friend he should understand the distinct roles lusty odalisques and loyal friends played in the life of an Ottoman Sultan like him who had the blood of Bayezid the Saint and Selim the Terrible running in his veins.

Ibrahim had also decided there was no reason for him to ask his friend nosy questions about his new relationship. Any such hint would oblige a Sultan to explain his feelings to a slave, and then a possibly superficial relation might appear much more important than it actually was. On the other hand, if this newly developing relationship turned up to be serious and long lasting, then by keeping a safe distance, he would have kept at least his dignity unsoiled enough to attract the Princess Hatidge's respect.

Right now it simply didn't make much sense to launch a preemptive attack against this unfamiliar woman, when he was at a disadvantage. The correct course was to prove his usefulness as long as possible, waiting for a more opportune occasion when firmer details about her true character had surfaced.

The previous events with the Valide Sultan had showed this Russian maiden was clearly her choice, and she should have also his sympathy and support. If he ever had a son who displayed preferences to the same sex, he should find a good whore for him too, and the Russian seemed to possess a remarkable ability to raise a sensitive man's moral. Right now, he had the black eyes of Hatidge Sultan in his mind, and if an Ottoman Sultan wished to share his bed with a Christian slave of dubious past, then, he would have every right to claim an Ottoman Princess to become the mother of his children.

With a careful analysis he could see that this promiscuous maiden could become his best ally, as she was cutting the Osmanli family down to his size. If an enchantress was elevated to the Sultan's bed then he, a hammam boy and a eunuch candidate, could entertain impossible dreams of the highest possible status.

He left the bedroom convinced that as long as the Sultan needed his advice, he had nothing to fear from any female slave no matter how attractive or lusty she might appear to be. If any of the Christian teaching made any sense, it had to be the eventual triumph of spirit over flesh, and he could surely provide both to lift his temperamental master's moral.

****

She had been following the entire conversation from the keyhole and as soon as the bedroom door closed behind Ibrahim's back, the girl returned to find Suleiman's mood entirely changed. He seemed very pleased his friend had found the solution to his problem and from now on, nothing could cast a shadow over their happiness. Without one comment more, he asked a scriber to come over and he dictated two letters in a hurry. The first was directed to the Janissary Aga to put Ibrahim's plan into action. The second manuscript was to be delivered in the hands of his mother. He reassured her that everything was under control thanks to a very wise suggestion of his precious friend she seemed to so actively object.

When he had finished his obligations, he felt somewhat less nervous, but still quite depressed. The truth was that all these days he had neglected a faithful friend and he had not too many friends he could rely on. His free time was limited by Allah from sunrise to sunset and from sunset to sunrise, and he wished he had twice as many sunsets to sunrises to divide justly among his two favorites.

"Who was that man?" the Russian girl asked.

"He was my Hasodabashi, Ibrahim. He normally resides next door in this very room, in case I need him. Urgent problems don't announce their existence days ago," he informed her and set her mind in motion.

She had already heard in the Harem the rumors Suleiman Khan was spending most of his nights with this particular servant. This unnatural behavior was probably the reason why his desperate mother had chosen to send her instead of any other concubine who might be more pure and beautiful than her. Her most important virtue that made all the difference was her erotic experience with aged men no other concubine or Kadin could outweigh with her virtue or beauty. She didn't feel offended by this choice. Hafsa was right. Her son needed a kind of woman who could convince him he was the manliest man who ever lived.

"That's so true! These days I feel too in the middle of the night a most urgent need for your flesh. I wonder if he would mind, if I was to move to his room until you make these urges of mine stop. Is he really as attractive as they say?" she asked continuing her teasing strategy.

"Yes, maybe he is, but he is much wiser than his looks might suggest," he countered her onslaught.

"Is he the one who arranges for our daily meetings?"

"No, I am the one! He has nothing to do with it. Why do you ask?"

"If he was, perhaps I should show him some gratitude with a tip, so he does not think I'm just an ungrateful bitch," she said indifferently. "Rewarding the capable servants is a way to encourage good performance. These poor eunuchs don't have much to live for unlike us."

The Harem vicious rumors claimed Ibrahim was no eunuch, so this was just a trap to test the Sultan's sincerity. She failed. Suleiman was so happy with her he didn't feel like hiding anything. This girl made him feel like a true Sultan, and a Sultan should not lie. His father's thunderous voice chastising lies still echoed in his mind.

"Ibrahim is not a eunuch. He may be a slave, but at the same time he is my closest friend and my most trusted adviser in all my affairs."

The Russian maiden was quick in recovering.

"If he is your closest friend, then you wouldn't mind much if I was to meet him. I think he would be very pleased to find out how much we love each other."

"I'm sure he already knows that much. News travels very fast in the Harem corridors."

"Indeed they do. I wish we could be all alone sometime, without eunuchs standing outside my door. Do you think Ibrahim could arrange that as a Hasodabashi?"

"No, he cannot! He can only enforce the Harem rules. I'm the only one who can command the Aga of the White Eunuchs, but I won't! It's a security measure that can save lives. All the members of my household must feel safe inside my Seraglio."

"Yes, but they say few sneaky eunuchs are eavesdropping to learn all of your secrets."

"Yes, few of them are indeed nosy, but this is my wish. My father had to know everything that happens inside his Selamlik, and I must know too," Suleiman declared with a tone of voice that didn't tolerate objections; but he was already outflanked.

"Indeed you must, and I am sorry to start this conversation. I was a bit selfish thinking of my reputation, but I shouldn't be. From the moment I make my master happy, I shouldn't worry if the entire world knows all the details of how I accomplish it."

It was a hit below the belt that struck home, forcing the Sultan to consider all the consequences.

"You are right. I never thought of every devious consequence of spying. If one day something leaks out, I will have their heads in a platter."

"No, you shouldn't be so harsh about an issue that makes us so happy. You have your Hasodabashi for such intimate matters. A noble sovereign should behave benevolently and his state officials harsh. Then, if something goes wrong, it must be a state officials' fault, not yours."

It was truly remarkable how quickly his favorite had discovered what had been wrong during Selim's reign. She was a true blessing. None of his concubines had ever made such profound suggestion. This creature somehow reminded him of his mother. Perhaps he should discuss her suggestion with Ibrahim too, and then, if he didn't have anything better to propose, consider suitable ways to apply it.

* * * * * * *

The Russian girl waited patiently for him to finish all his other official duties before she could claim back his undivided attention. She had a strange smile that pleased him so much that he asked her for an explanation. She kept her expression and asked with a pretentious air of submission:

"What should I do to make me the sole keeper of your heart and keep me here in his bed for one more night?" she asked and her smile was so irresistibly innocent that Suleiman never suspected she was well aware of the nature of his relationship with Ibrahim.

Actually, it was the very first piece of news she heard as soon as she came back to the Eski Saray from her first dancing exhibition for a change of clothes; but, she had kept her cool, and her impeccable composure had disarmed all the other concubines that had tried to hurt her feelings. At the moment, any previous affair that Suleiman had created was nothing but a minor distraction, as long as she could read in his eyes his unreserved adoration for her erotic skills.

Suleiman's behavior was extremely easy for her to analyze. The fact he

87

was bored of his harem was a clear sign his formal wives had failed to please him even though they were exceedingly beautiful, as everyone testified. This simply meant Ibrahim had something more to give him, when they were in bed and between two men there were just three possible options. She was wise enough to try first the most probable one between a master and a slave. Suleiman needed to feel like a conqueror.

She was also confident that within a week she would be carrying in her womb the irreplaceable ingredient of her plan that could fulfill all her ambitions, the sacred seed of the House of Osman. If all went well, she would be within few months in the same level with the other two mothers of Suleiman's children. However, very soon even this state of equilibrium was going to change in her favor. She was the youngest and being the fountain of youth was one of the most powerful arguments in the Harem.

Now, she had to be patient and avoid hasty moves, as time was her ally. Given time, she would be the winner in any such competition. She was the wittiest of them all possibly as much as she was the more lustful. The only fear she had was her oncoming pregnancy, as complications were very common. She was not also sure how pregnancy could affect her mood. Up to that moment, her only duty was to keep his bed warm and his passion fiery; but soon this was bound to change, as every newborn baby could become another powerful ally for her cause.

Suleiman for the moment did not seem to care whether her smile was an indication of gratitude for his affections or a sign of triumph. Therefore, as most frequently happens to proud young men in love, he naturally assumed the most optimistic scenario was materializing. He was now perplexed by one more thought. The day that a slave had entered his service, was the last day of her previous life and the beginning of the new. The Russian concubine had to forget her old Christian name and assume the name her master would choose for her. This custom was quite similar with the Christian baptism, as all the Muslims were named the same day they were born by their father.

Naming a child was a very simple ceremony for Allah's faithful. All that required was for the child's father to write down at the last page of a Quran the name of the newborn.

However, to name an infidel female slave all these religious ceremonial details were too much of a hustle, and common names that signified beauty were chosen, namely Spring Flower, Jasmine, Rose, Jacinth, Rosebud, Tulip, Carnation, depending on the mood and the preferences of the master.

All these days he had tried hard to find a suitable name for her, but could not make up his mind. All seemed common and overused for such an unforgettable woman; but, now as she smiled at him, she was so captivating he couldn't think anything more suitable than "Hurrem", "the joyous one", as he knew deep in his heart she was meant to be his everlasting smile. This would be the name for all the men who loved her too.

For those who despised her lineage, she would always be "Roxelana", the

"Russian"; but, for those who really hated she would "Rossa" for her questionable red tinted erotic skills.

****

As the days of happiness quickly piled up, Hurrem's optimism grew daily by leaps and bounds. There was no way after a week full of debauchery she wouldn't get pregnant. Of course, it was too early for any definite sign, but as it often happens, great expectations can even produce symptoms.

This new development did not make everyone happy, as sometimes foolish people consider rumors as facts. It was a setback for Mahidevran who could not accept this new period of negligence. She was a noble woman, a legal wife, and she had certain rights that could not be easily refused. Ibrahim as the Hasodabashi was the man to see and Zarafet her ablest ambassador.

"My lady wishes to have the pleasure of a meeting," she requested and Ibrahim took his time in replying.

It had been several years since he had become part of the Ottoman hierarchy and knew well what an official like him should expect when he was making a favor.

"I can assure you that my desire to see her is much greater than of hers to see me. However, I'm afraid this morning I'm on a very tight schedule," he calmly replied. "However, since it appears that my Master will be busy tonight too, I might be able to see her tonight for as much time as she wishes."

"I'm afraid my mistress cannot wait that long. From what I've heard she plans to meet the Sultan tonight."

"I'm not aware of any such meeting being arranged for tonight, but I will be the last man on this world to try to oppose such an enjoyable plan for my master. On the contrary, I will do my best to make it happen, if this is the will of my master."

"Then, my mistress will be forever grateful," Zarafet reassured him with a long smile.

"I wish I could live forever, because then I could wait patiently to enjoy my reward; but, life passes quickly, so people must be greedy rather than patient," Ibrahim pointedly remarked and the slave was sharp and well-prepared to respond to this subtle hint.

"When the masters are busy, the slaves are free to look after their own interests," she noted and fell on her knees to demonstrate her total submission to his will and she was not denied all the privileges that this position implied.

For a princess having pretty courtiers was an undeniable advantage. They could perform deeds her decency would not allow; but a slave would never do something her master would not allow. Therefore, her eagerness to please had to be a direct command. Mahidevran knew him too well and didn't mind bribing him in a way that pleased him most. By now everyone in the Harem should realize that money had no effect on him, if he ever took it, it was just to spend it in the most profitable way. Mahidevran was a Princess and Zarafet a commoner. He wouldn't mind treating her as a Princess, if she was not was not a courtier; but she was an intermediate carrier of a Princess' message.

Suleiman's problems with Mahidevran existed because he treated her as a Princess; but he was not going to repeat the same mistake. He was going to show Zarafet how dominant he could be, but in a very gentle way. Zarafet was indeed a very sensitive Tatar.

"You have the most sumptuous lips I have ever seen," he remarked with a tender smile, "but I would be the most deceitful costumer, if I failed to compliment your superb buttocks. I bet their firmness is the result of many hours of horse riding."

He was right. Zarafet was not only sensitive, but she had a sense of humor. Perhaps, it was a character she shared with her mistress. It was a risky supposition, but he was not the kind of man who would not risk everything to gain an advantage, so he added with a naughty smile:

"I bet your mistress also likes long rides. She is a true Tatar after all."

****

"This is unacceptable. I'm the Sultan and I will decide who I'll see and who will share my bed with me," Suleiman exploded the moment Ibrahim hesitantly expressed his suggestion for tonight's schedule.

"Indeed you are and I'm the last man eager to challenge this undeniable right! However, you are also the Shadow of Allah who does all he can to bring happiness and stability into this world," Ibrahim calmly replied, "and my duty is to assist you to the full extent of my abilities in distributing justly the content of your heart to each recipient, even if this means that I will get less than what I consider a just reward for my love and absolute devotion to your happiness."

"Actually, you are the only person I would most gladly spend some time tonight after such a long separation, not Mahidevran who is so demanding that she makes me feel like being her slave," Suleiman confessed.

"Would you mind if we postpone our meeting for a few days for the good of the Empire? Mahidevran is supposed to be fertile these days according to the Kislar Aga. She is so impeccably beautiful, she is just ideal for making sons. Now tell me, which foolish Sultan would say no to another son and simply waste his precious time chatting idly all night smoking a water-pipe with an intimate friend?"

Ibrahim didn't need to say anything more. Being just was the Sultan's greatest concern. It was the least he could do to equal his father's exploits for the time being.

****

Allah with all his wisdom knew well that distributing pleasure equally was an easy task, while distributing pain justly was an almost impossible ordeal. This was the reason why Allah made war much briefer than peace. He also knew that humans would always choose an easy task rather than a hard one. What He didn't appreciate was that most humans considered this evil trend as the wisest choice.

****

When Zarafet finished her report, Mahidevran did not seem content with the news. Ibrahim's subtle promises were too vague to satisfy her aggressive disposition; but, under the circumstances she could do nothing more than wait for as long as it took the slave to accomplish what he had promised. She summoned also Yabani to keep her company. She valued their advices a great deal even if they were often contrary to each other. This way they helped her take a more balanced decision.

In the case of Hurrem, Yabani had an inflexible point of view. Hurrem should be disposed somehow, as soon as the Sultan's passion resided like an overflowed river. For a nice sum she could find a eunuch ready to put his life in danger by slipping a deadly poison in her food. Zarafet on the other hand was considerably less violent. Time, she claimed, run in Mahidevran's favor. Sooner or later the Sultan would get bored of her the same way he did with all his other concubines. He was a typical man who valued greatly superior sex practices and everything she heard from the Eunuchs underlined this assertion. There was no trick in the book Hurrem didn't know. It was a very upsetting thought, but somehow this woman knew more tricks than all the concubines of the Harem put together and her trained flesh combined the virtues of a handsome youngster with femininity.

It was not the first time her courtiers used such a vulgar vocabulary when they were all alone. In fact, it had become almost an unwritten concubine rule inside the Harem to avoid using romantic, vague, or diplomatic terms resembling eunuch chatting, creating only suspicions of ambiguous insincerity.

"Do you suppose, Hurrem was a Galata whore before entering the Harem?" Mahidevran asked; but displaying hostile attitude was a subtle hint for her slaves to support her accusation.

"Of course she was a prostitute besides being a dancer!" Yabani claimed loudly. "Didn't you see her how she danced? As a woman I was ashamed just to look at her."

"How did you manage to see her dancing? The Kislar Aga practically threw us out trying not to see her shameful exhibition," Mahidevran asked with grievance.

"We both saw her!" Zarafet confessed. "When the Aga left to go to sleep, the White Eunuchs left the door open on purpose. They wouldn't lose the spectacle for anything."

"I simply couldn't come back and watch. It would be below the dignity of any Kadin," Mahidevran remarked in disgust.

"That's true, but I don't think it would do my mistress any good displaying

91

decency. The Sultan fell for her tricks completely as if he was a schoolboy and she his first time whore. All these Christian dancers are despicable witches. For instance, no Muslim wife would dare to take off her husband's clothes in a reception hall with so many spectators," Yabani continued.

"Is that what she did?" Mahidevran inquired. "Only whores do that to save time. For me watching a man getting undressed for the first time is an unforgettable thrill."

"For me too!" Zarafet and Yabani said in tandem, but their discussion was interrupted by the Black Eunuch guard asking permission for Ibrahim to enter.

It was unquestionably a gracious gesture from his part. According to the existing ritual, the Hasodabashi had the right to enter a concubine's apartment unannounced to check her conduct; but, Mahidevran and Gülfem were both Kadin of noble birth, and he had decided to honor this important distinction. Entering, he noticed they were all excited, a condition that made beautiful women even more desirable.

Perhaps, the three women should have worn their veils, but the fact that all the Hasodabashi were eunuchs had simplified the Muslim ritual in his case too. They were all surprised by his visit, and he couldn't resist the temptation to keep them wondering about the purpose of his visit.

"What brings you here, Ibrahim?" Mahidevran asked decisively, trying to put him into the awkward position of a servant giving a report to his superior.

"Your Highness has given me a mission, and I felt I should report at the earliest opportunity my sad failure or my resounding success," he noticed and immediately saw Mahidevran's eyes glittering with anticipation.

"What did the Sultan say?" she asked without hesitation.

"Is it true what the Kislar Aga told me?"

"What did this creep tell you?" Mahidevran said still furious about the role this eunuch had played.

"He told me many interesting things about the Russian maiden, because this is his duty as well as mine. I simply have to know everything that goes on inside my master's harem."

He didn't wish to say anything more before Mahidevran pressured him to.

"She is a whore, a piece of sold meat from a Galata bordello, isn't she?" she snapped back.

"This is not for me to say. I'm a piece of sold meat too; so, it would be unfair for me to judge what a concubine has to go through in her life first to survive and then prosper. The Aga told me she is a very skilled oriental dancer from the Galata district who knows how to use her belly to make the most mesmerizing promises."

"Then go back to the Seraglio, if this all you have to say," Mahidevran screamed at him in anger.

"No, that's not all. I came to tell you that since these are your fertile days, you are expected tonight in the Sultan's quarters and possibly for this entire week," Ibrahim announced, surprising everyone.

"What about that whore?" Mahidevran asked still furious for his leniency.

"As far as I know, she is not invited. Do you suppose I should make arrangements for her to dance for your pleasure too? From what I hear she is an enchanting dancer able to stir all sorts of desires to both men and women," he teased her. "There are even a few extremely poisonous tongues who claim she has even the Kislar Aga under her spell, and I wonder how she accomplishes such a feat. After all he is supposedly just a eunuch."

It was critical moment, as it always is when a human being is pushed to the limits of his endurance; but, Ibrahim felt now confidently enough to behave obnoxiously with every harem woman he encountered. Perhaps, the fact that Zarafet and Yabani were present increased his audacity beyond any previous acceptable limit.

****

Ibrahim was not the only man with a similar trend. Most men's appreciation was reduced the more they used a woman for their pleasure. It was one of the male characteristics Allah strongly despised. When He created the male gender He had hoped that men would appreciate the greatest gift women possessed, the only gate to immortality in this world; but, He failed in His prognosis. It was a curious effect similar to what Mehmet the Conqueror, His Shadow, had suffered. He had fought valiantly to demolish the Edirne Kapi with his artillery for the first time; but, since then and until his death, he could not remember how many times he had entered the Eternal City through this gate after a glorious expedition.

On the other hand, fearful of an old myth, Fatih had raised a wall blocking the Golden Gate the Roman Emperors used to enter Constantinople after a successful military expedition to block permanently such a possibility and used Edirne Kapi instead.

****

"I wonder if Kislar Aga is really a eunuch," Ibrahim hesitantly asked.

"No, he isn't. He just can't have any children," Yabani boldly claimed.

"How do you know?" Zarafet challenged her.

"He always goes to the hammam all alone. That's how," Yabani exploded. "There are few things every woman in the Harem should know about men. Fear is in the eyes of a eunuch."

Mahidevran by now was truly flabbergasted by every bit of news suddenly revealed. She didn't care much about the Kislar Aga, but she understood perfectly well Ibrahim had been teasing her, and she had fallen for it and blew her top, getting in a state of rage for a man who had accomplished a remarkable feat under the circumstances in her favor.

"Hasodabashi, I am grateful for your efforts!" she finally uttered as soon as she had regained her composure, but he was still in a teasing mood.

"Are you really fertile tonight? I have promised him another son, and I don't wish to appear a liar to my master. There were all these rumors circulating in the Harem about you being pregnant for a third time; but I can now see that you are as desirable as any virgin concubine."

Mahidevran was now well prepared to adapt to the overall atmosphere, and she didn't care to reply but just faintly smile, putting an end to this intimate and embarrassing discussion. She failed. Ibrahim was too excited for his success and pressed forward.

"Is it true Allah has imposed on women to become most desirable during their fertile days?"

"Yes, that's true!" Zarafet and Yabani replied in tandem ahead of their mistress. "Few of them can behave like real sluts those days."

"I don't suspect this is Hurrem's problem," Ibrahim wondered but he received no reply.

****

"Hurrem is not pregnant," Suleiman revealed with a sorry expression.

"It is not an important issue!" Ibrahim noticed to calm down his master's worries. "Women are very sensitive and temperamental creatures. In the old days, just for this reason Ancient Greeks assumed several goddesses were responsible for women's behavior. Hera was responsible for married women, Athena for the wise ones, Artemis for the pure, and Aphrodite for the lustful. If we were Ancient Greeks, we would now conclude that Hera was pleased with Mahidevran's conduct and displeased with your new favorite who followed Aphrodite's advices; but do not worry! Aphrodite bore many more children than Hera in the long run. This goddess simply could not refuse to comfort any attractive man even if he was a close relative. Now all that is left is for us to decide which role Gülfem plays.""

"I have no use for your Greek gods. They are so many of them it is confusing. One god, Allah, is enough for me," Suleiman replied and draw another sip of red wine.

"You are a hypocrite. Besides Allah you trust also Bacchus, Mars, and Eros! You may not wish to admit it, but deep inside you prefer Hurrem. This is why you wish so much to have a child with her."

"This is not true. Hurrem is just a slave of mine I use for pleasure. Mahidevran Sultan is my Kadin and so is Gülfem."

"That may be true, but you keep on asking me these days for Hurrem. This means she is a more pleasant company. This is also what the eunuchs tell me."

"The eunuchs are too nosy. If I am asking more for Hurrem, it is because I wish to be fair. Mahidevran Sultan has already given me two healthy sons. Hurrem must have her chance too to have a child. Children provide a source of accomplishment to most women."

"This is indeed very wise of you; but, it is much more than that. I feel you are madly in love with Hurrem, but you don't want to admit it. She is much more than a slave to you. You want her to become the mother of your children too," Ibrahim insisted. "That's why you are so worried she is not pregnant yet and failed to comment about Mahidevran's fictitious pregnancy."

"Nonsense! Hurrem is now my favorite consort because she can make me smile. Gülfem is always so serious she cannot entertain my worries about the oncoming Belgrade expedition. I also know all about Mahidevran's false pregnancy much earlier than you, believe me. This is one reason I haven't seen her for a month. You know well I cannot stand liars."

"If Hurrem is just a slave for you, let me have her for a night. Friends should share all their possessions, don't they? A concubine is not more important than a caftan, or is she?" Ibrahim audaciously asked and his casual suggestion was enough to spoil the Sultan's mood.

"No! A human being is not the same as a caftan. It has feelings," Suleiman replied grimly. "Hurrem will be hurt, if I treat her like a common slave."

"You are absolutely right! I was just testing the sincerity of your declaration. A slave is not a caftan indeed, even if she might be cheaper to buy. You did all you could to keep me safe from Selim, and I will be grateful for my entire life. However, a woman should not be just witty and pleasant like a man. To feel complete she has to bear children too. If Hurrem is sterile, would you lent her to me for a month, and I promise you she will be even better educated when she comes back to you? She will even speak Greek fluently," Ibrahim continued once more in a teasing mood.

"Why are you making all these absurd suggestions tonight? Women are like horses. A true Turcoman like me will never lend you his horse."

Ibrahim started laughing heartedly, while Suleiman became progressively tenser. Ibrahim knew it was risky to laugh when a Turk was serious. Suleiman might think he was laughing at him, not his attachment to Hurrem.

"No! A woman is not a horse either. No Turcoman can fall in love with his horse. He simply uses, cares, and appreciates his horse; but, he would not mind trading it, if he found an even better one. I'm not crazy to ask you to share Mahidevran, Gülfem, or even Hurrem with me for a night. They are your favorite women. I will not even ask you for a caftan or a horse because they are yours too, and I'm your slave. Whatever you give me I shall accept because you wish me to. I made all these silly questions just for you to realize that you need Hurrem's love so much that you will be very happy if you could transform your love into a living human being that will live even when you two lovers will be gone. Hurrem is certainly much more than a caftan or a horse to you. Now she is a slave, but in the future she will be the mother of your children. This is the true essence of a woman's love and happy is the man who can experience it at least during a single night of his life."

"One night was not enough for me. I cannot have enough of Hurrem these days," Suleiman confessed.

"Yes, I realize that too; but, do you know why you love her as much as you say?"

"Yes, I do! We are made for each other by Allah. There can be no other explanation!" Suleiman claimed with passion.

Ibrahim remained silent. He did not have any immediate comment worth saying. He only knew there were many as convincing explanations. He was threading on dangerous ground. It was apparent Hurrem had become a very important element of the Sultan's happiness, and the reason was at least to him obvious too, since his feelings for Hurrem were quite similar. She was the kind of attractive woman who could ignite suddenly extreme passions, a defining characteristic of every libertine woman, as everyone else realized but the Sultan. This meant she was inclined instinctively to try one man after the other until she had saturated her lust and stopped seeking. Suleiman needed a woman like her all of his own to drown in her endless passion the devils that broke free sometimes unexpectedly, the same devils he could not control too almost as often and as badly.

The Ancient Greeks believed that before the Olympians there were other gods who controlled humanity, the Titans. Greeks were very subtle. One Titan was Chronos that ate his children. Selim was controlled by Chronos. To avoid Chronos' fate Selim had used eunuchs instead of women that were eternally sterile and could not produce children he might on day have to eat; but he was not always successful. Even in his deathbed Selim was dreaming of serving poisonous caftans to kill a faraway child he couldn't reach, while he sought in his comma to touch eternity happily with the help of a divine female like Mahidevran. These were how he had explained in his mind all the random pieces of information he had managed to collect teasing Asphodel and promising redemption.

Now he simply could not utter a word more because there was no way for him to know how Suleiman would react to his assertions. Suleiman had many similar traits with his father, but being similar did not mean the two men were identical.

He also knew that Muslims didn't appreciate statues of Olympian gods almost as much as fanatical Christians who cut their noses and penises wherever they discovered them. He was a man not a statue, and the only way to reach immortality was making a woman like Hatidge fall in love with him.

Women in the Seraglio had become much more critical ingredients in a warrior Sultan's life than simply vessels of pleasure, or objects a sovereign displayed to terrorize his enemies with his male vigor. They had become even more central than simply caring mothers and protectors of their precious heirs. They demanded the much more vital role of a comrade, occupying a greater portion of a warlord's time and attention. It was not some kind of devious conspiracy to undermine Sultan's overwhelming power to command his subjects. It was civilization creeping stealthily inside an Ottoman warrior's tent.

Ibrahim's bold suggestion of sharing Hurrem was not as offending as it seemed off-hand. Slaves were hardly human beings in certain respects. Under different circumstances two close friends could enjoy simultaneously not only a woman but a boy too in a Galata inn, if they so desired and could afford the higher cost. Suleiman could not be offended if Ibrahim indeed meant the content of his suggestion rather than used it as a subtle trick, so that the Sultan's feelings for this concubine could be clarified. It was an old Harem's custom concubines who could not produce heirs or did not produce much satisfaction to the Sultan to be given away as presents to other noblemen. Nevertheless, Hurrem's case was something entirely different and this was the crux of Ibrahim's audacious request.   But many times it was hard to probe into a man's heart so deeply without hurting it.

"You are right. Hurrem is not just one of my many concubines. Sooner or later, Allah willing, she is going to be a mother of an offspring. I cannot share her the same way I could not share you with anyone else, even my father," Suleiman confessed melancholically.

It was a bold confession of a weakness, Ibrahim was ready to exploit.

"I hope you realize my request for using Hurrem was just a friendly gesture to help you realize your true sentiments about this remarkable creature," he repeated trying hastily to divert the discussion from Selim. "I have never met her, but from what I hear, she is the kind of woman that can make you happy and that's enough for me to love her too."

"Whom did you hear praising Hurrem?" Suleiman asked impatiently.

"I heard a lot of praises, but the one I value most comes from the lips of her Highness, your Valide Sultan, because a mother knows best what's good for her son."

It was a skillful diplomatic reply that pleased Suleiman immensely. He was still afraid Hafsa Hatun might defend Mahidevran's rights as a Kadin. Ibrahim's reassurance was a welcome surprise that relaxed most of his previous tension. This change of heart became more apparent when the Sultan made a nod to the waiting eunuchs and asked them to bring some sweets along with the nargileh. Getting high on hashish was usually the prerequisite of a long night, but Ibrahim had still Hatidge's eyes in his mind and her conquest was all he cared about. Nevertheless, he felt that night was a bit too early to make such a risky request. He was still a minor servant in his master's court, a liaison between the Sultan and the Harem.

Hafsa Sultan had not asked him again to visit her apartments for a week; so, he had to wait idly for her invitation. Perhaps, the Valide Sultana was testing his patience, perhaps the reason for this delay was another issue he was not aware of. Now all he could do was to wait and try hard to improve his status in the meantime. He didn't have to wait long, as the Sultan felt his slave deserved a present for this piece of good news.

"Now that you have become my Hasodabashi, you should ride an Arabian horse appropriate for your office. It's not fair for you to follow me on foot during the Friday parade."

It was an unexpected honor Ibrahim had not planned, when he started this discussion about the status of concubines and horses in a Sultan's household.

Greek civilians, as every other "raya" (subject) of the Ottoman Empire, was not allowed to ride horses; however, this reward the exact moment it was made after such a spirited discussion sounded as a concession. It was as if Suleiman wished to separate his concubines from his horses as a possible domain of male competition.

One day soon he would have to talk to Suleiman about his feelings for his sister, but his instinct told him this was not the right time. He had to wait first for Hafsa to make the necessary preparations; so, he decided to change the subject once more.

"I'm especially honored by this gift. I would not like you to start a war against the infidels and have to drag me behind your stallion in an ox drawn "araba" as if I was a cook."

"You are much more precious than a cook for me; so, I want you to be always by my side. As Homer wrote, a war cannot be always won by Achilles' valor; sometimes Ulysses' wisdom may be proven more effective," said the Sultan and drew one more sip of smoke from the amber mouthpiece.

It was a sign he should do the same as a matter of Ottoman courtesy. The taste reminded him of Selim. It was the same powerful stuff that had numbed his reactions. In this sense the son resembled the father, and the slave could not find a diplomatic way to deny the will of the master. He didn't really mind, because hashish made any sensual experience more enjoyable.

****

Suleiman had never reconsidered or forgot a gracious offer he made. Early next morning they both went down the corbelled stone alley that led from the Gate of Felicity to the imperial stables. There he let him choose one white Arabian mare, and then he ordered a nice saddle to be mounted made of white calfskin ornamented with gold decorations and semiprecious stones part of the Mameluke treasures.

It was a very bright horse that realized immediately there was a new rider on the saddle and showed her discomfort with a long whinny of protest.

"Do not worry!" the Sultan reassured him with a suggestive smile. "She is another female made by Allah to submit to the will of the rider. Soon you will realize she does not really care who her rider is, but who treats her right, feeds, and gives her presents, an apple, a lump of sugar, or all these shining golden jewels. Eventually she will get use to your caresses and whine full of sorrow each time you have to go away. All females were made by Allah to behave so from the beginning of time; but, do not try ever to mount my stallion, because it will kill you, if you give it half a chance. Male beasts are like that. They are faithful to only one rider to the death!"

Turks knew how to treat their horses, so Ibrahim took seriously this advice even though he didn't try to make a comment. Instead, he bent over to approach the mare's ear and whispered a few love words in Turkish. He then caressed the animal's neck under the ear. The horse's skin shivered and raised its tail to the Sultan's astonishment.

Ibrahim's thoughts raced to the Princess. Will she ever be so obedient and susceptive to his caresses? He was still wondering how the Sultan felt when he talked about the horses and the women in his harem. Up to now, all the nights they had spent together, he had never suggested they could share the love of one of his concubines, although many complaints were heard inside the Harem since the day Suleiman rose to the throne. What was the deeper meaning of his master's behavior? Was it perhaps an expression of jealousy or one more attempt to keep him solely for himself? Now it was not yet the right time to probe deeper into his mind. As time passed, a more opportune moment should surely arrive sooner or later.

During this chilly winter morning so typical of the weather of Constantinople, what was more noteworthy was that the very same day Ibrahim went out the Bab-i-Hamayun riding his very own proud, white, Arabian mare and this honor was by no means a trifle. From the times of the fall of the Eternal City no other Roman had passed this gate on horseback. However, no countryman of his who happened to pass by that gate this early hour could ever believe this handsome young man dressed in white wearing a light blue turban was actually someone from the same breed. They all thought he was probably the son of a rich Turk Pasha.

Only the Janissaries that were guarding the gate knew well exactly who he was and laughed silently under their long hook-like moustaches, whispering degrading insinuations. However, Ibrahim had stopped paying attention to any vicious gossip that reached his ears coming from Turkish or any other lips. The road he had consciously selected was lonely, and he did not expect the uneducated mob to acknowledge his risky struggle for success.

For the ignorant public proper was only what was described in old, dusty books written by authors who had passed away ingloriously long time ago; but, these very same historic days insightful young men had proven that the world was a sphere turning around an axis, and human imagination wondering in space could not be limited within the pages of few dusty books, and any effort to restrict progress was sooner or later destined to fail miserably.

Ibrahim might be a Greek slave, but he was not willing to waste his entire life waiting for the reincarnation of a Roman Emperor to pass through the Golden Gate with his victorious armies, as his foolish compatriots believed. If he was such a fatalist, he would have sneaked out the Bab-i-Hamayun on foot never to return to the Eternal City, the domain of Holy Mary. True Romans survived no more in the Balkans. The few remaining traces of Roman blood had retreated unwilling to their motherland, Italy, to claim back the fortunes they had inherited and wasted away after centuries of treacheries, conspiracies, and extreme excesses.

He was much more determined than any such degenerate Roman. He had made up his mind he had better virtues than anyone else. He was unquestionably blessed, and he didn't care if God or Allah was responsible for his creation.

All humans were made of essentially the same flesh and bones. Suleiman Khan, the son of a Turk and a Tatar, had saved him from the grips of a Dalmatian pirate and a Jewish hammam owner recognizing his talents. It was not really important they were lovers. In his mind this was one more sign the Sultan valued highly his company in spirit and in flesh. Even today, Suleiman had not hesitated for a single moment to give him one of his own mares, and Turks would never consider sharing a horse, their weapons, or a woman with another man.

The Sultan had proven he was an exceptional man worthy of his full respect and support without a doubt. It did not matter if the Sultan was a Turk, a descendant of ignorant shepherds, as long as the idol in his dreams was Alexander the Great. Such great men of vision like Fatih and Selim had advanced already very far within fifty years, and Suleiman followed their bold steps. After all, Ibrahim was not the only or the first Roman who had supported an Ottoman Sultan. Before him thousands of "Romans" had fought side by side with Turks to change the world in Anatolia and unite the Balkans. Leaders should never be judged on the basis of their lineage, their language, or their faith, but only on the value of their elusive dreams on how their followers could prosper more in flesh and in mind.

His mind now travelled once more to Hatidge Sultan. She was not one of the mares in Suleiman stable. She was his precious sister. Was a brother willing to share her with a slave? Realistically speaking sharing a sister with a slave was much more difficult than sharing a mare or a slightly used concubine. Only time could reveal how far with sharing his property Suleiman was willing to go.

****

Ibrahim did not try to go very far during his first ride, as he was not feeling comfortably on the saddle of a new mare yet; so, he left behind the walls of the Seraglio and came down all the way to the shore of the Cape of Saray Bornu. Arriving safely there passed the harbor docks, he left the animal free to roam wherever her heart desired. The mare seemed very happy to have on her back an inexperienced rider, and soon she left the hard corbelled stone road to walk on the soft sand between the Roman Sea Walls and the breaking waves. She wondered there under the latticed windows of the Selamlik enjoying every step. Her pleasure from the contact with the cool water was so apparent that even the rider submitted to the same temptation. He dismounted and felt once more the freedom of a child who splashes around the seashore.

Suddenly, the common pleasure of the man and the animal was interrupted by the harsh voice of a Janissary guard on top of the Sea Walls who informed him that the approach to the beach in front of the Sultan's Palace was prohibited to anyone else except the Sultan.

Only for an instant his mind was flooded by a rebellious mood; but by becoming an Ottoman he had accepted the idea that there were certain pleasures only the Sultan could enjoy, and every fool challenging this principle would be in mortal danger. Now, he could do nothing but follow orders and ride back to the imperial stables, as any desire for exploration and adventure was gone. Sympathizing with the animal he caressed the mare's neck to comfort her for this unexpected adversity; but he had also felt the reins of the Sultan around his neck.

****

That morning Hurrem was rather late getting up. She stayed longer in bed to plan for the immediate future. For few days she had remained deserted inside her room in the Eski Saray, while the Sultan distributed equally justice to his two Kadin, neglecting entirely the "sold meat", as she was now called in the Harem by practically every concubine envious of her deeds.

She had been crying for days, but now all her wounds had healed the moment the Sultan decided he couldn't resist the attraction of her memory, and needed another dose of ultimate pleasure only she could provide, asking for her skills early in the morning, breaking the strict tradition of night invitations.

Mahidevran Sultan was her main opponent, but she was not aware of any of her secret cheats. On the other hand, she had definite proof of Gülfem's indiscretions with Selim. Gülfem was not an immediate threat. In fact, she had been Mahidevran's vanquished opponent, so she was essentially her ally. It was not to her advantage to accuse her for anything.

Her own past was a permanent black spot, so it would be to her advantage to keep her mouth shut. First she had to prove that beauty was not everything in a harem. There was much more on a woman than what pleased the eye, as God had provided human beings with five senses, not just one. Vision was indeed the queen of the senses. It had exquisite effects, but it was greedy too. For how long a man could stare at beautiful scenery, a magnificent sunset, or a majestic mountain range without getting bored? The more primitive the senses the longer their pleasure lasted. An old man could still be pleased to utter exhaustion even death, when his eyes and ears had ceased to function properly. Touch was the cheapest and the longest in a man's lifetime.

Mahidevran might be gorgeous, pleasing immensely the Sultan's eyes; but inside the turmoil of love-making other senses became more important in total darkness. Now that the sun shone again, she decided she should drown her anger, and let the Sultan enjoy her smile once again. Sooner or later he was going to come back from the world of illusions that smoking opium offered into the harsh world of reality, where the mind took control over the senses, and conspiracies reigned supreme over seductive fantasies. Anyway the competition in the Harem was so intense she had to stay close to him as much as possible. She had to find a good excuse, so that it didn't appear she was running after him. The most important man in her life should never get the impression her love for him was a forever granted prize. Even a Sultan should learn how to beg for the love of his most favorite odalisque.

Everything in the life of the Harem was gradually making perfect sense to her. She was just a slave and she never would have the chance to freely select her mate. Suleiman was the only one who had the right to choose. This was contrary to Mother Nature's designs that gave woman the capacity to utter the last word. Thus, their relation had to regain its balance and the only way was for him to become jealous, as jealousy was the only way he could be forced to fight to win her heart.

Nevertheless, every male beast permitted to enter the Harem was a eunuch and hardly capable of making a Sultan jealous. The Sultan even followed this rule and never entered the Eski Saray court riding his stallion. Stallions could put the best man to shame with its stamina.

The only man that could challenge the Sultan in Eski Saray was the young nobleman she had met that day in the Valide's apartments. She still remembered the trick he used to take a good look at her face. Since then he had failed to make an appearance, but there was a malicious rumor claiming Ibrahim was also the name of Suleiman's Hasodabashi, residing in the adjacent room to his master. Was it possible they were the same man?

A Hasodabashi had to be a eunuch. Could Ibrahim, her knight in white armor, be a eunuch? Selim Khan had two eunuchs as favorites. Was it conceivable Suleiman, the future father of her children, to be a eunuch lover too like his father?

This morning as she was staring at the open sea from the Sultan's window, she saw him again. He was riding a white mare, wandering at the beach looking towards the Seraglio windows. Was he really looking for her, or was it just a coincidence?

She went out on the balcony and asked indifferently the few White Eunuchs tiding the Sultan's apartment, if they had ever seen him before. Soon, all the windows of the Selamlik facing the sea were filled with hungry eyes full of curiosity measured up the young rider.

He was blond, well-built and handsome. From his clothes and the golden ornaments on the saddle he must have had royal blood, but no eunuch was willing to add any more information than what she saw. They kept their lips sealed. To make them jealous, she mentioned she already knew him and he had the most beautiful green eyes she had ever seen. Then one maliciously said that whoever he might be, he was nothing but a fool that sooner or letter would lose his head, entering the forbidden seashore of the Sultan.

Indeed, it did not take long, before a Janissary guard came and expelled the rider from the domain her eyes could cover. Soon the beach was empty and lonely again, and only the horse tracks on the wet sand proved without a doubt that the white knight of her dreams was not a figment of her imagination. As any other woman she needed to be certain that Suleiman was indeed the right man for her, and unless she felt secure about his love, she would restrain herself from falling in love with him. Naturally she had many excuses, as all her insecurities were direct consequences of her inferior status in the Harem. In this Seraglio, only slaves who followed commands felt safe enough.

****

Returning to his room, Ibrahim felt totally exhausted. He closed the window drapes so that the morning sun would not wake him up early, locked his entrance door as he always did to avoid the intrusion of eunuchs, and lay down to get a well-deserved rest. Slowly but steadily he was moving up the Ottoman ladder. There were always unoccupied voids he could fill. He simply had to find worthy deeds to prove his worth. With these thoughts his eyelids felt as heavy as the lead roof.

****

It was pitch dark when in his sleep he felt he was not alone in the room. Among the shadows that gradually grew longer and darker as the sun was painting red the western skies, he sensed a black silhouette that was motionless and kept on staring at him with its shimmering eyes. His blood froze as the shadow bolted the door behind it.

"Who is there?" he dared to ask, fearing the worst, a Mute executioner.

But then a smothered giggle was heard that could never have come out the mouth of a Mute. The shadow approached him with slow deliberate steps and the only image he could recall was that of the evil doctor who performed the circumcisions and all the castrations in the Seraglio. Had the Sultan decided his harem would be safer with a eunuch Hasodabashi?

Soon the shadow towered over him as if it was a scarecrow. It had a black cape on its shoulders and a long hat over its head. A hand reached for him and started searching under the linen, freezing his blood. He simply couldn't move or resist succumbed by the primal terror.

It made no sense to resist during this dreadful operation. The doctor was skilled and any movement would simply prolong the torture or possibly create an even bigger wound or an even greater loss. There was always some hope for every slave that the doctor would spare something of value.

As time progressed with a torturing slow beat one issue became gradually clear. The visitor was carefully examining his gender. It was a realization that flooded his heart with hope.

That horrible night the doctor had acted rather harshly but effectively reduced the blood flow to avoid a deadly hemorrhage. This had to be another less

103

experience doctor, because his expert hands tried hard to attract more blood.

"Did I scare the fearless Hasodabashi?" the dark shadow whispered in his ear putting an end to this audacious charade.

It was an unrecognizable murmur he simply couldn't recognize the identity of the speaker in such highly exited state he was in. He could only discern an adventurous woman was waiting patiently for his reply. It might well be Yabani or Zarafet.

"Yes, you did, I have never been scared so much in my life by a woman," he admitted trying not to disappoint his visitor. "Are you looking to buy a good slave?" he asked her in much better spirits.

"No, I have one already;" she added calmly. "Are you for sale too?" she asked him with a pretentious throaty male voice that sounded somewhat familiar.

Could it really be Hurrem? Could a Sultan's favorite have managed to slip into his room?

His mind suddenly became too confused to seek believable answers. This portion of her plan had succeeded, as his passion gradually grew out of proportion. She was well aware of his change of attitude and her lips showed her appreciation with a long, wholesome kiss. Could she be one of Mahidevran's audacious courtiers? She had a similar aggressive attitude, but much more refined. She was made to please not threaten him to submission like a Tatar. Could it possibly be Gülfem? How was he to know? He was a novice with women and he was bright enough to recognize the great difficulty of even a very knowledgeable man to recognize a woman from her kiss. He could only say she was not a woman he ever knew. She was simply too eager to swallow his flesh like a hungry snake that eats a bird and the only one who had the capacity.

He simply had to find her identity; so with both his free hands, he searched feverishly to find other traces of her identity under her cape. It was the easiest task in the world because she was almost naked. As far as he could discern under her cape she was wearing only a corsage to make her waste as slim as possible to enhance her fertility. His hands touched her belly and suddenly all his doubts evaporated. It was as firm as a man's. Could it ever be possible the visitor was Asphodel?

Nonsense! The eunuch was not so desperate. He was free to roam around the Grand Bazaar in search of a handsome Janissary.

Just to confuse him the maiden lifted her black cape and covered his head to create absolute darkness. Then, she slipped his manhood deep inside her to smoother his last hope for resistance. He was too preoccupied with seeking a way inside the cape to make sure she was woman, while she was eager to push his hands away preventing a definite conclusion. Was she still teasing him, or was she truly trying to retain her anonymity?

He suddenly realized that nothing really mattered with such a promiscuous creature but the satisfaction of its thirst so completely that it would return time and time again until it felt so secure about his desire, she would recognize him as its most desirable lover. Was he becoming insane to be so suspicious or was the spirit of Selim still haunting him so long after his demise?

Now that she felt safe, she threw the hat on the floor and let her long hair free to fall on her shoulders. Her motion had the mixed air of liberation and female crockery.

"I came to thank you for all you have done for me," she said and with a slow and sensual motion, she unlatched the tight corsage around her waist. It slowly opened its leaves like a flower, revealing a long strip of white flesh that extended from her breasts to the long shadow between her legs, as her naked firm belly emerged seductively through the silken fabric. She did not seem to care about her exposure, and with one hand she caressed her free breasts while the other slipped lower to cover her groin.

Ibrahim tried to get up and seat on the mattress, but she extended her hands and pushed his shoulders forcefully to fall flat on his back.

"Do not worry!" she whispered. "At this hour all the guards are in the mosque praying before going to the kitchens for lunch. We have plenty of time at our disposal to satisfy all our infatuations."

He remained silent unable to believe his eyes, but every move she made seemed to be a part of a definite plan. With the flexibility of a seasoned Ukrainian Cossack, she mounted him and tightened her thighs around his waist almost cutting his breath. Now, her belly was staring him in the face as if she was challenging him to fill it up. The fact it was flat and firm was not a drawback for her, but an impressive weapon. She looked fearless and confident she would not bare the child of a slave despite appearances. To make it plainer, without hesitation she searched under the linen and took firm hold of what she was looking for, the source of his pleasure.

He remained motionless as every move she made was in complete agreement with his desire. He left himself entirely at her disposal and soon he felt the wet warmth of her body surrounding his piece of hard flesh. She let a sigh slip through her lips signifying she was now ready to devote her flesh to his service. He accepted her offer and grabbed her breasts with constantly rising desire. Only then her belly started its sensuous dance he yearned from the moment he saw her for the first time.

At the start, the movements were imperceptible, but gradually her urge increased as the passion kept growing inside her reaching deeper and deeper. She felt transformed into the white mare and first started walking, then trotting, and finally galloping unrestrained. Her motion was powerful, but in the same time smooth, harmonic and experienced contrary to the scent of youth and innocence that filled the room with the exquisite fragrance of a rosebud.

It wasn't too long before he realized she was teasing him, as every time his pleasure reached a peak, she would slow down her frantic rhythm to a whisper until she felt that his passion had subsided enough to be controlled by his greedy mind eager for more. He lost the sense of time, as every rhythm of his body, even his heart was synchronized with the undulations of her waist. Right then a primitive fear filled his mind that perhaps his heart would stop, if she decided to put an end to her frantic run; but, she didn't wish to harm him and gradually increased even more the vigor and the tension of her voluptuous dance as if she was seeking an explosive crescendo.

He felt his heart beating violently within his chest, as if it was trying to get free from the prison of his ribs; but without a warning she glided away releasing her firm control of his passion, as if she had a sudden change of heart, or if she was ashamed for her wicked deed as she sensed deep inside her the first few spasms of a long series of most violent explosions.

"Take me!" he begged and begged her unable to control his passion; but, received no response or other comforting gesture, as the moment he had nothing more to offer her, she dismounted him and swiftly departed silently like a thief closing gently the door behind her.

The sound of his voice made him open his eyes widely, but to his great surprise he found himself all alone in the room and her image defused among the shadows. He turned around and saw his front door securely bolted, as he always did to keep away his fears of an undesirable intrusion. There seemed to be no other way a human soul could enter his room, but through the other door leading to the Sultan's bedroom.

He tested the knob, but it was locked from the inside. There could be but one explanation. A concubine or a Kadin had used this door to sneak in his room the moment the Sultan left to visit the mosque. She was bold enough to invade not just the heart of the Sultan, but also infiltrate with her being the mind of the slave. She had to be Hurrem and from now on he could recall her lust back into his memory whenever he wished. Even his flesh had surrendered its control to her fleeting image and from now on, his only hope to regain command over his emotions would be to drown the sapphire fog of Hurrem's glance inside the dark abyss of Hatidge's eyes; otherwise, eventually he would become mad enough to try one night to invade the Harem, as her allure appeared inescapable.

****

Even free women who discovered the changes pregnancy has caused on their figure, needed a tender reminder that the love of their beloved was still alive despite the swelling body they have to suffer. However, this gesture was not enough to comfort the heart of a slave. The very first an enslaved woman had to experience was an inescapable but largely voluntary conquest to prove to her master he got his money worth.

However, a young slave member of the Harem needed something more than that to warm her heart. She had to be convinced she was something more to him than just an object he used for his pleasure. This was the only way she could fill the void of her heart, as it was always difficult to fall in love with a master who treated her like another piece of his property, a "sold meat".

This expression was the second degradation she had to endure without complaint; but it was not to be the last. Every time she was invited to the

Sultan's bedroom, the Padisah making love to her was not a tender expression of an emotional connection, but simply an effort to "award justice" to a concubine of his, as this act was characterized according to the Ayin.

The only logical explanation Hurrem could find for this degrading term was that by this choice the Sultan was awarding her a distinction of superiority over all the other concubines he had bypassed to choose her. Nevertheless, she simply had to achieve much more than plain justice.

The doctor had been very confident this time. It was not simply an inconsequential delay of her cycle. In her womb a healthy fetus was growing.

The first thing that came into her mind was to inform the happy father; but, the Sultan was not to be disturbed. She waited patiently outside his door for a while pacing back and forth. Perhaps, Mahidevran being his legal Kadin didn't feel threatened, but she was just a slave used for pleasure, and she knew well enough that for men pleasures did not last long. If male pleasures lasted forever, then all prostitutes would be called wives. This was the will of Allah and one of the telltale signs He was a man as the Prophet proclaimed.

Another indication was that women suffered to deliver a child and few times died, while men enjoyed the fruits of the preliminary debauchery. She was more sophisticated than any male prophet. She had found out early on that pleasure lasted for women much more than for any man; so Allah might well be a woman. The critical question was if women should limit their pleasure to one man or behave greedily like insatiable bitches on the street. It was a question every woman had to answer in her own way during her entire life by choosing if she preferred to be treated like a goddess or a devil.

****

After an entire month he still had the same doubts. Was her nocturnal visit one of the elusive dreams opium had created?

Opium was a substance with unpredictable effects. He still remembered quite vividly Selim's tense face staring at him full of the excitement of conquest. Many times he had asked Selim's second favorite eunuch and now his page, Asphodel, details about what exactly had happened in the hammam, but received no satisfying answer. Hurrem had proven beyond doubt that even who was on top might well be an illusion, as human body was so flexible the man on top may not always be the manlier of the two.

In the Harem sometimes even a eunuch was not a eunuch in close examination, and a man with strict morals had to be very careful. In the Galata backstreets one could encounter even men dressed like women to attract lovers to make comfortable living, comforting peculiar customers with confused preferences.

His senses after smoking opium were also so confused that he had to consider the possibility his elusive dreams might be skillful allegories his mind created combining unrelated events. Depending on his mood, his mind might recall even vulgar narrations he heard from Selim's exploits or naughty stories he heard from eunuchs in the Seraglio School, trying to prove that their lovers were the most viral men in the Eternal City.

After Hurrem's escape, when he eventually woke up in late afternoon, all doors were unlocked and Asphodel was staring at him more eager than ever to please him. Life in the Seraglio was simply too complicated, and the thousands of specialized servants with different duties to comfort the Sultan were the cause of this confusion of his personal interests.

Despite his slumber after a long sleep he was still aroused and experienced great difficulty imposing his will on a eunuch bold enough to pull away the covers to force him out of bed. He was not willing to accept his usual promises for future rewards and he was even more determined than Hurrem to use him. As he sat on top of him full of bravado with his back facing his master, there was no much difference between him and the lusty Russian.

"Please, please me," he begged and I will tell you everything you wish to know about Selim Khan," he promised and didn't hesitate for a single moment to reveal the truth, his truth.

In fact, the moment he realized Ibrahim was not in a submissive mood, he lied down in the mattress and slowly turned his back at him.

"Do you like my back? Selim Khan always had a good word to say, when he made love to me. Only Mahidevran has a more inviting back than me. Trust me!"

"How did Selim know anything about Mahidevran's back?" Ibrahim asked with frantic interest, but Asphodel delayed his answer long enough to gain control over his passion.

"How should I know that? He always dismissed us when he did justice to a female visitor. On the other hand, there is a rumor a secret passage exists in the Sultan's quarters, leading to the women's hammam in the Eski Saray. It is supposedly a portion of a Roman aqueduct, but I haven't seen it with my own eyes. The Kislar Aga has assured me it exists and he has never lied to me. I trust him blindly."

"Have you ever used this passage?"

"No, never! I'm not allowed to visit the Eski Saray. You ought to know that; but you have the authority to go anywhere and secretly do anything it pleases you now that the Sultan displays no interest to claim his right. No one will complain. I assure you. Why don't you ask the Kislar Aga to show you the way? Lately, he has become so damn lusty; he enjoys peeping couples in heat even more than me. I suspect he also spies on every Kadin and concubine to find out what kind of love affairs bloom every day in the Harem. You are the Hasodabashi and you should also be aware of all the concubines' traits. I'm you sure he will not deny you anything you ask."

"Then, I'd rather keep him at a safe distance," Ibrahim replied cautiously.

"Why, a man of the world like you should experience everything there is before making an educated decision. If you are willing to please a white eunuch like me, why should you be a racist? I don't know how you feel about it, but he has the most attractive flesh in the Saray for my money. All he is denied are babies. Hafsa Hatun is very wise to choose him now that Selim Khan is just a malignant spirit. His black skin is even smoother than velvet and his Nubian vigor almost inexhaustible."

****

As Asphodel's passion for his flesh had finally subsided along with his, Ibrahim had reached a state of complete emotional consolidation. The eunuch had blackmailed him to submission, but there were no hard feelings. He needed an emotional release too, after the stormy experience with the presumptuous concubine.

Everyone residing in the Seraglio considered that his duty was to serve the Sultan anyway possible to the best of his abilities, and presenting him as flawless, immaculate, invincible, or even divine, was an excuse for blind obedience. It created a state of mind where everyone who had a different point of view was dangerous to the overall emotional or mental stability.

Now, after what had happened with Selim's eunuchs, a new level of trust existed between him and the White Eunuch Corps. Now emotionally he was one of them. Now there was no way for him to impose any degree of moral superiority. He could only exert a superior degree of authority. They would obey his orders, but morally he was one of them. He was a conspirator too. He could demand answers, but he had to provide answers too.

"What happened to me that night in the hammam?" he murmured.

"How should I know? I only know what happened to me, and I have no complains. Your conduct was immaculate to say the least. You were in fact even more excited than today."

"Why?"

"I'm afraid you can only answer this question with absolute certainly. I can only guess that Selim or my brother had turned you on even more than that Russian bitch. This is what logic demands and logic is the most demanding master of our spirit. Every other master can do as he or she pleases with our flesh. This is what people call "The spirit is willing, but the flesh is weak," but all this is just the nonsense common men have to incorporate in their way of thinking. We eunuchs are wiser than that. The spirit may be willing to rise, but it is so closely connected to our rotten flesh, they are destined to die together."

****

Ibrahim must have realized by then the true reasons for her visit. Hurrem simply had to find out if he was a eunuch or a man. The approach would be entirely different.

He was not a eunuch! He was still a man; so, she didn't need to pay his cooperation with money but with an illusion of ultimate pleasure. She knew well enough that for a raped woman it was extremely difficult to love a man, any man. She also knew that most men were simply enchanted to attempt to surpass every obstacle. They were the fools who yearned for virgins; but they were also few even more foolish men who dreamed the impossible. Selim Khan had to be one of them, trying to conquer the world or impregnate a man.

She had a gut feeling Ibrahim was also such a rare kind of a man. The Kislar Aga had reassured her Asphodel was his most intimate servant. By now the devious eunuch must have found out what kind of man Ibrahim really was. She had to know similar intimate details. A hunter cannot be successful; if he does not know all the special habits the game he was after had.

Asphodel would be most grateful by now. He must have sensed how difficult it was what she had achieved during lunch time, escaping Ibrahim's fatal attraction so suddenly. It was as enjoyable for a woman as it was for a eunuch to combine business with pleasure as long as the possibility of an undesirable pregnancy could be eliminated.

She had recently become an exception to this rule. She adored every attempt for a pregnancy that brought her closer to every slave's goal, domination of her master.

****

Since the night when Suleiman had cut ceremoniously Hurrem's rosebud, Valide Sultan was delighted with Hurrem's dedication to her master's pleasure during the oncoming months.

The Kislar Aga kept on reporting all the devious tricks she used to get Suleiman interested. She was practically residing in Suleiman's quarters, constantly trying to seduce the Sultan with every possible way, using techniques he didn't even dare to describe in detail to protect her dignity.

Hafsa Sultan was so desperate to protect her son from Ibrahim's influence, she wouldn't mind if few of the Ayin rules demanding concubines to reside in the Eski Saray were bent. It was a good occasion for her to show she had an open mind and put the Empire's prosperity above inflexible outdated religious commandments. She had decided that under the circumstances she was obliged to listen to the Kislar Aga daily progress reports, but she was not going to put any obstacles to Hurrem's bold efforts. On the contrary, she would secretly reward this cheeky female for every victory she achieved against her son's affliction.

The good news kept coming week after week but her pregnancy announcement topped them all. Now Hafsa firmly believed this extraordinary girl was meant to make her son happy, and as a mother she needed nothing more to give her blessings to his new intimate consort. However, Hurrem was not a legal wife of the Sultan. She was just a slave his mother had bought from the bazaar, hopping that she could make her son see life in another way now that all the other concubines had failed to excite or keep his interest alive for long. In Hafsa's mind Hurrem was a choice of desperation and her offspring socially inferior to the children of a Tatar Princess like Mahidevran.

Nevertheless, hearing the results from the Jewish doctor's examination, Hafsa got up, embraced Hurrem with affection, opened a wooden box made of ebony and ivory, and took out a necklace formed by a series of roses made of rubies and sapphires. It was one of Selim's presents collected from the Palace of the Shah in Tabriz and Hafsa Sultan placed it around her neck.

"This is something to brighten up your smile whenever my son keeps you waiting," she announced tenderly.

Then, she was also kind enough to give her some advice about what she should avoid during her pregnancy for the safest possible delivery. Nevertheless, she let Hurrem know in a more sober tone that she was going to have the best care possible in the Harem, but even if she followed all the doctors' advices, bringing a child into this world was a dangerous process that often led concubines to their demise. Hurrem may not be aware of similar events, but the Harem had a backdoor used to carry out to the Bosporus dead concubines and their illegitimate children.

Hafsa did not forget to ask if her son kept on seeing her during this period, but the answer she received woke up her old fears. Suleiman's visits were gradually becoming sparser and that could mean just one thing. He was spending the nights with someone else.

It was quite easy for the Valide to find out with whom were these meetings, as the Kislar Aga kept exact records of all the Sultan's requests for the Eski Saray Kadin and concubine services. She knew how to take care of this problem and did not press Hurrem any further with unnecessary questions.

It was evident Hurrem was also upset for the Sultan's relapse, but Hafsa was curious to find the extent of her anxiety, so she asked her whether she was jealous. Without any hesitation, Hurrem responded eloquently with a single word:

"Extremely!"

Hafsa smiled and inquired if she would feel better if Suleiman was sleeping with another concubine, now that she would be indisposed.

"It is not for me to decide the Sultan's consorts. This is a decision of the Hasodabashi. He has to make all the necessary preparations," Hurrem said indifferently.

"You know well enough that I wouldn't hesitate to pull few strings to support your claims, if he neglects your pleasure for someone else's," Hafsa reassured her.

"I would never be so demanding for my pleasure; but I know well enough that few women in love may even lose their child, if they feel their beloved has lost interest because of their pregnancy. I also know your Majesty mean well. You are like a mother to me, or perhaps even better, because you are more open-minded than her. This is why I dare to tell you I need your son by my side now much more than ever before."

"Blood can't be turned to water. My children's happiness will always come first for me; but now that you are carrying a grandchild of mine, so you are my blood too almost as much as Mahidevran or Gülfem is. I know it is impossible for you to see them as I do, but it would not harm you, if you try to view every odalisque my son has as your sister. You all have your differences, but in the end the blood of the children you are carrying is the same, the blood of Osman. Anyway and no matter what happens, the Harem should not become another problem to solve these critical days for my son. He has a war to win, and this is the greatest concern for all of us right now."

Hurrem was no fool either. She knew Mahidevran Sultan was a Tatar and much closer to Hafsa's heart as she could ever be. The Princess also had produced two sons, so for the moment she was at least twice as important. Hafsa was lying, so it was fair for her to lie too.

"I realize that; so, I will do my best for my man to return victorious. I love Suleiman more than my life," Hurrem claimed, but such complete devotion did not make much sense for a Valide Sultan familiar with the prevailing harem mentality.

****

Allah knew Hurrem claims were lies. Humans loved most of all themselves. If mothers loved their children more than themselves, it was a unique exception in the entire universe because children were the extensions of themselves in time. Allah also knew that even the exceptions had exceptions, and few mothers would even kill their children; thus, in this faulty universe it was impossible to make universal rules. Rules had to bend to fit inside an expanding but finite universe.

The feelings of men for their children were considerably different and less stable, sometimes puzzling even Allah who was a man according to every male prophet. Was Allah another exception? He was unique and this was a prerequisite for being exceptional.

****

Asphodel's smile was triumphant smile was much more eloquent that his tongue. At last he had achieved his goal. He had twisted the will of the Hasodabashi in his favor. Now she had to make sure he understood that he owed her a favor too in return.

"I'm very happy for you. There will never be enough happiness in this Saray, unless we all learn how to share what we have; otherwise envy will be our ruin. Let me know what you need and I might be able to help you again in the future."

"You have helped me more than enough and I will always remember your kindness. Now your happiness has become mine. We have too much in common. Our kind hearts will never be fully content unless we can make everyone around us as happy as we are. Our masters desire to conquer the world in the name of Allah, but we are the true believers. We yearn to make the world better."

Asphodel words sounded absurd and blasphemous to the common ear; but despite her past she felt she had nothing common. Unknowingly, this sensitive eunuch had sensed a serious fault in her plan she had never considered until that moment. Fortunately it was very easy to eliminate it. The next time Hurrem saw Hafsa Sultan she would not fail to remind her that it was a great sin for a Christian to carry the child of a Muslim, and if this sin lasted for long, Allah the All-Mighty might decide to punish them all.

****

"As I was coming here, I think I saw Ibrahim. Is he still here looking to please neglected Sultan's consorts for his harem?" Hurrem inquired indifferently.

It seemed like an innocent question, but she was surprised to see the change in Sultana's face. She had become deadly serious. How was it ever possible that Hurrem could have found out of her little scheme? She was very careful to keep a secret all about Ibrahim's meetings in the Harem; but now Hafsa had to find out how much Hurrem knew about her plan.

"Ibrahim is nothing more than another slave of my son. He always does exactly what my son commands him to do."

"Yes, I know, but men are no good in this sort of stuff. I wish Allah could help you find a suitable woman for him to leave my man sleep in peace," Hurrem said trying hard to show indifference, but the words had painted Hafsa' cheeks red. "I do not believe an experienced and powerful woman like you cannot select few girls from Sultan Selim's Harem worthy of an inexperienced slave, so that he does not come so often to the Seraglio." she added trying to extract a promise.

Hafsa smiled for the compliment. Hurrem was right, of course.

"Indeed I can! Even in a very dilapidated harem like Selim's I'm confident I can discover not one but ten slaves to reward Ibrahim for his good deeds. His advices have been precious contributions to the stability of the Empire," she conceded.

"Indeed Ibrahim is most helpful as a Hasodabashi. In fact, there has never been a year when we had in the Sultan's harem two women pregnant at the same time," Hurrem noticed.

Hafsa needed several moments to realize all the implications of what it had just slipped off Hurrem's tongue; but, when she did, she suddenly became very thoughtful. Did Hurrem know about another pregnancy she ignored? In a harem full of frustrated concubines the presence of a young and capable Hasodabashi could be seen under certain very conflicting angles. Now, she had to find out most urgently what exactly Ibrahim's contribution was to the Sultan's concubine pregnancies. If a woman of her age and status could be tempted by a gifted slave, what were the chances of a lusty concubine not tasting the juicy apple? The old ways were well-thought to achieve old goals. In a harem full of young women eager to mate at every opportunity, the presence of an able young man was a risky enterprise. She had to hurry. She had to take control of the situation before another scandal surfaced, demolishing her son's reputation as a man and the proper man to ask about a concubine's cycles was the Kislar Aga who knew exactly, when these cycles commenced and when they ended.

****

The Kislar Aga was more than certain that the only odalisque carrying a child was Hurrem and since the day she had received the blessings of the Eski Saray Mufti, her pregnancy was progressing perfectly. However, few rumors had reached his ears that the cycles of the Sultan's Kadin were erratic, but he was too humble a slave to ask more details from the mother of a Sehzade (Heir). Any issue related to the blood of Osman, the Valide Sultan had the right and the responsibility. Nevertheless, now that he had realized his mistress' ignorance in this matter, he wouldn't be worthy of her trust if he failed to mention that every sign he was aware of proved that Allah was just. Mahidevran's pregnancy was a hoax caused by her insatiable desire to have a third child, while Gülfem's prayers for a second child had been answered.

"I didn't know my son was so prolific," Hafsa boosted with a long smile. "I always thought Gülfem had permanently lost his favor."

"I thought so too," the Aga added. "But as you may know, my master always sends me way every time he meets with any of his Kadin; thus, the only fact I know is that whenever he invites Gülfem Hatun in his bedroom, he always asks me to bring him a pair of nargileh too and some sweets."

Hafsa Sultan couldn't restrain a smile. This black eunuch was a priceless gem. He knew how to convey the messages without offending her dignity. She also knew well that a black eunuch's duties were to choose and transport the right consort to the Sultan's chambers. Whatever was happening in there was the duty of a white eunuch to know since the days of Sultan Selim.

A Kadin pregnancy was a very serious matter to be left to chance. Asphodel had not been left alive to spy only on Ibrahim. He had to become her eyes and ears in the Seraglio.

****

It was not very easy to terrify a eunuch, as for most death would put an end to their eternal torture. Nevertheless, a simple question that naturally came out of her mouth with great anxiety was enough to make Asphodel blush and tremble.

"Do you know how to dive underwater? From what I know your brother couldn't keep his breath long enough. So, tell me all you know about what happened in the Sultan's quarters!"

"I know nothing worth telling you, but many rumors have reached my ears that might interest your Majesty, if with your judgment you can discern any traces of truth among infinity of lies and slander. All you have to do is ask and I swear in my life that I will tell you all I know."

She had to accept Asphodel was very slippery even for a eunuch. Selim was very wise at least in this choice of a favorite.

"You must consider me a very foolish woman to ask you any specific question. You have to tell me all you know and then I will tell how I feel about your sincerity. You are not the only eunuch I employ to tell me all I need to know. I have kept an eye on you for more than I can remember; so search even the darkest corners of your mind and tell what you've found, unless you yearn to meet Selim and pay your respects in Hell."

She didn't have to say more and her eyes expressed more vividly the hate and contempt she felt for him. Women would never forget who wrong them. Now it was apparent Hafsa Sultan was searching for reasonable excuses to murder him.

To make sure he understood her intentions, the formidable Valide Sultan asked for the presence of the Kislar Aga. It was a sign Hafsa couldn't summon the Mutes, but somehow she was prepared to compromise. Mentioning Sultan Selim would be something more than a hint.

"I didn't wish to add to your sorrows, and this is the only reason I've never mentioned to anyone that Sultan Selim had the name of Mahidevran Sultan on his lips the moment he died."

Hafsa Sultan's face didn't twitch, but a cloud passed swiftly in her eyes.

"Is this all you know about Selim Khan?" she asked with an expression of infinite doubt.

"He did much more than that. He wrote her also a love letter. It said that her son was not going to become a Sultan after his death. He even asked my poor brother to prepare a poisoned caftan for your son, but Menekse never prepared it. Such a caftan must be soaked in poison at least for a day and my poor brother was strangled just few hours letter. I am not a doctor, so I cannot say if these were just fleeting dreams labdanum causes. I only know is that when I smoke pappies dust, I always see the dreams I have not fulfilled."

"And which are the unfulfilled dreams of yours, my foolish eunuch?" Hafsa asked as grimly as she could. "Do you also dream of Mahidevran Sultan?"

"No!" reassured her. "She would be my worst nightmare. She is such a demanding woman I would have to kill myself in shame for my inadequacy."

Hafsa could not retain her threatening stance. One of the most critical gifts Allah gave to eunuchs in exchange for their loss was their sense of humor. Most women in the Harem were too practical to have a sense of humor. Most had one track mind. They sought only pleasure; they were also exceedingly arrogant and had a great idea about their own significance.

"I dream only of men," he humbly confessed.

"Don't you dare tell me you are in love with Ibrahim too!" she warned him teasingly.

Hearing her question Asphodel took a deep breath. Hafsa's knowledge was not as complete as he feared.

"No!" he assured her as indifferently as he could. "I haven't dreamed of him for quite some time. I used to dream of him when he was still a student in the Seraglio School. He has changed a great deal since then. Now he dreams only of women. It is no use trying, when a man has become so indifferent. In Allah's world for the dreams of two people to become true they must at least coincide to a certain extent."

Hafsa Sultan was now favorable impressed by this eunuchs wits. He was not just a lusty beast as other eunuchs claimed. Perhaps he could help her find the solution to her problem.

"Enough said about Mahidevran or Ibrahim. I'm not interested in any of them. Tell me what you know about Gülfem," she sternly demanded.

"I'm not the one for you to ask. I have very little knowledge of her deeds. I will only repeat whatever I've heard. I saw her only once face to face, when she visited Sultan Selim in the Marble Kiosk."

This was a piece of news Hafsa didn't expect to hear. Now she could not restrain her curiosity, but she had to appear as sober and cool as possible.

"My son's Kadin has every right to visit the grandfather of her son."

"Indeed she has! This is actually why I was very surprised to see her come at midnight in disguise."

"She might have come to tell him a secret. Selim Khan was always very keen on keeping secrets. You must know that better than anyone else. Only when he died, tongues were untied and all sorts of secrets became public," Hafsa bitterly noticed.

"Indeed, now everyone knows Selim was a very lusty man, but he was also very just. Many women were very eager to use the seed of a mighty conqueror."

"I know you are deeply puzzled why I have summoned you here, but I am also aware you have been a very loyal and intimate servant of my last husband. Now that your master has died, I expect you will be as loyal to all the members of his family, especially me," Hafsa remarked as sternly as her gender allowed.

For Asphodel, a page trained to please a manly Sultan, having a woman giving him orders was an entirely new experience, but the fame of the Valide Sultana had preceded her. He knew well she was a Tatar and the daughter of a cold-hearted raider. He also knew that race dictated behaviour to a great extent. He was Circassian and submission was his second nature.

"I'm yours to command," he uttered as submissively as possible, ready to play any role this powerful woman might require, "but I must inform you that I've never chosen any of Selim's consorts anytime. Every time, I summoned the Kislar Aga to bring the Sultan's choices."

"Yes, I have never seen you face to face, but I know exactly what your duties were in Sultan Selim's Selamlik. I also know that my husband's orders had to be obeyed; so to be fair, I will limit my demands to the absolute essentials," Hafsa said in good spirits, realizing the awkward position of this strange creature, "and from all your remaining instincts I will demand only the sharpest, your sense for survival. Therefore, just tell me now all you know about my husband's final days, and be careful. Don't even think of hiding me even the tiniest detail of the services you provided. You are not the only spy with a long tongue in my husband's immediate surroundings. Remember that your dear friend Menekse was too, but he left us forever without tasting the sweat fruits of his lucrative profession. I sincerely hope you are luckier than him."

"As you know, my service has been very long and intimate. I don't know where to start," Asphodel uttered in a state of sincere bewilderment.

"Don't be afraid. I'm not a vindictive woman. I know Selim had been your lover for a while; but, as they say, there is no way a woman might know exactly what happened behind the Selim's Selamlik close doors. This great injustice must end tonight, and I will be most grateful, if you assist me in this quest."

****

Many times a man may feel so strong that he can face all the adversities fate can raise in his path, but it is one more illusion as life is capable of belittling even the mightiest of men.

It was less than a year since the day Selim died, and Death passed again the threshold of the imperial family. The first time it was the turn of Gülfem's son Murat to leave his last breath. He was the third son of Suleiman in the row legal heir to the throne.

Nevertheless, the death of young child was a rather common occurrence in the Eternal City. The water coming out of wells and springs was not always clean, not even within the grounds of the Seraglio. Thus, a simple intestinal infection that for a grown-up was nothing more than few days of discomfort, for a young child was often a death sentence.

However, this time the cause of death was more sinister, an epidemic of smallpox. It was a disease that often visited the Eternal City carried along by the camel caravans from Asia and Africa. One had to touch another victim to get infected. All the efforts of the Seraglio doctors were proven fruitless, unable to prevent the inevitable.

Since an epidemic was responsible for this death, the mother was judged innocent of any neglect. However, a solemn shade was cast over Gülfem as with every other woman who had bear and lost the son of an Osmanli. The death of a child had a way to degrade the reputation of a mother, even if the cause was bad luck. Luck was a vague virtue that played a serious role in human life and everyone knew that. Kismet was also a category of events that could not be explained by human reasoning or the holy books. However, many infidels claimed that even Kismet could be manipulated to obey a man's will, few even claimed there were ways for anyone to die simply by touching a dirty piece of clothes.

****

Every death creates a void; but Allah the Merciful must have wished the wounds of Murat's death to heel quickly, as Hurrem gave Suleiman a healthy son in his place. Mohamed was his given name, and if he Allah wished him to become a Sultan, he would be the third Osmanli with this blessed name.

Now that everything was settled fairly and Allah stood by his side, Suleiman Khan could go ahead with the expedition against Belgrade with improved confidence. Everyone in Europe who had doubted him and rushed to pass judgment based only on his fiery passions would soon feel the brunt of his reply.

For one more time an Ottoman Sultan would start a bold military expedition leaving Constantinople seemingly defenseless. Only the Ottoman Fleet stood on the way guarding the entrance to the Dardanelles and few Janissary Ortas on the Sea Walls; but no citizen fell threatened. Venice was a weakling. The Infidels in the West were divided, the heretics in Persia still licking their wounds after Selim's routs, and the Mamelukes a species in danger of extinction wandering the deserts of Sudan.

The shame of the Ottoman enemies was so complete after Selim Khan's triumphs that the young Sultan could leave his capital in the hands of a woman, the formidable Valide Sultan. Not many people knew the truth, but even if they became aware of this risky maneuver, they could not take advantage. The power balance had drastically sifted. The age of aggressive Crusades was gone for good, and from now on the best the Christians could do was defend their ill-obtained gains.

The era of payback had commenced inside and outside the borders of the Domain of Peace where Allah reigned supreme. The Shadow of Allah was now following faithfully the plans of Selim Khan in the Balkans, but in his absence in the Eski Saray the last traces of his passage had to be wiped out clean.

For the good of the Empire every illegitimate heir of Selim had to eliminate even if it was unborn. This was what the Ayin prescribed and a Valide Sultan should not appear disrespectful.

The easiest commands to respect of every god were always the ones that fitted your plans.

Chapter 7
In the Castle of the Knights of Rhodes

'Make war to all your enemies following the path of Allah
and always stay within its limits. Allah does not love all those
who cross His limits'
(Quran, Sura II, 190)

The Ottoman ambition to conquer the city of Belgrade was several decades old. Since the glorious days of Mohamed the Second the Conqueror, and just three years after the fall of Constantinople, the New Rome, they had tried for the first time to push this city to submission by a long siege. However back then, their efforts failed miserably as a surprise attack by the king of Hungary, Hunyadi, broke the lines of the Ottoman army, and almost captured Fatih who was wounded in the ensuing muddle and had to run for his life.

Now both these old adversaries had died and young ones had risen in their place. The Ottomans had now Suleiman the son of Selim as a leader,

119

whereas the Hungarians an inexperienced young king. This time the effort was focused on speed. The Ottoman armies appeared suddenly in front of the Belgrade walls, but they did not try to storm the fortress. Instead, they landed heavy guns on an island on the Danube, and started an intense bombardment of the walls. Then, using mines they tore down the defenses and finally by letting loose the Janissaries, they broke into the city. The entire operation was so brief that by the time the king of Hungary received the news of Belgrade's fall, he was still drinking wine celebrating a wedding.

The occupation of Belgrade with the ease it had occurred froze stiff the Christian Europe. Belgrade, the White City, was guarding the southern gate of Europe blocking the valley of the Danube. It was not that long ago that a young Turk twenty years old had taken Constantinople in a few months, the great bastion of Christendom, and now another young and inexperienced Sultan twenty seven years old had wrestled Belgrade from the Hungarians, the descendants of Attila and the mighty Huns. The heart of Europe, Vienna, lay now unprotected. Fortunately, the wet season was approaching, and the heavy siege guns would be very difficult to roll on the muddy Hungarian plains.

The Ottomans had very seldom rushed ahead unprepared. Their advances were well planned and only when the necessary war supplies were secured. They did not intend to grab a world in a few years only to return it shortly to another owner, like Alexander the Great. Time was running in their favor, as until then every new land they occupied, within few years became a new reservoir of men and supplies. The conquest of the world was not the accomplishment of a single brilliant, reckless leader, but a relentless sequence of outstanding warriors and wise tacticians.

It was not only the collection of the Christian children that had born fruits; it was the overpowering momentum of success that had pushed even old enemies to come and fight by their side. Within few years, fierce enemy nations like the Albanians, the Bulgarians and the Bosnians, who had previously fought bitterly against them, had now turned into the most trustworthy allies. The resentment for the Romans and their weak Jewish son of their God was such that many rushed to change religion and have a taste of victory after a long series of defeats by the Muslims.

Suleiman, exuberant of his victory, wanted to advance even deeper all the way to Budapest, but Ibrahim advised him it would be safer to spend the winter in the City and start a new expedition the coming year.

"It is preferable," he said, "we keep our first steps small and secure, risking no serious drawbacks. We are not as experienced as Selim Khan was, but we are still young and we have plenty of years for many more victories and triumphs."

"This is true, but Alexander was also young and death met him before he had the time to enjoy his conquests," Suleiman argued.

Ibrahim realized that his master was still upset and scared by the recent deaths in his family. His duty now was to encourage him, because the weight of the Empire might be too much for his shoulders.

"Every man has his own destiny that is as unique as the lines of fortune on his palms. Only the beginning and the end all men equally share, as all lines must have a beginning and an end. Whatever comes in between is unique and unrepeatable for every man, as each moment life offers us thousands of different choices. If Alexander's road led him to the East, your path may be crowned by glory in the West. Success is now all that matters, and the foundation of every new victory lies on proper preparation. You should never find yourself in the place of this incompetent Hungarian King who was caught napping. If we go north right now we might give him the chance to turn his defeat into victory. Let him fall asleep again, and next spring we will be better prepared for a new expedition. Let's go back home and let everyone know who truly the son of Selim is, now that this entire continent trembles hearing your name the same way Asia and Africa did with Selim."

That night they stayed up sleepless and talked for hours about their dreams and with every hour that passed, they felt stronger as each one tried to extinguish all the doubts of the other. Their love might be based on weakness; but, as they came closer and became one, they grew stronger as if they were Homer's heroes.

****

When Suleiman returned to the Seraglio, he was surrounded by flatterers that were eager to sing hymns for his courage and military abilities. They were the same ones who had advised him before to organize parades and celebrations. They were the same people that few months ago were questioning everything, even his manhood. They were as harmful as moths that fly around flames that shine bright at night, but dare to lay eggs on tree trunks foolish enough to eat their trunks that feed them. Now Suleiman had a trusty friend by his side that with his judgment helped him to make the right decisions.

"You are an exception made by Allah to make great quests that no one else has done before; but to complete this task you must aim also at exceptional targets. Leave commonplace actions to ordinary men. Belgrade was just the beginning for you. It was an unimportant capital of an obscure country, as obscure city as Edirne, or Bursa. What would people think about your glorious ancestors if your grandfather Fatih had wasted his time celebrating each capture of an Anatolian village, when his aim was Constantinople, the New Rome? Imagine how ludicrous Alexander the Great would look now if he wasted his time celebrating forever his victory at Granicus River, when in his future the triumph of Gaugamela waited in vain his bold advance. Only ordinary people waste their lives celebrating minimal successes, because they feel this is as high as their mediocre abilities will ever reach. You must advance further than any other man in history has ever stridden, and to do that you must dream only of monumental tasks. Imagination is the mother of reality. Reality is nothing but a frighten child tied on his mother's apron strings. We have plenty of time to feast, sing and dance, when we enter the capitals of every kingdom of the West, starting from that cursed Venetian democracy of looters that still hold as pawn the crown of the Roman Emperor."

He did not need to say more and Suleiman gladly accepted his advice. Alexander was the favorite hero of the Orient, and to repeat his exploits was not only his dream, but also of Fatih and Selim before him. Maybe the right time had come for someone to excel all their accomplishments by Allah's will. Thus, the only ceremony that disturbed the calm waters of the Golden Horn was the inauguration of Selim's mosque that was to contain also his mausoleum.

It was his father's decision to be built on the Fifth Hill of the City. There were no houses built up there yet and the fields were used as sheep pastures. The ground was covered by old ruins from the days of the Romans, and the view down to the Golden Horn was majestic. The eye could travel unopposed from the hills around the Eyup cemetery all the way to the walls of Galata and further north to the Thracian forest that was now named Belgrade Forest in his honor. If Fatih has chosen the Fourth Hill for his mosque, it was fare that Selim would have the peak of another hill for his grave. Selim was nothing less than the conqueror of five holy cities, Damascus, Jerusalem, Cairo, Mecca and Medina. He was now called the Shadow of Allah.

Entering the imposing mosque of Sultan Selim with its elevated dome that reflected the austerity and gravity of his character, Ibrahim felt a chill creeping up his spine. Only three years had passed since that frightful night he had spent kneeled before him trying to secure his life. That terrifying man with his unbending will who had forced him to submission was back then a dying man, trying up to the last hour to fulfill one of his dreams, while he was just a slave negotiating an honorable surrender. Since then many things had changed for him for the better. With his total submission he had gained his son's complete confidence.

He could still remember Selim's voice in his ear talking about the relentless force of human curiosity. Selim was now dead, lying under a heavy tombstone and a huge turban. He was unable to lift a finger to stop him in his quest for power and glory. Now he had everything, while Selim had nothing. Death had stolen everything from this mighty warrior with one stroke, his thoughts, his senses, his desires, and his heartbeat. The slave was right all alone in all his submissive choices, as staying alive should be the very first and the ultimate task for every human being. Nothing else mattered. Kismet could change a man's life with a single stroke. Everyone had to stay alive to give luck a second chance to correct even the gravest misfortune.

He was exceptionally lucky, and Suleiman had fallen in love with him at first sight. There was no other word to describe the Sultan's feelings. Selim, despite his victories as a champion of Allah, had suddenly run out of luck and died a horrible death as if Allah was punishing him for conquering the world in his name. It was a divine sign all gods were extremely temperamental.

On the other hand, Ibrahim the wretched Christian slave was now on a path to absolute authority. All indications suggested that rather soon he would achieve anything he set his mind on accomplishing, everything that made human life on Earth worth living. Soon he was going to taste unlimited power, endless money, luxurious cloths, exquisite women, even handsome men, if he so desired. As long as a man was alive, he should try to enjoy every moment, because a man's life could change drastically in a few moments for better or for worse.

All the innumerable nights he had spent in the Seraglio School thinking what he should do to survive unharmed, were not wasted. Flesh was both the temple and the obedient slave of the mind. The hands that touched his flesh against his will could never defile him, if he had not left open the gates of his mind and let the conquerors in to use him as they pleased. Now, if Suleiman desired his cooperation to be content, he had to pay the price for this weakness. His weakness at the moment was two black eyes as black as the deepest well, and he was willing to pay any price they asked to taste the red lips hidden behind the veil. If Selim had started his quest from women and ended in the embrace of eunuchs, he had decided to follow the opposite path.

During the process of living, victory and conquest were the worst possible tutors. They only taught the weakness of your opponents and how to grow fat from the consumption of the spoils. Far more crucial for your future was to realize your own weaknesses that during your last defeat had betrayed you, so you were going to become the victor in the next conflict that sooner or later you were bound to face.

The victorious future was much more important than a glorious past, a fact very few Romans had realized. Mother Nature's had developed mechanisms to turn today's masters into tomorrow's slaves. Thus, from time to time every nation had to taste defeat, foreign occupation, even slavery to be able to bear in its womb a liberator who would start a new cycle of victories and glories once again. Everything alive on this globe had to close its current cycle before starting a new one, as if earth's rotation imposed this motion on the lives of people too.

Ibrahim's thoughts were interrupted by the Muezzin's prayer. He was now a Muslim and had paid in full the price for it. He did not believe in Allah, or any other god. The entire universe was a creation of the Word, a law no one could ever decipher in its entirety. He did not dare to show disrespect to the god of the Sultan, because he knew well the punishment for every Muslim who changed his faith and became a Christian or anything else was death. Instead, he preferred to kneel and bend his neck deeply until his forehead touched the thick carpet of the imperial loge. His future life depended on total submissiveness to the power of Islam and its Caliph.

******

The Sultan was praying one step ahead of his slave. At last he had tasted his first important victory, and he was thrilled. He had to thank Allah for every honor he now enjoyed. He was sure that in some remote corner of this temple the jinn of his father would be proud to see his son following his steps. Up to that moment Allah had listened to every Ottoman Sultan prayer, so he found the courage to ask Him one more. Thus, he prayed that his newly born son by Hurrem would grow and become like him; however, nothing extraordinary happened. The ground under his feet did not shake, no thunder up in heavens was heard, and no water sprung from the Earth to prove Allah was listening to his prayers.

Leaving the mosque, they followed the same crooked road towards the Eski Saray. Suleiman would visit his newly born son by Hurrem next, whereas Ibrahim had requested a Valide Sultan audience. Before separating, the two men promised that they would meet again the same night. Ibrahim's plan was to try to see the Princess one more time and the proper excuse to enter the apartment of the Sultana was duly found. He had promised Hafsa to narrate all the details of the Belgrade expedition.

However, when he finally met her, he realized she was much more interested in extracting information about his relationship with her son. One of her spies had already informed her that during the entire campaign the Sultan had kept him by his side in his tent day and night; but, now meeting her face to face, even though she tried hard to find a chance to ask him about her son, Ibrahim skillfully turned the subject to Hatidge Sultan. It was a game that could go on forever, if Hafsa did not accept that in the end her losses due to the mutual ignorance of intents would be greater. After all, in the Ottoman Empire a son was worth much more than a daughter. The best she could accomplish under the circumstances was to try hard not to lose face.

"You must have missed her a lot after so many months of separation and you only talk about her," she tried to tease him, but her tone of voice sounded as if she was a bit jealous.

In this occasion she had demolished once more the Harem's strict rules, requiring the separation of the sexes by a latticed screen, so that a man's eyes could not touch female flesh. Much more important for the success of her plan was to be able to observe the expressions on his face, even though she allowed her opponent to have the same privileges.

"If something is boring in a war, it's to see all around you only fierce men eager to kill each other," he replied indifferently.

"I wouldn't mind be surrounded by handsome men eager to risk their lives for a worthwhile conquest. My experience has taught me that good company makes any kind of trip enjoyable," she countered boldly advancing a step further to reach him.

If she was any other woman, Ibrahim could have sworn she was jealous; but, now she was probably trying to lay another trap for him. Ibrahim decided some flattery might be useful for his cause.

"I wouldn't dare to doubt the expertise of an attractive and confident woman like Your Highness whose experiences with handsome men is surely more numerous than mine," he admitted.

"Besides being woman, I am also a mother; so, in my eyes the best looking man is my son. Is this an illusion?" she replied and her words sounded like a crude trap.

"No! My Sultan is indeed a very interesting man," he remarked, and the contrast between "her son" and "my Sultan" was distinct and noticeable.

Hafsa kept pressuring him for a confession his relationship with Suleiman was still alive, and he resisted; so, she suddenly lost all her patience and asked him directly:

"Are you still in love with my son?"

But now, he was ready to give her a taste of the truth and a subtle insult.

"Obedience becomes much easier for a slave, if his master is handsome. I am sure a wise Valide Sultan must know as much."

Hafsa decided to make one last effort to win the battle without excessive losses. She threw at him some more bait.

"Indeed it does, but life becomes even easier for a slave, if his mistress is attractive too."

Her words began to puzzle him. Was she seriously asking him to become a slave of Princess Hatidge? Was it possible Tatars were such a naïve race? He had to try his luck to the end, so he replied with the saddest expression he could master.

"A slave has no right to choose his master. Masters tend to select the slaves who offer them the most pleasure. This is the last judgment of Allah for the fate of all slaves."

"Maybe it is so, but what would you do, if Allah's will was a attractive woman to choose you for her slave? Would you submit totally to her will and forget every other bind?"

Ibrahim could not be sure whom she meant, Hatidge or herself. He had to be certain before committing himself. The idea he might be desirable to the widow of Selim was unnerving; but, he couldn't resist the temptation to be sure.

"I wish I were so lucky that a distinguished widow with delicate taste would select me as her favorite. Mature widows have so many lessons to teach a young and naive man like me, while a young widow has age as her stronger ally. However, no widow will be so foolish to buy a slave without thoroughly testing him; so, under the circumstances, a marriage is the best I can hope for, and my master has the last word for all my choices."

"Your master is totally devoted to his favorite, while you are now all alone and practically deserted to his fate. I think that if your master truly respects your feelings, he should let you free to choose the mistress of your heart too."

"If I was to ask for such a questionable favor after all he has done for me, he would have every right to consider me as the most ungrateful slave. However, if I could be sure who the exquisite beauty is that wants to become my mistress, then the prospect of such great happiness might make me lose my mind, commit the biggest folly of my life, and try to steal from her a kiss."

He paused briefly his uncommitted chatter and then threw his own bait at her.

"For many nights I've prayed to Allah to make me worthy of a wise and attractive woman like Your Majesty."

Surprisingly this new insolence was treated with great tolerance. Hafsa failed to detect or reprimand the flattery of an audacious man much younger her; but, in a harem full of younger women her feminine insecurities were still very much alive.

Her most secret wish was that perhaps, Allah willing, she would have again one last opportunity to steal a night of passion with a younger man, if Hatidge had changed her mind for some reason. One final night would warm her heart enough to last a lifetime and it would also by a fair revenge for Selim's last audacious deception with Gülfem Hatun. However, her racy thoughts made her blush, a sign of weakness she had to hide her embarrassment behind a pleasantry.

"Don't be so foolishly adventurous! It's not I the one who dreams of you each night. It's the Princess Hatidge the one you cannot forget."

Ibrahim pretended he was overjoyed and added with pretentious submission:

"For such a pair of sapphire eyes I would dare to claim my freedom even from Sultan Selim, blessed be his name forever."

Now the Sultana was puzzled. It was clear the slave was playing with her like cat and mouse. Hatidge's eyes were dark as coal. Was this claim a mistake or a deliberate act? Hurrem was the only girl in the Harem who had sapphire eyes, and she said so.

Ibrahim tried to excuse himself for his mistake. He had not seen the Princess for so long that he had forgotten the color of her eyes. Perhaps now that he was back, he should see her once more as soon as possible, because in a few months a new expedition would commence. If the Princess was kind enough to let him see her, he was ready to meet her even this very night.

Hafsa realized she was caught in her own trap and the intended prey was now trying to eat the trap's bait unpunished. Still, the happiness of her son was more important than a widow daughter's virtue, and it seemed possible to keep Ibrahim away from her son long enough for her plan with Hatidge to be successfully concluded.

Her daughter had displayed undeniable signs Ibrahim was a most appealing man. The arrangement was perfect, as everyone involved was too happy to follow her suggestions; but despite appearances she was not emotionally prepared for such a sudden turn of events. She had to find quickly an excuse to delay and she did keeping appearances.

Hatidge should be informed about the new developments and make up her mind. As she was the supervisor of the Harem, Kislar Aga would be most happy to make all the necessary preparation. For the time being, the slave had to leave her quarters; but, with a long smile she promised him that very soon he would receive a new invitation.

Departing, Ibrahim remembered the promise he had given to Suleiman for that night. He was excited, but this time the object of his desire was someone else, and this sensation made slavery feel much heavier than ever. Making love was for every human being the most appropriate time to express freely the will to build a better future of his choice.

****

As Suleiman entered Hurrem's apartments unannounced, he caught her breastfeeding his son. Her pregnancy had filled her breasts with milk, giving her figure the affluent Oriental femininity she lacked. Now, her every curve had a new shape and the beloved slim girl of his dreams had vanished forever, leaving behind a woman that scarcely reminded her previous self. Even her smile had changed as her lips were full of the saps that now circulated in her veins, and her eyes had lost the expression of innocence that used to ignite in him the flame of the first seduction.

This pair of deep lagoons with the dark blue waters seemed to know today what they needed to be content and how to get it. Now, they seemed deserted by passion, staring at him as an angry lioness protecting her cub. Her message was plain. She was still feeding her son; so, he should stay away at a safe distance until she had done her duty as a mother, before demanding the services of a concubine. It was a difficult challenge as the smell of milk rushed in his nostrils and woke up memories of his own childhood, arousing his hunger for her flesh.

Undeniably, Hurrem had been ambushed seeing him suddenly at her doorstep. It was a most irregular event, as a Sultan normally summoned his slaves to come to him and serve his wishes. This time he looked different too. His face seemed much manlier, as a light beard grew hesitantly on his chin. He guessed accurately the reason for her surprise and confessed this growth was actually one of Ibrahim's suggestions during the Belgrade siege. By growing a beard he would be even more terrorizing to his enemies still doubting his abilities and judgment.

She left the baby in the cradle and rubbed her chick on his beard. The sensation of his whiskers on her neck unleashed her wild imagination. Beards with their roughness diminished the differences between tender husbands and savage rapists.

With her mind's eyes she saw his lips wandering on her skin, and got more excited than her heart could hold after so many months of separation. With a voice made coarser by desire, she whispered that Ibrahim's idea was most agreeable and kissed her master passionately on his lips. It was the first time after the delivery that her beloved took her in his arms and she could not control her passion. They mated many times that night, and as any old maid in the City might claim, this was the reason Hurrem would give birth to a beautiful

127

girl nine months later.

Only when the sun was high up in the skies, Suleiman remembered the promise he gave to his friend, but he felt no remorse for his omission. After all, he was the Sultan and his favorite just a slave of the Gate of Felicity that had no right to make wanton demands on his master.

****

When Ibrahim arrived at the gate of Suleiman's apartments, he was informed the Sultan had not returned. They were surprised to see him smile turning his back to them and their master. Normally he should be angry, but that night he felt no feelings resembling jealousy or anger. He went back to is room to sleep off his excitement. His most pressing concern was if Hafsa would keep her promise the next few days. He did not know for how long the Sultana would keep him waiting, perhaps to punish him for all the worries he had caused her earlier on.

****

His worries vanished late next afternoon as a black eunuch came to his door and informed him that the Kislar Aga was waiting patiently at the Orta Kapi for his arrival. He was indeed there, holding a large bundle. He led him to a nearby inn close to Top Kapi entrance gate, where the Aga quickly revealed what he was carrying. They were woman's clothes and a black mantle with a hood. He asked him to take off all of his clothes and wear instead a pair of woman's trousers, a "salvar", and a pair of red slippers embroidered with golden threads and white pearls instead of his boots. He felt funny dressed like this, but he did not protest.

When he was almost ready, the Aga gave him a black veil with two eyeholes to see his way around. Finally, he pulled out of his belt a tiny bottle with a strong rose perfume and spread it all over his clothes. The scent was so potent his eyes started shedding tears. As the Aga explained, it was a necessary protection since all eunuchs could smell the scent of a man from many paces away. He then examined him closely and satisfied by the result, they proceeded for the Eski Saray in Valide's coach. It was quite late when they entered the Harem and most of the eunuchs had retired by then. The few of them that crossed their path scarcely dropped a second look at his direction. Concubines were coming and going; but despite his fears, eunuchs didn't seem to care much about his figure to turn around and make a note of his femininity or its absence.

Ibrahim became very excited and could not contain his heartbeat. Meeting a woman was an unprecedented feeling he had never felt with a man, any man. Back then he was afraid and felt uncomfortable expressing his feelings. He was waiting patiently for the other man to make the first move; but now he felt successive waves of passion flood his soul like a wild torrent after a winter storm that could not be contained within its banks.

128

Soon they found themselves in front of an engraved door inlayed with mother-of-pearl. The eunuch opened the door without knocking and nodded Ibrahim to go in. The room was empty and dark. Valide Sultan was nowhere to be found. The door closed behind him robbing his eyes from the dim light coming from the corridor. He was left alone and somewhat worried about what would come next, but not before long a piece of black cloth covering a lamp fell on the floor and miraculously the entire room was filled with stars. It was the light coming from a single oil lamp, burning fiercely under a bronze cover. The cover was full of tiny holes shaped like stars and created on the blue walls the illusion of a summer sky.

He heard a laughter coming from the shadows and embarrassed he left the mantel fall on the floor along with his slippers. His eyes gradually adjusted to the dimness and started penetrating the shadows. The lamp was standing on a low round table, the kind the Ottomans called a "sofra" next to a large pile of silken pillows. Deep in the shadows, he could now discern a woman he had never seen before in his life. She was leaning on her elbow holding her head. She seemed relaxed and confident at this highly suggestive position.

Her skin was pitch black and shining like the pelt of a black panther. She was wearing a semitransparent nightgown in a dark magenta color that matched in the darkness the shade of her skin. The white of her eyes was like a lighthouse inviting him to find shelter in the safety of her arms.

"Where is the Princess?" Ibrahim inquired afraid that perhaps the Kislar Aga had made a mistake in the room.

"My eyes have the same dark color," she replied with a smile that let a perfect set of white teeth make an appearance between her fleshy lips.

She was telling the truth. Her eyes were also pitch black; however, everything else was different, but equally attractive in its own merit. Her feminine body was blessed by fuller curves displaying openly its secret desire to attract a male. Being slave in the Harem had kept her away from this duty, but her body was proclaiming clearly Mother Nature's intentions to reproduce an exquisite specimen of the black race, the race every other envied for its vigor and sensuality.

He read clearly in her eyes the extent of her passion and realized that loving a woman was not as sinful as the teachers and the priests back in Parga proclaimed. It was the ultimate invitation for the creation of a private new universe for every human being. Her eyes begged him to spread his seed inside her and reassured him she would take care of it as best as she could.

"What's your name?" he dared to ask, trying to steal some time to decide what to do next.

"My name is Basm-i-Allem, which in Persian means the jewel of the universe; but they who loved me prefer to call me simply Basmi."

Her words sounded as a sincere declaration of a stormy past; but he appreciated sincerity above all female virtues. For him it meant she knew how to make a man happy and her list of lovers in Africa and Asia far exceeded his deeds.

Her deep sensuous voice touched his ears like a song from a long forgotten dream. He had actually underestimated Hafsa Sultan, and he had left himself vulnerable to her Parthian arrow. He realized that his duty this night was to prove on the body of a slave his worth as a man, before she would let him touch the flower of an Ottoman Princess.

He had no objections for any test an overcautious mother might devise. If he had a daughter, he would do the same and probably more, as there were all sorts of men in the world; but, he was angry with himself for being surprised once more by a woman. Up to this moment, he had never ceased to demonstrate his virtues, and by now, there was no test he would be afraid to undertake. Making love to a beautiful woman few years older than him would be another new experience, and he felt bold enough to treat it as a challenge.

"Basmi, I would not mind spending this night learning from your lips how to correctly pronounce your name," he suggested and her smile was the quickest expression of permission.

It was the first time in his life he was completely free to impose his desires on the body of a woman, being in complete command of his choices. He was now worried that perhaps he might commit a critical mistake; so he approached and sat next to her, hesitating even to lay a finger on her lustrous ebony skin. However, the slave was well-trained in the art of seduction. She sensed his profound embarrassment, and to encourage him, she took his hands and put them on her naked breasts, looked passionately at him, promptly responding to his insinuation with one of her own.

"My name is not difficult to pronounce for such skillful lips as yours. You only need to practice a bit harder many times, Basmi, Basmi, Basmi!" she advised him, and her last word was smothered by the aggression of his lips.

Her magnificent personal scent mixed with the potency of sandalwood had already fully engulfed him, raising his male aggression to an unprecedented level. Undoubtedly, her challenge had to be countered promptly and severely punished before she could form the impression his initial embarrassment was some kind of impotency. Soon his fears were proved unfounded, as with a trained slave he only had to make the first step in a new direction, being prepared to enjoy another kind of pleasure.

Basmi was capable to read in his eyes which portion of her exquisite flesh his heart desired, and she was happy to submit to every aggressive male urge for invasion. It was a struggle without a winner, as she was well-trained to be a pleaser exactly as he was. He was now sure she had also been an inmate of the Seraglio School for slaves, and she knew by heart the Persian miniature book. It was also clear that her body had not been invaded by another man for a long time, and he soon found out what the triple repetition of her name truly meant.

For a few hours, he felt like a master and a Sultan, as this gorgeous female slave tried every trick her rich memory could recall pleasing him. This feeling of total domination over a female body was a deeply satisfying sensation, an entirely new experience that surprised him with its intensity. Suleiman must have felt the same way with him long time ago. He could not clarify though completely if this pleasure was the result of mating with a female, if it had to do with the domination of the strong over the weak, or if it was something even more primitive deeply imbedded in his brain.

In her embrace he felt that beside the temporary triumphant sensation of the hunter that dominates the body of his prey, there was also a feeling of creation, as the union with another race lays the foundation for the formation of a new species with a unique shade of human skin. It was a divine signal that within the loins of a man the power of God resided. Perhaps, this was the reason why the Christian priests considered making love a terrible sin; but what else could a man do to proliferate the species? Should he have to wait for the god of the Christians to inseminate each and every wild flower?

It was a worthy goal for every human being to create an innovation, to make a new beginning for a better future as often as his feeble strength allowed. Since humans were clearly the most complicated beings on Earth, the love with a woman had the divine power of ultimate creation and a woman's body was the gate to Paradise where God resided, waiting to judge every man for his ability to plow and seed new offspring.

However, creation was a purely female accomplishment, and so, if there was a Creator, he could never be a man. All the religions he trusted had been lying, and a single lie was enough to falsify a god. All the doubts he had about God or Allah had been dispersed with each new wave of female aggression. There was a god hidden in every woman's body eager to create new images of their harmonious union. This was the only truth he could trust unreservedly.

He could hardly remember the number, but when the last wave of passion dissipated within his flesh, his body was immersed with the essence of black skin that smothered his sense of smell. In this highly saturated state, it was impossible for the delicate perfume from the Spice Islands beyond the Indian Ocean that gradually slipped into the room through the latticed screen in a dark corner of the room to excite his nostrils.

Nevertheless, the Princess was completely content with what she saw, and could not wait to take the place of her favorite slave. Only the fear of Valide Sultan's reaction and her self-respect kept her from exercising all her executive privileges of an Osmanli on a male slave right then.

However, her magnificent brother was going to find out the very next day all her wishes and act accordingly. He was the only man on Earth who now stood in her way to happiness, but she was convinced her status as a young widow could bypass any objection he might care to raise about the fate of his favorite slave. She only had to be patient, and spent all her desires to touch and caress on the immaculate fur of her favorite white Angora cat with the blue and green eyes.

****

Not too much time had passed before another death disturbed the peace and happiness of the Sultan delaying his military plans. Without serious cause his youngest son by Mahidevran Ahmet was found dead on his bed.

The doctor blamed the tragedy to spoiled food, but the mother's status was severely affected. It was an opportune moment for few poisonous tongues of the Harem to start spreading the rumor that Hurrem, the wicked Christian witch, had poisoned the child. The truth was that the investigations Ibrahim conducted proved no evil, and no one dared to accuse without proof Suleiman's favorite. Nevertheless, it was also true that from the days the Romans founded the City, poisons were sold that could kill a man in a few hours and leave no trace behind.

No imperial doctor worthy of his high post was ignorant of their existence. Thus, for security reasons the necks of everyone came in touch with the Prince's plate from the cook to the waiter were severed. It may well have been a coincidence, but since then no other death from food poisoning occurred in the Seraglio through the Suleiman's reign.

Suleiman was very distressed for the loss of a second son so soon after the first. The almighty Allah had not spared His shadow from the sad duty to throw once more a handful of soil onto the coffin of a close member of his family. Nevertheless, life does not stand idle for long and in every corner of the way every mortal may find happiness or sadness with almost the same probability.

For most people joy must be more frequent than pain, and this is why births are always more numerous than deaths. Suleiman soon forgot his lost children, as within a year a new child was born by his new favorite Russian concubine. This time it was a girl he named Mihrimah. Her name in Persian meant the Sun's Moon and soon she became the favorite child of the Sultan. He never failed to grant any of her wishes.

****

Every child born in the Seraglio brought about changes in the hierarchy of the Harem, as the status of a Kadin or a concubine was closely related to the number of children she bore.

A mother of many children had many things to gain from her good luck. It was a sign she was capable to exploit better the holy seed of the House of Osman for the benefit of the Empire. Naturally, the status of a mother of a son was even higher, since he might well become the next Sultan, if this was the will of Allah. However, even the birth of a daughter created a definite improvement of the mother's rights, social status, and financial rewards.

The duties of a mother never ended with childbirth. She had to raise the child and educate it properly until the age it was admitted to the Seraglio School. Then, her role was practically concluded, and she was entirely free to enjoy the fruits of her labors for the rest of her life.

On the other hand, the mother lost all her privileges, even her life, if her child died and its death was attributed to her fault. As any death might also be the result of Kismet, it made sense for any woman to take into account the possibility of a mishap. This was the best way the wisdom of a woman could be measured in the Harem.

****

In the School, every young Prince had to learn horse riding, archery, swordsmanship, and all the necessary martial arts that would be useful to defend his life in a battle, as well as everything of value during peace time, as woodcarving or metalworking, to be able to build houses, furniture or weapons. Suleiman, for instance was a capable jeweler.

On the other hand, a Princess had to learn embroidery, knitting, sewing and playing a musical instrument. For all children there were common courses in religion, history, reading and writing in Arabic to be able to read and copy the Quran, Persian to recite poetry, and Turkish to command the pages and the courtiers.

The birth of Mihrimah, the second child within a year by the same mother, put Hurrem a step higher than any other Kadin in the Harem, as the Sultan had twisted few rules of the Ayin in her favor, following his father's example. The unwritten laws of his clan advised against a second birth by the same slave, favoring one concubine over all others. It was a position Roxelana would never lose until the end of her life. Her example would be repeated by Osmanli many times in the future, because Allah allowed every novelty to linger for as long as there was profit or pleasure to be gained.

****

The birth of Suleiman's daughter delayed for a while the preparations for the new Ottoman military expedition. Consistent with the strategy of his ancestors to strike successively at different directions of the horizon, Suleiman's next target would be in the Aegean Sea. The Sultan had to avenge next his great grandfather Fatih's defeat in the island of Rhodes.

This island together Crete held the keys to the Aegean Sea entrance from the South. It was occupied by the Knights of Saint John, the infamous Hospitallers of Acre, expelled from the Holy Lands by the Mamelukes of Egypt.

Rhodes had become an obstruction on the seaways from Constantinople to Alexandria, Acre, and Beirut. Without its occupation the safe commerce between these three harbors now in Ottoman hands became gradually extremely difficult.

The Knights were transforming from pious monks to blood-thirsty pirates whenever an opportune occasion for plunder arouse, and together with the Venetians in Crete and Cyprus were pillaging even the ships carrying pilgrims to Mecca. Rhodes was going to be the first crack of the Christian military blockade in the Mediterranean for the Ottoman sails, trying to break out of the Aegean

Sea towards Northern Africa and the Holy Land harbors.

During the oncoming spring the Ottoman armies from East and West were amassing across the Bosporus. The Sultan's military banner with the seven horsetails was posted in front of the Üsküdar Gate that meant an eastern enemy would be targeted next. The command of the armies rested in the hands of Selim's third Vizier, Ahmet Pasha. He was now the "Serasker", namely the Field Marshal of the Ottomans. The Ottoman Fleet was following the orders of Hayreddin Barbarossa who was turning it from small raiding flotillas into a strong tactical force.

The landing in Rhodes was carried out without opposition with the help of the massive fleet that carried the troops back and forth from the Asian coast, and within few days the entire countryside had surrendered without much native resistance. Only the great castle of the Knights of Rhodes remained occupied by the Christian knights, but the fortifications were powerful enough to control this strategic harbor putting the entirely island under threat with frequent murderous sorties.

The siege started according to the successful strategy of Belgrade by bombarding and undermining the mighty walls. However, the Knights were experts in building strong castles, and after five full months of intensive and bloody warfare the results were minimal compared to the grave losses. The castle could be taken only by hunger, but that might take many more months and possibly through the winter, since the enemy was well provided in advance for a long siege.

During the summer the fleet could keep the Ottoman armies well provided too, but as days passed, the rain and the cold were more damaging for the moral of the besiegers living in tents than of the defenders who resided comfortably in their homes and palaces. The prospect of a failure kept Suleiman awake at night. He was not willing to accept his luck has changed so quickly; nevertheless, the Council of the Pashas had come to the conclusion that at least for this winter most of the fighting troops had to return to the City to rest and lick their wounds.

Especially the Janissaries were getting restless after their grave losses and ceased to attack with their usual determination. They also seemed tired of the long siege and longed for the comforts of their homes. The experienced Grand Vizier also feared that any possible setback on the battlefield could trigger a mutiny against his leadership. Only the Sultan still kept few traces of determination and ordered them for one more final attack at daybreak; but, the spirited attack proved more disastrous than any one before. A change of strategy was necessary.

****

That night after the end of all hostilities, Ibrahim entered the Sultan's tent. He had spent the entire day by the Sultan's side watching the one after the other all the unsuccessful waves of the besiegers' attacks against the Christian Crusaders' fortifications until there was no more strength left to fight in both combatants, thinking and taking notes.

His master seemed greatly disappointed by the resulting failure, as now only the shameful retreat of the Ottoman armies remained as a viable option. However, surprisingly the slave's face didn't feel the least depressed by the adverse events, and a wide smile was written all over his face that didn't remained unnoticed by the gloomy Sultan.

"Why are you smiling at our defeat? These monks are the worst kind of infidels. They are religious fanatics. Don't you realize that if someone sees you laughing, this might be considered treasonous?"

"Yes, it could; but, only if my Master was an ordinary, simpleminded man, and I know well enough he is not," Ibrahim replied. "A wise emperor should be elated too like me that this senseless slaughter of faithful souls will soon stop with our new triumph."

"What do you mean?" the Sultan asked in anger.

"I am smiling full of joy, because in a few days we will be going home victoriously after your second triumph."

"I am not that hopeful any longer. Today was our very last attack for this year."

"I know that, but this defeat doesn't mean we cannot win this war. Castles are like women, they can be raped, but they can also be seduced, if the terms are honourable. The Romans before you almost never had to fight, and when they fought, half the times they lost the battles. Only when they offered reasonable terms, they won the day. Raping a city by force is the worst possible option, because like a woman during raping there is no cooperation to achieve the maximum possible pleasure, but only confrontation that spoils it. Please tell me. Do you have to rape your slaves to get the maximum of pleasure? No, of course not! You are not a Western barbarian, nor a looting Crusader. You are a civilized Oriental sovereign. When you go to a bazaar you don't grab whatever you like, but you negotiate the price with the seller. These barbarous knights that stand against you are as tired of fighting as we are at sunset. I watched them from dawn to sunset. They also know that we will come back next year even stronger, while they would be weaker. They are pirates, so they know that from now on their trade post here in Rhodes will be ruined. They are few, and we are numerous. Their numbers dwindle while ours grow. Next year we will arrive with even mightier guns. They know they will be doomed sooner or later. They are religious fanatics and only in the Resurrection after death they can hope now. If they were Muslims and I the Sultan, I would give their leader my sister as a bride and make them my vassals; but, they are Christian monks who despise women, so I would offer them as the ultimate present their lives, their weapons and a choice, life or death, to find out how much they believe in life after death."

Suleiman remained thoughtful for a while as he considered carefully his response to the slave's suggestions.

"This kind of conclusion is not honourable enough after so much bloodshed."

"Bloodshed is never an honourable solution. Do you remember what your great grandfather did, when he conquered the Eternal City and saw all the destruction the Crusaders had done? He was appealed and did his best to find new citizens and built new palaces, mosques, bazaars, and public buildings. Are you so forgetful to repeat the Crusader's mistake? Do you prefer to be the conqueror of a ruined city, or would you rather be the owner of a prosperous one that year after year will flood your treasury with tariffs and taxes? Even if you were to conquer Rhodes by force, the Sultan's share is only one fifth of the spoils. All the rest of its treasures would be lost forever ending up in the deep Janissary pockets, and from there to every whore and dancer in Galata. Is this where you wish your riches to go?"

This time the Sultan was quick to respond.

"This is not what my father would do to a city after so many months of bloody siege."

"Your father was a just and wise man. He always offered honourable terms of surrender and never looted a city that stopped resisting him. He was also a poet. He would never rape anyone, if he could seduce him. Please let me go to the City of Rhodes dressed richly like a Vizier and seduce them to submission. I used to be a Christian, so they will trust my words more than anyone else's."

Suleiman remained silent. He was very disturbed by the idea that his second expedition might end up in failure; so he didn't have much of a choice.

"I will send you as my messenger with the most honorable offer I can make," he noted.

****

It was almost a miracle. After a week of negotiations the Castle of the Knights of Rhodes, opened up the gates for the defenders to board the pirate fleet and sail away to the West with all their standards, arms and belongings. However, the most amazing development was the fact that many of the fanatical Knights of Saint John decided to remain in Rhodes, changed their faith and entered the Sultan's service.

Rhodes had fallen; but, it was also saved. Ibrahim was right. There was no reason for a city to die first so it could be resurrected. The native people were the most grateful of all for this change of masters, as the Knights of Temple were cruel landlords, the dungeons were full of prisoners, and they demanded even heavier taxes than the Venetians and the Romans before them.

Only the Janissaries were sorry for the achieving a truce, because there would be no looting, and a war without plunder was an incomprehensible concept for their lot. However, this time they had no right to demand any reward, as they had failed in their mission. Their only option was to lick their wounds and wait for the next war.

****

The Ottoman momentous success in Rhodes had a great impact on the European sentiments because the way it had finally materialized was totally unexpected. Instead of a bloody massacre that would enhance the barbarous image of the Ottomans, as looters, rapists, and plunderers, Europe was faced with a much more dangerous reality, a bloodless surrender of the fanatical Christian knights who instead of dying for their faith had trusted the words of a noble and benevolent Muslim Emperor. Only time could now show, if Suleiman was a capable leader like Saladin bound to throw the Christians clear out of the Balkans.

The most characteristic reaction of a European sovereign was the words of Charles the Fifth at the time, who as soon as the details of the disaster became known, acknowledged that "**never before in the world something as precious as Rhodes had been lost in such an impeccable way.**"

It was indeed a most perilous development for the entire Christian world. Christian monks had preferred to become part of an Islamic empire, extending from the Land of the Nile to the Danube and from Mesopotamia to the Ionian Sea. It was as if the Roman Empire had been resurrected under a different name and a more powerful God.

Allah the Benevolent was already worshiped in the same Christian churches, as even the Fatih's Mosque was built by a Greek architect in the image of Agia Sophia. Ottomans had become the vengeful angels for the Crusade stricken Orient and the sons of the Devil for Christianity and Occident.

For a wise young man like Ibrahim this difference in people's minds was a sign Balkans and the Aegean Sea had become the center of the controversy and Constantinople once again the naval of the world. The fact that Suleiman was a pious believer of the Prophet was an insignificant detail for most of his subjects as long as he was victorious. Everything else was just a minor, meaningless detail only Christian Patriarchs and Muslim Ulema could ever distinguish. Now the greatest prospect was for other Christian islands like Crete, Cyprus and Sicily to follow the example of Rhodes.

Silently and subtly Venetians started to pay tributes to the Sultan to retain the use of the Greek Islands in the Aegean and the Ionian Sea; but they didn't stop there. They also offered their fleet to carry the grain from Egypt and the Ukraine to the Golden Horn, exactly as they had done during the Roman era. It was an agreement for mutual benefit. The Venetian Flying Lion terrorizing the Aegean few years back with a single stroke had turned into an obedient cat eager to be caressed and pampered by the strong Ottoman hands.

****

Just before returning to the Constantinople, Sultan Suleiman decided it would be a good idea to take a stroll on horseback around the town of Rhodes. Every ironclad gate was now wide open, and all the town folks locked up inside the walls for many months were out strolling and chatting freely on the harbor piers. It was a day of celebration and festivities for the new found liberty under a benevolent ruler. Few hours ago the last Venetian vessel with the Knights' leadership had started their long trip for Crete.

The weather was gradually turning bitter cold as the northern wind blowing hard turned the horses' breath into steam, resembling fire-spitting dragons from fairy tales.

"I long so much for home, now I have the illusion the northern wind is carrying to our nostrils the scent of the Golden Horn," Suleiman claimed.

"Wherever there are fireplaces in the Mediterranean that burn wood and roast mackerels and tenderloins of suckling lamb it will smell like home to me," Ibrahim replied. "Men are not trees to grow roots at one place. It's a woman's habit to always look for shelters and her duty to attract her man back to her bosom. True men are wanderers and settlers."

"You are right again. Indeed, I long for Hurrem too. For how long a man can survive without a woman? Perhaps you have been a slave too long to understand this simple truth."

"Perhaps I might have acquired indeed such a trend; but, a slave cannot be blamed for his choices. If someone is responsible for this preference, this surely must be his master and the orders he gives me."

"You are right; but, I am very happy I kept you all this time by my side. Without you this prosperous city would lay in ruins, or we would be returning home with our tails between our legs. Imagine all these happy people dead or in chains, merchandise for the slave traders. Isn't all this a fair exchange for just few months away from a woman's touch?"

"I really don't know the answer to this question. I am just a slave and the only touch I know is yours. Perhaps it is you a world conqueror the right man to answer a fair question. Is conquering the world really worth the shed blood and the toil, or should a man restrict his ambitions to just a single woman?" Ibrahim pointedly inquired.

"Now it's too late for me to answer such a question. I already have three wives in my harem," Suleiman acknowledged with a long smile. "Am I too greedy to desire you, three women, and the world too?"

"No! A mortal man has the right to demand in his life all the weight his back can carry. This is actually how the worth of a man is measured."

"I am very curious to find out how much your back can carry. Perhaps as soon as we come back home, I should give you permission to buy few slaves for your pleasure as a reward for your wise counselling in this expedition and see how much you enjoy the change."

It was a curious thought Ibrahim diplomatically refused to comment, staring instead absentmindedly in the horizon.

The horses had stopped short of the end of the pier scared of the angry sea that hit the huge boulders enclosing the ancient Rhodes harbour.

"Perhaps on these very rocks one of the Seven Wonders, the Colossus of Rhodes was standing, and now there is not even a trace of its glory. Life has a way to diminish every man's vanity sooner or later," Ibrahim replied subtly to his master's inquisition. "But there is no harm done if a benevolent master in trying to enrich life of his slave. Allah made the world so that happiness is a commodity that can be shared without diminishing its value as it is with women."

"Yes, and that's why the Prophet gave Muslim men the right to enjoy many women to use our endless lust for a good cause, the proliferation of the faithful. A Muslim slave like you should have the same right."

"I always wondered if the same teaching applies for women too," the slave countered, but his response was too ambiguous to be properly appreciated on horseback.

Perhaps the powerful wave that came crashing on the pier breaking into a million droplets was responsible for the long and perfect silence that followed as the two men tried to control their horses from rising on their hind legs; however; as the sun was setting, its rays gave birth to a brilliant rainbow that dazzled both riders and horses with its luminescent majesty, dispersing every possible doubt about the magic of the moment.

And as a second wave came crashing producing a similar effect, both men prayed that this moment would never end; but, fatefully it did, as the sun swiftly disappeared behind the clouds riding on the wings of the "tramontane", as the Venetian sailors called the northerly wind, behind the dark silhouettes of the mountains, extinguishing its spectacular pyrotechnics.

A setting sun can produce different feelings in two men's hearts. The Sultan dreamed this sacred hour about an empire where the sun would never set. His father had humbled the Orient. After the island of Rhodes in the East, time had come for him to humble the Occident.

For the slave from the Ionian Sea a sunset had more subtle, philosophical dimensions. Empires would rise and fall. The sun god had to be a man, because before rising again he needed a long period of recuperation. After the conquest of Rhodes the Ottomans needed a period of recovery too. Perhaps the time had come for him to claim the hand of the Princess.

Despite the distance, he could still feel her attraction even though she was many days of travel away. Women were blessed by this mysterious ability to attract men from a distance. Even worse was the fact that time acted in their favor, and as it progressed, their attraction grew even stronger, as the years remaining for a man to make the momentous decision of having a child withered away into fruitless memories.

Naturally, men had a different point of view of life than women. They were too often moody and unpredictable. They could drastically change attitudes in the spur of a moment. His relationship with the Sultan was too fragile to last forever. He didn't need a wise counselor to realize that. He could feel it in his loins that Suleiman's desire for him was dwindling. Their relationship to last should be transformed to something more permanent than simple carnal desire. There was no way he could challenge a professional enchantress in the battlefield of seduction. She was simply too feminine, the incarnation of Aphrodite blessed with the ability to turn desire into flesh.

If he was a eunuch, he would have just one choice, serve him in the same way the Roman eunuchs had served their emperors. Suleiman would be a god and he his guarding angel. Perhaps if Zarafet and Yabani had not raped him so decisively, if Hurrem did not visit his dreams each night uninvited, if Basmi didn't have so fleshy lips, or, if he hadn't read fiery desire in Hatidge's eyes, he could feel like an obedient angel to the will of his god; but, all these miraculous events had turned him into a lusty devil looking for new conquests like Selim Khan.

Perhaps the Prophet was right. One woman was not enough for a man. Perhaps he was just responding to challenges as any ordinary human being made by Allah to respond to an eye with an eye or with desire for desire.

"You are correct!" the Sultan consented interrupting his fantasy. "A war that conquers a piece of land by exterminating the people that cultivate it is meaningless. People are like sheep that graze on land. An emperor should behave like a wise shepherd who must increase his flock, not diminish it. We the Turks are great shepherds. It's a skill running in our veins together with our blood."

"That's a principle most wisely versed. The people need only a mesmerizing dream and they will follow the man who can provide them with the best laid-out plan leading to happiness. Their leader could be an emperor, a conqueror, or a prophet. He only has to provide an enchanting dream and a human flock will form and follow him to the end of the world."

"My race always preferred to enslave nations rather than to slaughter them; but there were also few nations who claimed they were the blessed ones, and someone had to bring them back to the sober reality. This is what happened to your Greco-Romans relatives. Fatih never planned of conquer you by force, blood and tears, but you were so damn conceited believing the words of foolish priests instead of your own reason."

Ibrahim felt the need to defend his race.

"Every nation is entitled to seek its moment of glory in its lifespan, and we Romans had the lion's share of triumphs in the world. Many nations besides us, the Persians, the Mamelukes, the Serbs and the Bulgarians decided that they should fight against the Ottomans, and lost their most precious possessions and even their lives. Other nations like the Arabs have chosen more wisely and decided it is to their advantage to bow down their heads and seek your mercy. Only Time will prove who was right and who was wrong. In my mind only one issue is certain and incontestable. Living is better than dying because as long as one can breathe there is hope. If History can teach us something useful for our future, this is not whether we should kneel or resist the will of our enemy to find if he is stronger or weaker than we are; but, that the blood of a nation weakens as the centuries go by, and the only way for blood to recover its vigour is to be enslaved from time to time by a stronger nation. If the Turks are so powerful now, it is because they were slaves for many years to the same people that now serve them. There are no nations blessed or cursed by God, master races, or nations of slaves. In a single moment a single worthy leader can change everything for the better or for the worst, cutting the umbilical cord of a nation with its past; but, to do that he has to be an exception, a man who doesn't wish to waste his one and only life hidden inside the anonymity of the crowd. Only weaklings feel secure lost inside a flock imprisoned in a sheepcote, yearning for the caresses of the shepherd until the time comes to feel the blade of the butcher. Today a Roman from the Ionian Sea is your most obedient slave. Tomorrow everything can radically change. History is such a complicated process I may not have to fight against Allah to the death to regain liberty. Perhaps a smile of the goddess of fortune might be enough for my liberation."

The Sultan was in such good mood that he didn't lose his smile with this new slave impertinence.

"I am not willing to get into an argument with you tonight, because I also believe that whatever happens is according to the will of Allah who now wants me to be your master and you my slave. I only wish to point out that a proud master will not relinquish his command without a fight, and if this time ever comes blood will flow like a river."

"I am not in the mood for fighting too. No one wants to lose his privileges, even when he knows that he is getting old and has to yield his throne to the new blood. Even if he is sick and wise as your father was until the very last moment, he may be under the illusion that a second life is coming. As long as we live there is always hope the next day will be better than the last. It may be an illusion we come to realize the moment of our death."

His answer set the Sultan thinking, as it reminded him of his duties as a descendant of Osman.

"I don't know what the best way is for a Sultan to solve the succession to the throne problem. In my case my father solved it to my advantage. I hope that when my time comes, you will be standing by my side to give me a wise advice how to choose the best sovereign among my sons. Then, I will need your wisdom and clarity of purpose more than ever. Even my grim father smiled content listening to your arguments, and he was the one who elevated you to the position of the Guardian of my Hawks rather than turning you into an obedient eunuch good only for keeping me company through the night."

Ibrahim was not certain if it would be to his advantage to disclose how he obtained this position; so, he remained silent. He decided it was not wise to try to be overly truthful, as lies were often much more digestible than truth.

Perhaps one day he might be confident enough to tell his lover the entire truth about his father, but right now Selim's advice to consider seriously the value of silence seemed the wiser option. His friend was not yet as foresighted as his father. His mind still roamed in the clouds of his momentous military success.

"True human wisdom is to avoid solving other people's problems first before your own. The man who can find the source of his personal happiness is the most sensible of all. For me you became the wiser of men the moment you realized that happiness is hidden inside the crystal clear sapphire eyes of Hurrem."

An expression of surprise appeared in the Sultan's face.

"You are right, but how do you know the color of Hurrem's eyes? I thought I was the only one who had seen her face."

It was a mistake Ibrahim had to neutralize and the truth seemed as the better choice.

"My Master, please forgive my indiscretion. I was lucky enough to see her eyes one day, when she was still one more humble of your mother's courtiers."

The Sultan seemed indifferent for his disclosure and asked him for his judgment.

"What do you think of her? Is she worthy enough to become the woman of my life?"

It was clearly a rhetorical question begging for a single answer. Ibrahim had no reason to disappoint his master in such a serious matter.

"Hurrem is worth much more than what your mother paid to buy her. She is an exceptional creature well fitted to become the very first one of your life's companions. Human emotions are like light. They become stronger when they are focused."

The Sultan was elated with his answer.

"Besides you who help me choose wisely, she is the only one who can make me happier and put a smile on my face. Everyone else bores me to death. I will always keep you two locked deep inside my heart."

"The word 'always' scares me to death, as time is invincible by us mortals. An earthquake has toppled even the Colossus of Rhodes and Agia Sophia's dome. What chance does a slave full of mortal weaknesses have against time in a wicked city that has dethroned even emperors?"

"There is nothing in this world that can change my feelings for the two of you. Only if there is an earthquake strong enough to topple me down, then you might fall too; but, your presence here by my side drives away all my fears about the future."

Ibrahim wanted to go on questioning his friend's feelings. Was a man's heart big enough for two? Islam claimed that a man could marry four women; but, the Holy Quran never talked in detail about passionate love, only respect for another's feelings. Love was much more than just blind obedience and respect. It contained the essence of uniqueness and possession as much as the birth of a child did, adding the essences of a father and a mother. From the days of his training in the school for pages, he had learned to distinguish between long lasting love and fleeing lust. For a slave experiencing lust was a rare event, because his life style was very confined. Generating lust for his masters had been his main asset in his struggle for prosperity. To make his life more modestly pleasant, he had adjusted his pleasure to that of his masters; but, as time passed and status improved, his heart yearned for something more permanent than temporary fulfillment. On the other hand, his master had less complex needs. In the Harem satisfaction of lust was for him readily available like eating, drinking or breathing; thus, it had practically no permanent value.

What his master needed was love. However, the best the slave could do now was to make a wish to a god he didn't believe, since these days Allah was the one and only god who made most of his wishes come true somehow.

"Il-hamdu-lellah, (In the name of Allah)," he uttered as it was more important from now on to have the last word even if it was just a common everyday Muslim wish.

****

The victorious return of the Sultan to the City of Constantine after a second quick success in a row raised Suleiman's star even higher than Fatih's who had failed to subdue both Belgrade and Rhodes fortifications.

Essentially, cities were for world conquerors like women they had to exploit. They could marry them, if they surrendered, or rape them, if they resisted. The fact that Hurrem had captured his master's heart meant she had been very comforting to his emotional and carnal needs. She had followed Ibrahim's approach and that meant she was a highly intelligent ruler of emotions.

Having intelligent enemies could be perilous, but having gifted friends was a valuable asset. He could not have any complain from Hurrem's behavior. To be a truly impartial judge he had to get into the defendant's position.

Hurrem had become extremely frustrated for her initial failure to get pregnant, and she had a very hard life up to that point. She had been admitted to the Sultan's bedroom, but she was not the only woman there. The competition was extremely stiff, and he could see how frustrating was for her the presence of such an exquisite woman like Mahidevran who already had two sons. If he was the Sultan, after having some fun with Hurrem for a change, he would surely return to his old love to give her a couple of children more now that she had lost a precious son.

Hurrem could never have guessed that Mahidevran would suddenly lose a son within a year, and she would be now the most prolific concubine in the Harem. If all the rumors for her dubious past were accurate, a "sold meat" facing dismissal after few satisfying orgies was perfectly justified to look for another customer for her assets; thus, having a taste of what was readily available was a logical choice, not an excessive display of lust.

Since then a lot had changed as Hurrem had not only managed to be elevated in the Harem; but he was also occupying now a position by the Sultan's side much more significant than his post as the Guardian of the Hawks. Indeed, within few months after Rhodes with a Sultan's firman he was named a Pasha, and soon after he became the "Beylerbey of Rumelia" i.e. Governor of the

Balkan Peninsula.

However, as it often happens, extraordinary honors create extraordinary resentment especially among the few who think they should be the ones to be honored instead. For the common logic this is the result of human envy, but for the wise ones this is Allah's way to keep the balance. The Janissaries and many other soldiers regarded war as the best way to get rich. The peaceful conclusion of the siege of Rhodes brought to them nothing but casualties, gapping wounds and constant worries. Without plunder war brought riches only to the Sultan who was the only one profiting from tax collection. For all the rest who fought in a war, the spoils, the slaves and the lands conquered and shared among the warriors were what made wars worth fighting for.

No one knew who or how it started; but, soon there was unrest about the fate of the Christians in the Eternal City in the Janissary barracks and the Islamic Schools around the Fatih Mosque. Then, a mixed committee of soldiers and clergy was formed and appeared in front of the Divan. They claimed the Islamic Law required the Christians in Constantinople who had resisted and fought against the Ottoman armies to change their belief at once by force or face death. As Allah was benevolent and forgiving, the Christians had to face at best two more days of loot, rapes and plunder, since it was known Fatih had allowed only one day of pillaging after the fall of Constantinople.

The plain truth was that Sultan Mehmet Fatih strolling along the city streets back then, became very depressed looking at the sorry condition of this great city and stopped its destruction. Most of the public buildings had been dilapidated and demolished during the Latin conquest two centuries before, and later many of the houses were deserted after a series of plagues, forcing many inhabitants to immigrate to Italy.

The great Roman City was reduced in size, becoming a small town and a trophy unworthy of the great effort and expenses invested in conquering it. Even Edirne and Bursa, the obscure provincial capitals of the Ottoman Empire, had many more residents back then than Constantinople; but, Mehmet was a man of vision, and soon he moved by force or incentives many people from conquered lands, or by offering a country to every religious refugee of the world. If this benevolent policy was reversed, the Eternal City might lose the most dynamic and industrious portion of its population, the Romans, the Armenians and the Jews.

It was a difficult decision for Suleiman, as whatever solution he chose would create an opposition not only in the City but in the Empire, as a great part of the Ottoman success was due to the freedom of religion they practiced. Christians, and Jews were highly prosperous communities in the Empire, and alienating them could be proven disastrous. It was also very unfair, as these people lived in these lands long before the Turks stepped on Anatolian soil. In a single stroke the success of Rhodes conquest would vanish; but if the Ottomans were to conquer Europe, religious fanaticism should be kept out of this conflict as much as possible. The critical issue was not whether the Holy Spirit came before or after the Son, as in the Roman era, but if the Ottomans could provide security and prosperity with fewer taxes than anyone else to all the citizens on the lands they conquered.

****

That night Suleiman was full of tension caused once more by the stress of indecision. To reach a viable solution he felt he had to ask for the help of the Seyh-ul-Islam, the chief Ulema of the Empire responsible for all matters related to the application of Sharia, the sacred Islamic Law. He was the first one who found out about the problem, and also the one who had warned the Orthodox Patriarch about a possible religious violence explosion.

That night the Seih had arrived secretly wearing his most imposing suit with the huge turban second in size only to the Sultan's, his best white caftan with the saber fur collar, and his most brilliant golden rings to honor the young Sultan and underline the importance of his visit. This was the first time the young Sultan had secretly asked for his advice and this honor was most important for him and his authority.

Long time ago the grandfather of Suleiman, Bayezid the Saint considered the position of the Seyh-ul-Islam even more important than his own, since he had to apply the laws of men while the Ulema the laws of Allah. Nevertheless, since the day Selim the Grim had risen to the Ottoman throne, religion had receded to the background, as the Sultan's authority became absolute. Selim didn't wait for the verdict of trials and carried out death sentences with his own hand. Perhaps now with the young Sultan Seyh-ul-Islam's old authority might be replenished.

The Mufti kneeled deeply in front of the Sultan and recited many of the titles the Sultan possessed according to the protocol.

"Greetings to the Padisah Suleiman Khan, son of Selim Khan, Master of Mecca and Medina, Lord of Damascus, Cairo and Jerusalem. I pray Allah illuminates your thoughts to the path of justice."

Suleiman was quick to come to the point bypassing formalities.

"I have invited you tonight to listen to your opinion about the fate of the infidels in the City. It is a religious matter and your interpretations are of great importance for the Caliph of Islam. In the Arz Odas we are all alone and we can talk freely and frankly. What are Allah's commands in this case, should I force all the Christians and the Jews to become Muslims?"

The Mufti became thoughtful for a while to add importance to his judgment.

"My Sultan, my duty is to explain the Quran, so that all the faithful comprehend the Prophet's teachings and Allah's infinite wisdom illuminates your thoughts. As you well know, it is plainly written in the Holy Quran that every city that refuses to accept the word of the Prophet, closes its gates and resist the will of Allah should be pillaged for three days, and its inhabitants should be enslaved and sold. However, in the case of the Eternal City, this punishment to be just should have been carried immediately after the conquest, not now more than fifty years later, when most of the perpetrators are dead. The Holy Quran also states that the Christians and the Jews who have done no harm against the faithful must not suffer. As far as I know many gates of Constantinople were opened to accept the victorious armies of the Prophet, and for this reason Fatih spared the inhabitants of these districts from slavery, while punished by death all who resisted his will by arms. Punishing the Christians of the City now is unfair and extreme, and Allah the Benevolent punishes everyone who exceeds the limits."

Suleiman seemed satisfied by the Great Mufti's reply. He had reached a similar conclusion, but he didn't need just a fair declaration of principles. He needed a practical advice how to enforce the law of logic on a furious mob full of murderous rage.

"Every word of yours spoken was full of wisdom and moderation, and I am in complete agreement with every word spoken. However, the rebels argue that the Caliph should always do the best he can to increase the numbers of the faithful; thus, I have to threaten the infidels into changing their faith and save their lives and fortunes."

"That is true indeed, but all the Ottoman Sultans abode by the law which states that all who submit to the will of Allah and bow to his majesty should not be harmed. There can be no exceptions to this fair law, as even changing a single letter in the Quran is a mortal sin," the Mufti sternly noted.

"How can the Quran prescribe at one point to kill the fanatical infidels, and in another to let them live and prosper? One of these two laws must be wrong. This is what logic dictates," the Sultan argued.

It was now becoming gradually apparent that Suleiman insisted on a clear cut solution that even the simplest minds could comprehend and an explanation that could not be contested by the religious mob. On the other hand, the Mufti insisted on the theoretical basis of the existing dispute.

"The Quran contains nothing but the word of Allah exactly the way they were relayed to the Prophet Mohamed by the angel Gabriel, blessed be his name. Everything inside the Holy Quran is correct down to the last comma. This is the truth and nothing but the truth, so help us Allah. Logic and religion do not mix, as human logic leads only to dreadful errors and heresies. The true faith in Allah commences where human logic ends."

Suleiman has been for too many years in the company of Ibrahim to be satisfied by similar simpleminded explanations. When he was younger he also remembered many of his grandfather teachings who had been greatly influenced by the words of heretical dervishes.

"I must have a simple answer no one can challenge. If the Great Mufti of Islam cannot make it plain enough for the Janissaries to understand, perhaps I have to seek advice elsewhere else, my Pashas," the Sultan subtly threatened.

"My final answer is one and crystal clear. The infidels inside the City should not be harmed in any way, because when Fatih crossed the Edirne gate, the Christian and Jewish priests did not resist his will and kneeled before his power. Only the Latin Patriarch escaped in a Venetian vessel, as the Roman Emperor and his Latin mercenaries fought to the death and lost their lives for their sins. This is how history describes the event. Even if Fatih was still alive, he would never consider punishing the children of the infidels for any sin their fathers have committed," the Great Mufti acknowledged offended by the Sultan's objections. "If the Caliph doesn't need my advice for any other issue, I would like to offer him my sincerest wishes for longevity hoping that the next time he asks for my advice his problems will have been reduced at least by one."

The Sultan rose and greeted with respect the Great Mufti of the Empire to show his gratitude for his advice; however, he was not content with the explanation offered. He also believed the infidels were innocent of any past crimes of their ancestors; but, the argument that the Sultan should exercise all his power to force the infidels to change their fate seemed unshakable in the simple mind of a fanatic Janissary eager to loot. Perhaps the opinion of an infidel on this issue would be more practical; so, he summoned Ibrahim to his quarters.

****

It was already past midnight when Ibrahim entered his bedroom visibly worried about the urgency of the call. The Sultan was still sitting on the low sofa, smoking silently his nargileh and tasting occasionally small pieces of sweet delights from the Chios Island. The atmosphere was already heavy with thick clouds of smoke and the scent of hashish was overwhelming. The Sultan nodded him to come closer and indicated that his pleasure was to sit next to him on the throne.

Since their return from Rhodes, they never had the chance to be alone together, as the celebrations for the victory required the Sultan's uninterrupted participation in all the festivities. Ibrahim was by his side, but there were always other guests present too. This time would be different and the servant had already his instructions to bring along a second nargileh, sweets and fruits. Suleiman was very careful to treat him as his equal only when there were no other eyes around that could mistake his care for weakness.

Few draughts of smoke were enough to warm up the atmosphere and as soon as the usual formalities were out of the way Suleiman explained him what the reason was for this nocturnal invitation.

Ibrahim listened carefully to all the Sultan had to say, but when Suleiman explained the Grand Mufti's preposition, he couldn't keep a straight face.

"Why are you smiling?" the Sultan asked him rather irritated.

"Introducing the mob into theological disputes is the best way to lead the Empire down the path of the Romans, ruining everything your wise ancestors have achieved in a single day. The crowds need commands not excuses. We both know and Grand Mufti knows too that for the Empire to prosper you need all of its citizens to work in harmony the same way two horses must be tied to pull the coach in the same direction. The Muslims and the infidels are for you these two fine horses. Since the days Fatih reigned, this City has prospered because all the nations that inhabit it cooperated. When nations cooperate then even the borders have no meaning. They are simply lines drawn on maps. The Ottomans should not have to suffer the same fate of the Romans before them with all their foolish heresies about the icons or the bloody conflicts about who has the Holy Ghost in his possession, the father or the son. The Prophet solved these problems with one stroke, no paintings, and Allah is one, not an entity split in three. The Empire is in danger only when the Sultan has no majestic dreams to share with his subjects. He must also unite and teach them that their best option is for them to follow his magnificent dreams. Thus, the Shadow of Allah should reward the believers of his divine order and punish the infidels working to promote chaos. This should be the only choice the mob has to make. Mobs must forget what religion, color, language, or what clothes everyone wears. They should focus only on who follows the laws of the Sultan and who doesn't. Whoever follows the laws must be allowed to enter the Sultan's Paradise, rest under the thick shade of trees and find pure mates on river banks, as we did long ago in the plains of Edirne."

The Sultan had still some doubts about Ibrahim's point of view.

"Yes, but someday everyone must become Muslim exactly like me and my master race. These are the words of Allah; otherwise, there can be no world peace."

"This is no world order. It's religious sentimental nonsense! It is the recipe for Hell! Imagine a world where every man looks like you, believe in the same god, speak the same language, have black hair, grey coloured eyes, a slightly bent nose, and has the same way of thinking. Look around you and you will find that Allah in His infinite wisdom has not created two things identical. There are not two men, nor two horses, not two women, nor two leaves, not even two grains of sand alike. Allah's World Order is the Harmony of Disorder and so should his Shadow behave too. Would you ever like me more, if I looked like Hurrem full of sensuous curves?"

The Sultan was surprised by this last remark and could not help but giggle.

"Tonight we may joke about it and everything may be smartly said; but, tomorrow I will have to convince a mob of angry Janissaries that what the Grand Mufti said about the infidels in the City is the truth, and you know better than me that when the Janissaries start arguing, logic stops."

"The Janissaries will be no problem for the Empire, if the Sultan and the Grand Mufti are convinced that what they have agreed upon is the truth. The religion is not the last argument but the first and logic follows. However, where religion and logic stop, there starts the edge of your sword. If the voice of Allah cannot convince a doubter, then Death surely can. Tomorrow morning the Chief Executioner should read a firman with Grand Mufti's interpretation of the Islamic law in front of the Janissary barracks and wait to see what will happen next."

The Sultan's face became brighter than ever before as the tension disappeared at once. Now he was certain the crisis would soon be over without any serious consequences, and he felt the need to offer a present to his slave for his service.

"Ask me a favour and I swear in Allah's name I will grant it at once."

Ibrahim, felt the need to reveal his feelings for the Sultan's sister, but he hesitated at the last moment. The Sultan might be offended by such an audacious request. Even if he was his most intimate friend, Ibrahim was still a slave and Hatidge a Princess. Perhaps his request could be versed more effectively by someone else in the same way the Grand Mufti's fetva would be better announced by the Chief Executioner.

"Only few days have passed since you made me Beylerbey of Rumelia. I would consider myself exceedingly greedy if I was to ask you tonight for another favor. As the Grand Mufti said, Allah punishes the greedy one who goes beyond the limits. I will ask no more favors from Your Majesty; but if you still feel you should reward me then make true whatever favour someone else you trust asks for me."

"Are you sure this is what you want right now?"

"Yes, I am sure, if you believe that it is a fair request."

"If a man is so rich that he feels he has no more favors to ask from the Sultan, then the Sultan must ask him a favor," Suleiman replied with a curious smile and Ibrahim realized that he had to comply that night with all the Sultans commands.

He didn't mind much because by now he had realized that everything in life had a price. That same night Ibrahim was taught two more lessons. Firstly, that he should never give promises for favors not explicitly expressed in advance and secondly, that he should never underestimate a man's lust.

****

Even when a man feels that he has followed every Allah's commandment, there are always few secret ones he will always miss, because only Allah is the Knower of All Secrets.

This night Ibrahim should not also underestimate the lust of a woman. As Hurrem spent the entire night waiting for the Sultan's invitation, early morning she realized that something was still missing from the complete conquest of Suleiman's heart. And if Ibrahim was full of male confidence as any Ottoman Beylerbey should be, Hurrem was full of doubts for her own significance, and she was so insecure she was never going to forgive her man's infidelities. Perhaps, she was still too immature to bear the burden that he should learn to share her man with another person, either a man or a woman. Perchance she was afraid that her children would someday find out the truth and try to imitate their father.

In this world, when something materialized, it was easy for anyone to explain why it did so. The true wisdom was to predict the future before it actually happened; but this is something only Allah could do, because He is everything, the past, the present and the future.

****

The Kislar Aga seemed surprised hearing Valide Sultan's last command. He had to summon secretly a certain White Eunuch in the Harem and no one else was supposed to know.

Up to this moment entering the Harem was prohibited for any White Eunuch, but he was not bold enough to doubt the wisdom of a direct order. He only knew well enough the reason.

All the Black Eunuchs were drastically castrated at an early age by Copt monks in the town of Asyut, as the slave traders transported slaves from Nubia through the Nile Valley to the Cairo markets. The castration was generally compulsory; but which Nubian slave would complain, if for some reason the slave trader chose to spare him?

On the other hand, the White Eunuchs were a much more diverse group coming mostly from Circassia on the Caucuses. They were castrated within the Ottoman Empire borders by Roman and Jewish doctors. In general, the prospect of serving the Sultan in close quarters acted as a strong motive for many poor subjects from the Balkans or Anatolia to enlist in this service and secure a high post in the Ottoman hierarchy. It was well known that when Bayezid the Saint was the Sultan, even two Grand Viziers were Janissaries and eunuchs. Many men among them had been sterilized simply to curb the natural tendency of all men to have children; but otherwise, they had everything a woman required to be content. Was this the reason why this eunuch was summoned in the Harem so stealthily?

It was not his duty to judge the personal choices of white men. If he was not enslaved, by now he would have used his own harem in Sudan to enrich his tribe with divine images of himself. Now directing the Sultan's Harem and denied the blessing of children, he looked with envy every man intact capable of enjoying women and having children too. His curiosity was so pronounced, he couldn't help but eavesdrop and his hearing had been greatly enhanced after his grave mishap.

****

Asphodel did not expect to be summoned so soon after his arrival. As the Kapi Aga he had to follow the Sultan all the way to Rhodes and didn't have time to adjust to his normal routines in the Seraglio. However, Hafsa's face had a long smile and a purse rested in her palm for him to claim it, but it was not all he got.

"I'm very pleased of your services. You were even more truthful than I expected about Gülfem Hatun. I could never imagine she could be so devious."

150

"I don't wish to contradict you, but she may not be as devious as you presume. From what the rumors claim, she simply wished to ask Sultan Selim to spare her only son back then."

"I'm afraid you are too naïve when it comes to women. There are always at least two reasons behind every act. The safety of her son was just the obvious one to sooth her consciousness. As you well know my husband was a handsome man and making love to him was always pleasurable; however, these were not enough reasons for that bitch. She decided that if she had two sons by two Sultans it would be even more certain she would become Valide Sultan one day; so, beware of women asking for favors. Only when a noble woman commands you, you may have no regrets for any action she demands simply because you will have no choice."

"I will treasure your advices much more than your purse," he claimed obediently and she giggled.

"Spend your coins well. From what I hear the Janissaries are very frustrated these days and the prices of women have fallen. On the other hand, the prices of boys have risen because of the increase demand for the uncommon."

"I'm still very young to retire; so I will buy a house and make a harem of my own," he replied encouraged by her friendly disposition.

He had made an accurate assessment. Hafsa Sultan's manners had immensely changed for the better since the moment she felt confident of his sincerity.

"I would be most willing to contribute to such a noble cause, if you were to tell me exactly what you know about Ibrahim, and how you assess his relationship with my son. I'm sure that as a White Eunuch you had more than your fair share of similar affairs between young men."

Asphodel sensed the tension behind her warm tone of voice. Hafsa was the Valide Sultan, but before that she was also a mother. She was a lioness that would think twice before attacking another lioness simply to gain the favors of a male lion; but she would try to kill even the very same male, if he dared to threaten her cubs. She was now friendly because she didn't wish to alarm him. Hafsa Sultan was leading him to a very dangerous path, and he was not sure, if she had not paid Menekse handsomely to kill Selim Khan and save the life of her son.

"I'm sure an experienced Valide Sultan knows that men's preferences change gradually as time passes. This is why Allah the All-Wise promises enchanting houri and handsome young men to his martyrs to satisfy all cases."

Hafsa could not restrain a long smile. Now she only needed to make a few questions to be sure.

"Yes, I know that Selim Khan had reached this crossroad. It's the only excuse I can find for his insatiable greed for conquests. If he hadn't died, he would have closed down the Eski Saray and sent me to my father's palace in Crimea."

"I didn't wish to sadden you, but men can be very cruel and forgetful sometimes. I'm sure if he hadn't died, he would have executed me along with my brother. Even your son wouldn't be safe, if Selim Khan lived long enough to carry out his threat."

"What threat was that?" Hafsa Sultan inquired with considerable interest.

"I think he had decided to abolish the White Eunuch Corps and establish a new one using only attractive young men like Ibrahim."

Hafsa Sultan was startled by this new piece of news he never expected when she started questioning. She wished to find out how well Ibrahim had kept his promise to let her son free from his influence; but now she had found another vein of gold.

"How do you know this was in his mind? Selim Khan was extremely secretive. No one knew what was in his mind."

"It was not entirely his idea. Selim Khan became so pleased with Ibrahim's charms he had no further use of us eunuchs!"

The Valide Sultan seemed terrified by the prospect, even though Selim's promise would never come true now. Even as a thought it was enough to paralyze her. It was such a monstrous concept that if she knew, she would do her best to destroy it. The eunuch understood her thoughts and tried to comfort her.

"Allah the All-Seer just in time averted this monstrosity by sending an angel to carry Selim Khan to heavens, Mashallah!"

Hafsa's face turned suddenly into stone. A horrific idea had sprung from nowhere.

"Were you this divine angel?" she asked.

"No! I was already gone when the Sultan left his last breath," he proclaimed with more passion that he should. "Ask the Grand Vizier, Piri Pasha, if you don't trust my word."

"I have already asked him and he told me you were already gone by then; but your own damned brother for some reason was left behind. This is one of the reasons why he had to die; but I had enough of Selim Khan. Tell me more about Ibrahim. How do you judge him as a man? Can he keep a woman satisfied too as well as a man?"

It was a question that forced Asphodel to think hard before answering. If he disclosed all of Ibrahim's talents, then Hafsa Sultan might be tempted to claim him for her own.

"This is very difficult question, because Ibrahim is such a complicated creature and my experience with women is practically nonexistent. I only know that few men can be extremely versatile with the right incentives. Allah made me a man, but then an attractive man came and made me feel like a woman. He had to be Allah's angel, because this change saved me from the scalpel. Who knows how I may feel, if another divine angel like Mahidevran ever shows kindness and gives me a kiss? Only Allah knows exactly how few miracles happen."

Hafsa would be fully justified to summon the Black Eunuchs and execute him on the spot for his vague reply; but she was much wiser than that and would never do something in the spur of the moment. She was like Selim. If she could find other uses, she would never resort to such extreme violence. She would rather hide her thoughts under the disguise of a joke.

"Is Mahidevran Sultan the only angel in this harem? I can easily recall the faces of half a dozen angels so benevolent who wouldn't think twice to resurrect the dead. I'm the Valide Sultan and this Harem is now under my command."

****

When Ibrahim left the Sultan's quarters in the morning, he was still dizzy by the hypnotic action of the smoking nargileh; thus, he didn't pay much attention to the presence of a black eunuch seating on the parapet of the "sendirvan", the intricately curved marble fountain of the third court. Anyway, even if he was fully aware of the surroundings, he would never have considered the possibility he was sent there to remember every night visitor his master had.

A hunter seldom associates his superiority with the inferiority of the game he is after and vice versa. Thus, Hurrem could never have guessed how Ibrahim felt that morning. The fact he went straight to the Janissary hammam to drive away the scent of another man she might consider it as a simple act of coquetry or cleanness. However, Ibrahim couldn't wait to get dressed properly and seek refuge in Hafsa's quarters in the Eski Saray.

This time the formidable Sultana didn't have him wait for long to receive him, and this gave him the suspicion she was actually expecting this unannounced visit. She also had a wide smile that was easy to discern even behind the silken veil, but it was not easy for him to figure out if this was an expression of a personal triumph after a battle won, or the submissive smile of the vanquished who tried his best to sweet-talk the victor to avoid the worst consequences of his defeat.

Nevertheless, in either case, even if they had to cross their swords, it would be fair to practice and increase their dexterity rather than fight to the death. He had to admit that after all these months he had spent among men in a military camp, the proximity to any handsome woman was a welcome change to his daily schedule. Anyway he didn't have many chances to have an interesting discussion with someone able to keep his interest acute for a long time.

Besides Suleiman and Selim, most other men he met had tried to set traps on his path, or were simply interested on how to make money out of his friendship; but as long as he was the Sultan's favorite, his career was secured and with it came a comfortable life many men would even kill for. However, women had always something to say worth listening, as they always concentrated their discussions on issues of practical interest that did not involve money or power as men did practically always.

"To whom do we owe the pleasure of this early visit Ibrahim Pasha?" she inquired with a long, pleasant smile.

153

From the announcement of his new title it was evident that despite the seclusion of the Eski Saray, she didn't miss much of everything that was happening in the immense Metropolis. He decided that her attitude had been sufficiently improved, and his instinct suggested he had nothing more to fear from the formidable Sultan's mother. He decided to be as much frank with her as it was practically possible under the circumstances.

"You are always in my mind, even though sometimes I might lose my way inside the dark corridors and end up in unfamiliar rooms," he replied in a teasing mood.

"I hope that your night roaming in the Eski Saray were as pleasant as your visits in the Yeni Saray," she remarked being sharper and better informed about his conducts than he expected. This fact made telling her the truth much easier.

"The truth is that all my visits to women's rooms have offered me a pleasant reward in the end, which is not always the case in my visits elsewhere. In fact, in most of my intimate meetings with men, I left their quarters yawning or in pain. However, today the reward doesn't have to be anything more but the pleasure of your company."

"If I didn't know what sinful desires are troubling you, I might have imagined you are trying to flatter me. What kind of favour will you ask of me this time, Ibrahim Pasha? Perhaps another even higher office is in your sights today?"

"Higher offices are indeed for many men the only way to stand out of a crowd; but, I can assure you I have other options."

"Such as?" Hafsa inquired.

"As a page, I have been trained to please perfectly only my master; but, in certain cases I am quite willing to exceed my limits as only Allah is truly perfect in all His tasks."

"This is a most interesting declaration; but an exceedingly suspicious character might characterize it as an empty boast."

"A simpleton perhaps might do just that, but surely not you or my wise Sultan, Allah's Shadow. You both have personal knowledge of my ability to rise to the occasion."

The extent of the impertinence of this slave would always surprise her. In fact, it was the main reason she found Ibrahim so interesting and attractive. He was the kind of man any woman would go out of her way to enjoy his company. Perhaps her plan to use Hatidge as bait could wait for one more day.

"You are an impudent and self-centred Roman who is blessed with all the merits and drawbacks of your race," she concluded; but her tone sounded friendlier than her words.

"It is true that our race has very often crossed the barriers of both virtue and sin, but isn't this excessiveness the very essence of what history is made of? Many people might consider even my presence here as a violation of basic moral principles, but we are both much wiser than the vulgar mob. We know that we can always find good excuses for our every deed, if we have to. The same act can be described as a momentary weakness, a forgivable expression of gratitude or a prize for services rendered, when the occasion demands it."

"Do you think that a mother should not care for her one and only son?"

"A mother's love is unquestionably the purest of feelings; but, it's not the very first sensation a son creates. There is also the agonizing pain of birth, and even before birth a painful violation must also occur that will remain in a woman's mind till the end of time."

"This sounds a lot like the puzzle what came first the egg or the chicken."

"If I didn't know you are a pious Muslim, I could have mistaken you for a Christian who trusts virtuous women may be impregnated also by sniffing flowers."

"I have never been a Christian. You were!"

"Yes, I was, and I still do believe that divine women have the power to perform miracles too."

"Such as?" she inquired in a playful mood.

"For instance, I believe that eventually Your Highness will grant me your full support in my quest because she knows that I may be a complicated character, but at least my intentions are honorable," he proclaimed.

It was again a case of ultimate impertinence, but she was more curious than offended.

"And why do you think that I would be willing to do that and take chances when I'm not certain of the outcome?" she asked with genuine interest and her tone had the professionalism of a Kapali Çarsi (Covered Market) rug merchant. "After all, a wise Muslim does not act, unless she is certain of a favorable result. I must leave the world more beautiful than I found it."

"This is me expert opinion, because I know I deserve all my promotions and because I will be immensely grateful for any further advancement to a new even more challenging role."

He had a supreme confidence and this was very disturbing. She had to humble him in some way before he became totally out of control. The Sultana looked at him from head to toes.

"To be absolutely sincere, I have not decided yet who should I support, you or your countless enemies," she confessed with a face as sincere as she could manage under the circumstances.

"I trust that as a caring mother you will support the man who loves and supports your son more than anyone else."

"There are many women in this Harem who could make the same claim and sound more convincing."

"You are not only a mother. You are also a formidable Valide Sultana. I am certain you can discern better than any young concubine which man can be more beneficial for the Ottoman Empire. You must have realized by now that all who hate me envy my position and would kill to be in my place. Please tell me! Would you rather have another man in your reception room right now? It is very easy for me to walk out of this door and disappear forever."

As Hafsa Hatun measured accurately word for word what she was to say next, not a single sound disturbed the absolute silence. This devious young man had pointed out two of her major duties. She was indeed a mother and a Valide Sultana; but, in her mind she was much more than that. She was also a woman and a widow.

All her spies had come back with the same reports. They had assured her that her son and his slave were spending an awful lot of time together in Rhodes, even the entire last night in Constantinople. They had even slept in the same tent throughout the entire expedition. This was not the duty of a Guardian of the Imperial Hawks; however, Ibrahim was more than that by now; he was also a Hasodabashi, which literarily meant he was responsible for whatever happened in the Sultan's quarters day and night. He had a very good excuse for sleeping in the same tent or an adjacent room. Occupying this new post was indeed a brilliant strategic maneuver carried out behind her back in Manisa.

Nevertheless, this excessive amount of preparation was encouraging. If Ibrahim and her son were indeed lovers they had thought of everything. All the Sultans as the Roman Emperors did before them never slept alone in fear of an assassin. Guarding the Emperor in his sleep was the duty of the White Eunuchs. Normally a Hasodabashi should be a eunuch; however, Ibrahim was not. This much she knew for certain. Basmi was very positive on this point. In fact, Ibrahim was a very passionate lover perfectly capable of satisfying any promiscuous woman, even a widow.

Perhaps Ibrahim was much more. He might just be the excellent counsel her son needed at the beginning of his reign. Perhaps as a mother she couldn't yet face the truth. Was it really so important with whom a Sultan slept at night, if in the morning he could rise and lead the armies to a series of military triumphs in battlefields even the mighty Fatih had been defeated?

It was a common secret that Fatih had also many male lovers. Would she rather have a loser for a son who slept only with a single woman? Women asked impossible tasks from their men. They had to belong only to them and no one else; but, being faithful to a single woman was it really a virtue useful for an Emperor? What did it really meant such a compromise on his imperial duties? An Emperor had to be able to satisfy the desires of many nations; so it was a widely accepted for every Sultan to take in his harem as many princesses as possible. Perhaps nations behaved like women who found pleasure serving extraordinary men and bearing their children. She was a woman and could not easily fathom a man's heart. With all the women in his harem, if a Sultan limited his choices to a single woman, this might mean he was afraid to respond to the advances of every other woman who sought to have a son as good as he was.

She had been in Selim's harem far too long to realize that every concubine did the best so she could to sleep even for a night with a Sultan to secure presents and become "Gözde", attracting the eye of the Sultan. For few women this was the high point of their lives.

She had been luckier. She was a princess. She was married to Selim and she gave him so much satisfaction the first night that he didn't leave her side for many days until he was sure she was pregnant. He appreciated her as a woman, so much he gave her three daughters and finally a son. Before becoming Valide Sultan besides living a life of leisure, she was also rewarded with a several nights full of lust more than any other odalisque in the Eski Saray. Should she complaint because when he was fighting valiantly in the East, he felt the need after each victory to conquer few daughters of his enemies to demolish even further their moral?

Perhaps she was a bit unfair being so demanding of her son. Even if he was emotionally attached to a man, it was not that important, if he was also a conqueror of nations. Perhaps her initial reaction was based only on female sentiments and not on pure logic. The pure logic of a Valide Sultan demanded from a mother to be careful. If her son was in love with a man, then pointing out this weakness would only make matters worse. Her son would lose his confidence and then the Janissaries might sense his weakness too. They were the ones who spent most of their money in Galata on rent boys, whores and belly dancers to demonstrate their overflowing manliness. Why should she blame all the women in the Eternal City that were attracted by this male show-off, when all the foreign armies were terrified of the consequences of a defeat?

As a Tatar woman she had to admit she enjoyed this type of wanton men too. Many times when she was bathing in milk, or her courtiers spread lotions and ointments on her skin, she had fantasies of being immersed in Janissary sperm. She had to admit that Allah filled female imagination with all sorts of sensual dreams she had to reject later, when she woke up and her decency returned to haunt her.

Making a woman feel guilty for even their thoughts was the work of Islam. It was a religion forcing everyone even the Sultan to become a slave of Allah, a man. She knew though that long time ago Tatars were uncivilized pagans who could not discern right from wrong. She could feel many times deep inside her the primal urge to be wild. It was in her blood and she could do nothing about. The Ottoman tradition also demanded every Sultan to become one with these Janissary brutes.

Suleiman was paid a monthly salary exactly like a Janissary, so everyone would think he was one of them. Few Janissaries became so devoted to their cause that they didn't want to make families or have children; so they sought to become sterilized. There was even a Grand Vizier of Selim, Sinan Pasha who was such a devoted Janissary, and he was killed fighting like a lion against the Mamelukes in Egypt. Being among singular men who behaved in a certain way was usually enough cause for a man to adopt their lifestyle. It was how societies, communities or groups were born characterized by special habits that made them unique. Thank Allah, there was no such a trend yet among Sultans. They had to be different, but better than anyone else.

Living most of her life in a harem, she had also fallen into the same social trap. Few lonely nights she had felt the need to seek pleasure in another woman's bosom the same way many other concubines fought solitude. She knew that Hatidge after the loss of her husband had succumbed to the caresses of a slave, Basmi, another devious present of Sultan Selim who had executed the man in her life.

Lending your intimate slave to someone else was a true sign of Islam's benevolence. Love was the way for human beings to reduce their loneliness by sharing it. When she was young, her mother's arms were her best refuge when she was scared. Was this abnormal? No, it wasn't! It was considered perfectly normal by all her tutors; but, what should she do when her father gave her away to a handsome prince without asking her consent? Were Selim's arms the embrace she always yearned for, or was she totally perverted? Every time she remembered how she felt when Basmi had used her long tongue for the first time to get in touch with hers deep inside her mouth she got goose bumps?

Time had a way to put down the flame in every man when everything combustible had been consumed. The more passionate the love the most quickly it receded, just like a firestorm in a poor neighborhood in the Eternal City. By making a fuss about, it she was simply turning a trivial matter into an international crisis. Silence was perhaps the better virtue in this case too. Perhaps all her worries were nothing but jealousy, as her son had sought gradually another intimate relationship rather than the original mother-to-son affliction he had when he suckled.

Ibrahim Pasha was right. Women were made for peacetimes, when tenderness was needed to heal the wounds of war. During a war a submissive man was a better companion than any other woman to excite the male aggression of a warrior.

Ibrahim looked strong enough to become her son's shield during the oncoming wars. As long as there was fighting to be done, a Sultan needed both types of consorts in succession.

A Valide Sultan above all had to be effective and practical. She could see now it would be wrong to treat Ibrahim like an opponent. As long as he was supporting her son, he was an ally and a valuable friend. He looked like one dynamic and highly motivated young man on his way to fame and glory. His degrading experiences as a slave had not demolished his spirit, but forged his will to succeed, despite all the obstacles he had encountered.

This was the stuff that made man a conqueror. She was not fully convinced her son had similar virtues. He was not as resilient and could be influenced by trifles, and this was a good reason to become a slave of his passion one day. His love affair with Hurrem had gone very well for the time being; but now Suleiman was spending too many hours with her, neglecting other important duties. Perhaps, the unexpected death of Mahidevran's child and Hurrem's second delivery had affected his judgment in her favor, but one more daughter didn't count for much.

Ibrahim might be the right man to cover up her son's shortcomings. The fact that Selim Khan had approved Ibrahim's appointment was the first sign he knew something more than she did. Now that Selim was dead and his threat extinguish, it was much easier to find his motive about this appointment.

Menekse had been executed, but Asphodel, the second of her husband close favorites, had been plain enough in his descriptions explaining why Selim had showed preference to this young man. It was his tenacity to fight to the end for a lost cause.

Asphodel had been more talkative than she prayed for, so she actually got more information than she was able to digest. When Selim was in a coma, he didn't cry her name even once. Was Mahidevran the woman of Selim dreams or was she simply the mesmerizing illusion of youth he recalled before the very end?

The only event Asphodel knew for certain was Selim had tried hard to summon his son's favorite, but Piri Pasha, the reigning Grand Vizier, dismissed his commands as the result of hallucinations induced by the opium he had consumed to sooth the unbearable pains of his illness. If she also smoked opium, what would her dreams be? Would she dream of Selim or someone else much younger, more vigorous and more readily available, like Ibrahim Pasha?

This thought completely unbalanced her disposition. She had to find out at once; so, she gave the order for two shisha to be lighted and filled with the stuff of the impossible dreams.

****

They had been smoking for several minutes in total silence before she felt the first signs her animosity was fading away like smoke. She now knew animosity was her last line of defense. To be safe, Ibrahim had to leave her room at once. Since her tongue was getting numb, she indicated it was time for him to leave by getting up, and he bowed deeply with respect in front of her. At last Ibrahim behaved obediently, she thought; but, she was mistaken and surprised. He caught her hand firmly and to her surprise he touched her fingers with his lips in the same manner the Venetians greeted noble women.

For an Ottoman lady this liberty was unthinkable, but she was a Tatar and she thoroughly enjoyed it. It brought back a feeling lost since the days she was a girl in Crimea. It was the turmoil stirred in a virgin's heart the first time she was touched by a strange man. She was clearly on the verge of hallucinations, since many years had passed since that day, but she remembered exactly when and what had happened. It was her wedding night. She was dressed in white and Selim couldn't wait to see her bare skin. He was always so violent and compulsive that he didn't give her enough time to adjust to the new state of a woman. Their union was much more of a ceremonial rape than the tender love she dreamed like a shy virgin.

Selim's behaviour was not exceptional, her mother had warned her. This was how every warrior behaved because of the long periods of isolation. Gradually she had adjusted to his rough ways of expressing passion. Perhaps this was the reason why she became so attached to her gentle courtier. "Do to others what you wish they do to you," was the way human minds operated.

"That's enough!" she ordered Ibrahim with trembling voice.

"Why?" he asked and she found very hard to seek for a proper response.

"I am a Sultana and you are my son's slave," she managed to utter, but it was clearly the wrong words to utter. Her tone was also too arrogant to be tolerated by a slave in revolt.

"If I'm a slave, then let me serve you to the best of my abilities," he replied and broke easily through her feeble first line of resistance, the will to keep her lips untouched by his.

****

Perhaps the detailed descriptions by Basmi were to blame, but as a mother she had to know if the slave was a man, or if he had queer tendencies. In the Harem, she had fallen victim many times to the various narrations she had heard about Selim's escapades with his most slutty concubines. It was natural for any widow to try to imitate the successes of a whorish consort like Basmi who looked so happy after serving him. Imitation was how progress and civilization was spread even though it was clearly not enough for true progress. Women as well as men had to exceed existing limits, violate rules, and if men treated women as an object of conquest, women could retaliate, as the urge to exceed the limits was mutual, universal and independent of gender, as the eunuchs' behaviour proved without a doubt. The human urge of filling the voids was relentless.

According to Basmi, Ibrahim had behaved very skilfully as a lover despite his youthful age. He could discover her weaknesses, and even if he couldn't find one, he could inspire new vices and then proceed to exploit them. He also had the vitality of a wild animal; but in a very refined way. After all, Basmi was a slave trained to accept the wishes of every occasional master; but, Hafsa was a Sultana and clearly not prepared for this overwhelming onslaught of male vigour. How did this slave ever knew what was inside her mind, when his lips touched her hand?

Did he sense the thrill his touch had created on her skin? Could he count all the chills that raced up her spine? There were few instinctive reactions no woman could control. Maybe he saw her goose bumps rising from her arm and spreading all the way down to her belly. Why had she chosen to wear such a revealing dress when Asphodel arranged this meeting?

Ibrahim had to be a very sensitive and perceptive man, because then, as he was still on his knees begging, while her majesty was towering above him, he embraced her thighs and pressed his head between her thighs like a frighten child. He might have felt her trembling knees, or sensed she was a mother and could not resist caressing his golden hair; but, this instinctive motherly reaction was all he needed to turn his hold into all the alluring caresses a lonely widow might desire, moving his fingers under her dress up her buttocks one imperceptible step at the time, as if a slave was humbly requesting the unreserved approval of a Valide Sultana for his punishable by death indiscretion.

She gave it away with tender sighs, and she had no excuses even though the greatest part of her behaviour could be traced back to her motherly instincts. If Selim had impregnated her few more times, then she might have been much more resilient to another man's touch. If most men needed many women to satisfy their lust, most women needed many children to subside their divine motherhood urges. Perhaps this was the reason why her mind suddenly was filled with the long days past her pregnancies. Back then for as long as she was breastfeeding, she couldn't stand the hands of Selim on her body.

Women had to bear children. This was Allah's will according to her mother's advices, and a woman had to accept every ceremonial rape her husband was willing to perform to please his instincts without any concern for her own pleasure. However, Ibrahim showed no intention of raping her. He was doing all he could to please her, exactly as he had promised. Getting her pregnant was not his immediate aim. His aim was clearly to offer her so much pleasure that she would start crying, realizing the extent of her weakness; otherwise, he would not have lost so much time massaging her breasts to set her body on fire.

Was it ever possible that she would become pregnant again? How would she explain such an event now that she was a widow? Her blood was still coming regularly, and the Holy Book gave explicit instructions of what a widow should after a proper period of abstinence when the moment came to seek a companion for her bed.

Most rich widows at her age in Constantinople bought much younger slaves to satisfy their divine urges for motherhood; but, her position was different. If Suleiman was not emotionally involved with Ibrahim, she could buy Ibrahim for her household. She was certain the Sultan would never agree with such an arrangement. He might even exile her in Manisa. He could accept the idea of sharing a slave with his sister, but with his mother it was incomprehensible. Under the circumstances, Ibrahim had been wiser than her, because he had kept his head even when she lost her mind and demanded his total submission to her needs.

"What do you want of me?" she asked him as if she had the strength to resist or the will to negotiate.

"I would love to earn your complete trust, and I would be greatly honored, if I could serve you in every way you desire to be happy for the rest of your life," he replied without releasing his gentle hold as his fingers slipped deeply under her undergarments taking control of her senses. The suspicion Ibrahim was possibly doing the same to her son surprisingly did not disgust but excited her further, as her son was part of her flesh.

"Do you realize you could lose your head, if the Sultan came in right now and saw me in your arms like this?" she threatened him in a last effort to curb his aggression.

"Only if you were to tell him exactly what I'm doing; otherwise I intend to take all the blame and protect your reputation. I have sneaked in your room under false pretenses, and seeing you all alone and depress by your recent loss I overcame your deliberate but desperate resistance by brute force."

Now she was perplexed with his intentions, but extremely curious to find out where his boldness would lead them. The slave was subtly insinuating that she though his intentions were dishonorable.

"Why are you touching me? Why are your lips so bold and your tongue so intrusive? Don't you have any respect for me?" she asked him in a teasing disposition.

"Indeed I do, but I feel this is what Your Highness wants me to do, but is too ashamed to ask."

"You are mistaken. I am a Valide and the mother of the Sultan. This is a fact that many times has slipped your mind," she whispered feeling her resistance weakening under his onslaught.

"You are all that and much more. You are a woman, a very lonely woman who never had a man kneeled at her feet ready to obey all her commands, a woman who has spent all her life obeying the orders of a cruel and violent husband."

"You are wrong again. I had many slaves at my feet since the day I was born; but I grant you that you are the first male slave who had the nerve to touch me so intimately," she claimed as she felt his hands feverishly massaging her buttocks.

Ibrahim, still on his knees, raised his head and stared at her face. Her hair was black but grey hair had made their appearance at her temples. Her eyes were black like the night, a common characteristic with both her husband and her daughter; but, now they were sparkling as bright as the flames from the chandelier reflecting on their wetness. It was impossible to hide her profound excitement to become molested.

"I may be caressing you, but have a very good excuse for my position even if the Sultan opens up the door right now."

"I am very interested to hear it," she snapped back with a long smile.

"I am now begging you on my knees to forgive my impudent request to become your clandestine lover," he replied with an imperceptible smile.

Hafsa exploded in laughter and he followed her, but he did not release his firm grip.

"I have an even better one. You were begging me to ask the Sultan for his sister's hand," she countered, caressing once again his blond hair.

"I should have known that I could never compete with a woman in excuses," he acknowledged. "Perhaps that's why I also want to become your most secret and intimate companion. I need a competent tutor to teach me how to disguise the truth as well as you did through all these years your flesh yearned to be caressed and was harshly deprived by an extremely egoistic man."

His hint of absolute intimacy was the kind of service expected from any decent slave a widow might consider buying. Was this the arrangement he was aiming for? If she was in a slave market looking for a slave, the Black Eunuch accompanying her would be the one who would ask all these embarrassing inquires; but, now she had no eunuch to carry out this task.

Fortunately, she didn't have any still lingering questions about his bedroom capabilities. Basmi had been most explicit, and she had seen the eyes of Hatidge reflecting the same excitement. They both were much younger than her and they were more easily impressed. Hatidge had already hinted she wouldn't mind marrying her brother's intimate friend; but, she was not as young and naïve to lay her daughter's entire life in the hands of a greedy man like Ibrahim. As a carrying mother she had to give her motherly advices of what kind of man Hatidge should look for. Men like Ibrahim were like hungry bees that collected honey from every flower they found with open petals.

Suddenly she realized why he was still holding her tight with his head pressed between her legs. Surprisingly she didn't feel like pushing him away. Only Selim had been so close to the center of her being; but he was now dead and buried. This was the kind of intimacy the slave was referring to. She felt extremely weak to push him away. She could feel now the warmth of his body penetrating her heavy brocade cloths all the way to her silken undergarments.

For the time being he was still very discrete and didn't make a move that would offend her with its boldness. Was he as excited as she? Perhaps he had sensed how weak she was and expected her to make the first move. Perhaps he was not discrete, but just patient. He had her surrounded under siege expecting her unconditional surrender. Indeed, she was desperate for a bold man who would overlook her superior status and treat her like his slave.

"You've better go. The Sultan may decide to visit me this morning," she suggested, but immediately she realized her request were her unreserved surrender. He was no longer a slave, as slaves existed to be ordered; but, by now he must have felt her knees trembling. Realizing her declining sense of morality, he tried to improve his status and rise, holding on to her clothes; but, his weight suddenly became unbearable for her trembling knees; so, she let herself go down to his level and knelt on the rug just to feel his head slip between her breasts, like the Bosporus passes between Europe and Asia.

She was almost certain the black eunuch's eye would be stuck now in the keyhole, curious to see what was happening inside the room and earn few gold coins for his silence. The fact she had sent away all her attendants must have enticed the Kislar Aga's curiosity even further, but her curiosity was even greater than any damned eunuch. She simply had to find out if youth had passed her by forever.

Ibrahim seemed to be a most submissive slave and she could order him to do just about anything; however, even if the submissiveness of a servant was infinite, the willingness of a mistress to give him orders was limited.

Being a master was as unnatural as being a slave. Today she had decided to be neither one. She had decided to be what the slave had suggested, an intimate companion and a model of cooperation for mutual benefit.

She felt his hands pull down her white laced brassiere. It was the triumph she was hoping for. His lips reached gently for her right nipple, and with his eyes closed he looked as innocent as a baby. Only his beard made his touch unmistakably manly. She needed that confirmation. In the Harem any kind of bodily hair on women and eunuchs was unthinkable. A Hasodabashi with a beard was absurd too till Ibrahim arrived to the Seraglio.

As now both his hands milked her half-exposed breasts, the roughness of his skin was another sign that with the appearance of Ibrahim something had drastically changed in her life for the better forever.

She felt his hands trying to find ways to slip inside her lace underclothes, but his struggle was hopeless. The undergarments of Hafsa Sultan were pointlessly intricate as Sultan Selim's visits were rare, but the dress she had instinctively chosen was not as difficult to shed away. Perhaps the next time Ibrahim would visit her, she should wait for him dressed as simply as an overheated mistress coming out of the hammam.

Would there ever be a second time? If she didn't give him some help, the young man might never return. Surprisingly this challenge made her feel alive. She was again a novice concubine trying her best to become the Ikbal of a Sultan. It was a great chance to take revenge for her entire youth wasted in the Harem waiting for a man's invitation, as even the Galata whores had won the right to have men knocking on their door. Asphodel's disclosures about her dead husband had been the last stroke.

She reached behind her back and unbuttoned her dress all the way down to her buttocks, but still her corsage was held in place by innumerable stays. Even she could never take it off without the help of a maid. And then she panicked. Was Allah the Keeper of Morality punishing her for her insatiable lust?

By now she had found many excuses for her outrageous acts. A woman could find a million of excuses, if she had to convince himself that by following her urges she was doing the right thing. She was a widow and no dead man's memory had any rights on her lively flesh. She had been frustrated for many years, and Ibrahim, this impertinent slave, had seduced her and by pulling down her dress had broken her will to resist.

Twenty years earlier Ibrahim was just a baby and she a young mother. In her nomadic tribe if any child was hungry, no woman would refuse to give him a breast to suckle. The time passed could not affect the immortal feelings in a woman.

Even if Ibrahim behaved like a Viking raider invading her tent, her mother had instruct her never to resist a rapist. Men were animals and any kind of struggle made them even more violent. Men in their passion could even slaughter a woman, if she offered spirited resistance.

All she had to know about men was subtly noted in the Quran in a way a Mufti could not explain. If a woman closed the gates and did not accept the one and only god, Allah gave a man the right to rape her for three days and then sell her as a slave.

On the other hand, if she opened up the gates and accepted Allah as her god, then he would not harm her. If Ibrahim was to return into her bedroom for one more time, today she had to please him as much as he was pleasing her. A good deed deserved another and the best way to enslave a slave would be to treat him as a master. To take off his clothes Ibrahim needed no servants, only a whisper that she was his to take was enough, or perhaps even less than a whisper.

He got up and slowly threw his clothes on her bed one by one as if he was still in the Avret Bazaar enticing his buyers. She could see he was extremely confident about the way he looked.

Part of this personal pride had to be his high price in the slave bazaar. Becoming a slave had few distinct advantages. He knew exactly what his worth was. Free people had illusions about themselves, and the black eunuch courtiers were constantly trying to give pleasant answers to every question she ever posed about her looks. Perhaps, if Ibrahim became her intimate companion, she could discover her true value in life.

Of course, it was also possible he would never return, considering the excessive risk compared to the reward. Being a Hasodabashi, he had many opportunities to exchange favours with any concubine or even a desperate Kadin like Gülfem; but she was not just any ordinary Valide Sultan. She was not naïve. She had formed a network of spies and spent plenty of money to loose many tongues.

Being a Kadin was the best way for a woman to become the object of envy in the Harem. For her, whatever a concubine did to improve her status was of no consequence, but the reputation of a Kadin had to be impeccable, as she was a mother and a legally bound wife.

Now that Hurrem had become a mother of two children and Mahidevran had lost her youngest child, tension was in the air. Mahidevran had to do her best to even up the score, and Ibrahim's position was critical for her plans. It was a common secret Mahidevran was desperate for the Sultan's attention. Who knows what she might do, if her son kept calling only for Hurrem?

Gülfem and Mahidevran would become infuriated and justly so. A zealous woman might explode and Ibrahim was the obvious choice, the best friend of a philandering Sultan.

Why was her mind trying to escape to other thoughts and bypass all the wild desires she felt as the slave explored with his tongue her gates to a Sultan's paradise few moments ago? Perhaps she was hesitant because if she didn't take this precaution, the entire Harem would find out that her morality had descended to the level of a Galata whore who could not refuse anything to a big spender.

All her worries about her son, his sister Hatidge, the Kadin and the Empire had to wait now until the slave was fully content. It didn't look as an easy task as the slave standing up in front of her looked proud and impressive as much as Selim in his prime. Perhaps the only difference is that he had light complexion and green eyes that made him look like a Frank, so different, but at the same time so desirable.

Perhaps he was of Norman seed, when long ago in the times of the Romans the Franks had conquered Byzantium and raped all the women they could find; but, all these were questions only men asked who could never be sure if their sons were really theirs. A woman kneeling before a man had other priorities. She has to humble his pride, and this is a task a woman could accomplish even when she was dressed with the most intricate of garments.

Ibrahim had already claimed the rights of a master when he pulled her veil off. The next few hours he was going to be her master until all his immense impertinence had been diminished to a proper size.

****

"Am I pleasing you?" Hafsa asked interrupting his thoughts as his gaze traveled on the decorations on the ceiling.

He turned around and saw her naked body still and plump, ready and willing to be conquered once more. Only the on-rushing blood on her cheeks and breasts bore evidence that a bearded man had tasted all she had to offer.

For his taste Hafsa Hatun was not much different than Basmi. Only her skin, her taste and her scent were drastically different. At the moment the gray hair on her temples was only a sign that she was more skilled and less spontaneous than the younger black slave. After this memorable morning, she would probably grow a few more gray hairs, but only her hairdresser could see the difference.

Her desire for a man's touch had transpired something unexpected for such a powerful woman, a sense of desperation. The death of Selim had been for her a warning that even the manliest mate would eventually fade away, and as a woman she had to keep on tasting a passionate man's love till her last breath.

He didn't have similar fears yet; so, he was very patient enjoying calmly the pleasures every part of her body could provide. From her question it was clear she had considered his patience as a sign of boredom. This was not true, but he wasn't sure if telling a woman the truth was always the most advantageous policy for a young man on the rise. Hafsa Sultan could become infatuated with him, make impossible demands and even put his life in danger.

"Immensely! Let's just say that if you were a slave, I would pay dearly to include you too in my harem. Innocence and virginity is simply not enough. Experience is essential too."

She laughed at his impertinence, because it wouldn't pay any dividend to make him angry. Somehow the slave knew by instinct what to say to please her; however, she was not going to remain passive anymore and as long as she had the upper hand.

"I am very glad I'm pleasing you. I feel the same way and whenever your master gets bored of you, I will be the first to buy you out. Of course, you lack the stamina of a mature man, but this is something exercise may cure promptly."

She was realistic and practical. He was no match for an experienced woman and he knew it. He should have expected that aging women would still have a constantly growing appetite.

"Would you advise me to buy few concubines and start my harem?" he countered. "Perhaps, I should also employ an old whore for a while to teach them all the tricks."

She knew he wasn't going to be easy outmanoeuvring him, but there was no harm in trying it.

"If I were in your shoes I would try both. Experience is better than gold. It never gets lost. It simply accumulates becoming even more precious."

"My lady, this glorious morning you've taught me this lesson well. I promise you on my life that I will never stop sneaking into your quarters for advice for as long as you willing to teach me. You simply have to summon me. I'll never go back to my word, and I'll be your intimate companion for as long as you want me, even if the Sultan never decides to put me on sale."

His face was sober and she knew he was telling the truth. Perhaps he had some Norman blood in his veins. Perhaps he was not just another treacherous Greek. Now she had to make a decision and she was old enough to distrust miracles. She could see that Ibrahim's visits in her quarters could never become as frequent as she would have liked to, each and every night; but, Allah had advised his followers not to be greedy. As long as Ibrahim was his son's page, he could come and go as he pleased in the Eski Saray, supposedly carrying secret messages between her and the Sultan. Even if he got another higher office, the interest of a Valide Sultan for the affairs of the Empire was also well understood and tolerated by the Sultan.

Should she get upset for Ibrahim's insinuation that she was as useful to a young man as an old whore? A widow in her age was wise enough to know that women were treated like whores anyway, even if for the eyes of society the price a man paid for their services varied. As Selim's wife for her contribution to the Empire's longevity she was rewarded with fame, riches and power. If she was Selim's concubine, he would simply have paid her a few gold coins for the same services and few more to breastfeed his son. What she had done as Selim's Kadin was exactly the same only her compensation was considerably richer. Now she had the power to put this impertinent man in his place.

She reached to a small locker she had by her bed, opened it and picked up a leather purse. She then left it in his lap with care trying not to hurt him.

"My dear Ibrahim, you have pleasured me immensely today. I actually think we are a perfect match, because we are wise enough to understand each other's needs. This small purse is just a small token of my appreciation for the tenderest love I have ever experienced in my entire life. Spend it as you please. You can buy a young slave for your harem or go to Galata and rent the services of an old whore. You can even rent any slutty boy you desire or get drunk in a tavern with an Orta of frustrated Janissaries. As long as you care for my household, you have nothing to fear of me, because I know the full extent of your true devotion."

Ibrahim was very surprised and impressed by her little speech. Hafsa was indeed a most intelligent woman and a worthy opponent of Selim. With a few well-chosen words she had countered his sauciness and put him in his proper place. Contrary to his insinuations, he was indeed a male whore whom powerful men and women could reward for his services. However, he had accepted gladly this derogatory mission the moment he had entered the Seraglio School for pages. This acceptance of reality was his true power. When other slaves were sorry for their moral descent and lost their self-respect, he had adapted to his duties and was proud for his accomplishments.

Now this remarkable mature woman seemed also proud of her accomplishments, assuming a woman would always be the last standing in the battlefield of human lust. She was wrong. Whatever a woman could do a man could match if he was properly instructed. Her body was fully exposed confident of its superiority. Allah was right. A woman was just too vulnerable when naked, so she should wear every bit of cloth she could lay her hands on. Without her elaborate garments, any experienced man had Valide Sultan's total submission at his fingertips.

"I would be a total fool to leave the warmth of your embrace and search for pleasure elsewhere, when Paradise is so close at hand. With your purse of golden coins I am going to buy me a pink ruby ring, so every time I stare at its glimmer I will remember the colour of your wide open lips."

This was a response she didn't expected and before she could cover her nudity his lips had taken command of her passion. Only her most intimate courtier had ever tasted her passion, but the taste of dry red wine she served made her lose her mind much more than the taster. She was now at his mercy and had to bite the pillow to keep her from announcing to the entire Harem that Ibrahim had turned her into a muezzin, proclaiming there was a new god to be worshiped in the Eski Saray. All she could do now was to try to turn this fight into a tie and give him a taste of his own medicine.

****

She now felt too exhausted to fight and too relaxed to have any trace of animosity. She was in finally in peace with the entire world. Men were not just the violently piercing creatures she always thought. They were the lips of Allah that could thrill any woman to accept their divinity.

Ibrahim was now resting with eyes closed in her bosom as if he was a child that had satiated his hunger for milk for a while. She was a mother and knew hunger would return, if not in a few minutes or perhaps in a few hours at most. The only question in her mind was if he would come back to her room another day to have again his fill of her wine.

Men were like animals only a woman could tame. Ibrahim was a young man, so their relation could not last for long. Now she had the choice to exhaust his desire in a few days, or keep it alive for as long as it would last. At the moment she could not make up her mind which of the two solutions fitted her mood best, and predictions were a very risky undertaking and living by them even riskier. All she could remember was the advice of her nanny long time ago. A woman's flesh memory lasted only for nine days. After ten days there was no sign left on it the most sensitive eunuch could ever discover.

However, regaining fully her elasticity was not her main concern. Sooner or later Ibrahim would need a son, and she was not the woman who could provide him with all his heart desired. On the other hand, the need for variety was natural not only for a man but for a woman too. After an hour of vigorous passion, now she was longing for the gentle massage of her courtier and the rejuvenating sense of feminine total submissiveness. She was as warlike as the Ottoman Empire. She needed a period of peace to enjoy the fruits of her violent struggles.

The human species was too greedy; it had discovered ways to find pleasure in times of war as much as in time of peace. Tension was concurrent with expectation as pleasure was with relaxation. She was a mature woman and still didn't know what was more pleasurable, expecting or tasting pleasure.

Her current concern was how much of this exchange of feelings a man like Ibrahim would appreciate. Perhaps, his teachers at the Seraglio School who had longer experiences with him could inform her; but, she had to have the courage to pose the right questions. Perhaps she could fathom his intentions by offering him some bait. His eyes may be now closed, but the rhythm of his breath was just too rough to be asleep.

"Now that Selim has passed away, he left many widows and concubines who need an intimate companion," she started, but he cut her off with an ironic smile and a compliment.

"Now that I have met you, I simply cannot be happy with anything less exquisite than a magnificent Sultana of noble birth."

"Don't be too hasty! Few of these beauties are much younger than me or are even virgins eager to bear a child for the first time. Now that the old Sultan was dead, they had a choice. They could remain locked in the Harem in the Eski Saray or get married to a Pasha. This is not much of a choice as far as I am concern. Sooner or later you have to start a family too, and these gorgeous girls have extensive training and excellent manners. I propose that you should think about it. It never pays to make hasty decisions. If I were you I would go next and ask my master whether he objects of you having a few of his neglected concubines. If you are in a hurry to choose them, my Kislar Aga is ready to take you to a trip in a dead Sultan's paradise."

"I'm already in Paradise. I am totally content right now just to think of nothing else, but how to serve your highness in the best possible way until you get bored and dismissed me."

It was clear he was up to her scheme.

"What exactly do you want of me?" she calmly inquired.

"I have realized too that our affair cannot last for as long as we desire right now. Therefore, since our marriage is just an impossible dream, if I was to get married soon, now that I am still drunk with your wine, I couldn't be happy with no one else but a woman of as noble birth and impeccable breading as you are, Princess Hatidge for instance," he replied with ample courage, "because whenever I am in her arms she will remind me of you."

She was expecting this audacious preference, and a wise Valide Sultan should plan ahead. From the moment the word came out Ibrahim was not a eunuch, with all his virtues he was in great demand, as women of all kinds tried to take advantage of a slave's virility. A woman of her age could not hope to keep a man like him forever tied to her bed. However, the more women Ibrahim had the better for the Empire, as any future indiscretion he was bound to make would be simply added to the old ones, creating confusion about the past.

"Is the Sultan's sister enough to satisfy your sickly arrogance? As her mother I know well enough that she is a spoiled brat; so, perhaps a woman of a lesser stature would be the ideal choice for a man like you, starting his harem. If Hatidge Sultan ever finds out all your escapades, she will be extremely jealous. She wouldn't stand it, if you ever were to cheat on her with anyone else but her slave Basmi."

"She doesn't have to find out everything. Loose tongues have plenty to lose by talking, and frequent wars create many opportunities for long separations and passionate reunions."

"Peace too, and I want you to know that I am not jealous of you anymore. I used to be, but a maturing widow has no right to demand fidelity from such a young lover."

"I am not your lover, and I will never be. I am your intimate companion and you are my counselor. Love is a bad word. Whatever happened between us was not love; it was a sincere exchange of inspirations."

She couldn't do anything but admire the extent of his diplomatic skills.

"A woman needs to feel she is loved even when she realizes that's no true and that she is just another conquest," she complained.

"Conquest is another ill-chosen word that brings back bad memories. We the Ottomans must be careful with the words we use to avoid unnecessary reactions. How can a mutual agreement on our future be a conquest? I view our relationship as a sacred union of purpose, and my acceptance in your quarters as a wise concession to promote trading of a variety of goods. In fact, I would be very happy if I was granted the same privileges as the Venetians have who are permitted to come and go into the Golden Horn as often as they have something to trade."

Hafsa Sultan had to admit he had a rare sense of humor Turks lacked.

"As far as I know, similar privileges have the ships from Genoa and Pisa. Does that mean I should increase the circle of my visitors?" she countered with a suggestive smile.

He had to admit that Hafsa was equal to the task and a most interesting woman. He could learn a lot about the balance of power in the Seraglio simply by being close to her. Ottoman women were much more exciting than men or eunuchs. Men had taught him only how to obey, and eunuchs how to please without demanding pleasure in exchange; but, this powerful and sensuous woman had showed him there were also other civilized ways to achieve contentment.

"Let's don't excite our greed by talking only about how to please our own passions. There are many more frustrated women than you think in this damned Harem. For instance, Gülfem's recent loss has removed every past blood connection with the House of Osman. I'm certain my even-handed son is now favourably considering a divorce, as the proper punishment for a mother who didn't take proper care of an heir. Therefore, considering Gülfem's present inferior status as a Kadin, how would you feel, if the Sultan decided to divorce her? As far as I know, he has not visited her for many years since Hurrem materialized in his harem. In terms you men use for women, she is less used than the Princess. Would you consider her a trophy worthy of your ambitions?"

Ibrahim took his time before answering. He was faced with an obvious trap. Now that he had gain access to Valide's bedroom, in Hafsa's mind the prospect of offering him her daughter as a bride had greatly diminished. It was a clear sign his greed and urge for vengeance had been detrimental for his immediate future. Was Hafsa so devious, or was she trying to fathom his lack of scrupulous before accepting him as a bridegroom of her daughter?

"I would never consider such a marriage possible. Gülfem is still emotionally involved with my master. She will never respond to my advances right now. Perhaps later, when she realizes Hurrem is going to become the sole Sultan's favourite, she might be less reluctant."

"Do you really think Hurrem will become so powerful?" Hafsa asked with suspicion.

"Yes, I do! This is why I intend to give Mahidevran a second chance to produce another Prince heir replacing poor Ahmet, Allah bless his soul. If I was a Sultan, Mahidevran would be my only choice. She is almost as dynamic and faithful as you are, and she is not a widow yet."

Hafsa could only admire this new explosion of diplomatic fireworks and devious flattery. Ibrahim had skilfully changed the subject and expertly delayed giving a definite answer about Gülfem. It was fairly obvious his aim was still her daughter, Princess Hatidge; however, praising Mahidevran so highly meant unconsciously he desired her too. She simply had to find out more. Thank Allah she had been wise enough to offer two Tatar servants to serve Mahidevran after her marriage with her son, and Tatars were very faithful to their members of their clan. There was no way Yabani, or Zarafet would not know which man was in Mahidevran's heart.

"I'm sorry! I didn't wish to appear too pushy. If Gülfem is indeed so devoted to my son, then Hatidge will be my next choice too, and from what I hear she is very fond of you, so there is one obstacle less. I don't have a firm objection to this union. I was simply exploring different alternatives, to free you from the embarrassment of having slept with both a mother and a daughter."

Ibrahim could not but admire this new twist. Hafsa was a truly relentless negotiator, and from the very beginning she had been trying to develop a sense of deep trust between them only insatiable sex could generate. His new rise in the Ottoman hierarchy meant she felt she needed his support in all her plans.

He didn't have any objection in offering her a helping hand provided he knew what prize exactly she was after. At the moment one fact was incontestable. Securing a young lover were not her sole concern the same way taking revenge on Selim was neither his goal this morning. They both were simply too greedy and tried to combine pleasure with hard work.

He felt they had nothing more to say at this moment, and prolonging his visit may put everything he had gained in jeopardy; but, he was still a slave and he couldn't just get dressed and leave. He had to be dismissed by his mistress.

"Is there anything else I can do for Your Highness this morning?" he asked without moving a muscle.

"No! Our exchange of inspirations, as you call it, has been most invigorating. I feel the next few days I will have many intriguing details to recall of this unexpected encounter. I must confess I had misjudged you. I never expected you were such a refined manipulator of emotions. When I found out why my dead departed husband thought so highly of you, I did my best to find everything there was to know about you. When he was still alive, discovering what happened behind his close door was an almost impossible task; but now that he is dead, it was just a matter of few gold coins as oaths to a dead sovereign were automatically dissolved. Fortunately for you I was the first to find out the truth and now the old oaths to Selim have been renewed to me personally. They will surely last for as long as I'm alive. I'm glad I was the first one to learn about Selim's death few days before my son found out he was the new Sultan, and I'm not just boasting. Menekse's death has released me too of all my oaths. He was indeed my most loyal spy inside the Marble Kiosk. I laughed my heart out when he told me of your escapades. He was also quite explicit when he described to me what happened when you fell asleep in the hammam. Maybe one day when we have nothing more pleasant to do, I will let you know how hard you tried to resist the Sultan's advances. Today is not that day, because I still need you, and I'm a pious Muslim bound by my oaths even to a dead eunuch. Don't worry. I have not uttered a word to my son about all this, because it is not to his advantage to know as much as it is for me. Nevertheless, since we are partners now, I have to give one more advice. Trust no one in the Seraglio. They are all out to get you."

Ibrahim needed some more time to think Hafsa's revelations. If Menekse had been her agent in the past, it meant Asphodel might be too now. The fact that Menekse had been executed meant he was not one of the Grand Vizier's secret agents. The fact that the Grand Vizier had kept his high post also meant Suleiman was not displeased by the eunuch's execution. Nevertheless, Asphodel was not harmed during the messy days of Selim's illness. Who was his true master now that Selim had departed? Perhaps, it might be useful to get in touch with this eunuch and make him an offer difficult to turn down.

"I'm truly indebted for accepting me into your trust. I wish I knew what else I could do to show my gratitude for this great honour," he noted and looked deep into Hafsa's black eyes searching for an answer.

Hafsa could not keep a straight face after his new audacious suggestion.

"When I first met you I could never have imagined you were such a prick," she claimed with a pretentious severe face, and as she tried to get up turning her back at him.

It was indeed her best view. Was it her Parthian Arrow? It could be just about anything, even an advanced invitation for his next visit. Now that the Sultana considered him as a member of her team, he could visit her as often as it pleased him.

She turned her face and noticed the point of focus of his eyes. He was nude too, and quite incapable of hiding the effect her milky white flesh she had on his. It was a present she seemed grateful to receive. Perhaps, accepting him as the new husband of her daughter had raised a few obstacles in the nature of their relationship. As the Valide Sultana she had to retain a certain degree of morality, no matter how difficult it was in a harem where total lack of scrupulous was the norm. He had to admit she was much more practical and conniving than he was, but this was hardly surprising. She was a versatile woman in every sense of the word.

"Since I know now what touches your heart, I intend to reward you with a wedding gift I know you will use time after time; but, now you must let me alone to think out all the objections my son might raise to your unlikely match with his sister."

"I have no worries that you'll succeed. Successful matches are your specialty," he said with subtle irony.

They had nothing more to say that day and Ibrahim, retreating slowly towards the exit, bowed his neck with allegiance. It was the first time they were separating as two old friends who had nothing to divide, but many things to share. A new era had started. Now Ibrahim was not just a slave of the Sultan, but an honest partner in sharing his possessions.

****

Once Ibrahim closed the door behind him, Hafsa felt deeply the extent of her loneliness. Up to this morning many years had passed since her looks made a young man turn his head at her direction. It had been a momentous feat filling her nights all these years with thousands of hallucinations that had been eventually refuted as Selim Khan's infatuation was the conquest of the world, not her happiness. Now that this violent man, Sultan Selim, had died, she had realized that all these dreams were nothing but ephemeral creations of her

173

imagination. From now on she would be forced to fill her life with the excitement, the happiness and the love affairs of others.

The words of this gifted slave still echoed in her ears. By removing the luxurious veils of her grandeur, he had discerned the desperate nakedness of her heart. Her specialty was now arranging marriages. Distressed by this thought, she sprang up and ran to the door to beg him come back and share her loneliness that night too; but, he was already lost in the darkness of the corridor's depths. She could send a slave to recall him, but something deep inside kept her idle.

She lay in bed to think better. Maybe the sparkle in his eyes she noticed every time he looked at her aging body was not nothing more than the reflection of the lamp. Perhaps the warmth of his hand was an illusion caused by the burning coals of bronze brazier. Even the sweat on his palms may not have been a clear sign of desire, but of embarrassment for the outrageous behaviour of a Valide Sultana who had retreated from the splendour of the Eski Saray to the shame of a brothel.

The only sensation she could fully trust was the unyielding passion she felt when he smothered all her towers and conquered the one after the other all her gates. Only Selim had been so passionate and so hasty when he knew his days were numbered. If he was right, then there was no moment to lose.

She stopped at the last moment. Really how raunchy she would feel, if she invited Ibrahim to sneak back in her bedroom one night and he refused claiming he had a previous engagement with the Sultan? It would have been the last stroke eliminating even the last traces of her self-esteem as a woman and as Valide Sultana; thus, she preferred to sacrifice this sudden urge of lust for the sake of posterity.

She closed her eyes to avoid seeing another depressing scene from a Sultan's widow sober reality. It would be unthinkable for a Sultan's mother to be married to a Pasha, as any other of his concubines was entitled to. For a Sultan's young widow in the Eski Saray surrounded by Black Eunuchs the only available possibility to rediscover love was to resort to a form of prostitution. If she needed a man for a night to be happy, she had to find him in a caravanserai around the Grand Bazaar, where many married women were daily employed to earn a living better than their poor or lazy husbands could provide.

In such a lodging shelter only foreigners resided, and a disguised widow could easily rent a room for few hours no questions asked. Then, for such a desperate woman it was simply a matter of exposing few of her charms by the gate to attract a suitable consort among the occasional customers, members of the numerous caravans that arrived in the Eternal City from every corner of the globe. Ibrahim as a Hasodabashi must have known this sorry fate of widows, and decided she should be spared from such an embarrassment.

She got up and went to the window. Beyond the high walls of the Eski Saray she could see the roofs of the many caravansaries in the neighbourhood a stone-throw away. It was a view that surprisingly warmed her heart. If Ibrahim neglected her, she wouldn't spend the rest of her nights all alone. Even if she grew old, there would be always young, hard working men carrying loads of commodities up and down the hills looking for a good break.

She laughed ironically at the indecent way her mind now worked from the moment she had Selim's widow and found out he had died with Mahidevran's name on his lips. Suddenly her heart was full of vengeance for all her lost years of Job's patience. This unexpected affair with Ibrahim had filled her mind with all sorts of crazy dreams of fictitious clandestine affairs. The simple truth was that for a mighty Valide Sultan there were all sorts of intriguing opportunities. With enough cash the Kislar Aga could lead in her bedroom any handsome Janissary she fancied. These adventurous men would do anything for money even satisfy a woman in total darkness.

She went back and lay flat on her back on her bed. She closed her eyes and took a deep breath to calm her overexcited senses. She had been so frustrated for so long an attractive but inexperienced young man in a few hours had almost turned her, a middle aged woman, into a sex maniac. How could any frustrated young concubine refuse him? This madness should end. No complete man should be allowed to enter the Harem under no pretences.

But as she pushed aside his tantalizing naked image from her mind, in her nostrils a breeze brought the smoke of a hookah along with the scent of Samian red wine and the breaths of drunken sailors from the harbour. It was useless for her to resist reality. It was the will of Allah. Few men existed that could turn even the most virtuous woman into a whore. It was not her fault. This was how Allah had made the world. Everyone was born with weaknesses he had to try to eliminate, but being virtuous was hardly enjoyable; so, only in heaven angels resided. Earth was the domain of the Devil.

****

And Allah the Knower of all Secrets of the Heart made one more miracle. By shutting her eyes Hafsa Sultan suddenly found herself in the middle of endless hall and felt all over her naked skin the eyes of every drunken tavern patron, searching feverishly to find openings to sneak through the silken veils covering the object of their dreams. She still did not wish to do them the favour to pull them off all at once, because not enough silver coins had fallen on the floor as many as the tavern owner had prescribed each of her dances should cost. Only then she was allowed to expose first her breasts and her round buttocks for every sailor to enjoy, as she searched for the best dressed customer to sit on his lap. If she was lucky tonight, he would show his appreciation for this free treat by opening his purse to pay tribute to her art of seduction. Then, anything was possible, but usually most men found impossible to resist the attraction of her firm buttocks that were even more perilously tight than the Bosporus Straights.

She had no complaints for her life, and could dance even ten times each night until morning without feeling tired. Perhaps, it was the energy she drained from men during the intermissions; but, that evening everything was different.

Among the customers the keeper had recognized the disguised Roman Emperor. He had seen him in the Hippodrome and couldn't be mistaken. His presence meant she had to try to make her dancing routine something special, dedicated only to the Emperor's green eyes and blond hair. It implied she had to take everything off, as if she was a cheap whore.

She had an entirely different opinion. She had to look remote and expensive; so this time her dance was shortened. She didn't even pull her veils off, but showed how a shy dancer should behave to make a good impression to an aristocratic audience. She didn't even rush in the end to sit on his lap, as she always did with every attractive sailor she yearned. She simply stood in front of him still sweaty from her great effort to appear as flexible and well trained as possible.

He took his time judging her face and impeccable curves, and finally with a long smile full of anticipation he slowly pulled from his girdle a leather purse. He picked out a handful of gold coins and left it on the counter without bothering to measure it. Then, looking into her eyes, he put the pouch back in his belt. With a quick look she judged the amount of gold was much more than her regular dance worth. The move raised up to her cheeks the blood of shame. He knew that despite her young age she was a prostitute. It was the second time she felt ashamed for what she had become. The first time was when her mother offered her first night of lust to a nobleman passing by the village during a difficult year and she had to wipe off her blood with her white nightgown.

That night it was not proper to try to hide the truth, offending his intelligence; so, she led him by the hand into the humble of the bedroom to give him his money worth. Now, she ought to pull out her best performance to empty his entire pouch in her hands. It was an easy task for a woman of her youth and experience. The virgin courtiers of the imperial court may be as beautiful as she, but their training was inferior. What chances could have a girl raised by monks against a Galata prostitute trained to please even the grumpy old sailors of the Seven Seas? Knowledge could not sneak through a monastery's walls. It travelled on the waves and the caravans that wandered deep in the wonderlands of the Orient.

The combination of youth, beauty and intelligence was simply overwhelming for a Roman Emperor raised in an environment of Christian purity. Thus in the end, to reward the divine dexterity of her fleshy lips he didn't just empty his purse, but invited her to the Grand Palace, hoping that perhaps in few weeks he would exhaust her repertoire. Most men were incurably naïve. In the palace, within a few days she was transformed during the day into a noble lady to save him from embarrassment. With all the experiences from the hard periods of her life, soon she had him asking her for advice more often than his eunuch councillors. Only during the nights when even the eunuchs retired, she turned into a maenad eager to feast on male flesh.

Now what remained to be seen was what more a Sultan expected out of a gorgeous young woman who could turn into a wise whore after sunset to make her into his Birinci Kadin.

****

Hafsa woke up and felt once more inside her silk nightwear the sticky sweat of desire. What was this strange dream Allah had sent to disturb the sleep of a desperate widow? She remembered an old story she had heard in Selim's harem from the lips of a Greek eunuch about an Empress who was a dancer in Galata loving every sailor, before realizing her fate in the hands of the Roman Emperor Justinian. This night her mind had given life to this old story with unexplainable ways. For a little while, she had become in her dreams the prostitute of a Roman Emperor, while in all her life she was so proud she had not mated with a common man but only a Sultan. If this was not a divine sign sent be Allah that she had sinned becoming for a few hours the whore of a slave, she must have lost her mind.

Deeply embarrassed by her dream, she swore to do a hundred prostrations in the mosque the very next morning. Ibrahim may have thoroughly disgraced her, but a Valide Sultan should not blame a slave for her own weakness. All slaves obeyed promptly their master's commands; so, the masters were responsible for being so weak. If they could do nothing but succumb to their weaknesses, it had to be their own lack of power that prevented them from improving themselves.

****

The power to overcome weaknesses was always a chimera proposed by the prophets to test people's faith in their elusive words, and had nothing to do with the actual demands of Allah who distributed randomly virtues and vices to all his creatures.

People were made by Allah's hands to see dreams all alone and share reality with others. Thus, Valide Sultan's dream had nothing to do with her own reality. It was simply a stern warning of how a magnificent Roman Emperor might fall in love with a whore and make her his Empress.

Old wisdom distilled for many generations prevented Emperors to marry women of common birth simply because ordinary women would always be wiser than noble ones. Wisdom was the result of experience and knowledge, and commoners had a much more difficult life and many more chances to make mistakes and learn from their heartaches.

The Ottoman Empire was the continuation of the Roman in the East. The Seraglio operated following the old Roman rules adjusted to Islamic Laws. A Sultan should marry only Princesses to make many sons to avoid the inglorious termination of a dynasty. Concubine was a more polite name for whores and harems for private bordellos. The human species didn't really change, only its vocabulary did. This was Allah's will that obeyed the primal Law that existed even before Prophet Mohamed made his dramatic appearance in the minds of humans to turn beasts into humans.

****

Suleiman was dazzled when he was handed the invitation of his mother. The letter did not say much. She was asking him to come and discuss urgently a serious family problem that should not be postponed. He feared that his mother might have learned something from the recent evolution of his relationship with Ibrahim and would start a new round of annoying reproaches.

However, Hafsa Sultan pleasantly surprised him with her warm greetings and sincere congratulations for his new success during the Rhodes expedition. The sudden joy was so great he did not hesitate to offer her a substantial part of the revenues of the port of Rhodes for her charitable foundation; but, the surprises did not end there that day.

"Thank you my son for your most precious gift; but, I suggest you rewrite this firman and transfer the full amount of your donation to the income of your sister to cover the expenses for her oncoming wedding. I do not have as many needs as she does in this life or the next."

Suleiman was left speechless by this announcement and with great difficulty he found the words to ask for the name of the future groom, expressing his amazement because no one had thought of asking him if he approved of this union. He was not only the Sultan, but also the brother and the guardian of the bride after her divorce. However, the formidable Sultana had come well-prepared for such a fight that day. She had all the answers ready and her aggressive style signified she would not tolerate objections from her son. She had never flinched in her life, even before her violent husband, and she was not willing to start now, when she had revolted against male oppression at last.

Of course, she was not going to explain the exact reasons for her boldness. The Sultan may easily decide that his honor was greatly offended, execute Ibrahim and exile her. Her revolution had to be expressed gradually in more subtle ways during a longer period to allow for better digestion.

"I didn't wish to distract you from your military duties, because I was sure that especially for this groom there was no reason to request your approval. You have already chosen Ibrahim for the highest offices of the Empire, and he is also your most loyal friend. Therefore, I was certain you will approve of him wholeheartedly. Moreover, immediately after your victory in Rhodes you made him a Pasha that means he is also a trusty military leader. Now, am I wrong to assume that you intend to choose him next as your Vizier too, so that your sister will not be married to someone socially far below her last husband? In fact, if you ask me, I think you are wronging your extraordinary friend with this lowly title of an ordinary Vizier. In my opinion with the qualifications he has, and all the services he has offered to the Empire up to now you ought to make him your Grand Vizier, overlooking any possible objections offending your absolute authority that may pop up. How can you expect someone to serve you faithfully, if you have mistreated him?"

Suleiman felt the ground below his feet tremble and remained silent, trying to regain his balance; but, with this passive attitude he gave his relentless mother the right to start criticizing the choices of all his Viziers that had resulted in so much unnecessary bloodshed and misery during the Rhodes expedition.

He tried to interrupt her by referring to the precious services the current Grand Vizier had offered him during the risky times of his succession, but nothing could stop the torrent of arguments against Piri Pasha. It was not just his old age that mattered, but also his too outdated and conservative ideas that made him useless as a counselor of a young and ambitious Sultan like him destined to surpass Fatih and possibly his mighty father. It was indeed a tour de force of a well-coached opponent who had attacked him unexpectedly from the rear.

However, her argument that ultimately gave him the final blow was that during this era of radical changes they lived, when from one moment to another the old flat Earth was proven round, a wise Sultan would never chose a Vizier who was good during his father era.

And slowly Suleiman began to see the entire proposal with the different eye. Of course his confidence in Ibrahim's abilities was absolute. Moreover, the new higher office would be another excuse to see him whenever he wished, and a marriage with his sister Hatidge would close many poisonous mouths still bitterly gossiping them today. Eventually, even though he was convinced his mother was right, simply from inertia he persisted on his objections. As a competent military leader he knew the importance of rearguard action during a planned strategic retreat. Of course, it was impossible to manifest openly to his mother the jealousy he deeply felt for this union that from now on he would share his favorite with his sister; so, he simply uttered.

"I will agree only if my sister wants him and tells me so. After all she is a Princess and he is my slave."

It was the only excuse he could find in the confusion of his retreat; but, instead of a new argument Hafsa Sultan surprisingly agreed and overbid him adding with a slightly ironic smile:

"Of course he is your slave; so, we not only have to ask your sister, but Mahidevran, Hurrem and Gülfem too and all the other women in your harem, whether they can ever be happy without having Ibrahim as their Hasodabashi. From the moment he started managing your harem most of their complaints have stopped. Let's wait now and see what all these women will say, when they find out that you kept next to you at the night an unmarried slave who is not a eunuch."

After this indirect blackmail, Suleiman realized he had lost the game and he most likely was facing the conspiracy of three women. To keep up appearances he decided to follow the advice of his mother. What remained to be seen was how willingly each of his Kadin would accept this proposal. It would be very interesting indeed to find out if his protégé had managed to gain the confidence of all these women, so from that day on, besides Allah, Ibrahim the slave would also have a shadow.

****

Gülfem was very pleased to receive Ibrahim, but she was careful enough to keep up appearances, and asked a Black Eunuch to put a mashrabiya screen between them, so he could not see clearly her face. Of course, this was just another Islamic hypocrisy, as the screen worked both ways and the person losing most of the spectacle was the one sited further from the screen; however, Gülfem was fair and sat in a sofa at equal distance.

Since he had requested this meeting, he had to disclose first the reasons for his visit and he didn't feel like beating around the bush.

"Hafsa Sultan has complained to me that I have wrong you, leaving you aside. I have explained to her this choice was intentional to give the Sultan enough time to forget your recent loss. Now, that enough time has passed according to the words of the Prophet, I intend to be as fair as I can, for as long as I am the Hasodabashi of the Sultan's harem."

The prospect of him losing this post was a piece of news Gülfem did not expect to hear, and she was visibly upset. After all these years she was probably under the impression Ibrahim would be her Hasodabashi for as long as possible in a similar way the Chief Black and White Eunuch were employed, in other words for as long their services pleased the Sultan, or until they retired, or died.

"I did not know you have displeased the Sultan enough to demote you," she rhetorically asked.

"As far as I know, I did my duty as best as I could; but from what I hear, recently he thinks I might be more useful in another post."

"I hope all this is for the better," she noted rather indifferently.

"I'm not sure yet, because I have the feeling the higher one is raised the greater the dangers of a painful fall. Anyway, for a man like me would rather be surrounded by exquisite flowers like you than rebellious Janissaries," he argued and discerned through the screen lattice that Gülfem seemed pleased with the compliment, and her smile gave him the courage to continue: "I only wish I knew the way to make them all bloom, because a garden is more beautiful the more kinds of flower it has."

"Everyone knows what a flower needs to bloom before bearing fruits. It's good soil, plenty of sun, and enough water," she said suggestively.

"That's true, but in the Eski Saray even the sun is difficult to shine under all this shadows, the water is sparse and the soil may be rich but not plentiful," he argued. "I'm sure your Excellence feels as restrained as I do."

He knew she was an Albanian woman from a noble family given as a present to a young Prince Heir by her family to secure his favor. Albanians had many common virtues and vices with Greeks; so, Gülfem must have felt too the effects of oppression.

"In my country the soil is poor, but we have plenty of sun and rains," she noted and he was aware she told the plain truth.

"As you may know I'm from Parga, and I value freedom as much as any other slave. I also know that all the birds do not sing living in a cage. Few like nightingales and birds of prey may even die. Now tell me, are you a blooming rose, a singing bird or a bird of prey?"

"My name is Gülfem. This says it all."

She was right! Despite her age that was now advancing beyond the second decade, she still looked like a blooming rose that any man would be delighted to pluck. Under different circumstances she was a worthy trophy. Now, the question was whether the Sultan would be willing to lose a flower he didn't wish to smell anymore its hypnotic bouquet.

****

Mahidevran was expecting him and seemed very pleased he kept equal distances from the two Sultan's Kadin. Perhaps this was the reason she didn't use a screen during this meeting; but maybe she was more certain of the favorable affects her beauty would have on a man capable of influencing the choices of the Sultan. She was right. Ibrahim felt indeed more relaxed avoiding a direct confrontation with her eyes; but, she did not seem like a woman who would not pursue a retreating opponent until his eventual unconditional surrender.

Observing her body language, Ibrahim could fill the immense pressure his master was under in her presence. The dress she was wearing was chosen to attract the eyes of her husband, and her entire attitude was not as subdued as Gülfem's. She didn't seem to consider the recent loss of an imperial heir as a source of personal shame. For her it was more like a challenge, a step back that should be the starting point for a faster pace. For her a screen was a superfluous obstruction. It was unquestionably a bold and optimistic approach, but it was questionable if the Sultan was ready and able to perform according to her wishes. He was at war and he needed every bit of authority he could master.

Suleiman had lost recently his father, and then shortly two of his youngest sons. In cold blood Mahidevran was the fairest of them all and should be the Sultan's first choice; but, Suleiman had tried his luck with Gülfem too, and when they both failed to keep him fully content, made another try with Hurrem. The fact he spent more nights with her could not be easily explained simply by appearances. It had to be the result of other factors.

He could not say with confidence anything about Hurrem's past, and he still remembered vaguely her bold raid in his bedroom to earn his favor. His mind was quite confused at the time and many minor details had been erased. All he could say now with complete confidence was that residing permanently in a harem, made young women desperate for love after a while. In such an environment, a woman was pushed to the limits by seclusion, envy and loneliness.

He had been a victim too of similar urges when he was a student in the Seraglio School trained by Selim to become his favorite. When Selim was away fighting, he had chosen the next available substitute, a handsome Janissary who had winked at him to show his interest. After years of frustration, Hurrem had sneaked into his room and took advantage of his limited resistance due to the hashish smoking.

These days he was quite content, so the presence of the divine Mahidevran could not affect his judgment so much; but, he could easily imagine what would have happened, if one day Allah sprang a miracle and returning from a long military expedition he found Mahidevran naked in his bedroom. Surrounded daily by death, and after many months of separation from female flesh, how could he ever refuse soothing his desire and not drink few mouthfuls from the source of immortality?

As a Hasodabashi he had the chance to talk with all the Harem's midwives. They had assured him that after a long separation women were inclined to bear sons rather than daughters. It was a fact that could only be interpreted in a single way. Allah had made the world in such a way that a war created the preconditions for more wars.

On the other hand, slaves were forced by their masters to behave rebelliously. It was as simple as that and Mahidevran was a noble lady used to be surrounded by slaves. How would she react, if he ever flirted with her? Hafsa's resistance collapsed after an elaborate kiss on her hand. Only the ominous presence of a Black Eunuch in a faraway corner was a stern reminder he was still inside a Sultan's harem and not a luxurious brothel.

****

"It's nice to see you again so soon, Ibrahim. What brings you to my chambers? I hope I have not done something so wrong to be exiled," she remarked with considerable audacity.

"I'm afraid you did, but it appears that the Shadow of Allah is as benevolent as Allah and has forgiven you. In fact, he needs your love so much; he cannot wait to meet you again and make a new start," he noted as sternly as he could, but with a long smile he added: "Only if you refuse, I might suggest exiling you for a while until you come back to your senses."

Mahidevran rewarded him with a smile to demonstrate her pleasure for receiving after months the Sultan's invitation, but she didn't reply at once accepting it. It was clear there was something missing of importance.

"Who has the Sultan been seeing all these months?" she asked, but Ibrahim was certain she already knew the answer.

"I have no reasons to hide the truth from a Sultan's Kadin. His only visitor had been Hurrem."

"Is he with that whore again?" she asked rhetorically. "Ibrahim, please tell me. What does she have that I don't? A competent Hasodabashi like you must know our differences."

It was another rhetorical question, because at least in his eyes Hurrem was mediocre and extremely licentious, while Mahidevran was a gorgeous creature of impeccable morality. However, unquestionably Suleiman's preference to Hurrem's charms was also an undeniable fact.

"I'm the last man to know the differences, but I'm sure differences exist, because my master is a reasonable and deliberate man; so I can only guess."

"Then, please make a guess for my sake," she requested, "so I can do my best to improve my appeal for the benefit of the Empire."

"A fair man can make logical guesses only based on his experiences," he claimed diplomatically. "Otherwise, there is a great danger his guesses might be wild."

"Many people in the Harem say that your experiences are already quite extensive," she argued.

"They may think so, but who can say with confidence what is extensive and what is limited? I personally believe that an ordinary man is always willing to extend further the limits of his knowledge, while a woman is much happier when she can turn every experience into tangible results."

Mahidevran smiled rewarding his audacity. In this harem it was almost an unwritten custom that beautiful women needed as many compliments as they could trigger to reinforce their confidence in the constant struggle to secure the preference of the dominant male.

"You are right, but I believe in this harem the Sultan is the one who makes the norm."

"Indeed he does, and it is very dangerous for any slave to challenge his status," he argued continuing this small talk.

"That may be true for ordinary men, but as far as I know you claim you are extraordinary, and recent events prove that even the Sultan believes so; thus, pick up your courage and make a wild guess for my sake. Who knows, your answer may be rewarded. As far as I know, the Sultan has honored you many times by saying you two have many things in common as if you were brothers," she gladly continued their flirting.

"Indeed he has, so if I was to put myself in his place, I might consider a Galata whore more exciting company than any Princess, because she is trained to satisfy her customer, any customer, while a Princess demands to receive all the satisfaction she feels she is entitled to."

It should have been a fully satisfying response, but surprisingly Mahidevran's face showed displeasure, and Hasodabashi had to know the reason.

"I believe I have offended you. Please let me know what I did wrong, so I will never do it again," he said submissively.

"Yes, you did hurt me, but you did nothing wrong. Truth hurts! And the truth is that I have no hope to win my man back. The Black Eunuchs claim Hurrem is very experienced and she knows all the tricks that can make a man fully content. She knows much more than the book of the 'Forbidden Pleasures',", she said sadly, and Ibrahim felt the need to turn her frowned grimace into a long smile.

"I'm not so sure she is that good. As far as I know my master is very demanding. I believe if we try hard enough, we can make him see what is best for him and the Empire."

"I always knew I can depend on you. If you can get rid of Hurrem, you may ask me any favor you want," she assured him.

It was a general statement he couldn't accept at face value, so he repeated its conclusion with a question mark.

"Any favor I want?" he inquired; but, he got only a long smile as an answer.

****

Leaving Mahidevran's apartment he was sure that by now everyone in the Harem would be discussing each of his morning visits. Unquestionably the time he had spent in Hafsa's apartments extended the most; but, who could object a Hasodabashi investing his time discussing the current Harem's problems with the noble woman in charge and his superior?

Everyone, from the Black Eunuchs to the last cleaning woman, could see that the recent infant deaths had multiplied the existing tensions, as Hurrem was now the most fertile woman, besides being the one the Sultan visited most.

For most residents it was an unexplainable phenomenon since this woman was less attractive and noble than the Sultan's two Kadin, but he knew why. She was voracious and she had convinced his master he was the cause of her avarice.

Ibrahim entering her apartment noticed the presence of the Kislar Aga, and with an inquisitive look made sure the eunuch had to provide explanations for his visit.

"Padisah asked me to prepare Hurrem for tonight," he explained and Ibrahim felt a bit annoyed by this unexpected infringement of his rights. He could start complaining but complains were a clear sign of weakness.

"Great! You save me the time of informing Hurrem was my choice not only for tonight but for the entire next week," he replied with a smile of relief. "Do you have to convey any other message?" he inquired, indicating that the Kislar Aga had to return to his other duties.

****

The moment the Aga was out the door, Hurrem smiled seductively and sat next to him on the sofa.

"Thanks for the preference. I knew you were a wise man perfectly capable of realizing who the best company to entertain our Master is."

Ibrahim grasped her hand that seemed too lonely resting on the sofa and turned it over to take a careful look at her palm.

"What do you see?" she inquired with a giggle.

"That you are a very interesting concubine capable of pleasing even the most eclectic man. What else?" he replied and offered her the most seductive smile he could master.

"Are you an eclectic man?" she inquired with an imperceptibly ironic smile.

"Why should a slave become eclectic?" he replied with a question and lay her hand between his thighs, forcing her to pull it as if it had touched a scorching flame.

"Simply because everyone you omit will instinctively become your enemy," she managed to utter.

"No, they won't. Hope dies last," he replied with confidence.

"What are your hopes right now?" she asked him matching his confidence.

"Nothing! When I'm doing my duty I expect no rewards."

"We are different. I always expect a reward, when I'm doing my duty."

"I used to be sold meat too, but as I grow older I have evolved into a careful seeker of exquisite pleasures."

"You live in a world of illusions. Everyone is a sold meat, even when the price is pure love. Whatever we do creates a reaction. With a single touch I can enslave any man. This power is what I call a reward."

"I wonder what kind of reward you expected when you left me in the cold," Ibrahim asked sincerely puzzled.

She rewarded him with an enigmatic giggle.

"The greatest pleasure is anticipation. Men are most certainly made so. The prospect of a kiss turns them on much more than the kiss itself."

"Indeed it does, but that morning waiting indefinitely was far beyond my endurance."

"You don't say! I thought nothing was impossible for you. You are disappointing me for a second time today. I thought a man like you would have a much more productive imagination. In my mind what happened between us was just the beginning of a masterpiece you could complete with your mind's hands at your leisure any way you pleased time and time again until you reached perfection."

"It was the wrong assumption. I'm just a novice while you are a true artist. You have such an extensive experience you can turn yourself into any man's dream."

"What you say doesn't make much sense. How can a novice like you judge the extent of my long experiences?"

He had to admit her logic was impeccable, but he had not said his last word.

"I have used my imagination along with my logic. A virgin that captures the interest of an exceptional man like a Sultan must be exceptional too. She is as rare as the immaculate Virgin Mary of the Christians, a true miracle of creation."

"I'm sure you are joking. You can't mean that. You were a slave too before evolving into a Hasodabashi. You know that every slave who passes the Seraglio gates claims she is a virgin to improve her chances. A wise Emperor should have realized by now what kind of a big scam this is."

"There are few men that cannot face the reality about the people they love, while few others don't even care."

"When I'm in love with a man I simply don't care if I'm his very first woman. All I care is that I'm his last. Why should he care what exactly I had been before meeting him?" Hurrem noticed.

"That's hard when your beloved is a Sultan."

"You may have accepted that, but I haven't. I'm more romantic than you despite my obscure past."

"What is your past?" Ibrahim asked grabbing the occasion.

"I'm a priest's daughter."

"With your achievements this sounds like a lie!"

"No, it isn't. It's the truth. Your question is simply a dumb one. Daughters take after their mothers not their fathers. A competent Hasodabashi should know that," she teased him. "But a man's past is usually more interesting than a woman's. Men have so many opportunities to experience and sin. It's unfair!"

Ibrahim suddenly discovered he was not the hunter but the prey. Perhaps Hurrem had been asking about him.

"For a slave doing whatever his master asks is no sin. It's a virtue."

"This is a very critical point and I'm very glad we agree on this issue," she remarked.

"But if a slave takes certain initiatives bypassing his master's commands may be sinful," he snapped back to test her reactions.

"Do you really believe that whatever two slaves do to entertain their slavery is an improper violation of their master's rights?"

"No, but their master may think it is and punish them."

"No, it isn't! Slaves should try to win their freedom even for a moment each day," she noted with conviction defending her rights.

"Whenever you feel like revolting, let me know so I can see what I can do to help you," he suggested with a long smile.

Hurrem could not keep a stern face, and she turned her mouth into an open invitation with a friendly smile.

"For a revolution to be successful it has to occur the right moment."

It was a subtle promise. He could feel her desire for him was growing again. Whatever she had found out about his deeds had not diminished the attraction she felt for him. However, after two deliveries she was careful not to take chances. The entire harem knew he was visiting her and time passed quickly. His visit had lasted more than hers, and at least he knew what a woman of her talents could do in such a short time.

"Are you happy this coming week Suleiman will be all yours?" he inquired.

"Will you always sleep next door?" Hurrem replied confusing once more his feelings.

"Why do you ask?" he asked her. "Do you intend to pay me another visit?"

"Why should I even try to complicate your plans? Now you have many more lucrative choices, and it will be to my advantage if you marry a Princess or if you seduce any of the Sultan's Kadin. Thus, make your choice and I will keep the Sultan busy."

"Aren't you afraid I might inform the Sultan of your wicket suggestions?" Ibrahim said sincerely surprised about the turn of events.

"No! Why should you? If you considered it carefully, we are partners. We are both slaves looking for a better future for us and our children. Why should we behave like opponents when we have nothing to share? Are you truly in love with the Sultan? No! That was indeed a silly question. How can a slave be in love with his master?"

It was a question Ibrahim had no reply. Hurrem was right. Love had to be the result of freedom of choice among many alternatives. After his initial confusion, now he realized the more choices he had the stronger the love he felt.

Hurrem had been a true revelation. She may have been a young whore in the past; but, she certainly knew how to manipulate men to her advantage. With a few kisses she could turn even the Kislar Aga into her instrument the same way she had clouded his judgment. He simply had to get married as soon as possible with the Princess. He was simply too vulnerable to a prostitute's advances, and it was easy to see why. When a woman was easy, then it wasn't easy to find excuses for not enjoying her as often as it pleased him. Was this another reason Suleiman spent so much time with Hurrem?

No! This kind of logic didn't make sense for a Sultan. For him all women were easy. Hurrem's attraction had to be something else he still couldn't figure out.

****

Asphodel was firm. He had not opened his mouth to anyone. The leak must have been someone else. In the Seraglio, there were hundreds of pages of all kinds, so it was practically impossible to find out who knew what. Even if the Sultan locked his door of a dark room, there were ways a page could guess what was happening behind a closed door.

As Ibrahim knew quite well, there were all the lower grade pages that took care of cleaning the rooms and washing clothes. If he so wished, they could easily find when a woman's period started or when a Sultan became excited. There were telltale signs the nose or the eyes of a eunuch could discern.

"Give me your underwear tonight and I will tell you, where you have been all day," he proposed, but Ibrahim refused. It was then when Asphodel fell on his knees in front of him as if he was prostrating. He was rather astonished by the move and failed to react promptly when the eunuch embraced his thighs and pressed his face on his abdomen. When he managed to push him away it was too late. The eunuch had a naughty smile on his face.

"You had a very busy morning," he announced. "There are all sorts of perfumes mixed up on your clothes. Next time you visit these whores don't seat on their couches or their beds."

"I didn't sit on their beds!" Ibrahim insisted, but Asphodel's grimace indicated plainly his misbelief.

"Don't lie to me, so I won't lie to you. Valide Sultan invited you to her quarters this morning. Her scent is very heavy and it is all over you, not just your clothes. She is a good fuck, no doubt about it. Sultan Selim used to tell me she was draining him better than anyone else. If I were you, I would take all my clothes off and I promise I will wash them personally, so no one else would know what you have done. But be careful. Do not repeat such foolishness ever again. Marrying Hatidge Sultan is a good excuse for you to improve your morality."

Ibrahim was now very impressed, and with all these developments he had many things to ask.

"What do you think of Hatidge Sultan?"

"Don't ask me such general questions about any woman. In general they are all whores. They all give you everything you desire in return of for everything they desire. Hatidge Sultan is a widow. Her previous husband did not last long. This is a bad omen for every future lover. Now she is lonely and frustrated. If I were you I would try to turn her too into my slave the same way you did with everyone else. Having everyone yearning for you is a great accomplishment. On the other hand, pleasing everyone makes you cheap and disposable sooner rather than later."

"I don't agree. Pleasing everyone is what I call the perfect trade. Everyone is happy and no one complains," Ibrahim remarked rather annoyed by a fatalistic or superstitious assertion.

Perhaps Asphodel was telling the truth, perhaps he was lying. It was not important who leaked the rumors. What counted was that there was no way for anyone to keep a secret inside the Seraglio. Sooner or later time would come to put the pressure on the knowers of all the secrets. This eunuch certainly knew too much as he next asked with a long smile:

"How are His Majesty favorites doing this morning? I bet they looked and smiled like flowers for your sake."

****

Allah is the Knower of All Secrets, and whoever tried to replace him was a grave sinner who sooner or later would be punished. Allah had made the world so few secrets were meant to be eternal. This was also the reason why no matter what outrageous gossips leaked in the Eternal City from the Harem, there was always at least a grain of truth.

****

"What did he want?" the Kislar Aga asked the odalisque as she suckled her newborn baby.

"He wished to tell me that for the next week I will be the Sultan's favorite."

"And why did you think he did this special favor for you?"

"I don't know, but I wonder if I have misjudged him."

"You are a fool. This coming week Mahidevran has her period. Few women become very aggressive and lose their minds with lust during their fertile days. With a bit of luck she might get pregnant once more. What if she bears another son while you suckle a daughter?"

"As long as my children are well fed and healthy, I can get pregnant again too. This is why I keep breastfeeding my children. I couldn't stand losing a child I had to suffer so much to bear it. I have all the time in the world to make another son."

"Unfortunately, I cannot help you much to achieve this goal. I can only excite your fantasies, since everyone knows that hot women get pregnant more easily; but, in your position the final question is whether you can kill, so that one son of yours may live."

"Is giving me advices the only reason you came to me this time of day?"

"No damned woman! I love seeing women breastfeeding their children. They remind me so much of home and my mother."

"Does that mean you are going to leave me all alone when I finish? Don't you know that when a woman has a suckling baby, her urges diminish to almost nothing?"

****

Hafsa Sultana leaving the Sultan's apartments went directly to Hurrem's bedroom. She found her looking after her children under the supervision of the Kislar Aga.

The newborn Mihrimah slept quietly in her cradle, while little Mehmet was trying to make with Hurrem's help his first steps. He was already one year old, but the boys usually have difficulty walking and saying the first words. Seeing Hurrem's efforts, Hafsa Sultan felt content. Choosing Hurrem for her son's life partner was proving unexpectedly successful. Her efforts had been justified. This girl was not only the embodiment of eroticism, giving her son sheer pleasure on every occasion, but even more important was the fact that her hunger for love was not a manifestation of selfish passion for carnal satisfaction, but sprang from an intrinsic, desperate need for motherhood her son felt obliged to satisfy for some reason.

She had met several concubines in her life that handled men as

189

effectively as Hurrem, perhaps even more, but their motives were different. They adored sex and enjoyed love with any man they could lay their hands on. They were so degenerate when darkness fell, they would embrace the first Black Eunuch who would wink at them, or molest even the next woman lying on the hammam pedestal.

All the men in the Harem may be castrated, but they still had tongues, fingers or even fists. During the long summer nights, when the Sultan was always at war, no one in the Harem could sleep with open windows because of their passionate sighs. A harem was the kind of prison where an unscrupulous woman could lose every bit of self-respect, a wicked institution that pushed women to the limits of their endurance against evil.

When during the winter months, Selim came back from the wars and got bored or tired visiting them after few weeks, they did all they could to sneak out of the Harem in search of other men. Eventually the Kislar Aga had to look the other way, because there would be trouble even for him, if the Sultan found out what they were doing within its walls while he was absent.

However, the Harem's rules did not allow the Sultan's concubines meeting secretly other men and the punishment was death by drowning in the Bosporus Straights in front of the Seraglio. The guilty were simply invited to the Yeni Saray never to return no questions asked. Despite this obstacle, it was not impossible for a concubine to bribe a guard and get out of the Eski Saray for a few hours, when the Sultan was at war or resting inside the Topkapi Seraglio with another concubine and discipline relaxed. When the sun was setting, which Janissary guard on the walls of the Eski Saray would say no to a fast engagement with such an exceptional but utterly promiscuous creature? If she was not the Birinci Kadin even she would be tempted to try. The jealousy of knowing that the only man you were allowed to mate was mating with another woman was too much to bear even when you were pregnant.

Under these emotional stresses, gradually a simple trend became a habit and a habit a lucrative profession. Then, the more money a wicked concubine could earn in the neighborhood caravanserais the more guards and Black Eunuchs she could bribe, as there was always a great demand in the Eternal City for beautiful and licentious women. However, the excess of desires made them dumb, and risked not only their lives but their lovers' lives too.

Hurrem was drastically different as the Kislar Aga who tutored her reported. She was undoubtedly yearning for men too, but not just for her pleasure. She was wise enough to realize that pleasure was just a fleeing sensation, and this was not a woman's mistake. A woman could go on practically forever. It was always a man's shortcoming.

Hafsa Sultan was the best witness of this phenomenon. Even the fearsome Sultan Selim could not compete in bed with the average virgin in her puberty. Perhaps this was why when he grew older, he finally associated only with eunuchs he could totally dominate. Being defeated by a young girl was unacceptable for the self-respect of a world conqueror.

Hurrem was earthy and practical most of all. She was unquestionably a lusty bitch, but her aim was to bear children. She was like Mother Earth that the deeper a man pushed his plough in her flesh the more fertile she became. And now that she had become a mother, she would never put the future of her children in question for a man other than her son. This was not just her impression, but Kislar Aga's expert assessment too.

Every indication available pointed out that in her mind love had a single purpose, namely to bring into this world something tangible, a new life that would be the living proof that her love for the man she had chosen was eternal. When she danced for her son the second time, she couldn't contain her curiosity and watched stealthily the entire divine seduction ceremony. Her dance was nothing less enchanting than the movements of a flower that opens its petals, and the eroticism she emanated nothing but the inescapable scent that invited her son to pollinate her obediently like a bee. Hurrem was devilish attractive but divinely inspired and she had to be tolerated.

In Hafsa Sultan's mind, in the Ottoman garden of life women should be like the different kind of trees planted in Allah's Paradise. Many trees were cultivated for the beauty of their flowers, others for their dense shade they provided, few others for the usefulness of their wood, or the value of their fruit, but Hurrem was an exception that combined every possible use.

This was not just her opinion but Kislar Aga's too.

****

Allah the All-Seer laughs His heart out when people gather, build cities, shape nations, and exchange information, thinking that by adding dubious opinions you may approach the truth. If this was indeed the truth, then He would have only a son, a Holy Ghost and no daughter. He would be surrounded by psalm singing angels up in heavens listening to monks reciting hymns in his name exactly as the Council of Nicaea had concluded after a "democratic" vote under the supervision of Emperor Constantine the Great, a vicious killer who had murder both his son and one of his wives. This was at least what the barbaric Christians believed.

What was true was entirely different and much simpler. People should gather, collaborate and coexist unified, because it was the only way they could face the perils of the violent, unfinished universe He had created. Many people believing that a fleeting dream was true, was the only way to realize it irrespectively if the dream was peace or war, creation or distraction. Good and evil had equal chances of success, as Allah is the fairest of all gods.

****

The moment Hurrem saw Hafsa Sultana entering, she rushed to greet and kiss her hand, but her lips that day had lost their bright smile. It was obvious something was tormenting her. Hafsa had no time to lose in half-truths and half-

191

lies, so she immediately inquired for the true cause of her distress. Hurrem that up to that moment with great difficulty contained her emotions, burst into sobs that rattled her full breasts.

Hafsa began to worry that something serious had happened to one of her children, and motioned the Kislar Aga to summon her personal doctor; but, as Hurrem quieted somewhat her sorrow down, she confessed that Suleiman was still spending many nights with his slave, and the previous evening had refused to invite her or any other of his concubine into his bedroom.

"I do not know what else to do to convince him to quit this strange affliction with his audacious slave. Even our two children are not enough to keep him close to us at night."

For a woman of Hafsa's experience, it was easy to discern Hurrem was deeply in love with her son and was hurt by his peculiar behavior. She was in such troubled psychological condition she could not see what kind of behavior to choose that was best for her interests.

"If I were you, I wouldn't be particularly worried about this condition," she finally noted, "I had to go through the same heartaches with his father too. My Suleiman is your Sultan and being his slave means you are the favorite of a man who has the power to demand everything in this world and still remain unsatisfied; but, all these troubles will eventually pass, and then you will realize that in a woman's life other feelings are more precious than the husband you now adore. In Allah's world everything has a beginning and an end. In the end you will both lose your desires that seem so potent right now. All fires are extinguished when there is nothing left to burn."

"I could bear this torture, if I didn't have any children with him; if my sole purpose in life was to soften his heart with my tenderness."

"Don't curse your luck because it might abandon you! Your children are the blessing of Allah to your womb. Even if the Sultan deserts you for a while for a lusty woman, a man or even a eunuch, do not worry. Sooner or later they are destined to become separated, as this kind of relationships does not last long because they are contrary to Nature. However, if your wish in life is to have Suleiman back in your arms as soon as possible, you must faithfully follow my advices as you did last time and won his favor. I am his mother and I know how he thinks."

****

The formidable Sultana spoke for a long time and after the last advice silence fell in the room, as the two women were immersed in their own thoughts. From the Aga Mosque in the courtyard the voice of the Muezzin rose for the afternoon prayer, but they were not willing to interrupt their chat and pray to Allah because they were both convinced the solution was not going to descend from Heaven.

Hurrem had realized that despite her hurt sentiments Hafsa was essentially right. Her status in the Harem despite her two marvelous creations was still relatively low. She was still a slave who had attracted for few evenings the eye of the Sultan with her dance and her tricks and nothing more than that.

All the rights and privileges she enjoyed today stemmed from her son, Mehmet. Without his existence soon another Ikbal would make her presence felt, as every month younger concubines arrived from the Avret Bazar. Then, her status would be endangered depending on the charms of every new inmate.

From one week to the next, the eye of the Sultan might be lost forever among the charms of another even more deceitful concubine who would mimic or improve her tricks. At this disquieting thought she felt her stomach muscles tightening. This madness had to stop because it led nowhere she wished to go.

Ibrahim Pasha instead offered the Sultan something more tangible than a fleeting sensual relationship. He had proved that in any crisis he could find a better solution than any other proposal that reached the ears of Suleiman from the lips of any Vizier, Serasker (Field General), or White Eunuch.

Sultana's idea to marry him with the Princess was not bad at all. It had hidden virtues. This marriage ought to put an end to Ibrahim's intimate relationship with Suleiman. Perhaps, she ought to develop good relations with him and influence the decisions of the Sultan relating to her son. Suddenly, her mood changed radically for the better.

If Ibrahim became Grand Vizier with her help, he would feel obliged to repay this favor with one of his from his new position in the same way she had reward him the only way a novice concubine knew. Maybe this marriage would be indeed a great opportunity to improve her status too in the Seraglio. Ibrahim was a slave and he would surely sympathize with her struggle to promote her offspring.

"I will do my best for Ibrahim to get married. If you think, that Hatidge Sultan is the best choice and not Gülfem Hatun, who am I to contradict a mother who wants her daughter to be happy. My only concern is to make sure that as my son grows up, he should not have to feel the shock of seeing his father in bed with a man as Suleiman did. Sons imitate the ways of the father as much as daughters try to become like their mothers. This is the will of Allah and to believe otherwise it's much more than foolish."

"I couldn't agree with you more; but now tell me. Wouldn't you rather have a woman helping you take care of your children than the Kislar Aga? If you wish, I can always provide you with a nanny. Daughters don't need so much their mother's milk as boys do."

Hurrem had to admit that she was more efficient manager of the Harem than Ibrahim or the Kislar Aga simply because she was an experienced woman. Hafsa knew that the moment she stopped suckling, her urges would start a new cycle of fertility.

****

Maybe it was coincidence, but Ibrahim's promise came true. As he promised the same evening, Suleiman asked his servant to bring Hurrem from the Eski Saray to the Marble Kiosk. Perhaps this night he felt the need to have a woman by his side for a change. From the day his favorite had delivered his only daughter, he had not found free time to spend a night with her, and maybe he felt remorse for this cruel indifference.

Perhaps, unintentionally Suleiman had remembered the firm advices of the Book for Princes that he should prefer the company of women than men during the cold winter nights. Then again, it might simply be the will of Allah. Only Allah knew the truth in its entirety.

****

There was a severe winter that year, and the "Garbis" (Northeastern wind) was blowing hard from Scythia across the Black Sea. It was carrying along with him the frozen breath of Tatar steppes mixed with the fine droplets from the exhalations of the vast pine forests beyond the Urals. The wind had begun to blow since early this afternoon, but back then the sun was still above the horizon and the atmosphere tolerable; thus, many folks made the mistake and left their homes dressed with light clothing.

However, as night fell and the light weakened, the wind grew stronger, the initial moisture turned first into rain and then into fine snow the wind whirled over the rooftops, giving the impression that even the wind was filled with clouds of stars; but the magic of the night didn't stop there. In a few moments all the branches were covered by a thin layer of ice the few oil lanterns illuminating the streets turned into glowing Venetian crystals.

Inside the Seraglio the atmosphere was warm and cozy. In all the rooms the fireplaces were lit with dry wood harvested in midsummer and stacked in large warehouses away from any trace of moisture. On top of the lead-covered roofs the endless chimneys gouged clouds of black smoke and sparks as if the Seraglio was on fire. And if someone dared to remain outdoors and stare at the Tower of Justice that towered over the Divan, he would have imagined that through the funnels thousands of evil spirits escaped, disguised as fleeing dark clouds of smoke that spread and covered the Eternal City; but nobody was mad enough to risk pneumonia, wandering around the courtyards of the Topkapi Seraglio. Only the Mute Executioners stayed awake so late, dodging the raindrops from falling onto their grim face, as if Sultan Selim was going to rise again and hand them for one more time death sentences.

The Mutes were hallucinating recalling previous glories. However, this was a magical night the young Sultan considered fit not fit for distribution of death sentences but for planting the seeds of a new life from the oblivion of the frozen winter to the germination of the oncoming spring.

Suleiman examined Hurrem as she hurried into his room eager to meet him, following submissively his command. Perhaps, it had been too long without seeing her eyes, and the feverish desire to see them drowned in an ocean of lust was now resurrected as if it was the insatiable urge of an opium addict.

What did Hurrem have that attracted him so much? She was not as tall and slim like Mahidevran, and her breasts bore the consequences of her recent double pregnancies and her passionate insistence on breastfeeding both her children. Her face didn't have the aristocratic features of noble Tatar Princesses exhibited practically since birth. Her eyes were undeniably true mirrors of her never-resting mind; but, women were seldom loved for their brains. If something was superb on her was her back with her two adorable dimples over her firm, manly buttocks; but as a Sultan he couldn't enjoyed them as much as he desired, because no slave besides Ibrahim was permitted to turn his back at him.

That night he was hopping he was going to quench his desire inside her flaming lips; but what he faced was deeply frustrating. Hurrem had brought along their two children, holding Mihrimah in her arms, while Mehmet was walking erect grabbing the edge of her dress. Together they all sat on the carpet by his feet, while the Kislar Aga who had accompanied them from the Eski Saray kneeled by the door waiting for orders.

He did not wish to begin the night with a quarrel, so he pretended that everything was a pleasant surprise for him; but Hurrem surprised him with a depressing reply to his gracious greeting. She ought, she claimed, now that she had two children to raise, to remain permanently in the Eski Saray for there was always the fear in all these perilous trips her most precious offspring to catch a cold or a deadly disease and infect all his children.

Another death should not be the cause of depression for her master now that he was designing with Ibrahim a new military expedition in the Balkans. Each child of the Osman breed was precious to the Empire, and the House of Osman had already lost two able heirs from other more frivolous mothers that valued the pleasure of making love to their master more than a healthy son. Perhaps, to be perfectly safe, she and her children should move to Edirne away from the dangers lurking in the Seraglio and the Kiosks of the Eternal City. In this way he would be free from any family worries, and could devote all his time to the success of his next campaign in Europe.

Suleiman tried calmly but in vain to change her opinion. Her perseverance was adamant and her arguments properly prepared. The truth was that the Ayin traditions had an inviolable rule. When a concubine bore a Prince Heir, she ought to be withdrawn from the Sultan's life, because it was certain his interest for her would be limited from then on; thus, it was best for everyone to remove her from his life entirely, so she could devote all her energy and care to the welfare of her children and let the Sultan free of any family obligations to find happiness with other younger favorites and less used.

Anyone could see that her breasts were deformed by milk, becoming useless to offer pleasure to the man of her life thrilled much more by untouched virgins. This was going to be her last sacrifice for the sake of their everlasting love. She did not forget, of course, her low position. She was just a piece of purchased meat from the Avret bazaar, and her destination in life was to satisfy all the Sultan's desires, even the most unusual. But, if he placed any value on her feelings, all he had to do right now was to remove her entirely from his direct intimate environment and spare her the pain of seeing other younger women, much more wicked than her, take her place in his bed.

The Sultan had been ambushed by her torrent of suggestions; so, he tried to buy some time until he was able to discern what the root cause of her complaints was. Despite his young age, he had enough experience of female complaints. Already he counted more than ten years of living with several women in his harem, as Hurrem was the eighth consecutive protégé. This experience was already greater than the lifetime experiences of any ordinary Ottoman husband.

It was clear Hurrem's passionate plea was not caused by typical feminine coquetry which could easily be forgotten with few jewels or dresses. The recruitment of children was the ultimate weapon for a woman, and its use indicated her goal was something much more important; so, he tried to find out what exactly bothered her in the Esky Saray.

He first reassured her that nothing had affected his feelings. He then added with a bit of irony that he was very content with her accomplishments, and it was not among his intentions to buy other more licentious favorites. The desire for the mother of his children was as strong as during their first night, when she offered him so much pleasure his heart almost burst.

Hurrem realized she had no reason to hide her intentions any longer. The period of strategic maneuver had achieved its purpose and had weakened his defense. Now it was time to hit the main target.

"The master of the world and my Lord has no reason to hide the truth from an odalisque madly in love with His Majesty," she said with ear-caressing voice as she kept looking at him straight in the eye with gut-enflaming passion.

"If you have extinguished the flame of your passion for her, you should let her find a new higher purpose in life, raising her precious children the Shadow of Allah had bestowed to her care, rather than spend every hour of the day trying to find new ways of milking a bull," she said and finishing her sentence, she ducked her head and lowered her eyes to look with affection at her baby daughter in her arms.

It was a posture that reminded him the old Roman mosaics of Virgin Mary he had seen in old churches he had visited in the Eternal City out of curiosity, when he was young. Her image awoke the Turk raider inside him. He motioned the courtesan to take the kids to an adjacent room leaving them alone.

When the door closed behind them, he sat next to Hurrem and leaned her gently on the carpet. He then mildly grabbed her chin and sought her gazing eyes, but she lowered even more her eyelids. He kissed her half-opened lips passionately, but she did not reciprocate his kiss. She just lay down on the carpet, but did not show any reaction to his caresses, but simply accepted pathetically his every intrusion into her personal space.

However, this passive attitude awakened in him the violent emotions of the conqueror. He tried to caress her breasts, but his clumsy fingers entangled in her pearl necklace finally broke it, spreading its beads on the carpet. It was right then when Hurrem first reacted by unbuttoning the laced jersey that covered her breasts. It was the first but also the last obstacle he had found in his way, since that day, Allah willing, she was wearing a simple dress that allowed her to breastfeed without having to undress.

The Sultan seeing her naked breasts, his passion overflowed; so he pushed aside hastily all the clothes preventing him from reaching his ultimate goal. On the other hand, Hurrem did not try to resist, nor share his passion. Her eyes remained closed, depriving him of the pleasure of plunging his glance into the crystal blue waters of her pupils.

When his passion for her flesh had subsided, he found himself lying next to her, staring at the ceiling trying to recover the rhythm of his breath after the struggle of the previous intense moments. Instinctively he stretched his hand and touched tenderly her left breast to count her heartbeats. As far as he could remember this was the first time he had ever made such an affectionate gesture as passion was always greater than curiosity.

He discovered her heart was calm and rhythmic without any particular excitement. He looked at her half-naked body, but could not find any distinct signs of passion. Her nipples were soft and even the sweat on her skin was his own. Her eyes were now like the flat surface of a lake that was faithfully reflecting his image.

This kind of behavior was something new. Up to this night he always ended what she had began; but, now the roles were almost reversed, and she had distanced herself away from him, as if she was merely a sex toy for a single player. Surprisingly her refusal had not affected negatively the pleasure he felt. In fact, his desire to conquer her had grown even stronger.

He saw her now as a wild animal, a mustang he had to lasso and tame enough to ride; but in the end, he was left with his own needs unmet, because his offers that best suited his needs the woman of his life had not accepted.

It was not important she had not resisted. The attitude seemed just the fortitude of slaves. The conclusion was clear. He, a magnanimous Sultan, had been ejected by a slave. And to make things even worst, Hurrem summoned back her Nubian slave. Did this mean it was time for her to leave?

Somehow, since his father came back from Egypt, Nubians had proliferated in the City of Constantine, but he had not noticed this change before that moment. Both Nubian men and women had impressive physic, no doubt; so, he considered a natural phenomenon that the prices of Nubian slaves were raised considerably since then. Personally he didn't appreciate such affluent proportions; but, he could certainly sympathize with any male Nubian slave who liked women to look like statues of fertility. Primitive people had deeply rooted ideas of what looked exciting. He was a Turk and Turks always had to ride horses and be as slim as possible for the poor animals to carry less weight and travel further and faster. As far as he knew Nubian women were not allowed to ride either horses or camels.

His thoughts jumped for no apparent reason from Nubian slaves to Ibrahim. Perhaps, he obeyed the wishes of his master too, keeping himself distant and untouched from any emotional engagement a passionate erotic act could trigger.

If he ever realized Ibrahim pretended excitements, with his knife he would take his head off; but, under no circumstances he would bear to see life fading away from her sapphire eyes under the sword of the Chief Executor. Now he recognized what he had missed most this evening. He had not read in her eyes the passion of love. He decided to capitulate, since despite the invasion of her body, he had not conquered her soul.

"What do you want from me anyway?" he asked in despair.

She opened her eyes wide to fathom his. Seeing his state of emotional turmoil she coldly administered the last stroke.

"Now that I have your children, I don't want anything more from you! Now, I just want you!" she said and her eyes ejected brilliant sparks of jealousy. If this was the majestic lion of the Ottoman Empire, she was definitely an angry lioness, and the protection of her children made her much more determined and dangerous.

He spent much of the night trying to convince her he was solely hers; but, she did not change opinion. She wasted no time believing his claims that whatever she heard in the Harem for his friend was a lie, and she paid no attention to the promises her children will always be under his protection. Only when he took an oath in the name of Allah that above everyone else he put their children, Hurrem showed somewhat reassured and relieved; but, she did not stop her demands. She discreetly dodged in the nature of his relationship with Ibrahim. She was determined to clarify the situation once and for all, even though any confrontation with the Sultan was always a risky business for any concubine.

"If every rumor I hear about you and your beloved slave in the Harem is a miserable lie," she argued with the stern tone of a judge, "then nobody will dare to continue circulating lies that Ibrahim is your most desirable Makbil (favorite), if you find a suitable woman to marry him as soon as possible. And what better option do you have than to offer to such a gifted man your sister as a wife? She is a widow after all for several years and a real man like Ibrahim must be what she yearns for."

He tried again to evade another empty promise, but Hurrem interrupted him with unbending determination.

"If you value your friend as much as your attitude and the time you spend in his presence shows, you couldn't find another bride that suits him more a true man like him than your sister. And don't worry. She will raise no objections.

There are rumors in the Harem that she has already sneaked him once in her bedroom, and since then she cannot sleep unless she hugs a hard pillow between her legs. I don't believe these rumors, even though I know how good a pillow feels to a lonely woman missing a man who has gone to fight the holy war."

Suleiman now realized Hatidge might be the reason for all this strange behavior. Indeed this new affair was not a trivial matter. Such a marriage meant that now the blood of a Roman slave would join the blood of Osman. If the marriage produced a son, this son would have some of Selim's blood in his veins, which in the future may be proved dangerous.

On the other hand, such a marriage would put an end to all these devious mouths that today were making ironic comments about their relationships. Now, even Ibrahim's advancement in the Ottoman hierarchy could be explained in connection with the Princess and not because of any kind of weakness of his. Nobody could blame him any longer in the Eternal City for all the distinguishing offices he had offered to the groom. However, what still escaped explanation was why Hurrem was trying to ensure Ibrahim would climb another step higher. Perhaps time or luck would reveal the reasons. Perhaps a conspiracy was brewing, but still it was too early to tell; thus, he decided to consent and said with a trace of bigotry:

"If Hatidge wants Ibrahim Pasha for her husband and he has no objections, I will not become an obstacle in their paths to happiness."

His words were heard decisively, but deep inside he still had the hope that something could happen and this marriage would be canceled forever. It was then when Hurrem realized the right time had come to seek a favor of her own.

"I'm very curious to meet this man who has imprisoned the hearts of the entire Osman family. Perhaps he has a lot to teach me too."

This implicit claim under other circumstance would be an insult to the Sultan's status; but, this time it went unnoticed, because Hurrem bent her neck and lowered her eyes. It was a submissive posture of a slave in front of the omnipotent Sultan that fitted perfectly the occasion, a body gesture that skillfully hid the intentions of the mind. With her eyes focused on the floor, the Sultan could not see the triumphant expression that passed over her eyes as fast as lightning, or give importance to the trivial fact she was now uttering the last word.

Hurrem had discovered one of her man's weaknesses, and from then on every time she desired a serious concession, she would use a simple cocktail of an adequate dose of sexual coldness mixed with a generous portion of motherly instinct to achieve her aims. It was the same phenomenon as few drops of water turned magically "raki" into a milky-white, alcoholic drink that could transform gentle wandering dervishes into heartless, bloodthirsty Janissary warriors. One more drop could have a severe effect on the outcome; so, Kislar Aga's idea to have a cute black slave always present, while she was seducing the man of her life might become useful one day, when she didn't feel like pleasing him. The Aga claimed all men were lusty creatures and the divine images of a goddess of fertility improved immensely their disposition.

Hafsa's advice was useful too. The men were molded by Mother Nature to become lovers and fathers for the perpetuation of the species. To start this magical process, a wise woman needed only to determine the correct proportions of mother and mistress that suited her man's character.

A wry smile for the stupidity of the mob shaped her lips as she remembered the silly popular rumors that had reached her ears, claiming she was a witch who secretly poisoned the Sultan with potent erotic filters made from the glands of female hyenas.

This smile did not pass unnoticed. Suleiman, like any other man, was unable to determine each time he met her why the woman in his heart was smiling. Forced by the naivety of his imagination he assumed it had something to do with her erotic disposition, another telltale sign she was ready to mate.

However, Allah had devised a way for a woman to measure man's naivety by the dose of optimism he beheld in his life, namely that if he sweats enough, the best possible scenario will always materialize. Thus, this very evening, all the Sultan desires were realized as Hurrem did not refuse any part of her body he craved. She had no reason to do otherwise. What had happened earlier was another very pleasant erotic game played to make him believe he could always find shelter in her arms from all the family demons that pursued him.

****

After nine months, Suleiman acquired another son to remember forever this fateful night. Perhaps this was the will of Allah; but possibly her very own pretty African goddess of fertility was responsible, who silently slipped under the covers to offer her two helping hands and a pair of lips, when the man of her dreams momentarily lost his drive and fell asleep.

The Kislar Aga was indeed a precious jewel. When she had shown him the book of the Forbidden Pleasures and asked him what he thought about it, he simply laughed and asked for the second volume where two women seduced a man.

He was indeed a wise man and a credit to his race. A promiscuous man's dreams could not be contained in one book. Always something was left out to provide employment to another, even more imaginative author. Unfortunately he didn't know how to write, but he could narrate very vividly, how he seduced his many wives in his native hut. She was not the only one who heard his stories. According to his claims, this was the way he used to keep concubines from complaining, and it had never failed. He was so audacious he even claimed humans were not offspring of gods or Allah, but of a certain breed of meat-eating monkeys that lived in herds and roamed the savannahs in search of food like the Tatars and Turks. These monkeys had also Sultans and harems, but when their Sultans aged and became weak, their harems were usurped by more potent males that turned the old Sultans into slaves younger males of the herd used as sex toys, when females were not available to provide relief.

****

The very next day Suleiman, still overflowing with confidence, asked Princess Hatidge to pay him a visit. These two close relatives of his had not particularly close relations, as men and women lived in different worlds in Constantinople since the days of the Romans. Since the age of circumcision, the boys had more freedom of movement in the city and the countryside, and in the case of Suleiman, future military obligations forced him to spend much of his life in tents.

On the other hand, Hatidge Sultan's life was restricted from the outset between the Eski and the Edirne Seraglio, while few sorties in the streets and bazaars of the City almost always in closed carriages heavily escorted and only on holidays. Thus, the hours they were both living under the same roof were very limited. Their relation allowed by Ayin was largely formal, without the usual cordiality characterizing the relations between close relatives of ordinary people, constantly sharing both space and time.

Hatidge entering the Sultan's apartment, stood awkwardly in front of her brother. She had prepared her appearance several hours before her visit. She had studied not only what to say, but even what to wear. She ought to wear a modest dress highlighting her beauty, as beauty was a desirable asset for every woman because it impacted the minds of men like a powerful rejuvenating drug. Today she had to convince the Sultan she was no longer the irresolute maiden he remembered during her first marriage who followed the commands of her unbending father, but an adult woman who knew exactly what she wanted without appearing unrefined or vulgar. After all he was no Selim the Grim.

She had picked up from her closet a dress made of purple Bursa silk brocade with low cut neckline exposing her frustrated femininity; but, to show she was a Princess and entirely different than any of the promiscuous concubines who tried to attract the Sultan's attention for a night, a dense cover made of white lace protected her full blossoming breasts that manly eyes should not penetrate unrestricted. It was indeed a dress made according to the Prophet's command that a woman should not expose to the public scrutiny anything but her face, leaving the imagination to complement all the unseen details that set her apart from other women of her age. Her brother should surely appreciate the sincerity of her appearance. After all she was the widow of a rich Pasha, and she had everything a distinguished man needed to become inspired and knew how to present it. Despite her youthful looks, her two children proved she was not a naïve virgin any more, but an experienced warrior in the battle of the sexes who had already claimed the life of a less capable opponent.

Present during Hatidge's crucial visit was their mother Hafsa. The reigning Valide Sultan would not miss the opportunity to underline her newly acquired status and influence, as Hafsa had successfully wrestled this title the moment Selim expired.

Hafsa Sultan did not wish to leave the Princess alone, in case something escaped that could threaten her plan. But now, as Hatidge was standing in front of her brother, the Sultan seemed uncomfortable as if he had forgotten what he wanted to say and how he should exercise his absolute authority. She was kind enough though to pay her respects by kneeling in front of his throne with respect as if he was Allah.

Indeed, after his coronation Suleiman had ceased to be just an ordinary Ottoman Sultan from Anatolia and the Balkans. He had now become also a religious leader, the Caliph of Islam and the Shadow of Allah on Earth, a powerful icon worthy of the honor of prostration. However, Suleiman did not wish his authority to spoil the warm family atmosphere, so he quickly got up to his feet and grasping both her hands firmly, he pull her up and set her straight on her feet. He had not seen her so close for a long time, and his sister was at an age, when every passing day changed her looks as a bud that opens its petals and becomes a rose overnight. And he was not willing to let anyone deny him the pleasure to be confronted by a fragrant flower.

She was rather slim but sufficiently curvy to fulfill the dominant Oriental female beauty standard. She also had fine features and a long black hair flowing freely down her spine all the way to her waist that amplified rather than concealed her apparent sensuality.

Her dark eyes were slightly slit and along with the dyed red protruding apples were undeniable signs that part of her blood had reached Constantinople all the way from the endless Parthian steppes between the Black and the Caspian Sea.

Wishing to appear playful and familiar, he asked her with a pretentiously austere tone, if she had any complaints from the services of any slave in the Eski Saray, so he could punish him as severely as he deserved.

Hatidge Sultan lifted her head and looked at him straight in the eye. Her black eyes, shining behind the veil like basalt, revealed better than anything else her resolution unbending like steel and reminded him the eyes of his father. It was a grim reminder of the old days that forced him to unconsciously lower his gaze like a child caught doing something naughty.

"Your information is true to the last word. These damned Eunuchs in the Eski Saray are hardly the proper company for me now that I became a widow by Selim Khan's will. They talk too much and they are the source of all sorts of vicious rumors that damages my reputation. Thus, I need the most discrete page of yours to keep me company at night. I met him by chance, and I feel he is the right kind of slave my needs. I believe his name is Ibrahim and he is not a eunuch. From what I heard he is a good counselor with superior wit, and an excellent collocutor. Chatting is just what a widow like me needs to forget the executed father of her children," she demanded with conviction and her tone of her voice and attitude had lost at once every trace of submissiveness she displayed before; on the contrary, she had the style of a victor imposing his terms, even though under the circumstances it was just a show-off counteracting his pretentious display of absolute authority.

Suleiman tried to smile-off his embarrassment, but her all-demanding expression did not change at all to suit his wishes.

"Do you wish a slave to serve you or another husband?" he asked in amazement, trying to regain his repose.

She understood his inner thoughts and her demanding style softened to give him some breathing space.

"You are my guardian and my Sultan; so, you should decide what kind of husband is best suited for me; but whoever he is, he should know that my heart shall belong to this Ibrahim slave of yours for as long as I wish."

It was another answer his sister posed to subtly test the limits of his determination.

"My wish is to reach a fair decision, even if it's difficult, that completely satisfies my beloved sister who seems to desire to leave my household for the second time."

Hafsa thought she had heard everything till then in the Harem, but she was mistaken. The blood of Selim running in Hatidge veins had spoken loud and clear, as she calmly replied:

"If Your Highness does not wish to marry me with anyone else because of politics, please lend me Pargali Ibrahim as my slave for as long as I want his services! I can't stand any more being surrounded by eunuchs," she replied aggressively, making Sultana's cheeks turn red.

Suleiman more remained silent contemplating just for few moments which would be the best solution to this conflict of interest. Then, he calmly replied that if she was so determined to have this slave, she would have to marry him to keep her reputation intact. Ibrahim was a Pasha now, but he was still his slave; so, he would belong to her to use as she pleased after the marriage ceremony.

He sincerely hoped that all would end there; but she had not finished all her terms.

"If you wish to retain him as your slave, then this decision is something you must announce to your precious slave and Pasha! He has to hear from your lips that for as long as I wish, among his other duties, is to follow my orders too," she replied, emphasizing her words one by one, and her tone was stern, indicating she meant exactly what she was saying.

It was an outrageous demand by a woman, but completely legitimate in all cases where two masters decided to share the services of a slave. Slaves were another piece of furniture masters could share according to their own arrangements.

When Hafsa Sultan and Princess Hatidge returned after considerable time to their apartments in the Eski Saray, Suleiman took a deep breath and sighed with relief. They had discussed everything about the wedding, from the immense dowry the bride and the groom would possess after the ceremony to the tiniest details of the wedding parade. Arguing against two women who knew exactly what they were asking for, any objection was condemned from the beginning. In the end however, they all agreed the marriage would be a good opportunity to demonstrate the empire's wealth and military might to friends and enemies alike. The marriage expenses were not a critical issue since Selim Khan had occupied the country of the Nile, because all the taxes from Egypt went directly to the Sultan's treasury.

The only concession he managed to extract from this bargaining in return of all the expenses of the marriage, was the right of Ibrahim's ownership, despite Hafsa's suggestion to buy him off. He would never give up this priceless acquisition no matter how many silver coins someone offered him. Now all they had to do was to announce the family decisions to Ibrahim the slave.

****

When Ibrahim started his steep ascent from Makbil of the Sultan to Hasodabashi and Pasha and from Beylerbey to Vizier, the degree of independence from his master gradually increased. These offices were not simply honorary titles, but accompanied with significant financial rewards. The affluent Ottoman state established by Fatih and developed by Selim had very high expectations from all the slaves of the Sultan, and any special service was rewarded by exceptional rewards to attract the best officials. Now Ibrahim had the financial capacity to spend his own money and satisfy his daily needs that made life more comfortable and bearable.

After the ceremony, the most important of all his assets would be a sumptuous palace to reside he and Hatidge Sultan and later, why not, their children. Certainly he did not wish to reside too far away from the side of Suleiman. The imperial power was like the sun and the closer someone approached the more light he reflected; but, he had to be careful approaching it so that he would not burn his wings in the flames. Thus, he chose to build his palace on the At Meidan next to Agia Sophia to be close to both the Divan and the Seraglio, if something happened and his services were urgently needed.

This marriage was a great boost for his confidence despite its drawbacks. Soon there would be no official in the Seraglio with Turkish blood who would not envy his position and would not try in every possible way to undermine it with whispers in the corridors. Despite being anonymous, sooner or later these rumors were bound to reach the ears of the Sultan, but this was not great concern of his, as he was just a slave and everything his was doing was to serve his master. Already they had tried to spread rumors about his alleged love affairs with other men, but the idea proved unsuccessful, as never anything as serious could escape the eye of the Sultan's spies that followed him closely day and night, when he wandered away from Topkapi.

When that approach failed, they had tried unsuccessfully to challenge his leadership skills. Now that none of these plans had worked out, he suspected they would try to undermine the confidence of the Sultan spreading rumors he had secret contacts with the enemies of the Empire, Venice and Charles, the Roman Emperor in Spain or the Persian Shah. He was not particularly worried of any such conspiracy, because he had confidence in his abilities. He did not believe that among these boorish and uneducated pashas with the unsophisticated minds there would be someone who could surpass him in intrigue. Anyway, Orient without intrigue would be awfully boring for his intellect.

****

Ibrahim did not expect Hafsa's invitation so soon, but he should. Tatars were famous for the suddenness of their raids. This time her approach was much friendlier. When she saw him entering she got up, and he closed the door behind him, she rushed into his arms.

"I have very pleasant news," she assured him. "In two months Hatidge will become your wife. My son was no match for her firm determination. You must have really made a good impression to my daughter for her to fight so hard for your hand."

"I'm very happy to hear it because she has enslaved my heart too."

"This marriage is going to change many things. I hope you realize that. My daughter is a very demanding woman and she knows exactly what she wants."

"This must be a family trade," he replied with a long friendly smile. "A master must know what he may ask from a slave, and if this is within the slave's capabilities."

"I'm very glad I don't have to waste time to elaborate further on this issue. I will only say this. When this marriage is finally consumed, my daughter's wishes will be your commands."

"And what if her commands are contrary to my Sultan's?" he asked teasingly.

"Inside the Topkapi Seraglio the Sultan is the Shadow of Allah. He commands and we all have to obey."

"What happens here, in the Eski Saray? Who is in command here?" he asked knowing in advance the answer.

"In here I'm the Shadow of the Sultan. Whoever crosses this gate will have to answer only to me," she noted firmly, but it was clear she was going to be reasonable.

"I want you to know, because sooner or later it will reach your ears that I have tried to buy you off, so that no one blames the Sultan for having an intimate friend he calls occasionally in his room, but I failed. Nevertheless, I believe he has decided to appoint another Hasodabashi in your place, a real eunuch this time. Hatidge made certain your nightly visits to her brother quarters will be sparse from now on. The Sultan has also agreed to build a palace for her sister on At Meidan as a dowry. Behind its gates you will be her slave. This is our deal."

"I don't mind serving her needs as a woman. Women are made to have children and I would love to have few children too of my very own."

"I'm very glad to hear it. This is indeed the divine duty of every married couple."

****

Mahidevran seemed delighted to see Ibrahim bow his back in front of her, and he was equally glad to relay the message he was carrying. She was invited tonight to the Topkapi Saray. He was about to excuse himself and leave when she stopped him with a question.

"Is it true everything I hear about you?" she asked vaguely.

"I am not sure. In every piece of news I hear about these days there are many things that are true, but there are also few lies and several exaggerations."

His dubious answer triggered her curiosity.

"What do you consider as an exaggeration?"

"Eunuchs say your lust exceeds even your beauty. This is the reason the Sultan does not see you as often as he should, and prefers to invite Hurrem whose lust is more manageable."

"That's a damn lie. She is the lusty bitch. This is what every eunuch you'll ask will testify. No one in the Harem knows what kind of tricks she plays to win the Sultan over, even now that she is breastfeeding her daughter," she replied in anger.

"As a Hasodabashi I believe only what I see with my own eyes; but I will do my best to find out. I promise you," Ibrahim reassured her calmly.

"And what have you seen with your own eyes, ex-Hasodabashi?" she replied pressing on her interrogation, making perfectly clear that her sources of information were reliable.

She knew he had advanced to a higher and less controversial post. Having an able man as a Hasodabashi had been too much of risk for his master so he made him a Pasha with military duties. Nevertheless, he was not mad to reveal all he knew about Hurrem; so, he bypassed her inquiry with a hint rather than a revelation.

"I have seen many things, but what puzzled me most was when I saw there were few licentious women who would rather blind a Hasodabashi with a towel than let him witness their rare moments of weakness," he replied with an imperceptible smile.

"This is how a man would describe the scene; but, my trusty informants claim in the end this blessed man gladly capitulated in front of superior forces, surrendering willingly all his essence. Even a powerful army does not have any hope when it's surrounded. A Pasha should know as much and stop fighting?"

"Yes, it is! I wish there was a way I could prove both your informants wrong, but till then I may need a lot of training."

Mahidevran could not resist the temptation. She could only postpone it.

"Behold! Maybe in another space and time every wish of ours will be granted by Allah," she said choosing to remain uncommitted and leave Kismet take command of their destiny.

It was a reasonable standpoint under the circumstances. Mahidevran was the Sultan's Kadin and he was just a slave who had a meteoric rise that could just as easily be reversed. She simply could not put all her trust in his words. He had to win her confidence step by step, exchanging favors and information.

"People in the bazaars claim she is poisoning him with erotic filters made from hyena's glands, but I don't trust hearsay."

"All rumors have a trace of truth to make them believable. In the Manisa bazaar such a rumor claimed you were the favorite slave of a rich widow. Was it ever possible? As far as the eunuchs say in the Seraglio, back then you were their best student," Mahidevran asked with an expression of profound disbelief.

Was she referring to Princess Hatidge as the widow or someone else?

"Your informants are correct. Show me a young man who claims he is not attracted by young widows, and I will show you a damned liar. Allah made widows an easy prey for bold men like me."

"Good references can go a long way in a harem where frustration and boredom reigns supreme. We all know there are few widows in this Saray. Are they all under the ultimate peril of seduction by a bold man?" she asked him teasingly.

"Allah the Benevolent blesses every man who eases the pains of a widow."

"This is not what I've witnessed. Your eyes don't make many distinctions. They keep searching deep inside every woman's bosom every chance they have. This is why I still consider you an infidel who pays no attention to what the Holy Quran says," Mahidevran teased him.

"This is one explanation but not the only one. After all these years away from home in slavery, I must be missing my mother," he said mocking her tease.

"Aren't you a bit too adventurous? What will the Sultan say if he finds out you are mesmerized by his women?" she asked adopting his teasing style.

"I don't know what he might say, but if I was him, I would be flattered. Having the most attractive concubines in his harem is a worthy cause for anyone to become a Sultan."

"That's what men say, but women feel otherwise. The more concubines a Sultan has the more disappointed all his women would be, as it happened with Selim Khan and the moment he died Hafsa Hatun became Hafsa Sultan. This is a very unfair attitude a Kadin who knows her worth will not accept for long."

"That's a fair complaint and as a Hasodabashi I did whatever I could to keep both his Kadin happy. Buying more sinful concubines was not my choice but Hafsa's. I hope my replacement will follow my example."

"As far as I know both the Sultan's Kadin have no complaints from your attitude, and I did all I could to reward you for your consideration," Mahidevran remarked with an imperceptible smile. "I don't know if you have ever felt it, but noble women can be very supportive to any logical ambition of a man, if his dreams are their dreams too. This is what being noble is about. You must be fair and reward your courtiers according to their performance."

It was a curious statement that set Ibrahim's mind in motion. Mahidevran had already a son named Mustafa she obviously dreamed that one day he would become the next Sultan. It was a natural ambition as Mustafa was Suleiman's firstborn son and had the best chances of reigning.

Among all his impossible dreams of imperial grandeur he would never have dared to include such a fate for his unborn son. What kind of common dreams among a man and a woman was she referring to? Was it possible she was referring to the dreams Hatidge had for her sons he might share in the near future?

Since she was a Princess, any son of hers would also have Osman's blood in his veins. For the time being he had no son, while the Sultan had two, but no one but Allah knew what time might bring. The recent two deaths was an indication of the drastic changes life could bring about without a warning.

****

Meeting Mahidevran was always a challenge for him. She was so desirable it was hard for any man not to start daydreaming; but, she was also very bright. With her attitude she was encouraging a bold man to make bold dreams. Under these conditions a man could do nothing but do her favors, hopping that one day she might return the favors.

Since a Sultan preferred younger women, it was almost certain he would die well ahead of them, leaving many mourning widows behind seeking relief. The Harem had fair rules, after few months of mourning every widow except the Sultan's mother could seek a new husband. Was he Mahidevran's dream as much as she was his?

Women in the imperial Harem had to dream luscious dreams to remain faithful, while the Sultan had every chance to make his modest dreams come true as often as he pleased. Becoming a Sultan's favorite was an unfair deal. Nothing had been said clearly inside the Harem, but unconsciously having as a Hasodabashi a complete young man was a logical choice. It was very unfortunate he had to abandon this post after his oncoming marriage; but being too greedy may not be the safest policy.

****

Full of questions this afternoon Ibrahim took the ferry and passed across to Galata on foot, as the steep uphill passages practically excluded riding horses in this district. If this was the sole reason why European sailors favored this isolated suburb of the City of Constantine it was doubtful, as the freedom to drink wine was a graver reason to be considered among few others as taverns for sailors had become very licentious places only the Galata district allowed. On the contrary, brothels constantly popped up around the Eski Saray and the Janissary Barracks where also the Grand Bazaar and the many inns were also located.

The continuous contact with the Ottomans and their oppressed state of mind under the Islamic Laws depressed him too, and occasionally he felt the need to breathe more freely even for just a little while. The interaction with them was intolerably dull with very few exceptions. He could not predict the future, but until then the Ottoman contribution to the human civilization had been limited to belly dancing and a shadowy puppet show.

Their ideas about new ways to progress were also too conservative for his taste, without any possibility of exceeding the limits of the strict Muslim religion. This was a severe restriction that did not help them evolve as rigorously as they should. Even the measurement of time was restricted by the agents of religion, the Muezzins, who governed their lives based on the five prayers of the day no one should miss according to the Prophet's instructions he purposely failed to follow.

In all their discussions, the constant reference to proverbs and the wise advices of elders and heroes of the Islamic tradition was equally unbearable. He believed that every nation that was building its future by looking only backwards, it would surely stumble sooner or later on the first obstacle it found on its path. Even the naive idea that Allah, a supreme omnipotent being, had chosen among all the people on the Earth an illiterate trader of Mecca to reveal his commandments on how people should act and live, when so many brilliant spirits had passed away in the Orient, was incompatible with his Roman logic.

Of course, at this point of his life he could not find more convincing the Christian beliefs about the divinity of another Illiterate Jewish carpenter from humble Galilee. At least the god the Jews had chosen to manifest his ten commandments was a gifted leader, a Prince of Egypt, Moses. For these reasons he felt much closer to the dishonored Zeus who favored with his seed only beautiful Princesses, lusty Queens and handsome youngsters, giving a worthy example to his followers to imitate and emulate.

Since the first day of his life he could remember, his mind obeyed the power of doubt and reason, so he could not accept either the superiority of the misguided Christian faith with the foolishness of the Holy Trinity, or the insane contradiction between religious faith and human reason preached by the Sunni Muslims. For him, if God existed, he had to be unique and impartial, favoring none against the other, leaving meritocracy to dominate survival and progress. The only question still open was what kind of merits was important for prosperity.

Of course, all these views he had kept strictly for himself, as he did not dare to express them openly even to his friend and Sultan before being fully convinced his mind was ripe for such radical ideas. He had a very good reason for this cautious approach. From the very first day he had realized Suleiman had the false impression the Osman family was something divine that set them apart from the uncultured hordes of Turks that had demolished the Eastern Roman Empire, a lonely bright spot among the great variety of barbarians that came to Asia Minor.

Unquestionably his master Suleiman was a special man. Like his father he was intelligent enough to promote merit, and he was as just as Selim was, but considerably more sensitive. He also had imagination he expressed in many ways. Despite his warlike attitude, he liked fine arts too and valued a great variety of human virtues, as loyalty, wisdom, beauty and creative power.

However, sometimes Suleiman's way of thinking spooked him, because he was a combination of the trends of his parents. He was devoted to his mission as his father, but he was also benevolent and kind hearted as his mother who as soon as she became a widow, she started spending Selim's looted riches for the benefit of her subjects. If Selim was just, she was too and the combination of this common virtue made Suleiman a just sovereign despite his immense authority that if sidetracked, it could easily lead him to excesses.

At every given moment Suleiman was equally capable of the best and the worst, if he felt this was a just reward or a severe punishment for an act a subject of his had committed. From the moment his subjects complained, his action to repair the damage to his image and honor as a supreme ruler was swift and remorseless. In a strict way he was right, but on the other hand, mistakes could be made by anyone anytime, even by the Shadow of Allah. Something that seemed fair for a man might be considered extreme for another.

Under a certain prospective their relationship was contrary to common logic, but on the other hand, considering they were both extraordinary men with exceptional virtues, they deserved something special too.

For any Grand Vizier, becoming the husband of a Princess was normal and easily digestible by the common man, but why should such a high official refuse the services of pretty courtiers like Mahidevran's Zarafet and Yabani too, for instance?

Every man had weaknesses and there were adventurous women eager and capable to exploit them and reversely. Who would dare to go against the will of Allah the Benevolent who blessed every creature that did his best to make another creature happy? Which Muslim should deny Allah of more soldiers to spread the word of his Prophet? Who would refuse the master's the right to have more slaves? Who could blame a benevolent man who tried to ease the loneliness of a widow or possibly satisfy the urges of a beautiful Kadin neglected by heartless husband seduced by a devilish concubine?

With very little effort he could find a thousand similar excuses to explain the Sultan the reasons for his escapades; but he knew well that if Suleiman felt he had offended his honor, he would not hesitate to execute him as any other offender. The Sultan was a hypocrite, but every human being was too without a doubt. Having limits was the honorable prerequisite the Prophet Mohamed obliged his faithful to have, but wisely enough he had failed to define them. These mysterious limits had nothing to do with race, skin color or religion. It was simply a matter of point of reference, as everyone saw the world from his own prospective. Even the most ugly and repulsive rascal would become furious if his children didn't look like him.

However, what looked like a blessing could also become a curse in another occasion. Suleiman was singular no doubt, but he was a Sultan and no one should dare say it at his face.

In a sense he was singular too, but he had a good excuse. He was a slave and in theory he had no will of his own. The sole truth was that he was a hypocrite too. He never regretted what he had done or what he was forced to do. He would have done the same because he liked variety, and in that respect he resembled the Sultan. His only drawback was his birth as a slave.

Now after many very stressing moments, he was on his way to glory. It was natural for him to feel free, and become bolder with every higher position he acquired. It was not just his boldness that made the difference, but also the fear and the power he projected all around him that made other people behave submissively to his will. Women were the first to acknowledge his superior virtues. If Asphodel had become now his most trusted associate, it had to be a further recognition of his superiority. Most people were like dogs eager to find a patron to serve, anyway, and for him having a eunuch under his authority was like stealing a bit of Selim's authority.

Passing across the Galata with the ferry, had fooled the Sultan's spy following closely every move he made for several months. When the Sultan revealed this fact to him, he was originally surprised and offended. He even blushed from shame for all the despicable acts he might have done that deserved the expenses of a personal spy; but, soon enough the Sultan offered him an excuse. He trusted him, but he had given him the honor of a spy to protect him, as recently a piece of reliable information had reached his ears on the existence of a conspiracy against his life.

At first Suleiman's attitude had flattered his coquetry, but eventually he felt once more ashamed. What kind of treachery his friend suspected against him? He couldn't have suspected his harem escapades, because there was no way a spy could follow him inside the Eski Saray. Inside the Topkapi, he was also followed everywhere by eunuchs until the bedroom door closed and the pages dismissed. The Sultan was a jealous fool. Simply locking the door of your bedroom in the presence of a man was all the proof needed for rumors to spread. Sneaking in the Harem was also forbidden, but a Hasodabashi needed no permit to go anywhere, even the Eski Saray.

It was his duty to visit any concubine he felt would please his master. Giving him this post was the best proof the Sultan had no suspicions of any fallacious behavior in his harem.

The announcement of his marriage must have been a revelation for his dear friend. How could the Princess know enough of his virtues to desire him as a husband? She was not a romantic, virgin fool. She was a widow full of experiences. She had also a very intimate Nubian courtier, Basmi. Who knows what kind of orgies Basmi had witnessed with his Princess? They were among the very few who could go for a stroll in the Grand Bazaar whenever they felt like it.

He suddenly stopped and burst into an uncontrollable laughter. He was going crazy. His rampant imagination was blowing up his mind. He felt everyone was as lusty and sinful as he was, but the truth was that every human being was unique. It meant that people around him could be less or even more licentious than he was.

He looked around and saw a cheap whore staring him from a window of the second floor. She must have heard his laughter and went out to see who that happy fellow may be. She did not seem to know who he was, as for the time being very few people had seen his face. Soon, when he had become the Grand Vizier and the Princess' husband, many people would recognize him and would have to walk the Galata streets in disguise surrendering much of his freedom. Through this entire evening he wanted to be left alone and perfectly free to think without interruptions. Since he had set foot in this city, the district of Galata was the one he unconsciously never wished to visit. It was there he would end up, if Suleiman had not purchased him. Now with the days of his marriage approaching, he realized how important was to have the freedom to make your own choices.

He had not yet decided what he wanted and neither knew where to find it. This far he had been wandering through the streets in an unfamiliar area, hoping that sooner or later his inspiration would make its appearance. The professional enchantresses with the European clothes that smiled defiantly in the entrances of taverns and whorehouses did everything they could to keep his optimism alive with their glances. Many were slaves brought to Galata from distant countries, while others showed they had arrived consciously and willingly desperate to make a living; but, all of them were not wearing scarfs in their hair, meaning that the oldest profession in the world was not included among the popular choices of Muslim women. However, all of these women seemed eager to have him as a customer. Were his looks that attracted them or his expensive clothes? This was one of the disadvantages whores had compared to ordinary women. A man would never know if he was really attractive to a prostitute, unless they gave him a free ride.

Beside them the gate of a steam bath was open that promised relief from the pressure of everyday life with all the distinct treatments a young man's hands could offer. He had little time to think and decide what would be his final choice. Now that Suleiman was lost from the face of the Earth, he was completely free to choose. The hammam was for him as familiar as the palm of his hand, while with whores he had still many unanswered questions to sort out.

He felt his cheeks blush as he realized a cute whore was winking at him, waiting for him to make a decision. He hated making decisions under pressure.

To make things even more difficult a pretty boy appeared from the dark interior of the hammam. Maybe if he had more time, he would make a more sensible decision, now the boy exerted the most powerful attraction as all the women for rent were mediocre specimens compared to the exquisite creatures of the Harem.

He had to admit he was a very weak character, whenever he was feeling lonely and felt the need to be loved. Love was a feeling people shared when they needed energy and optimism to face the future. He was certain he could love Mahidevran, Hatidge, or even Hurrem under different circumstances; but they were not there to take him into their arms and reciprocate his tender feelings. They were away restricted by all sorts of bindings, protected by formidable fortress he had to breach to satisfy his urge to be loved, the most natural feeling of a lonely slave.

On the contrary, this boy was at an arm's length smiling at him, eager to show him that he was willing to share an hour of his life for a minimal fee and no hassle. Under these strenuous circumstances he was a bargain.

****

Hurrem never had the chance to see a White Eunuch from so close, so she spent few extra moments to measure the effects of his misfortune. His face had some of the sweetness of a woman. It was nothing that had to do with the excessive red dye he used on his cheeks, the shadows on his eyelids or the red color of his lips. It was something deeper only her femininity could fathom. Despite his good looks he stirred no reaction.

Why did the Kislar Aga asked her to meet him it was not clear yet. Asphodel was supposed to possess secrets that could tumble the Empire, but the Aga had not offered her more clues of what to ask him. He only assured her he had done his best to drag them out, but he had failed. Now it was up to her to try.

"You may not know it, but I wish to become your friend, a very close friend," she noted with a friendly smile, but she didn't notice any change in his blunt expression. He was probably thinking that the friendship of a concubine did not mean much for a White Eunuch of his high stature, so he didn't even bother to break his silence.

"Do you like women?" she ventured next and he rewarded her attempt with an ironic smile.

"Are you in love with him?" she continued following a sudden inspiration. This time she saw a sparkle in his eyes.

"I'm too," she admitted, "but there is nothing I can do about it."

"No, you can!" he replied firmly. "You can wait! Even this will pass," he snapped back referring to the common advice for perseverance from the Quran.

"I'm not that patient. I need relief as quickly as possible. Am I too greedy?" she asked exposing her breast. "Please help me out right now."

****

Suddenly without any warning a familiar figure from the past burst-in in front of him in the distance. He immediately recognized the stranger from his unusually broad shoulder cut. He was Sinan, the tall Janissary who had spared him from the blade in the Avret Bazar that fateful day, when his fate had changed so dramatically. Since then he considered him a lucky charm.

He decided to follow him and if he found the right opportunity, to approach and talk to him. The Janissary peeked briefly at him, but he did not seem to recognize his face. The day was cold and the hood of his cloak covered with its shadow his complexion. With a fast pace the Janissary arrived at the threshold of a mosque, washed his hands and feet at the fountain, left the rustic shoes at the entrance and disappeared in the opening beneath the heavy leather cover that hid the interior from the eyes of the occasional passersby.

Mosques always scared Ibrahim since he was a boy. He connected them with the devşirme and the evil people who came to his village to grab the children of Christians. He still remembered the advice of his mother: "Do not pass near them, when you are going to the priest's house."

It was the only school in the village. Now he was a Muslim too and a Vizier had nothing to fear inside a mosque. Moreover, in the City of Constantine five decades of cohabitation had mitigated most of the religious differences. Now even the Christians of the city could enter into a mosque if they wished to, provided they did not agitate the prayer of the faithful of Allah, and removed their shoes respecting the cleanness and the sanctity of the temple.

For Muslims getting into a Christian church had never been a problem since the moment Mehmet Fatih broke in the Agia Sophia on horseback; but, now most of them respectfully entered Christian churches that had no rugs to soil. Christ was for Islam an important prophet who had spoken about the one, true God, like Muhammad had done and Moses.

For the Muslims Jesus was not the son of God, as Allah had neither sons nor daughters. He also never handed lilies to beautiful women like Zeus. Jesus was a Jew who had died on the cross in the hands of the Romans, suffering all the weaknesses of the flesh, while Allah was an all-powerful spirit that had molded the entire world in six days. Religions were an accurate measure of people's naiveté.

Ibrahim realized Jesus had no special magic powers the day he was told how the Eternal City, the most magnificent bastion of Christianity for a thousand years, had fallen in the hands of the believers of Allah. This simply meant that believing in Allah's power made more sense under the circumstances. It was simply another case where one belief became dangerous while another beneficial.

He pulled-off his boots and walked in too, pushing aside the leather cover of the door. It was prayer time and all men inside were sitting on the carpet, forming a circle in the middle of the mosque under the central dome to hear the sermon.

Ibrahim reading the Islamic inscriptions on the walls realized that he had unintentionally entered a mosque of Mevlevi Order, a mystic sect following the principles of Sufism. They got their name from Rumi, the poet they called Mevlevana, and followed his teachings that considered love an extremely important element of human life.

He did too believe in the power of love; however, the Orthodox Islam of the Sunnis looked suspiciously at any sect that added new meanings to the words of Quran. Nevertheless, in Suleiman's empire certain dervish orders had been allowed to exist and prosper, since with their benevolent work and charities helped turning infidels into faithful.

His first reaction was to turn back and flee; but now the Janissary had recognized him, and with a gesture invited him to sit in the empty space next to him to close the circle.

Ibrahim did not wish to appear rude or coward without a good reason, so he followed his suggestion. Soon enough an aged Imam appeared, sat at the center of the circle, and began to read the sermon from a manuscript book with gold bindings.

Arabic was often used in the Seraglio in elaborate religious speeches and very few words were unknown to him. Usually the meanings of the sermons were simple, and he had no trouble understanding the fundamental concepts of the teachings. This sermon suggested the faithful should struggle constantly in a great war with himself, Al-Jihad-al-Akbar. He had to try for his remaining life to avoid committing acts either in a state of rage, or exclusively for his personal satisfaction. Only under these rules it would be possible for any follower of the sect to achieve the completion of his inner self. This completion was possible only through the union with Allah the Omnipresent.

This was in fact the only way a man could hope to escape the feeling of depression which brings in a man's thought the inevitable prospect of death. His association with Allah was the sole purpose for a man to succeed in life.

To Ibrahim this entire sermon sounded contrary to what he believed in and sought after. For him personal satisfaction was the source from which he drew the essential energy to keep on living, and without it his life would lose its meaning. He thought of leaving the mosque, but curiosity for the unknown kept him stuck in his place. Sultan Selim had not been wrong. At critical moments in his life curiosity had showed him which path to follow.

In his case, total submission to the will of the Shadow of Allah was his conscientious choice, in a similar way as Islam demanded every faithful should do to the will of Allah. The other choice he had rejected was to resist Selim Khan and face the consequences. Selim had most graciously accepted his submission and rewarded him with a lucrative position next to his son.

Perhaps his total submission was the telltale sign Selim demanded that he would never betray his son or the entire House of Osman; however, he was still wandering what would have happened if he had decided to refuse him that night.

Now in this mosque the answer became crystal clear. Despite Rumi's teachings of the beneficial effects of love, his suspicions were fully vindicated. As Selim Khan was no Rumi, if he dared to resist, he would be raped, looted and discarded into the Bosporus Straights. This kind of fate was not particular to either Islam or Selim. The Christian Cross had applied similar or even harsher dilemmas, as even after total submission death was administered by its Crusader Knights, as he had witnessed in Rhodes. Submitting to Islam was the right choice for him. Selim was cruel but he was also just and rewarded both submission and excellence.

Islam was not ideal, but it was definitely an improvement over the Christianity of his era.

****

When the sermon was finally over, one of the faithful began to play a slow piece with a flute and immediately few followers stood up and started spinning slowly with outstretched hands. Symbolically one palm was facing the Earth and the other the sky. Gradually the rotating speed increased until the entire floor under the small dome was full of bodies spinning with absolute accuracy around invisible axes.

He retreated to the background not to be in anyone's way, as the pace gradually quickened. Then, he noticed for the first time the smell of burning opium in a censer with the narcotic incense mixed with other aromatic herbs. The smoke gradually filled the room until he could hardly distinguish the dancers still swirling incessantly. He started feeling smothered and unbearably dizzy as the entire room started spinning around him.

Through the dense fog he noticed a swarthy form coming menacingly towards him holding a sharp blade. He tried to defend himself, but he discovered he was unable to move any of his members. He felt an unbearable pain inundating his being, and then he saw a torrent of blood discharged as a fountain, painting the walls red. Together with his blood his life was slipping away from him too. It was strange how calm he felt as the oncoming death was welcomed by his brain, because as he drew closer the awful pain declined too.

Bathed in cold sweat he collapsed unconscious on the mat.

****

The first image he saw when he opened his eyes was the bearded face of the Janissary. He was bending over him, trying to cool his forehead with cold water.

The flute had stopped blowing and as he looked around, he noticed the small mosque was now empty too. Unknowingly he touched his body looking for huge open wound, but he found it intact. He tried to get up, but his legs betrayed him and buckled.

He would have fallen on the floor, if the strong hands of the Janissary did not hold him straight. He relied on them and made a few uncertain steps. Gradually, he regained his strength and went stumbling out of the mosque to the courtyard. He took a few deep breaths and the cold air helped him take back control of his senses.

"Thank you!" he uttered, but he did not get any response.

He tried to start a conversation.

"What's your name?" he asked the soldier and this time got a comprehensive answer.

"I'm Sinan from Ağırnas!"

"Are you Greek?" he asked him again.

"My parents were Greek. Now I'm as much Greek as you are."

It was an ambiguous answer he ought to expect from a Janissary.

"I've never imagined a Janissary could ever become a Dervish."

"Dervish in Persian means 'someone who is threading on the edge.' The edge is the threshold between human consciousness and the world of God. Even a Grand Vizier can sometime become Dervish as long as he wants to submit wholly to the word of the Prophet."

Ibrahim did not want to hear of another submission and he changed topic.

"I will never forget what you did for me in Avret Bazar, I owe you my life."

"Whatever I did that day, I did it because it had to be done, and not to win praises. To become a Dervish one does not need to keep torturing his self by remembering unpleasant past events. Each tribulation that does not kill us makes us stronger; so we should be glad we have encountered it; but, no matter how many such tests we might pass, eventually we all are going to die; thus, the very last test is the most crucial."

The tone of Sinan's voice was manly and despite his high position Sinan talked to him as if they were equal, two comrades and friends from long time ago. It was a pleasant change from the strict ritual of submission imposed in the Seraglio or by Islam.

"I feel today's test brought me one step closer to my demise."

"What dream did you see tonight?"

"It must have been my death," Ibrahim replied still confused by the shocking revelation.

"If I was you, I would not pay any attention to any dreams," the Janissary reassured him. "I have seen my death many times in my dreams and it's always the same. Death is a good adviser who keeps reminding me every time I meet him in a battle that he can take me any time it pleases him."

"How did you dream your death will occur?"

"Unfortunately I am on my bed dying of old age. This is the most slow and torturous death of all and a disgrace for a Janissary. Every day that passes I lose another precious piece of mine. What was your death dream all about that scared you so much?"

"I will die drenched in blood. A sharp blade cuts the thread of my life."

"That's a handsome death and nothing to be scared of. In a few moments everything ends; nevertheless, a quick death does not leave enough time to prepare yourself for this transformation; thus, you should start planning for the best way to meet your God even now."

Ibrahim thought Sinan's aims were confusing. Now he was young in the prime of his life, and every day that passed he was searching for a different enjoyment. However, when he aged, this constant search for new pleasures would be terminated. Then, the deeply buried memories of his youth would surface to torture him, as a body that no longer functioned could not satisfy the mind's insatiable hunger ever again.

"I do not know if the dream I saw will ever come true; but, when I'll grow old, I'll have all the time in the world to begin then my own Al-Jihad-al- Akbar," Ibrahim replied with disdain.

"No! The best time for anyone to start the war with himself has already passed," the Janissary said sternly. "The remaining of your life will progress much better, if you are prepared to die in advance. If you die before you die then you will not die when you die!"

It was a confusing game with words that made sense too with many other verbs besides die.

"I cannot believe it will ever be too late for me to change my life. Anyway, the best years for a man to sin is when he is young, and to repent when he is old. When I'm old, I promise you I will start war with myself," Ibrahim argued still in an optimistic mood.

"For young or elder people age does not really matter much. A man never loses his ability to create and creation is the source of the greatest pleasure. Allah's universe is in a constant process of creation and death for all its creatures," Sinan argued in earnest.

"If creation is an enjoyment, then creating pleasure is also a worthy kind of creation, and we are talking both about the same thing in other words. However, I'd prefer to stop living the day I'll lose the ability to enjoy some kind of pleasure."

Sinan stayed skeptical for a while.

"I was sincere when I said I'd like to die the moment I'd lose the ability to create; but sadly, no one knows when the time of death will come for him and prepare in advance for his departure. You must remember how suddenly Death came and struck you down in your dream and take notice. The sooner we are united with God, the more painless the process of dying will be for us then. The road of life may be long for some people and short for others. It is unfair but injustice is inevitable. It's a road that begins when what is yours is mine too and ends when nothing in the world is either yours or mine. You'll know you have arrived at the end of your road, when you and I will become one with God and Truth, another shining speck of dust that travels through space and time among the stars of the Milky Way."

"My death will be even more painful, if until then I have not experienced all my dreams to completion."

"And I promise that if you take a step to get closer to God, he will start running to greet you."

******

The night had advanced by then, and the waning moon had risen for some time behind the mountains of Anatolia. He said Sinan goodbye and promised him to return once again to the dervish tekke; however, now he wanted to be alone and think.

The dream of death he saw had profoundly shocked him, dispersing any urge to visit the hammam; but, he was also glad he had found now someone else who could share his solemn thoughts about life and death. The open doors of the hammam inviting him with all kinds of promises exerted no attraction any longer on his enflamed flesh. Without a warning or fanfare the critical duel with his consciousness had already begun.

That night it was not particularly windy and the humidity of the Golden Horn penetrated his flesh all the way to his bones. Ibrahim pulled the cloak over his head and sunk deeper in his thoughts. Many difficult years had passed since the night the privateers had brought him "meat for sale" in the Eternal City, and he was now ready to become the Sultan's sister's groom.

He should be very pleased for the path through life he had chosen. It could raise him as high as the stars, but if he was bound to fall, it would surely be painful. Many times, even now, he felt an impulse to swap clothes with the first beggar and become lost in the crowd, without turning his glance to look behind him. He knew the hand of Sultan was long. Perhaps he could never escape remaining under Allah's Shadow.

On the other hand, his newly acquired power inside the Harem filled him with self-confidence that gradually he would be able to resist the attraction men exerted on his flesh. Now he felt he was one step before the last on his way to fulfill his destiny. His marriage with Hatidge was the antechamber to the absolute authority of the Grand Vizier. Nobody would be any longer higher than him in the Ottoman hierarchy except the Sultan himself. Long gone were the days that a handsome Janissary could summon him and use him for his pleasure.

However, this position of power was attainable for as long as he was useful to the House of Osman. Often a Vizier lost his position along with his life, if he exceeded the limits of his authority. However, this ultimate fear did not affect his daily disposition anymore. He had faced mortal danger many times along the way during this voyage by being an exception to the existing rules. Nevertheless, with each passing day raising his status became more and more risky, as he had to balance his actions and emotions with Suleiman and all the members of his household that claimed a piece of his existence.

Up to now he had tried to please everyone that showed interest to know him deeper; but which were going to be the consequences if someone felt cheated?

In the Seraglio School the teacher of history had taught him that an ancient Greek philosopher postulated that the truth could be found only deep, at the bottom of the well of knowledge, but as usual there were many interpretations to every ancient Greek oracle depending on the prevailing conditions.

****

When Ibrahim finally arrived at the Seraglio, he found a page of the Sultan again waiting by the gate to relay him a message. Suleiman was seeking for him for some reason the servant was not in a position to know. Rather worried he rushed to the apartments of the Sultan and found him in the Throne Room, the Hiounkar Sofasi to emphasize once more his authority.

He was pacing left and right visibly annoyed; so, Ibrahim bent over his back and bowed his neck in front of his master, addressing him formally as Suleiman Khan son of Selim Khan, Padisah and Caliph to show his respect and total submission. However, Suleiman angrily interrupted the lengthy address asking him with a rude tone in which hole exactly he had disappeared.

Ibrahim had no reason to hide his stroll to the Galata district and revealed his visit to the Mevlevi Mosque to pray.

"From now on", he said in a tone that allowed no objections, "and whenever you leave my side even to pray, I want to know in advance where exactly you intend to go."

Ibrahim calmly replied that he presumed he already knew what his wishes were, but he was obviously wrong. Now that the Sultan had bothered to explain what he wished, he would obey his orders to the letter.

Suleiman did not seem to be satisfied by the answer and said so in plains words.

"That's not enough for me! I should know exactly what you're doing, if you wish to keep this beautiful head of yours in place. Do not forget that no matter what you think you have accomplished, you will always be a slave I bought from the Avret Bazaar for my pleasure."

Ibrahim was alarmed discerning deeply in the eyes of Suleiman the dark pupils of his father, and once again lowered his head with submission; however, the Sultan continued undeterred:

"Don't you know that I'm fully aware of everything that happens around me? I'm the Shadow of Allah, and if anything exists, it is because I wish or I tolerate it? Do not ever imagine that any man or any woman may come between us."

Ibrahim kneeled and leaned his back even lower. He did not speak at all, because he knew that when the Sultan was angry, he always had to say the last word to be content. He had not yet reached the time to claim this right too.

Nevertheless, for the time being it appeared Suleiman had completed expressing his demands.

"Tomorrow morning, Allah's will and mine is to make you the Grand Vizier of my Empire," he announced. "My precious sister Hatidge Sultan cannot marry an ordinary Vizier like her last husband. You may have enslaved the heart of my sister, but tonight I will teach you the real meaning of what owing allegiance to the blood of Osman means."

None of what he heard from the lips of Suleiman was something new that found him unprepared. The entire debate was nothing more than a violent jealousy scene triggered by the new relationship that had begun with the Princess without his permission. Since money had no value for him, the Sultan would happily give him the greatest gifts with one hand; but, he could not bear to lose something he already owned. His marriage with Suleiman's sister was going to be a very delicate affair that would surely tax all his diplomatic skills, as not only the Sultan, but the Princess too was determined to exercise their rights.

For one more time the Osmanli proved they were extremely greedy and their desires silent and demanding. Ibrahim had to learn that the driving force of his master was not the thirst for power, for money, or for glory. It was his need for love. Everything else was just an insignificant pretext.

Fortunately for him this passion was still alive; therefore, in the depth of his eyes shone not fear, but satisfaction. He felt safe because this Sultan could never reach into his soul as deeply as his formidable father.

Chapter 8

In the Divan

**"Thee do we serve and Thee do we beseech for help.
Keep us on the right path.
The path of those upon whom Thou hast bestowed favors."
(Quran, Sura I, 5-7)**

Early next morning in an outdoor ceremony at the Gate of Salutations, Ibrahim kneeled once more by the feet of the Sultan in front of all the high officials of the Ottoman Empire.

The Great Mufti of the City of Constantine was there, together with the three lower Viziers, the Kapudan Pasha, the Aga of the Janissaries, the Aga of the Spahis, and the Agha of the Executioners. There were also representatives of all the important foreign countries and every representative of the affluent families of Turks who lived in the Eternal City.

The words of the oath of the Grand Vizier were established long time ago, and no one could change a word; so, Ibrahim took the oath with the proper dose of allegiance just as befitting the occasion.

"I swear in my life and in my head to put all my energy in the service of

the most fair and charismatic Emperor, as long as he does not withdraw His Clemency and His Excellency from the insignificance of His servant."

Finally, he did not forget to kiss the gold-embroidered boots Sultan, the edge of the kaftan and the ring with the emerald signet on the right hand of his master. Then, Suleiman took from the hands of a page, the so called the Keeper of the Sword, a gold binding damascened sword adorned with precious gems, and placed on the extended hands of Ibrahim Pasha.

Then, Suleiman Khan got up and grasping Ibrahim's hand led him to a post which was to his right. This gesture was something that was not included in the traditional ritual, and it made a deep impression on anyone who was there and watched; but, even more impressive were the words that slipped at the end from the lips of the Padisah that were also unusual.

"I swear that Ibrahim Pasha will be the Grand Vizier of the Ottomans for my entire lifetime, and if a charge against him ever reaches my ears, I'm not going to believe it."

Then the voice of the army officers was heard as they shouted together:

"Pray peace and Allah's favor always accompany you."

In prayer the arrayed soldiers then answered.

"We wish luck follows you forever! We pray Allah protects the Sultan and his Vizier, our masters."

The ceremony ended just as simply as it had begun. Everyone present bowed before the Sultan and his Grand Vizier, and left stepping backwards to avoid turning their backs to the Sultan; but Ibrahim had now the power to make every Turk obey and kneel before him.

As he had learned from the lips of Suleiman before the ceremony, to open for him the position of the Grand Vizier, the former one, Piri Mehmet Pasha, was forced to withdraw on the grounds of his advanced age.

At the same time, the lower three viziers had also waived their rights to replace him on the basis of the hierarchy, when the Sultan lay in front of them the dilemma of resigning or immediate dismissal for incompetence. Their answer to this question could only be the one the Sultan wished to hear.

Ibrahim was convinced that after this exceptional ceremony his enemies would try harder to destroy him than ever before; but, at the same time he was also now more powerful and determined to succeed in his mission, countering their actions.

Before his rise he was indeed an easy target anyone could eliminate by poisoning or simply stabbing him to death at night, if he set his mind into it. Now after this unexpectedly high promotion he was under the strong shield of the state, and any conspiracy against him could not touch him. Only the Sultan could demote the Grand Vizier, but Suleiman's oath that they would be together until the Sultan's death was binding.

He had revealed his fears the previous night to the Sultan; but, he had reassured him that once he remained loyal to his master, he had nothing in the world to fear. The word "loyal" was spoken in a very emphatic tone. Suleiman made clear that the sense of freedom and power he had gained occupying this highest post had specific limits strictly defined by the wishes of the Sultan. However, compared to everyone else, Ibrahim's power was infinite, since he could now punish by the death penalty every accused criminal, from the lowest slave to a Vizier.

The only entity that exceeded his authority was Sheik-ul-Islam, the religious leader who was also president of the Superior Court on religious issues. His decisions called "fetva" could not be overturned by an order of the Grand Vizier, because this Mufti was the only true interpreter of the Holy Quran, the Laws of Allah.

The Sheikh-ul-Islam and the Grand Vizier were the only Ottoman officials directly appointed by the Sultan and Caliph. All others courts would be now accountable to Ibrahim.

He was not the first Grand Vizier of the Ottoman Empire who was of Roman descent; but, he had risen to this office from the lowest level of a slave. He was not a converted high tanking Roman official as many Viziers had been in the past.

The Romans had advanced a great deal since the day Mehmet Fatih had crossed the Gate of Agia Sophia on his horse. This was a profound change and many Turks had not enough time to fully digest. For how long this experiment might be extended on the basis of meritocracy only time could tell. The battle that had just begun was for many not just a conflict to harness the people's power, but a struggle of gods.

******

Hafsa Hatun was the first to invite and congratulate him for his new superior post. Perhaps when he received her invitation the idea she wanted a return favor passed his mind, but the moment she saw him, she made perfectly clear her role to this result was minor. It was Hatidge who had fought hard to turn the Sultan's opinion in his favor. She also made clear that from now on she would be his immediate superior. He had to please her before anyone else.

"I can't say why she pressed my son so hard for you, but she really did. I wonder if she is truly in love with you," Hafsa added and her tone was stern not playful as usual.

"I must have made her a good impression to Basmi. Good references are essential ingredients for a quick ascendance of any state official," Ibrahim claimed audaciously, but Hafsa knew how to cut him down to size.

"Don't be so arrogant, because any clever woman should be able to see through your veil. You appear as too ambitious to have any consideration for the feelings of someone else."

"That's not true and your highness knows as much; but today you sound as if you have repented for showing me the full extent of your favors."

"No, I haven't. For me you were just perfect at the time. I needed a boost of my moral, and a young man was what the doctor ordered; but, my daughter has different needs. She needs a husband of her own, a man she can depend on for the rest of her life. I'm not so sure you can be that man, because despite your apparent charms, you are emotionally unstable and greedy."

"And who isn't? We all are, so that we may adapt more easily to all the obstacles we have to face as we move forward in life. Who doesn't wish to be loved? But love has its proper price, and can be redeemed only by an equal amount of love, not just a fleeting display of excessive passion."

"This is exactly what I meant. What I'm afraid most is that you are not willing to pay the price to earn any woman's love," Hafsa challenged him.

"Is exclusivity and absolute fidelity what she requires of me?" Ibrahim asked.

"No, I don't think so. She can have as many lovers as you can, if she really needs them, but she doesn't. My daughter needs lots of love rather than many lovers."

"Indeed, if she had many lovers this would set a bad example for every widow of the Ottoman Empire that uses the House of Osman as an example and a role model. More than ten lovers may create a state of jealousy between her and the Sultan. As far as I know he kept less than ten concubines and two wives in his harem in Manisa. Now in the Seraglio as a Sultan he has many more options, but he has limited his choices to just two."

"You are very well informed; no wonder they considered you the best Odabashi in Manisa. My spies also said there were no complains since you were chosen for this duty."

"Then, you must also know that I always tried my best to serve his Excellency."

"Yes, I know that. You were very efficient even when blindfolded."

This revelation caught him by surprise. He had been a fool not to suspect that the mother of the Sultan would not have posted a spy among the courtiers of her son's most favorite wife.

Posting a Tatar slave as a spy was the best choice. Now the question was which of the two Zarafet, Yabani or possibly both were Hafsa's informers.

"I am flabbergasted by the efficiency of your spies. I could swear that both all they had in mind at the time were to please me, not test me out."

Suddenly Hafsa's smiling faced turned red from rage, but she refused to make another comment before she was in full command of her emotions.

"Did you say both? My hearing is not as good anymore."

"Yes, I did. And if you ask me who the better of the two was, I am not sure I can give you a fair answer, because their styles were quite different. The first was swift and demanding, while the second most patient and considerate. I can only say they were both perfect for my state of mind at the time."

It was quite clear he was missing something, as with every new praises the anger in Hafsa's grew. Thus, he was now obliged to ask:

"Did I say something wrong that has ignited your jealousy?"

"No, you didn't; but someone else did and this is quite unacceptable."

He had never seen the face of the Valide Sultan so grim and solemn, but it was also clear that whatever else he tried to say, he might worsen her disposition even further.

"I hope this story will not reach my Princess' ears. Few women become awfully jealous, when they find out of their husband's past flames."

"Yes, indeed they do, but there are all sorts of women in this world. The few wise ones may even appreciate a husband full of experiences they could also share," Hafsa replied seeming now much more relaxed. "Sharing has been a long tradition of the Osmanli family."

"Everyone in the Harem says you are a wise and open-minded Valide Sultan," Ibrahim boldly continued.

"This is a flattery hard for me to accept at face value, because I am also aware I can be very temperamental sometimes. Few days I behave wisely and few others I may take foolish chances with slaves of low morality; but it is difficult even for a sensitive man to realize how a woman locked in a harem feels."

"It may be difficult for a common man, but I'm a slave. So, few days I am fully content within the safety of the Seraglio, while others I cannot stay under lock and key for one extra hour. It is right then when I might do something as foolish as falling on my knees and beg a mighty Valide Sultan to show pity for me."

Hafsa looked at him intensely as if she was trying hard to read the content of his mind.

"That was indeed an act of a perfect fool. I could ask for your head for touching me," she acknowledged but her tone of voice was not threatening. Perhaps, threats were one way for her to become aroused.

"Indeed you could ask for my head for taking advantage of your perfect loneliness," Ibrahim said exploring his chances.

"No, I wouldn't do that, because I would be totally ungrateful for providing me with an unforgettable experience. Every descent woman must feel at least once in her life like a whore; otherwise, she would die wondering what kind of pleasures the other half enjoys. However, going through my life, I found out that total freedom is a very dangerous state of mind, and both women and men have to respect certain limits to be safe. I'm sure you have felt this way too. As you've said, I'm wise enough to know that the more times I'm testing these limits the greater the existing danger I might break them. One more time is always what it takes; but let me now ask you this. What would you say if an aging widow asked you to free her from her loneliness once and for all? What would you say if one day I asked you to follow me to the Seraglio in Edirne? What would you think of me if on the way there I asked you to change course and go instead to the Redestos harbor and get aboard a ship to Venice? Would you be willing to lose everything you've earned for my sake?"

Ibrahim could see in her eyes the sparkle of madness, the temporary madness that comes once in a lifetime. She was not sincere. She was only testing his resolve; but, she seemed so excited with the prospect, if he was to say yes, she had the power and the resolve to set this madness into motion. By now he had advanced too much to put everything in jeopardy. Perhaps, if Hafsa had bought him from the Avret Bazaar instead of her son, he would be willing to follow obediently her mad dream; but, now he was wise enough to know that the more he aged the fewer dreams he could realize.

Asphodel's narration about Selim's final moments and his yearning for Mahidevran's magnificence were quite revealing. A dying middle-aged man still had mad dreams he begged to be fulfilled. It was not Selim's mistake. It was simply a law of Mother Nature. Dreams were like vines that when young they crawled on the ground to every possible direction searching for a host; but when they found a suitable tree, they entangled its trunk and followed its growth. It was a dangerous cohabitation, as the tree might be strangled by such a powerful entanglement.

Hafsa liked the parable he had quickly composed. She admitted she had fallen victim too of such a choice, and she added:

"Now that Selim Khan, my proud tree, has fallen, I have to crawl again searching for a new host."

"I am not as lucky as you. My tree has not fallen yet, in fact it keeps on growing; so, if I ever wish to claim my freedom, I have to split in many branches and entangle whatever trees lies close."

Hafsa exploded her frustration into a cataract of laughter.

"It's always stimulating to chat with you, Ibrahim Pasha. You are the kind of man who can find an excuse out of every moral difficulty. If my son had not bought you, I'm sure that by now you would be the Grand Pezevenk (Pimp) of the Eternal City. You can always find a way to manipulate women and turn them into whores; but, today I feel better being a mother and since my son seems perfectly happy with all his promiscuous lovers, I have no reason to risk my reputation any further in his favor. You cannot imagine what kinds of rumors start spreading in the Harem, when a woman invites a man into her chambers and locks the door behind him."

"You have not locked the door today," Ibrahim remarked audaciously.

"You should remember that once is not a sin in the Harem. It's a test of virtue. Now I suggest you vanish out of my sight, and do your best to become the best mate for my daughter, and when I say best I mean the most faithful. Despite her sins as a widow, she surely deserves as much. And try to stay away from women who have to blindfold you to guard their virtue, because blindfolds are not always enough to hide the truth forever."

It was time for him to leave, but now that he had become the Grand Vizier he felt he deserved to have the last word.

"You've have always been very sincere and fair with me, and you have never hid from me behind a veil your enchanting eyes or your mesmerizing lips. I hope you realize that it would be unfair if I was to do anything less today but offer you my head, if this is what you need to be content. However, as you've said we are all unstable creatures, and what we choose to do today is completely different than what we might decide to do tomorrow. There is nothing wrong with this emotional instability of ours. This is in fact how Mother Nature wants us to behave, so that our past treacherous enemies may become our future loyal friends. This is the reason why from now on I will often come knocking on your door seeking guidance before every crucial step make for the good of the Ottoman Empire and your entire household."

******

Ibrahim left Hafsa's apartments deeply puzzled. What was the meaning of her comments about blindfolds, and why had she suddenly become so upset? After all he had done nothing wrong in Manisa, but simply succumbed to the overwhelming advances of two very determined and exceedingly lusty courtiers that took him by surprise in a man's hammam.

Perhaps it was exactly these memories that guided his steps to knock also at Hurrem's door the same day. She seemed surprised but very happy to accept him. Only her transparent veil showed she was keeping appearances according to the Harem's ritual.

"To what do I owe the pleasure of this visit, my magnificent Grand Vizier?" she asked him rather cautiously, but then she teasingly added. "Is this visit some kind of strict ritual you have to follow in accordance with your recent inauguration?"

"No! I try not to follow strict rituals but develop all my friendly relationships strictly on the basis of freedom of choice."

"I feel exactly the same way. Why should I feel any differently? I'm a slave too and certain choices have been imposed on me. If I was free, my choices would surely be different. I hope you have realized that."

"I surely did, but I still cannot understand why you disappeared so suddenly and unexpectedly. I believe one of the greatest satisfactions a woman may enjoy each day is to see a man melt in her hands," he pointedly replied.

"Indeed this is true, but wise women should not take unnecessary chances. What would have happened to me if I was to bear a child with blond hair and green eyes?" she inquired with disarming sincerity.

He simply had to show her he was sincere too.

"Wise women have all sorts of explanations for few natural phenomena and Mother Nature supports them. A child may resemble one of his grandparents. I bet light eyes or blond hair is common in Ukraine."

Hurrem could not keep a straight face and offered him a long smile that displayed a perfect row of pearly white teeth.

"I was too excited at the time and my mind couldn't think as straight as yours."

She was obviously lying and he told her so to show her impeccable looks could not cloud his judgment.

"You are right. I lied but this is simply because I didn't trust you. People say that men who are attracted to men cannot be fully trusted even by men. Perhaps, if you gradually change your preferences, I might be tempted to believe you."

"And I believe that every man or a woman is an individual, so rules don't apply universally. For example, common people say that men trust only the women they have fucked, but I still don't feel I can fully trust you?"

"No, you shouldn't. As far as I can remember you have not fully fucked me. I fucked you."

"Yes, and it was a very cruel act. You also left me in dire straits."

"The feelings were mutual, but it had to happen this way. Trust me! When I get very excited, I scream too much. That would have led us to our death."

"Nonsense! I would have sealed your lips with mine. There must be another more devious reason."

"You know how to push a woman to the corner. Is this how you convinced Hafsa to give you her daughter for a wife? A widow can be very susceptive to the image of a horny young man the same way a man cannot resist the sight of a woman's breast dripping milk."

This day had to be for him a most memorable one having to face a series of unexpected revelations. He surely could not admit his guilt. It was simply too dangerous to confirm her suspicions about his relationship with the Valide Sultan. If Hurrem became certain, then she could possible find other witnesses among the eunuch guards of Hafsa's apartments using bribery. All doors had very large keyholes, if one was curious enough to risk his life and become indiscrete.

"Why do you make such an absurdly unsubstantiated claim? Why would such a powerful woman do such a thing, while she is trying so hard to find another husband for her daughter?" he argued.

"This is what trying hard means for women. When we are desperate, our bodies become our ultimate weapons of seduction," she responded to his inquiry.

"I can certainly believe as much; but, now tell me, why were you so desperate, when our Padisah was completely at your mercy?"

"I thought you were cleverer than that. Perhaps I have overestimated you, but I couldn't help it. Screwing a Sultan's Kadin under his nose in Manisa was indeed a formidable task."

"What are you saying? Have you lost your mind?"

"Yes, I have; but now tell me this. Is it true that today the Sultan plans to visits the Janissary barracks?"

"Why do you ask? The Sultan's exact plans are a military secret. I'm not going to reveal it to such a conniving concubine like you."

His words sounded like a severe accusation, but she was much wiser than that. She knew he was just fooling around. She could now read in his eyes his excitement.

"I'm not conniving without a reason. I'm simply taking the chance that if I was kind to you and let you treat me like your whore, I might gain your complete trust. Isn't it what the Sultan does to you, when he has doubts of your fidelity?"

Hurrem was once more pushing him to see how far he might go, so remaining inactive he would force her to expose more of her weapons.

"Don't look so surprised. I'm sure you have heard I was a sold meat before entering the Harem exactly as you were. Old habits are very hard to break," she challenged him for one more time and he was well aware her apartment had just one door.

He went there and locked it, making sure the key covered the keyhole. When he returned, she was waiting for him on her knees naked. She had to be overly excited because when he came closer, she didn't wait for him to take his clothes off, but simply raised his caftan and slipped under it. Then, she turned him around and pushed him on her bed.

In this precarious position he could not deny her anything, and her lips expressed more fluently her most urgent desires. He was no match for her dexterity. With a few strokes she made him lose every bit of control he had over his emotions.

This time everything was different. She didn't stop and when he stopped the turbulent cascade of his passion, she pushed his caftan over his eyes, mounted him, and started once more her frantic gallop time and time again. Each time she reached a peak she sought to find his lips to muffle her sights, and when she failed, she used her teeth and his caftan like a moonstruck being that had to bite on something, so that she didn't bite-off her tongue.

He couldn't take much more of this punishment, so he pushed her away. She fell on the mattress with a wild look on her face having a hard time to catch her breath. Was she going to collapse in his hands?

No, she wouldn't. She was still perfectly capable of making new demands. She grabbed his hair and pushed his head between her legs, at the center of her being. It was a bold gesture of complete abandonment, as if she was begging for his lips to be as aggressive as hers had been few moments ago.

It was very hard for him to judge time as her strokes had replaced his heartbeats. He was not sure even about that count. Perhaps she had timed her strokes to match his heartbeats. However, now she was at his mercy, and his lips showed her he could be as sincere and elaborate as she was.

Suddenly the salty taste of her blood lingered on his tongue infuriating him. Was this morning one of her special days? If it really was, then her body was a fair game. Immersed in an ocean of passion she had no strength or will to resist him. He lifted her legs and placed them on his shoulders.

She understood his plan and to help him accomplish it she slipped off her bed and rested her head on the carpet and her back on the bed, while he got on his knees and plunged as hard and as deep as he could into her womb as if he was stabbing her time and time again.

She couldn't have enough of him and made him wonder if she was a Maenad in a fury. Now only his flesh could quench the primeval thirst of hers, and he could not deny her his essence. Only when her flesh had sucked his last drop, she stopped her plies for more and a fully satisfied face with her sapphire eyes open wide stared at his face more boldly than even a man.

"Are you now fully pleased of your slave?" she asked.

"I couldn't ask for anything more," he humbly confessed.

"Do you trust me now?" she asked with an imperceptible smile.

"Yes, I do."

"Then, now we can be partners, or can't we?" she inquired.

"I'm not absolutely sure just yet. Someday soon I might need another confirmation of your loyalty," he teased her.

"You are a greedy man, but I like greedy men. We have a lot in common."

"Suleiman is a greedy man too. Perhaps this is why we are both so attracted to him."

"No! You are much greedier than him. You desire also his sister for your wife; but I don't mind. In my village we have a custom. A groom must prove his worth with a whore or the village's widow before he is allowed to marry a maiden."

"You are not a whore. You are a concubine locked in a harem. I would have done exactly the same, if I were in your position. Frustration has forced me many times in the past to yearn not only a woman but a man too, even a eunuch."

"You are a man. You cannot really feel like a woman no matter how hard you try."

"I don't have to try hard. It comes to me naturally from time to time."

"Then, you are mad. I have never felt this way with any man in my life."

"And I have never felt this way with any woman but you."

"Don't lie to me. You have felt great with one woman blindfolded. This was the reason I played this trick too. When the eyes are blinded other senses take command of our emotions. You can use this trick with your new bride too, but don't tell her who has taught it to you. She loves her brother and who knows when she might decide to open his eyes."

"I must be going. The Sultan may be coming back any moment now."

"So, what? I can always say this is one of my special days, and send him away without unlocking my door. Muslim religion was made for women like me. I have a very unstable cycle."

"Indeed you might have. I got a taste of blood few moments ago."

"That may be so indeed; but, sometimes when I'm very excited I have few drops of blood. You may not know it, but I could even get pregnant after this magnificent rape."

"It was no rape. It was condescending sex between two very licentious individuals."

"No, it was rape, and if you insist denying it, I will tear up my cloths, unlock the door and summon the guards," she teased him.

"Why would you do that? I thought we were partners."

"If we are truly trusty partners, then trust me. It was a rape. Just say it and I will give you a present."

"OK! I love presents. It was rape! In fact, it was the best rape of my life. I plunged and plunged my sword deep inside you and you could do nothing about it."

"Good! You don't know how happy this confession makes me."

"Why? Rape is not the best type of sex a woman might feel."

"It's the worst. I was a virgin, but the Tatar raiders who grabbed raped me one by one for days. By the time we reached Constantinople, I had become their best whore. After this experience, I cannot enjoy anything else but another rape."

"Then, how on Earth the Chief Black Eunuch bought you for the Sultan?"

"I don't believe the Hasodabashi of the imperial harem can be so simpleminded. For your information black eunuchs know many tricks. In Africa they pierce their lips and their ears. Men in the city of Constantine are also extremely naïve. After each birth she suffers any woman can be turned into a Holy Virgin with a few stiches. Trust me. Trust me and don't ask the Chief Black Eunuch. He will deny everything I said. His head is on the line as much as yours. One scream of mine and you are dead man."

"Why would you wish to kill me? I did all I could to make you happy."

"Indeed you did as much and I'm grateful for all the fine, unique moments we shared today."

"Then you must invite me back," Ibrahim requested testing the extent of her voracity.

"Eventually I will, but only if you prove you can be trusted. I am a woman and I have other obligations besides simply seeking pleasure as you do. I'm not as greedy as I look. I'm a mother. I have to give more than I take."

"I know what you mean. You have an important obligation towards your children."

"And I'm very happy we had this chance to talk. I want you to know that I did all I could for your marriage to move forward. Now you have to do the same for me. For my children to have any chance to survive when my Suleiman dies, I must become the Sultan's Kadin too. Fratricide is the most foolish law this damned Seraglio has."

"I may not have any children yet, but I know exactly how you feel. Trust me."

"I trust you, but it's simply impossible for any man to feel like a mother. For him a child is just the consequence of a sinful night. For a mother her children are part of her flesh."

"For a man his children are his dreams for the future. Without them soon he will be past, gone and forgotten. Children are my true legacy."

"If this is how you feel about children, perhaps you should know that few of my children may be yours too."

"I'm not so naïve. Until today I had not surrendered my essence to your lust."

"Are you so sure about that? No man can be sure of anything with a woman. That afternoon I felt you starting to melt inside me, that is why I jumped up and left you cold; but who knows if I left one drop too late? Do you? Next time you come over I will have my Mihrimah for you to discern your signs. Her eyes are green and her hair is like chestnut. When she grows older, she is destined to look like her father. We only have to wait and keep our mouths shut. Time will tell which child belongs to which father. This is another unwritten law of the Harem."

****

Common people were right in their judgment. She was a witch, and she had bewitched him too as much as his friend. Firstly, she had used skillfully her body to enslave his, and when he had surrendered his essence, she had given him the coup de grace, claiming her daughter was his. Perhaps, she would claim next that one of her future child would be his too.

She had also modestly claimed she was raped by the Tatars and turned into a whore. This much might well be true; but the moment she was employed, no brothel manager would try to resell such an exquisite slave in the Avret Bazaar. Her price there would be just a fraction of the income she could produce in a month. On the other hand, any exquisite whore of Galata would be a well-known celebrity many people would recognize her face. Perhaps if he found a Christian painter, he could describe him how she looked and have him make an accurate sketch. Then, he could wander around the Avret Bazaar, show it, and find exactly where she came from.

Her last stroke against her own honesty was her claim she felt she had become pregnant once more by him few moments after their shameless orgy. He had to admit that her shameless lies made her even more attractive. It was a mysterious effect that pushed him to her bed simply to punish her blatant lies. If she already had a child of his, why not give her one more?

Now, to escape away from her attraction he had to marry the Princess and forget all about Hurrem the magnificent dancer. Beautiful but unscrupulous women were just too dangerous for a slave in high places like him. They could make him imagine he was a free man and lead him into peril. Who would the Sultan believe; his best friend and the Grand Vizier or a Tatars' whore?

The answer was painfully direct. These days of slavery, rape, loot and plunder, men could very easily turned into rapists, as slaves had no right to resist their masters. Suleiman had made it perfectly clear. The Hasodabashi was the master of the Harem. Thus, to please her he gave her everything she demanded and promised her he would be her slave for as long as she would be his.

He was serious, but she didn't believe him. She kept smiling no matter what he did to mesmerize her all the way to his conclusion. He knew this kind of attitude and she knew he knew. It was the very same smile he had each morning he woke up in the Sultan's bed. It meant he had no worries about the future.

At least he had now discovered what made her so attractive to conquerors and rapists. No matter what they did to sweep it away, she never lost her smile. It was a smile that fluently expressed her audacious claim: "No matter what you do to me, I will be the last standing."

And she was damned right! After such a satisfying experience he simply couldn't wipe the smile off his face. Hurrem could put a smile one every man's face.

****

Ibrahim may be a complicated mind and a knowledgeable man, but he was no match for a complicated mind and a knowledgeable woman from the Ukrainian steppes. She knew as well as any Tatar that the precious man's substance could last only for few days in a woman's womb but practically forever stored in freezing snow.

****

Now his mind was full of worries and vising the Princess to find comfort in her arms was still out of question. The Ottoman customs prohibited any contact between future married couples, as if the ceremony was the crucial detail that turned a natural act into a dreadful sin.

He was crossing the garden towards the entrance of the Eski Saray, when he came face to face with Mahidevran and her two consorts that were strolling along the rose garden.

He stopped and bowed his head in respect still used to the rules of behavior of his past office as a Hasodabashi, but Mahidevran seemed well acquainted with his new position and lower her head too. Among the roses she simply looked divine.

She greeted him according to the official protocol she now had to follow, but since there were no other onlookers she pushed aside pomp and congratulated him for his future marriage with surprising warmth, adding that she was very happy he was going to be soon another member of the imperial family.

"The Sultan must think greatly of you," she added.

It was a subtle challenge he couldn't leave unanswered.

"I believe the entire family has honored me with their respect, so I can be nothing else but greatly excited for this preference."

A flash passed quickly illuminating the black abyss of her eyes. Unquestionably they were the most responsive feature, even though for him her lips, her cheeks, and her delicate nose were the most attractive ones, revealing a generous portion of Mongol race in her blood. Instinctively she sensed his preferences and smiled sending shivers down his spine. Now he couldn't restrict any further his weakness and admitted that today she looked even more beautiful than ever before. Her cheeks turned red as she was clearly not accustomed to similar praises by men other than her husband, and her sense of fairness unconsciously pushed her to ascribe his praises to the proper recipient.

"They say that pregnancy improves a woman's complexion."

It was an unexpected revelation that was to be expected, as the competition of fertility that was going on among the Sultan's Kadin and this remarkable concubine was heating up.

"Congratulations!" he said not because he wanted to say it, but it was the proper response to such a happy announcement.

"I'm not so sure I should be congratulated yet. The midwives told me that in pregnancies beauty was a definite sign the child would be a girl."

"A baby girl is then another good sign that you will get pregnant once more soon after her," he added trying to moderate her distress.

"I don't think this game can go on forever. After all, no woman can compete with a damned sow!"

His mission as a Hasodabashi prompted him to moderate her insult. Calling Hurrem a sow was a bit too much considering the Muslim religious distain for pork meat.

"It's not for me to judge the taste for meat of my master," he remarked diplomatically, but devouring sows is prohibited by the Prophet."

He had a flirty attitude he was hopping he could transmit it like the plague, but Mahidevran was not in the right mood.

"You don't have to say anything more on this subject. I know you Romans would rather eat a suckling pig than devour a spring lamb."

This was a bit too much for his nerves. How was it possible Mahidevran to know the exact nature of his activities half an hour ago inside Hurrem's bedroom?

Had he been dangerously naïve? If he was naïve, there had to be some kind of peeping hole inside Hurrem's bedroom besides the rather obvious keyhole. The Black Eunuchs had to know whenever he visited the Harem. Now, the question was whether they were going to report his indiscretion to the Sultan or burry it among the many other secrets of the Harem.

The answer was not obvious. They could possibly decide that keeping the entire matter under wraps was for the best of their interests. Any successful attempt to violate the sanctity of the Harem meant they were incapable to enforce the strict rules. Additionally, if he was executed for offending the Sultan's honor, it would result the ascendance of another Grand Vizier. Unquestionably this would have been a step in the wrong direction as he was unquestionably the best man for the post, and he had Asphodel's assurances for this fact. However, it soon became clear Mahidevran had much more to say.

"How do my courtiers look to you? The Holy Quran obliges us to treat as tenderly both masters and slaves, or am I wrong?" Mahidevran inquired.

"This is exactly how I feel too. This is why whenever I can I intend to make all my choices as a Grand Vizier blindfolded."

Mahidevran could not resist his wit and challenged him.

"They say that a wise man should treat a noble woman as a slave and slave as a noble woman; but I don't know if there are many wise men who can distinguish between a noble woman and a slave in total darkness. My Grand Vizier, I wonder if you are as wise as they say."

"I'm wiser than they think. I can distinguish even between two slaves," he boasted.

"And I say you are another Greek full of hot air. How do you find my two courtiers? Close your eyes, kiss them, and prove it," she challenged him further and offered him her shawl.

"I don't need even that," he claimed. "When we are so close, I could distinguish a woman's scent among hundreds, and my memory does not easily fade away."

It was a statement that turned Mahidevran's face pink, sending waves of blood up her cheeks.

"Memories are often pleasant, but they can also be proven perilous," she warned him.

"Yes, but in few cases they are priceless jewels. Life would not be worth living without them. I will cherish them forever safe under lock and key in the deepest crevice of my mind."

Mahidevran sent him a faint smile to show him that she accepted his assurance.

"The trouble with long past memories is that after a while one cannot even prove they had ever happened," she remarked.

"A beauty mark, even in her back, can reveal the identity of a woman, but I never felt the need to prove anything. It is more than enough for me to know the truth than share it with anyone else. Sharing simply degrades the value of knowledge. As a Grand Vizier I know well enough the worth of a state secret."

"Some state secrets are best being forgotten. One of the virtues of the old Grand Vizier was that through aging his memory grew naturally weaker and weaker."

It was a curious statement that for the time being didn't make much sense; but it was not the right time to search for an explanation. They had been talking for some time now and sooner or later an indiscrete eye might monitor the event.

"Since as they say everything has its price in the Harem, I wonder what kind of reward a weak memory can bring to its owner."

"What kind of present would you like for your oncoming marriage?" she asked him, "one of my two unforgettable courtiers perhaps?" she suggested to close the deal.

"That's a very enticing thought indeed; but, I'm not sure my bride will agree. She has the blood of Selim Khan too and Sultans have not become powerful by sharing their property. This is why frequent use is a safer alternative than ownership for a slave of the Gate like me."

Mahidevran widen her smile in approval.

"Widows are very insecure creatures indeed. Very few are wise enough to distinguish between a once in a lifetime stroke of luck and a reiterative duty."

This was another curious statement that didn't make much sense to him. What was Mahidevran referring to? Was she talking about Hatidge Sultan or perhaps herself? He had to search deeper into Hatidge's past at the first available opportunity.

"Repetitions may be painful sometimes, but they are the foundations of deeper knowledge. Are you always visiting the rose garden this time of day?"

"No, but I intend to turn it into a habit," she promised him and summoned her courtiers to follow her. "Long live the Grand Vizier," she wished and her tone indicated she meant it.

****

Allah made the world in such a way that people can dream and then work harder to make their dreams come true. If dreams don't come true, it's not only because the people who dreamed them did not work hard enough to realize them or that their dreams were unrealistic and unrealizable. It may also mean that luck was against them, or even that other people who had dreamed against them had a simpler dream, as Allah favors simplicity over complexity, and if chaos often erupts, it is because chaos is the simplest development of all because it requires no preparation.

****

Perhaps it was better that he was promoted to Grand Vizier. Now he had only men to command. As a Hasodabashi he had to be in control of numerous women and hundreds of Black and White Eunuchs. Men were much easier to accommodate and he was trained to handle men one way or another. It was even easier, if these men were soldiers.

War was like a game of chess. There were only black and white pieces. Pieces were also able to perform limited and specific movements. Women were much more complicated beings than men. Even the flesh of men was rigid. A woman's flesh had numerous degrees of freedom. Their long hair could follow and give substance to the wind. Their flesh could bounce like springs or travel like waves. Their eyes could promise eternal happiness, their lips temporary pleasure, but they could also both lie and set deadly traps, if a man was not careful.

He was not. He had played with fire and it was a miracle he was not roasted yet. The marriage was a brilliant maneuver to put an end to risks and he had Hafsa Hatun to thank for it. She must have been informed of his escapades and chose the less painful alternative, to keep him busy with her audacious daughter for a while until the intentions of the Sultan became clearer.

Eventually Hafsa had been very compassionate with him. She must be seeing him like a son despite his affair with her true son. Women often behaved this way. They adopted an orphan and treated it like their child. This was essentially what she was doing. Despite the worries he had caused her, she had been very patient, generous and considerate. She did not behave like a Tatar. She was very sophisticated and used her intelligence to bring order into many people's lives. She had found the perfect companion for her son, and she had done her best to make also her daughter happy. She had correctly diagnosed her daughter's trends and found the husband who could set her emotions straight. Just a little while ago, he was blinded with by her beauty, but now he could clearly see that Hatidge was slowly drifting to a world of illusions.

Since that momentous night, he had asked Asphodel to find more details about Hatidge and Basmi via his eunuch connections, and he didn't beat around the bush. The two women were in intimate terms. No White Eunuch knew exactly the extent of their intimacy, but they were using opium as often as Selim Khan. It was a development Hafsa Sultan was determined to stop before it created permanent damage.

"What about Hurrem?" Ibrahim asked and the eunuch's faced turned pink all the way to his ears.

"I'm afraid she has the Kislar Aga under her spell," he hurried claiming. "I have to find out who blackmails whom. Since he became Aga, I have been worried. They say he was not properly cut, but no one knows for sure since he goes to the Aga Hammam either all alone or never."

"What kind of fool made such a choice of a Kislar Aga?" Ibrahim wondered.

"It was Selim Khan, following Menekse's suggestion, if I remember correctly; but he may have selected him looting the Mameluke's Sultan harem. Many times Selim was tempted to make a choice because of someone he yearned to conquer like you or instance. All he cared was to have obedient people he trusted serving him."

"That's insane! Why would Selim choose such a Kislar Aga of all cases?"

"Don't be a fool. It was a very logical choice at the time it was made. My master was fed up with all Harem complaints; but, it was not the first time such a dubious choice was made. The rumors claim Fatih was the first to reside away from his harem, when he built the Yeni Saray at the edge of the cliff away from the Eski Saray, so that he was not constantly disturbed by his women, while he was building an empire. Few people claim he wouldn't be Fatih, if he didn't have a Grand Vizier like Mahmud Pasha, but in the end he got separated even from him, because he lost his trust in him."

"As far as I know he executed him too like the worst traitor of all, Çandarlı Halil Pasha the Younger, after the fall of Constantinople," Ibrahim added.

"Yes, he most certainly did, when Mahmud Pasha divorced one of his Kadin, for cheating him with Fatih's son Mustafa. When few months later Mustafa died of poisoning, Fatih did not need any other proof that Mahmud Pasha had poisoned his most favorite son and Prince Heir."

"I wonder if Suleiman Khan knows all this malicious gossip," Ibrahim wondered.

"It's not gossip! It's the truth! Everyone in the Seraglio knows that."

"I didn't know that," Ibrahim humbly confessed.

"You are naïve. Hurrem knows all that and possibly more. She keeps on having long discussions with Kislar Aga behind locked doors after midnight. I'm sure by now she knows everything there is to know about the Harem's traditions."

"I wonder what they talk about. Perhaps she is giving him also dancing lessons," he ironically noted. "He yearns to become more attractive anyway he can."

"I don't wonder. I'm not as naïve as you are. A bolted door inside the Harem can mean just one thing. Something outrageous is happening behind it. Seducing your guardian is a successful strategy for any slave, and we both know how effective it can be. Who knows if Hurrem haven't found out what you have done to have the Sultan eat out of your hand and imitates it to the best of her abilities? Actually when Selim was ill he asked me to entertain him by belly dancing. He claimed my back was as seductive as Mahidevran's. As imagination plays the greatest part in a man's pleasure, sometimes after smoking hashish it's easy to fool a man's imagination with a copycat. Tell me, could you discern my back from Mahidevran's after a smoke?"

Ibrahim could not deny the logic of this assertion. Also locking a door was a rebellious act against Allah's or Allah's Shadow's strict harem laws. Asphodel knew well he had also revolted few times against Selim's wishes. He had failed on purpose in all the belly dancing lessons in the Seraglio School.

He did not stop resisting similar orders even now that Suleiman was Allah's Shadow and he his slave. He had a good excuse. If Suleiman had revolted against his father's absolute authority, why shouldn't he? No one could feel happy under a state of oppression.

Asphodel was feeling oppressed too. This was perhaps the reason he went over and locked the door. Now it was simply a matter how good negotiator he would be and find out the most about Hurrem. He could discern in the eunuch's eyes Asphodel was eager to talk. One of his first actions as a Grand Vizier should be to limit the excessive salaries of all the Eunuchs. If a slave ever became rich, he became even lustier. He was feeling it in his loins. It had to be another law of Mother Nature no one had spelled out until then; but there was a limit on how much lust a Harem could handle before exploding into chaos. Now he could see clearly they were all approaching this limit.

As Asphodel slowly removed his clothes he couldn't help but ask the critical question. Was it just insatiable lust or was his final aim different? He could see now more clearly why Asphodel was trying to prove to him how obedient he was and how devoted to providing pleasure to attractive men. What was he aiming at when he mentioned with any provocation his backside was as attractive as Mahidevran's?

For a superficial mind it might have been just an expression of the constant rivalry between concubines and eunuchs, black or white for more power, honing their skills to provide more pleasure to any eligible male who had power or money to spare. He was very stupid not to see that earlier. Asphodel was aiming for the empty position of the Hasodabashi. Now that he had the suspicion it was very easy to find out what the eunuch's plans were, so, he gently pushed him away.

"Please stop. I want to think more clearly what Hurrem is after," he said and waited.

He was right in all his assertions. The eunuch was now too excited to think clearly.

"If I was in your position, I wouldn't trust that whore. Trust my judgement!" he remarked and hugged his waist even tighter. "I know much more than your imagination can fathom."

"If I was in your position, I wouldn't trust her either; but, I have something you don't have that she craves; and it's something that makes all the difference in the world, trust me!"

"I do trust you, I do! Don't you see I'm your slave now and no one else's? I want you to become the greater man in the Empire," the eunuch cried full of passion.

Ibrahim had to admit that Asphodel seemed totally devoted to this cause.

"I can certainly feel your unreserved devotion. This is why I have decided to make you the new Hasodabashi in my place as soon as possible. The Sultan should be served by true eunuchs now that we are at war. In times of peace we have more freedom to relax even our unwritten laws."

"That's a very wise decision. You need someone you can trust to keep an eye on Hurrem and this damned Kislar Aga, and I am this person. I swear I'll do my best, so you won't regret this moment," the eunuch said and came even closer.

He had indeed an attractive back and two dimples over his loins. It was not a rare feature for both women, and men. Only Hurrem had dimples also on her cheeks that made her smile so damned irresistible.

Suddenly it all came back to him in a flash. Menekse and Asphodel were twins, so they both had dimples on their backs. It was a gift of the licentious goddess Aphrodite, as the ancient Greeks believed.

Another gift of gods was Apollo's belt male athletes had shaped by hard abdomen muscles. He had it too, but neither of the eunuchs twins had it. He smiled at the idea he was gifted by both Aphrodite and Apollo. Perhaps this was why Asphodel was so attracted to him. If he was looking for a good excuse to submit to his desires, now he had found it. A man could trust completely only the men he had conquered completely. Was he slowly becoming a sexually confused man like Selim?

****

That evening the Sultan was not infected by the desire to summon Ibrahim to sleep with him. He had also noticed his passion for Ibrahim was like a torrent overflowing its banks after a heavy rain following a long period of drought. On the other hand, his passion for Hurrem was more like an ever-flowing river. Occasionally it might increase and overpower his resistance, while sometimes it could also reach a low point, but it never dried up.

It all had to do with her behavior. If she was obedient and submissive strangely enough his passion regressed to a lower point, and if she approached him overexcited, his passion reached a nadir. The truth was that if he needed hot women to quench his thirst, Mahidevran and Gülfem were more than enough to satisfy him; but, this was not the kind of woman he needed most often. What he needed most of the time was not obedience but resistance. It was this reason that made Ibrahim also so exciting. He could not say anything without him offering a better option to counter his.

However, his favorite slave was never fully pleased. He always behaved as something important was missing to be fully content. Few nights ago he came to visit him with the air of a free man hoping that he could gain his freedom by hording the women of his life against him. Demolishing this rebellion made it the most exciting night of his life; so, he decided he would retain his slave through all his life along with Hurrem. If they rejected their slavery, this was enough reason for him to prolong it.

Tonight it was one more of these nights. Her arguments were plain enough and quite incontestable. Why should he invite other concubines and Kadin in his bedroom, if she was the one who gave him the greatest pleasure? It was simply a waste of time and the Prophet had spoken plainly enough on this critical issue.

The greatest sin a man could commit was to waste time. It was an advice that made sense. Time on Earth was limited and the worst factor was that no one knew how much time he had left, so every day and every night were precious.

She must have been brewing these ideas for a long time, because when she came in instead of prostrating and kissing the corner of his caftan, she appeared agitated. Even if it was fairly obvious what the purpose of this visit was, she pretended she did not know. Having him to tell her the reason for this short trip from the Eski Saray was one more way to underline his weakness. She had to lower him to her level.

"Why have you invited me here tonight?" she asked.

"I want to rape you! That's why!" it was the rude statement she was waiting for.

"Why would you want to do that? From what I've heard you have another son coming."

"No one knows if it is going to be a son," he ventured.

"The doctor knows. Doctors know these things after a thorough examination. If he didn't say so, it is because Mahidevran asked him not to tell," she explained.

"Why would she do that?"

"Don't be silly. She is dying to come to your bed more often than I do; but, if you know she is pregnant, you will never invite her until the delivery, and she might get so depressed she might lose the child like the other one. Women are very sensitive when they are pregnant. Any strong excitement can terminate a pregnancy. This is not my words but the doctor's. He examined me well too. It was just an awful experience. Despite his shortness in height he has very big hands and he enjoys stretching all the Sultanas to the limit. Few concubines enjoy it, but I don't."

"Relax! For his excesses I will give him a spanking he will never forget. The Prophet says clearly no one should try to break the limits."

"He is not a Muslim. He is a Jew, that's why enjoys so much to crucify Christians like me."

"Then, I will crucify him too early next morning."

"No, please don't. If he dies, I'm sure Ibrahim will hire a Greek doctor in his place. They are the worst kind. Few months ago, I've heard a story about a Greek doctor who fucked every poor woman who visited him because she couldn't bear children. In my country I knew also of a damned monk who performed such miracles, but for a doctor to do that it's an outrage. If I was to believe all the rumors that I hear, then no man in the Eternal City can be sure he is the father of his sons. Many women become very excited when a doctor's hand reaches so deeply, but what can they do with a Sultan who is so fruitful and impregnates them once every year?"

"The truth is that Allah has blessed me with fruitful wives too."

"I'm not as fruitful as I could be, and the reason is that the Eski Saray is so far away from your bedroom. I don't know how other odalisques feel, but I am very temperamental. Sometimes just looking at a mushroom growing in the Gülhane garden makes me horny and I dream of yours. Then, I have to do my best to forget you, because I become so unstable my legs are trembling with desire. There are moments I need you so much, that my eyes close out of passion and dream of you. I wonder what would happen if one such day I wake up, open my eyes and see another man filling my womb with his sperm taking advantage of my frustration. Thank Allah for giving you the wisdom to make Ibrahim Grand Vizier instead of Hasodabashi. Now that he is going to marry your sister, I hope he will stop sneaking in the Eski Saray with every possible opportunity. Mahidevran and I are the more content, but this is not what I hear about few other concubines of yours. Most of them you have never visited and they have become desperate for a pregnancy, any pregnancy. Few of them are

243

so desperate they are even more licentious than lonely widows like your sister. Do you know that in Christian monasteries virgins are called Brides of Jesus? Perhaps we should also call your concubines Allah's brides."

"Don't be impertinent. There is no such possibility. The Holy Quran mentions no such provision," he scolded her sternly.

"And I say the Holy Quran cannot cover every contingency. The sons of Osman have become great because they provide exciting new ideas that solve old problems. The Quran never said that a man's harem should be so far away from his Selamlik, but Fatih dared it, and instead of wasting his time with lusty women, he kept them away at the other end of the City to conserve his might and use it for a good cause. A true leader should sacrifice his pleasure for the good of the Empire as your father did when he started a new war. Of course, several concubines don't think this was the true reason and do not recognize the sacrifices a Sultan has to make to bring prosperity to his people. You may not know it, but there are few women so benevolent they will do everything they can to make happy every man who knocks on their door, even for free like the cheapest of the whores."

"If something like this happens to my harem this odalisque will meet her creator. Just tell me her name."

"Why should she? The duty of every woman is to bear children. If you deny this right it is you who must be punished."

"This small talk leads nowhere. I haven't brought you here to relay other women's complains."

"This is not just another woman's complain but mine too. It would be infinitely better if you moved all your odalisques into the Seraglio. There your eunuchs could supervise them better, and every time you needed me I would be in an arm's distance to comfort the stresses of the Empire better than anyone else. As it is now, it's almost impossible for me to get ready for you in time. You may not know it, but I do because I resided in the same house with my father. After a certain age, men cease to behave like wild stallions. They gradually need more time to get aroused, and so, by the time they are ready, it's time for them to go to sleep. I believe this is why you need Ibrahim's advices to last till dawn."

He had to admit her tongue was even sharper than her mind. From the moment Ibrahim had managed to seduce his sister, she had revolted too. Was this the beginning of a female conspiracy? It was a remote but distinct possibility, but now it was not the right time to investigate such a contingency. Hurrem's cheeks were red and her eyes where sparkling with excitement. As she was talking, she was constantly wetting her lips with the edge of her tongue.

"Take your clothes off," he ordered her firmly, but she didn't rush to obey his command. Was it possible she was not in the mood, or was she resisting arousing his passion?

"I have a splitting headache tonight. It was rather cold tonight and I didn't have enough time to dry and cool off after visiting hammam, so I caught a cold. Every time I come to meet you all dressed up, soft and scented, you may think everything I do for you is an easy task, but you don't know how much time it takes me to peel away my old skin, remove every bit of hair, or get thoroughly clean, so I don't look like a man but like a rose ready for you to pluck. So, please tell me. If you really like what you see tonight in front of your eyes, give me more time to prepare. Let me move in your quarters permanently and I promise you, I will be ready any time you feel like giving me another child. This tension is simply killing my desires for you."

She seemed sincere enough and he could see her hair was still wet.

"You don't seem to believe me, do you? Men make all sorts of crazy thoughts sometimes to degrade women. They see a woman fresh out of a hammam and their sick minds make all sorts of crazy stories. The most devious ones think she went to the hammam to clean her skin from the sweat of another man."

"No, I never made such a thought for you," he declared embarrassed by her ludicrous suggestion.

"I'm not sure about that. There are all these vicious rumors in the Harem. Ask the Kislar Aga and he will tell you if I'm lying. Few nasty words must have reached his ears too."

"What do the rumors say?"

"They say that I have stolen your heart because I'm a witch, a whore and a professional enchantress. They say that Kislar Aga didn't buy me from the Avret Bazaar, but from a whorehouse for underage girls where I danced and danced until the customer's bidding for my favors stopped. Do you believe such vicious lies for the mother of your children? Please tell me and if you do, let me and my children free to leave never to see us again."

"You are crazy. These children are mine too. My boy may become my heir, if Allah so wishes. You will never leave this palace as long as I am alive; but who says those vicious lies? If I find out who he is, I will offer you his head in a platter."

"Yes, I'm indeed crazy for you, but I don't know who this liar is; however, even if I knew, I would never tell you. I only know he hates us so much that he is determined to do whatever he can to separate us, because he is jealous of our love and will do anything to kill it. He knows that the more children we have the stronger your hold on the Empire will be."

"Do you suspect Ibrahim?" he asked hesitantly.

"Ibrahim is the last man I would suspect. He is your most devoted subject, and you have benefited him more than anyone else. He is not crazy to conspire against his benefactor. After all, the conspirator might well be an evil woman for all I care."

"Are you suspecting Mahidevran Sultan?"

"Are you insane? Mahidevran loves you so much she would never put her children into jeopardy for such a crazy plan. She can have no complains of your attitude. Despite loving me more, you have never failed to invite her to your bedroom. You are perfectly fair with both us. For every child she had, you gave me one too, so I don't get jealous. If now she has one and I have two, she cannot blame anyone else but Kismet. No woman can go against Allah's will. If He wants to take her child to heavens, then all she can do is to make one more for the one she lost. I don't know if you can ever manage to please us both, but if you wish to convince her how much you love me, then you should invite both of us one night together on this very bed. This is what true fairness demands. If you don't believe me, ask the Seih-ul-Islam."

"That's a crazy suggestion. He will think I'm insane and release a fetva to dethrone me."

"You may be right. The rumors say he is a worse pedophile even than a Christian priest."

"I will ask Ibrahim to investigate these charges, and I will appoint another one the moment these charges are proven; but, now it's getting late. Let's go to sleep."

"No, I don't want to sleep here. Every time I sleep here, we make love. I cannot bear the thought that tonight you'll not take me in your arms and show me who is the one and only conqueror. I'm afraid that I will not close my eyes all night waiting for your tender touch."

"I promise you the moment I blow away the flame, I will take you in my arms and make you mine."

"No, you won't put me to such torment. You love me too much. With a headache such as the one I am having, you will simply spare me from any more excitement that will send all my blood to my brain. Instead you will let me sleep in the Hasodabashi bedroom which is now empty. I cannot promise you anything tonight, but who knows what exactly Allah's wishes are? He is so powerful and benevolent he could blow away my pain with a single breath. Then, don't be surprised if you feel in the darkness a hungry pair of lips. The greatest torture for a concubine in a harem is the thought that in the next room a Janissary is sleeping all alone, dreaming in how many ways he can rape her."

"I am not a Janissary," Suleiman uttered totally confused.

"Yes, you are! Yes, you are! You simply don't know it yet."

She was right. The moment she took off her clothes, turn her back at him and put a closed door between them the excitement was simply too much to bear.

He rushed to the intermediate door and tried to open it. It was locked, but it was too delicately made to block his way for long. He simply kicked it open and saw her trying to hide her nudity behind a silken bedcover. Now it was his turn to take away his clothes and with every move he made his excitement grew in bounds. It had nothing to do with any mesmerizing moves she made or any passion he read in her eyes. It was the sheer terror her eyes reflected back that excited him as she stared at him unable to move a muscle.

He raped her time and time again that night trying to make her stop this mesmerizing game she played. Many times he felt she might be serious as he saw tears of pain running down her cheeks; but finally when he had given her everything he could from his existence, her lips smiled full of tenderness.

He had heard many times the same story, when his Solaks gathered around a camp fire before a battle. He didn't believe them back then, but now Hurrem had proven it was pure truth. When his Akinji during a raid slaughtered the man of a household, the woman became lost and didn't react to whatever her new masters did to her extinguishing their battle rage. Only when the last man exploded his passion and smiled full of delight, she would smile back at him certain that her ordeal was over.

He hadn't smile at her recently full of delight. In fact, he was still furious of her attempt to invade his privacy. He was also mad at Ibrahim whose absence had permitted this attempt for invasion. This damned marriage was bound to change a lot of things in his life. Ibrahim would feel very embarrassed to come and see him any time it pleased him. He would have to send a messenger, and knock on his door like a beggar. He was not a Sultan anymore. He was an ordinary man who had a wife to serve him in his bedroom. If Hurrem moved next door, he couldn't even invite Mahidevran and Gülfem without reprisals.

"You may stay here tonight, but next morning you have to go back to the Eski Saray."

"Why?" You have never fucked me so well before. Admit it! It's the first time I felt you as my master. I hope you realized that."

"By the way, why did you cry?"

"I couldn't help it. My mind simply could not contain so much pleasure."

"And why did you smiled at the very end?"

"I was very relieved my heart didn't burst out of passion."

"You shouldn't be so selfish. Allah will punish you for being so greedy. I have the obligation to please two Kadin besides you from time to time," he notice but his voice sounded as if he was negotiating.

"I promise that when I'm sleeping next door, I will never interfere. Only if you summon me to help you pleasing them, I will come in. If they can please you too once in a while when I have a headache, I can only be grateful."

"This is a preposterous proposition. They would not accept it. They are not slaves. Then, they would have every right to seek a divorce. This is what the law says if I'm offending them."

"You are the Sultan. You make the laws. If this is your pleasure, they have to accept it. If they ask for a divorce, it would mean they don't love you as much as I do. If they deny you the pleasure of an orgy, you have every right to ask for a divorce too. After all you are the mightiest Roman Emperor. You have every right to ask not only Mahidevran but also Gülfem and me to your bed, if this is what pleases you more. I bet Ibrahim will have no problem to join us, if this is your honest desire."

He could see it was just a crazy idea, but he had no more arguments left. He was also exhausted and his eyelids felt awfully heavy.

"Before falling asleep, I suggest you call Ibrahim and ask him what he thinks about my idea for an orgy. I'm sure he will have no objection also to share me with you. I'm just a slave you know and he is too. You can order us to do just about anything that pleases you, and we have no right to deny anything you desire, even me having a child with your friend. This is what true friends are for."

She was like a torrent that swept away everything in its path, and he had no way of stopping her mouth from producing the one more audacious idea after the other. In the end she was practically screaming her frustration and he was helpless to make her stop.

"I've told you, you are a Janissary and so is he. You shouldn't be ashamed to share your loot with any comrade in arms," she continued undeterred. "Why don't you go to your bed and sleep it over? I will not bother you anymore. Let's wait. You don't have to take a decision tonight. Tomorrow will be another day."

"And I wonder who gave you all these crazy ideas."

"Your sister did! The Kislar Aga told me that one night Hafsa Sultan ordered him to lead Ibrahim to your sister's room. She was there together with her Nubian slave. No one knows what happened in there; all the Aga knows is that they locked the door. I may be crazy, but the next time you ask me to come over, I will bring my Nubian slave along. My master the Sultan should not have any less pleasure than his slave Pargali Ibrahim."

He slapped hard both her chicks with a broad sweep of his right hand palm and its swift return to make her stop. She silently sought for the hand that had stricken her and when he accommodated, she licked his fingers like a faithful canine. Then, with the coarse voice of a woman still in heat she begged him:

"Please hurt me as much as you can. Show me you are my master and no one else!" she said and her eyes were shimmering like an insane maenad.

****

When the Sultan's Kadin met him in the garden, Gülfem Sultan was very direct.

"I need to talk to you," she said, but it was more like a plea than a firm request.

"We can talk here. I'm not in a hurry to leave. The Sultan asked for Hurrem tonight again."

"Good! It's about her mostly that we have to talk; but this is not the right place to talk for long, trust me. There are too many Black Eunuchs around us and they know how to read lips," she claimed and she looked scared enough to be believable.

"What do you suggest?"

"There is inn close by. The name is Kürkçü Han. You can't miss it. Everyone knows it. They have nice furs from Russia. You can always use a good fur to keep you warm in a bazaar."

It was not clear whether she knew his adventure at the Avret Bazaar, but for the time being it was not so important. The old story was all but forgotten. Now, even the dubious tale with the widow in Manisa had started to fade away. The Prophet was right. In the end everything was bound to pass, as people's memories were emptied not only by death but by oblivion to free space for new memories, another sign that there were limits in everything.

He was now the Grand Vizier and one of his new duties was to be in command of the Janissaries. It was a rebellious corps with extreme discipline as long there was a war in the immediate horizon. They were a dangerous, wild animal feeding on loot, rape and plunder. If they could not find food across the borders of the Empire they sought flesh inside the Great Walls of Constantinople.

He knew of Janissaries all too well. In the Seraglio School he had heard from the guards too many offers full of greedy lust; but, as every other group of people, they included every kind of folks within their ranks. Thank Allah, he had denied them all; otherwise, now he would have been in a most compromised position, if something had leaked. Many of them had died in Rhodes needlessly and despite their complaints about signing a peace treaty, many of them were grateful they had come out alive. There was also Sinan. If he was the purest, he couldn't say; but, with the oncoming wars in Europe their performance was critical, so he had joined the corps too to secure their support.

In times of peace and prosperity it was relatively easy to handle their rebellions as long as you had a full treasury and Selim had accomplished that and much more after looting Syria and Egypt.

He didn't have any trouble finding the Han. It was in the adjacent Mahmud Pasha district. He had to find more about this man. He only knew he was a Christian who became a Grand Vizier right at the Fall of Constantinople, fought hard in east and west for the Sultan, but later fell from favor, when he was slandered by another Christian who turned Muslim to prosper. There were indeed luxurious furs in this Han and he didn't hesitate to buy a fur coat from wolf's hide. If there was a war in the Balkans, it would be useful.

She came dressed in a black cloak with a hood that hid her chestnut hair perfectly, but she also used a thick veil to cover every feature besides her eyes. She seemed tense and she made a nod that meant "follow me". He picked up his coat and followed her suggestion. In one of the four corners of the Han there was a staircase that led to the second floor away from the busy ground floor where men, animals and merchandise mixed incoherently.

In the second floor there was a long series of locked iron doors. She knew where she was going and few times it seemed as if members of the Han staff recognized her; but she didn't stop to talk to anyone and went directly to a corner door and opened it with a key she took out of her purse. Just before getting in she made sure he was right behind her leaving the door barely open.

He went in and bolted the door behind him. Gülfem didn't complaint but took her cloak off and left it on a chair. The room was well appointed with an unexpected degree of luxury for a caravanserai.

"How do you like my home away from home?" she asked him with a naughty smile.

"It's very cozy," he replied and went straight to help her start the fireplace.

"I'm glad you like it. If you ever need to use it, just ask me for the key. I don't come here very often; but, if you ever need it, sent me a note."

"I cannot send you such a note. If it falls into the wrong hands and the Sultan finds out what we share our secrets, he will execute me."

"Nonsense! Just send me a note saying 'Allah is Great' and I will understand."

He didn't feel he had much to say. It was up to her to explain the reasons for this meeting, so he left his coat on the bed, attracting her attention.

"That's a nice fur!" Gülfem concluded after testing with her hand the quality of the pelt.

"Yes, it is. It's not very easy to find coats like this with a double lining. It feels very warm inside it."

"It's also very soft," she added trying to prolong this initial period.

"Try it on," he suggested. "If it fits you, it's yours," he added.

"No, thanks, it would be wasted on me. I don't get out in the cold so often like you."

"Maybe you will soon. Times always change for the better and freedom grows."

"Maybe for you, but for me years have passed without any good news. Allah seems to favor other more wicked souls."

"A friend of mine said that today is the first day of our future, so we have to fight hard and win the next battle," Ibrahim remarked.

"Your friend must be a romantic fool. Some things never change. You and I shall always be slaves of the Sultan."

"That may be true most of the time, but things may change for the better for us. Look at Hurrem for instance. In a few years she rose from a cheap dancer to a Sultan's favorite," he remarked to focus the derailed conversation.

"It's not Hurrem's doing. These days is simply the right era for whores to progress and nobility to recess," she asserted, but her tone was friendly and it contained a hint she include him in the progressing group.

"If nobility is recessing, maybe it's its fault for not being aggressive enough," he snapped back.

"Does the suggestion include me? What should I do? Take my clothes off and dance in front of His Highness, begging for few drops of his divine essence? Even then I would have no hope of matching the performance of a professional dancer from Galata."

"That is true, but women can be attractive in many other ways."

"Yes, they can and they are, but recognition depends also on the mood of the audience, not just the skill of the performer. The Sultan behaves like a deranged perverted beast with women. When he likes to hear poetry, he can summon the best poets, but most of the poets like Rumi are of dubious preferences, you know. They give him strange ideas and dubious visions he must share and experience."

"Yes, I know. Selim Han was one of them and my master likes poetry too; but these are grave words I don't like to hear against my Sultan or any other Osmanli Sultan. They have a treasonous tone I must reject, because the House of Osman is my only hope for magnificence. Anyway, you cannot judge a man on the basis of only one fault. Hurrem is very clever besides being beautiful. She could inspire any man to seed a better world in her womb."

"She is not that beautiful. She is simply deviously clever and she has the ability to turn even the most capable men into fathers of her children."

"Do you know anything more about her?"

"Yes, I do. First of all, she is sold meat! That's usually more than enough to know of a woman; but I know much more."

"I am also a slave, sold meat, but what does that really mean? Words can become very misleading especially when they slip through the crack under a closed door."

"Most Sultans are hypocrites, but slaves may not be as low as their position implies. For instance, you are a magnificent male specimen and a most competent leader. I know how to judge human characters. I've learned it the hard way. I wish you were the Sultan."

"How hard is hard for you?" Ibrahim asked trying to change a dangerous subject.

"I've been raped by the Sultan in my honeymoon exactly as you have been. One night Sultan Selim also invited me to the Marble Kiosk. Isn't that's hard enough for you?"

"It depends. It might have been softer than it seems, if the price was high enough. Allah made us wise and flexible, so we can use both our spirit and our flesh to prosper. If I were in your shoes, I would ask my master to set me free, if he does not wish to use me any longer for his pleasure."

"I have tried that, but it didn't work. He told me that whatever he had conquered he will never let free."

"These are hard words too, but time gradually turns hard men softer. You may simply have to wait a little longer. Everything passes sooner or later as the Prophet warns us. I can even say that what feels hard now will become soft soon enough, perhaps too soon sometimes," Ibrahim added with an imperceptible smile.

"I'm well aware of a woman's duty, but this is exactly my torture. How much longer should I wait, one month, or six months? He hasn't visited me for more than a year. Even a widow's mourning should not last more than few months."

"I believe he is the one who is losing the most."

"No, it's me the greater loser. My youth is fading away. Few years more and I will have to pay dearly to attract men to my bed, or spend all my income in buying young slaves."

"No, your youth is still blooming. If I had the Sultan's permission, I would welcome you into my harem any time you wish. You would be my well cherished rose, I promise you. I will give you all the sons you need to be fully content with your life."

"As they in the Harem say you are quite a prick. You can turn every woman into a whore; but you are wasting your time with me. Suleiman was my first man and I still love and care for him. I know it's silly, but I cannot help it."

"I love him too, but his love cannot fill entirely my heart. I still have empty space left I have to fulfill to feel complete."

"Do you think Hurrem can provide you with the kind of love you seek? Few kinds of loves are very dangerous. You are playing a dangerous game, Ibrahim Pasha, staying for so long inside Hurrem's apartment even in midday. The Kislar Aga is watching you closely."

"Danger is a very thrilling feeling. It keeps me alive. Even by meeting you I took chances. Did I make a mistake? Can you tell me anything more besides Hurrem being a whore and an exquisite dancer? I know all that, but I don't care."

"I do, but you have to promise me to keep this secret to yourself. Suleiman is not the kind of man who shows appreciation to heralds of bad news. I have tried to warn him vaguely, but he didn't wish to hear what I had to say."

"I am not that kind of listener. In every piece of news there are at least two sides provided you are bright enough to use the news to your advantage."

"This is indeed a piece of good news," Gülfem ironically noted.

"What's the story of Hurrem? How did she end up in the Harem from the Avret Bazaar?"

"She was never sold in the Avret Bazaar. The rumor says she was sent straight to Kislar Aga's brothel by her parents. That creep runs also a special kind of brothel by the Galata Tower with under aged Christian lads and lassies for the affluent elderly. They say Seih-Ul-Islam is a regular customer of this charitable establishment for orphans."

"This gossip sounds a bit too much. Are you sure this information is correct?"

"It's correct! Would you like to visit the place to see what goes on in there with your own eyes?"

"I would like that indeed, since I have to know everything before I close any brothel down. I have to because if it belongs to a Janissary, I may start a revolt."

"Closing brothels is a waste of time. If the demand is there, a new one will pop up next door. This is Galata for you. Without taverns and brothels this town would have disappeared centuries before. The capital of an empire should satisfy all its residents otherwise they will move elsewhere. In the Eternal City they worshiped the Virgin Mary, so all the brothels moved to Galata."

"You may be right, but from what I've heard till now, I can only feel pity for Hurrem. Do you know anything about how she uses female hyena glands?"

"I know that many women use them mixed with perfume, perhaps as many as the men who use musk, or the eunuchs who get inspired by jasmine," she replied ironically.

252

"I don't have to use anything to attract women. It's in my nature to be attractive."

"The simple truth is that after what has happened, there is no woman in the Harem who doesn't dream to sleep with you, but very few are bold enough to try it more than once."

"What kind of dreams are you dreaming my sweet Gülfem when you close your eyes the moment of ultimate passion?"

"I dream I could have another son soon."

They didn't have anything more to say, and they knew it. As long as the master remained possessive, the slaves could only enjoy fleeting glimpses of happiness when he was preoccupied with increasing his magnificence.

Ibrahim walked to the window. The snowing season of Constantinople had started. His coat would be useful every time he went out the door, but as the fire place was blazing hot, his clothes felt like an extra weight he could dispense of. The window was facing the street, but in the distance Agia Sophia and the Seraglio closed the view to Asia with their ageless splendor, reminding every resident or visitor that many years ago few extraordinary people had materialized their wildest dreams. Their steaming breaths would soon make this mesmerizing scenery invisible. He could already feel the heat of his growing passion burning his guts. It was too strong to be quenched by itself.

Gülfem's information did not tip the scale heavily against the Sultan's favorite. It simply explained Hurrem's unexpected success. In a few years she had risen from the gutter to the magnificent peak of Topkapi. It had to be some kind of ability he could do nothing but admire. If women could ever become Grand Viziers he might be worried; but, there wasn't a single incident of a woman becoming Keeper of the Hawks, Hasodabashi, Pasha, Beylerbey or Vizier. Their orbits might be parallel but they were asymptotes, so there could be no conflict. In fact, the only conflict he had to parry until now with a woman was with Hafsa Sultan, and she was now literarily eating from his hand.

He slowly turned around unsure of he was about to see.

Gülfem was waiting for him lying naked inside his fur coat on her bed. She had her eyes closed as if she was ashamed of herself, but she shouldn't be. Her goal was sacred and he should be cursed if he denied the most gracious and flattering offer any woman could make to a man, turn his seed into a human being.

Allah was not truly just and benevolent. He was extremely hard on women and overly complacent to men. Men could waste away their seeds daily, but women had only few days every month to put firm foundations to the future of humanity. Allah was extremely partial also in favor of the Sultans. He made the entire world complacent to their greed. He must have thought they were completely useless and unattractive; so he made slaves to be obliged to serve them.

In a sense he was lucky. Suleiman was an attractive man; but, he appeared not willing to pollinate again an exquisite flower like Gülfem. As her name suggested, she was indeed like a rose that now bloomed once more in the middle of a snowstorm seduced by the flames in the fireplace. She was completely hairless, well scented, and sparkling clean. Even from this distance her skin smelled like a field of Bulgarian rosebuds.

Her belly was firm and the ruby in her navel gleaming every time the flames reached a crescendo. Her breast looked practically untouched. It was not as affluent as Hurrem's, but considerably fuller than Hatidge's. The Sultan was insane for leaving such a rosebud to wither away. If beautiful women were not utilized by man, human beauty would gradually fade away.

He absentmindedly took his clothes off, as her image was breathtaking. Perhaps she got a bit worried for the delay because she boldly opened her legs to show him where to aim. It was the wrong kind of move as it offended his judgement. He didn't plan to aim anywhere else even though her henna dyed lips were even more inviting. He had decided to do his duty as a man and leave the rest to her care. She was caring enough to place a fluffy pillow under her waist to promote her chances.

He never worried if a concubine got pregnant. The Quran was plain enough how such an issue should be settled by the man. The Sultan wouldn't mind if he pleased a woman he didn't care much about. However, Gülfem was a Kadin, and a pregnancy would disgrace Suleiman, but she was clever to choose him for this task. It was easy for him to convince him that he had to be fair with all his Kadin to a certain extent.

On the other hand, since he was still free of legal obligations, Hatidge had no right to say anything. Their marriage was destined to proceed, and the fact she already had two children from her departed husband gave him plenty of excuses for this debauchery.

Gülfem got even tenser and opened her eyes briefly not to embarrass his nudity. She was a bit too Muslim for his taste. He was not Hermes of Praxiteles, but the training in the Seraglio School had been a blessing for his body. Now she couldn't keep her eyes closed, and he enjoyed her moral weakness.

He always had the opinion that vision was the sense that should be served first, because it had the greatest effect on appetite, even more than taste or smell. As she watched his passion for her grow, she couldn't resist the temptation to add some more henna on her lips to make them more inviting.

Suddenly an idea was born in her mind that sent chills down his spine. Gülfem had come fully prepared for this encounter. Was this immaculate preparation for his seduction her daily routine? Was their meeting in the garden of the Eski Saray a random event or a carefully orchestrated? Now it was too late to start examine all the existing possibilities. He was not sure how it happened, but he was more than sure that Gülfem didn't have any evil plans. She had lured him in a Han of dubious reputation; however, he could not hold that against her. It was a sign of intelligence. Expensive Han owners would recognize both him and her, and this would create unnecessary gossip in few aristocratic circles. She was wise. He had become a Grand Vizier, but a bit of modesty could bear tasty fruits.

Gülfem had made perfectly clear he would be welcomed some other night too. She had to be modest. She could never be certain a one night affair would produce fruits.

"Take your time. We have an entire night at our disposal," she assured him. "But don't forget to tell Asphodel to arrange an appointment for me with the Sultan soon. Today is one of those days for me to catch a son. Who knows?"

She was careful and practical. She also had a sense of humor and the correct attitude any mother should have. She was nothing at all like Hurrem. Even without other pieces of evidence Hurrem's haste was a clear cut sign of a professional on a tight schedule.

Gülfem's torment had to end. He kneeled on the edge and slowly lifted her legs all the way up his shoulders. They were spread open and as light as feathers. Another flight through the clouds of happiness had started. She was more down to Earth. She knew this visit would be for him a boost of confidence and another occasion for sheer pleasure.

"Give me all you have. I also need to feel wanted as much as you do."

Only time would show now if she was a person to be trusted or a conniver even worse than Hurrem.

****

Hurrem had kept her promise, but Suleiman's sleep was troubled. He saw so many dreams that in the end he could recall none whatsoever. He got up and went to the next room to make sure she was not a dream.

She was there sleeping happily with a pillow in her arms. He went to the other door stepping lightly on his toes. The door was open! Anyone could push down the doorknob and walk in. Slowly he bolted the door and went back to his room.

Where was Ibrahim? Why did he stay away? Where did he sleep that night? He could raise a hundred questions but could find no answer. Since the door was open he might have slipped silently in the darkness not to disturb him and lay down in his bed. Finding a naked woman's body sleeping there, he would be greatly surprised, but it was conceivable he might have thought the woman was a present from his master and enjoy her in every way that pleased him as he would do with every other prostitute he enjoyed during all his frequent visits to Galata brothels. Hurrem would not resist him, thinking he was her master. Then, it would be simply a matter of choice which seeds the woman of his life would choose to turn it into a Prince Heir of the Throne.

Suddenly life had become too complicated. For the time being he could do nothing but ask the guards of his door if they had seen Ibrahim Pasha that night. He opened the door and saw their sleepy faces. They were awake now, but who could be certain they had not taken a nap? His only solution was to ask the spy of the night shift where Ibrahim had spent last night.

He ordered one of the guards to go to the barracks and wake him up. Now he had few minutes left to decide what to do.

****

Suleiman went back to the Hasodabashi bedroom and saw Hurrem still sleeping. She must have being seeing a dream because she was caressing the pillow with passion. Was he going crazy being jealous of a pillow? Was he really a Sultan from the glorious Osman family?

His introspective contemplations were very disturbing. His mother was right. Ibrahim had to get married. His presence here in the Seraglio had only complicated his life. In his home Hatidge Sultan would be guarding her husband. He knew his sister. She was very possessive. She was constantly complaining about her last husband; but he was a Pasha and had every right to go out and have a night away from home with his friends. He was a military man after all and in every battle he was putting his life on the line. Women simply had no consideration for a man's feelings.

He suddenly heard Hurrem talking in her sleep. She was sighting full of passion and whispering names. He came closer to discern the name of the man she called for. He couldn't be mistaken. Her voice was loud and clear.

"Fuck me Ibrahim; fuck me any way you want. Let me have it all. I can take it. Please have pity on me and don't stop now! Rip me up, I need it!"

He simply couldn't believe his ears. Hurrem had not only slept with Ibrahim last night, but she had really enjoyed it. He had never heard her scream like that. The blood rushed in his brain with such pressure, he thought his scull would bust. He simply was stunned and had no idea what to do next. He simply couldn't keep on staring at her as she moved her belly up and down the pillow, so he looked away trying to regain his composure.

But suddenly he couldn't believe his ears, even when he heard her laughter gurgling and translucent like a brook cascading down a waterfall.

"Next morning, don't make so much noise, visiting me. I don't mind waking up early for another round, but I rather have you start my rape with a kiss. Grabbing my breasts next will also send chills down my spine."

She looked very sensuous with her fleshy lips just a bit apart so her white teeth showed like pearls in line, but he was still so upset his heart kept pounding in his chest.

"Come here," she ordered him. "You are too excited. I don't want you to die in my hands. Your mother had me trained me for months how to arouse men and then comfort their passions any way they chose."

He obeyed because his heart was pounding like never before, but soon she left him no doubts she was telling the truth. Unconsciously he counted time with his heartbeats. He had recovered all his male confidence after no more than a hundred strokes. He was her master again and asked her to get dressed because he was waiting a visitor.

"Is Ibrahim coming this morning?" she asked with pretentious excitement that got on his nerves.

He refused to answer. Then, the spy came in with his report. He was still yawning, but the Sultan didn't seem to care. Ibrahim after leaving the Eski Saray he had slept in a nearby caravanserai. He didn't know the reasons for such a choice, but he was grateful he had not sought his old residence as a Hasodabashi.

Suleiman's great grandfather Fatih had turned the district around the Grand Bazaar into a shelter for merchants. He didn't know exactly where this caravanserai was located, but the name he remembered well. It was the Kürkçü Han, the Caravanserai of the Furriers. His slave had to provide adequate explanations for his actions, but he had no doubts they would be convincing. It was natural for a man like Ibrahim to visit such an ill reputed place before his marriage. Now all he had to do was to exert his authority.

"You better go back to the Eski Saray at once," he ordered her to show he was in command.

"I need a carriage. The Kislar Aga who brought me here must be still sleeping."

"Go to the stables and tell them you need a carriage at once."

"I will, but do they know who I am?"

She was doing it more difficult to test his resolve.

"Why don't I stay here and when you finish your work, we can have lunch together," she proposed next.

"No, my wish is for you to leave my residence at once," he ordered her sternly.

"May I spend some time in the Grand Bazaar on my way back to do some shopping? I've heard they brought some new fabrics from India," she pleaded.

She was just teasing him to test his nerves again. To stop her meaningless objections, he finally gave the kind of order she desired. The carriage would take her back after a stop in the Bazaar for shopping. Leaving she gave him a kiss. Surprisingly she was still hot with desire.

****

"Take me to the Kürkçü Han!" she ordered the coachman.

She simply had to know what exactly was going on with Ibrahim. He had an effect on her as if he was her pimp and she was getting awfully jealous of his escapades.

****

As Ibrahim woke up his hand instinctively searched the pillow beside him. It was empty. She was simply too scared to take unnecessary chances.

Gülfem had every right to be upset, bitter and vindictive with the Sultan. The child that was lost was hers too. Now that he was all alone he tried to recall the entire experience and gather the memories he should retain. There was nothing of an entire night to discard. Up to that moment he was always making love like a thief; but she had made him a master and he fully enjoyed the privilege. It was a completely different experience. She had all the time to raise deliberately the level of pleasure to the highest possible and then let his pleasure explode.

It was completely silly, but he felt several times like Fatih when his huge gun sent stone after stone his projectiles to weaken the structure of the Great Walls, and what immense pleasure engulfed him, when he saw her tension subside as he melted inside her womb.

Gülfem was not too lusty, and he never regretted for a single moment her insistence to utilize his every drop to water the tree of life in her guts. It was one more time when the end justified the means. This was their silent agreement from the very beginning and he didn't have any objection to fully comply with her emotional needs that were his too.

She didn't have to say it, but there would be other times where she would be more open to suggestions. Her lips were ruby red and her proportions ideal. Her legs were light but they were also firm, as firm as his. Her village must have been up in the Pindos Mountain Range, and when she was young, she had to run up and down the slopes as much as he had in Parga.

The thought of Parga broke down his audacious fantasies about his future escapades. He had not visited Parga all these years, and now as a Grand Vizier he ought to program such a trip. Unfortunately Parga was a fortress still in the hands of the Venetians, so a formal visit was completely out of the question. A better idea would be to invite his immediate relatives in the Eternal City. Now he was on his way to become so rich that his parents could spend their last days in perfect comfort. Perhaps a house next to the Rumeli Hissar would remind them the hilly slopes of Parga.

Birthplaces had a silly effect on people. Every human liked to be buried in the place where he was born. He didn't care enough to preserve such illusions. All he cared was to have a happy death. If his mind had such ability, he wouldn't object if tonight he fought Death not at the marble threshing floors of the old Roman legend, but on the Great Walls where his cannon had demolished Gülfem's last line of resistance several times.

Was Gülfem sincere, when she said she had never felt like that, or was this the usual gracious comment of every noble lady the result of her aristocratic training? Her request they should meet again soon just before she went out the door was very flattering. Hurrem had never uttered any such complement. She must have had greater thrills in the arms of a gang of marauding Tatars with their long mustaches. Perhaps next time he should ask her to clarify this point. He was perhaps a bit silly, but he was also very competitive.

A soft knock on the door interrupted his contemplations.

"Who is it?" he asked and tried to get up to open the door, but there was need for that. Gülfem leaving had left it open for the cleaning ladies to change linen and set things straight.

Hurrem walked in as if she owned the place.

He wouldn't take any more of that. Gülfem had been a model of good of good manners.

"Who do you think you are to come barging in my room like Mehmet the Conqueror?" he noticed in a mocking disposition.

"I'm your guarding angel!" she claimed. "The Sultan is looking for you. He knows you are here and he intends to send his Janissaries to fetch you. I simply had to warn you and save your neck."

She didn't have to say anything more to get him out of his bed and she didn't miss the chance to examine him from a closer distance.

"You seem exhausted. I bet making love inside a double lined fur coat makes all the difference."

"Don't be silly. The woman makes all the difference, and this woman was truly exquisite. She was the best fuck of my life. She was even better than Basmi."

"How about Mahidevran, was she any better?"

"I've never touched Mahidevran on my word of honor."

"That's not what I've heard in the Harem, but I don't care who you screw. These moments are past and gone. My only worry is the future. Who was your bride tonight? Did you please her enough to come for a second serving like me?"

"It's none of your concern. I don't know even her name. It was so unexpected!"

"But I do and her perfume is unmistakable. I have a nose for such delicate tasks. Now please tell me, if Gülfem is so good, how come my Suleiman never invites her to his bedroom?"

He had to admit Hurrem was something else. She was not a witch but her abilities exceeded the norm.

"Let's go!" he ordered her trying to exercise his dubious authority.

"No! I want you to fuck me too inside this fur coat."

"Are you crazy? You've just said the Janissaries are coming."

"I don't care. I'm a concubine of the Imperial Harem and no Janissary has ever seen my face. If they come in, you should simply say that I'm just another whore you've hired for your pleasure. If they insist to test my charms as a whore, they will have to wait in line. I can handle all of them. In fact, I'm looking forward to such a test of my sincerity."

"You are a whore, no doubt about it."

"Yes I am. I enjoy men a lot almost as much as you do. That makes you a male whore too. Just tell me how much it will cost me this visit."

Hurrem was clearly trying to provoke him, and to prove that her intention were serious, she picked up and wore his coat. He had to admit it fitted her better than Gülfem because she was much more voluptuous and thus closer to his dimensions; but then he realized he was still nude and every change on his body was clearly visible. It would be ridiculous to try to hide the inspiring effect she had on him. She was not that kind of woman, who would feel embarrassed staring at a naked man gradually coming under the spell of the Holy Spirit, as Selim Khan mocked his carnal trend for procreation. On the contrary, he felt that with Hurrem he should become more offensive.

"So, how do you rate me as a man? Am I better than a bunch of Tatars?" he asked to challenge her, but she was not the kind of woman who would back down from a vulgar brawl.

"You are definitely a bigger man than any Tatar or Turk I know, but both come in hordes!" she replied most audaciously.

He simply couldn't stand her impudence any more. He grabbed the edges of her sleeves and turned her around as if they were folk-dancing. Then, he lifted her coat to check her degree of preparation of any courtesan to meet her client. Under her dress she was stark naked to save time. He made the connection more violently than any other time in his life to hurt her, but he failed to achieve this goal, because she didn't make any move to resist, but simply enjoyed his vigor until it was too painful for him to continue hurting her.

He was so hasty on purpose, trying to deny her every bit of pleasure, but he could never succeed inflicting any pain. The more violent he was the more she enjoyed. It was a confrontation that couldn't last for long. Compared to her, Gülfem was an angel of patience, tenderness, confidence and sheer determination. Gülfem had been taught early on that men enjoyed more decent women than wild ones. Even if they both had lost their virginity, they offered the illusion of purity to every marauding raping male they found in their lifetime.

Perhaps the idea of starting a dry run to balance out her act was exciting at first, but gradually, as the circular motion of her waist proved without a doubt she had repented, accepting that his anger was justified and had to be properly quenched, his initial fury finally subsided. She started moaning full of submission and this kind of attitude was translated in his mind as an offer to surrender he simply could not resist. She was willing to try anything to soften his heart. Her intentions were peaceful. She had come to trade pleasure rather than rob it.

She didn't seem to raise unreasonable demands on his vigor as time was short and this was more her doing rather than his. After all, as a Galata dancer she was trained to provide and accept the maximum pleasure in the least possible amount of time. Soon her screams practically dictated his next action, but it may have been just a show to amplify his pleasure to a new, higher level.

When he asked her to be less noisy, she explained that her show was not for him, but for the Janissaries who may have arrived and spied outside the door. Finally, she became very content with the result and he did not regret for a single moment her surprising visit. If something worth keeping from his entire Ukrainian maiden experience was that the surprise attack was the basic element that practically guaranteed her success and his unconditional adjustment to her wishes. He also had to admit that Hurrem had transformed prostitution into an art as he had a hard time distinguishing what was real and what a skillful act. Her mind was now focused on adding more illusions to her repertoire to make sure her customer would return; otherwise, her final suggestion didn't make sense.

"Next time you decide to fuck Gülfem, invite me too. I will hide in the closet. It's the only way you can convince me you like to fuck her more than me."

Now, he simply could not resist posing the critical question.

"Why are you such a whore?" he inquired and practically forced her explosion of passion in a cataract of laughter that seemed it would never end as even the Janissaries were not willing to interrupt out of oriental curtesy.

"My mother made me what I am," she finally confessed. "A wise Hasodabashi must know daughters take after their mothers," she explained the moment she became sober, but seeing his doubts written all over his face, she changed her tune in a flash. "No, I'm lying. My mother had nothing to do with my choice to become a tramp. Hard pricks like yours truly made me what I am."

****

There was a firm knock on the door and then, when nobody cared to answer, a stronger one erupted that shook the iron-clad door on its hinges.

"OK, guys!" she screamed at the besiegers. "Be patient! You wouldn't like interruptions too, so do not interrupt. This is what sweet Jesus preaches us all."

He rushed to get dressed, while she helped him perfectly calm to sort out his clothes. Eventually, as he opened the door, she pushed him quickly out with her fur coat wide open, since the Janissaries obviously had no eyes for anything else.

"Listen guys, today is my fur coat day. If you like what you see, just go down to the first floor, buy me a coat each and then form a line," she ordered before she slammed the door in their faces.

She was unbelievably bold and he was the Grand Vizier.

"Do you know who I am?" he asked them just to be sure.

"Yes, we do! You are the Grand Vizier Pargali Ibrahim Pasha," they all screamed in tandem.

"Good! If you forget what you saw, then you are up for a tip and a transfer to the new post of your dreams, the Galata harbor," he declared and opened his purse distributing equally the content.

They all thanked him for the tip and the transfer except one Janissary who seemed thoughtful and said nothing.

"Didn't you hear what I said?" Ibrahim asked him.

"Yes, I did, but I think I'm in love with this whore. How much a fur coat like that will cost me?"

"Comrade, I don't wish to scare you off, but it might cost you your life," he sternly replied.

****

Was he crazy for taking such risks with the Sultan's favorites? What was again this curious Hurrem's statement about him and Mahidevran Sultan? His straightforward reply hadn't convinced Hurrem. Sooner or later he had to clear his doubts directly with the Princess; but, how could a slave ask a Sultan's legal wife whether he had ever made love to her unknowingly? Perhaps, asking Gülfem Sultan if she heard something would be much easier.

****

The Sultan this time was much calmer than any recent time. He didn't ask why he had disappeared, but just what had happened. He seemed very relieved he had not spent last night in the Hasodabashi's bedroom but with a whore, and this was contrary to the recently established pattern of insane jealousies.

"Since I am to marry in few months, I thought of enjoying my liberty for the last time. In the mountains of my district, when the Ottoman armies appeared under the leadership of Mahmud Pasha, the native Albanians attacked him screaming 'Liberty or Death' and won many brilliant shorthanded victories. However, I am not so fanatic about liberty. Complete liberty means also loneliness. I would never trade my slavery in Constantinople for total freedom on a mountain peak," he replied confidently with a long smile.

Suleiman seemed happy with his answer and showed his appreciation with a conciliatory smile.

"Perhaps my mother is right. Perhaps it's best for both of us, if we reside in different households. Hurrem actually asked me to move my harem to Topkapi now that you are gone. She claims it would be best for our children to live in the same environment with both their parents. This of course means that I have to build new extensions to my apartments, or even raise a separate building for all the concubines and Kadin in my household. What do you think about such an arrangement?"

Ibrahim didn't have to think for long to reply. Having all concubines under a single house next to the Sultan's Selamlik sounded like a terrible idea. As the arrangement was now, a Sultan's messenger entered discretely the Eski Saray relaying the Sultan's wishes to the Aga of the Black Eunuchs who informed the lucky favorite of her next engagement. Then, during the day the favorite was led secretly to the hammam quarters where in total privacy she was prepared to be as presentable and as desirable as possible by the Black Eunuchs and her courtiers. Then, at night in total secrecy to avoid gossip she was transported to the Yeni Seraglio in Topkapi to entertain her master in privacy and seclusion.

If the same procedure was carried out in close quarters where everyone could see what was going on this would lead undoubtedly to endless quarrels among the concubines and possible violent confrontations; thus, he didn't hesitate to say so.

"Maybe you are right," the Sultan said after a brief contemplation.

"Of course I am right, at least theoretically; but, I'm not the ideal person to ask such a question. I don't even have a harem yet. Perhaps you should ask also the advice of your mother on such a practical matter, Her Excellency Hafsa

Sultan. "As I see it, your harem operates now in purity, discretion and isolation. Only if you wish to organize orgies, having all these lusty women under the same roof would make any sense," he asserted with ironic disposition, but the Sultan didn't care to laugh, he looked very worried with the prospect of such perilous cohabitation.

Somehow in his Muslim mind the word "orgy" was related to the abomination of Christianity or paganism.

****

Hafsa Sultan was much more theatrical in her reaction.

"Over my dead body!" she exclaimed and laughed sardonically. "I know men as well as I know women. This suggestion will demolish a century old tradition. Any young Sultan would be overwhelmed by his greed, if he has so many women living next door. My son, you are undoubtedly a fair man. Only if you wish to die of exhaustion you should invite more than one concubine in your bedroom. Their competition will literally break your heart. Even your father Selim the Just had constant trouble with his harem, and in the end he was accepting visits from virtuous princesses only if he was convinced they might lead to worthy sons. The rest of the time he was just fooling around with his damned eunuchs in total darkness fully sedated, so he couldn't tell the difference."

"It was not my idea. Hurrem has suggested this new arrangement, so we don't waste much time traveling back and forth at night especially during the winter. At the moment only she has to move with the coach, not the entire harem."

"I can sympathize with her request. She loves you a great deal and she wants to serve you better, but she is too selfish for comfort. She doesn't think coolly as I do; but, I am a mother and I think only for the good of my son; so just forget her suggestion and respect the Ayin of your ancestors. They knew best."

"What do you think if I was to dismiss all my other concubines and restrict my harem only to Hurrem and Mahidevran?"

"And what will you do with Gülfem? She is very pretty, obedient and extremely well-mannered. She also made you a worthy son, poor Murat who was so fair Allah took him up in heavens to serve Him. She does not deserve to be expelled from your arms for life simply because Allah stole her son."

"OK! I will keep her too in the Seraglio and visit her occasionally only."

"My answer is still no, even though I can see few practical advantages. For instance, you will save all these big salaries for Black Eunuchs that are now wasted. However, if you limit your harem to just three women, then you are just a common man not a mighty Sultan. The more women you have locked in your harem the more your enemies will respect you. Respect is a subtle form of envy."

****

263

The Sultan didn't feel very confident announcing his decision to do nothing. He could see that his mother and his friend were right, but deep in his heart he felt he needed Hurrem now more than ever and anyone else. His other two Kadin were useful as mothers, but not critical for his everyday happiness.

He didn't know what kind of new arguments Hurrem may have, but to sooth her heart he decided to show her he was ready to make few changes in their lives. He decided to visit Hurrem at Eski Saray the same night to make this preference known by breaking at least one rule. He would visit her apartment at night unannounced to surprise her and show her she was always attractive to his taste no matter what she wore or how extensively she had been prepared to please him.

If everything went well, he was going to spend the entire night there, and show her how much he loved her also in the morning. If he was indeed a Janissary as she claimed, he would show her his unbending will to exercise his body at daybreak each and every morning fairly for her pleasure.

****

Arriving at the Eski Saray, he found the two Black Eunuchs guarding her door dozing on a bench and woke them up. The slaves seeing in the oil lamp's flame who was he, they fell down on their knees to worship him, but he beckoned them not to make any noise and wake up his children sleeping in adjoining rooms.

He went next to their beds and looked at Sehzade Mehmet. His precious boy slept quietly and his chest rose and fell rhythmically; but suddenly his breathing stopped forcing the father's heart to leap off its tracks. Fortunately, quickly Mehmet resumed breathing freely and quicker with minute anguish.

The boy must have been seeing a bad dream. He bent over and kissed him, and the little boy woke up briefly; but seeing the face of his father over him, smiled faintly and fell asleep again this time much quieter. Something had changed and he felt proud of his accomplishment. If he had seen his father's face in the middle of the night leaning over his bed, it would be a nightmare and he would lose his sleep for weeks.

Many years had passed since he had his first son, Sehzade Mustafa, but through all these years he never had the chance to observe his children while they were sleeping as any ordinary father could.

During his childhood years, Selim Khan was simply too busy planning victorious wars, or inviting dubious visitors into his bedroom after midnight in the Marble Kiosk he had built for this purpose. Few years ago he might have been able to sleep next to his father's bed, but now this chance for such an emotionally soothing experience was lost forever.

He next wondered how many years would pass before his children missed their chance too, thirty, twenty, ten or maybe even less, if he kept living away from them. Death could come and knock on their doors anytime.

The poisonous snakes of anxiety encircled him once more after the death of his children, his father and his brothers. Death was lurking behind every human's back like a Mute Executioner. This much he knew well, living for years under his father's shadow; but when he was younger, he had hoped Allah would look after his Shadow.

Hurrem was correct in a way urging him to move the Harem next door. He should live indeed like any other ordinary man, since ordinary men enjoyed many more daily pleasures than simply the illusion of a Sultan that he could invite a new virgin to their bed every week. It was an illusion that couldn't last long. Virgins were mediocre lovers anyway. Hurrem was simply a genius when it came into his life to offer him a much greater variety of pleasures. Without knowing it with her tricks she was providing him with everything a refined man needed to feel he was special. With the help of the midwives, she became a virgin after each birth to please the insatiable vanity of an Ottoman Sultan.

This was one of the tricks she used to satisfy his lust for the unusual, the extraordinary. She was as wicked as the most devious eunuchs who masqueraded wearing the clothes of a concubine to excite the passions of his father, as Asphodel had admitted. It was one of the old tricks eunuchs used, even Sinan Pasha, Selim's favorite Grand Vizier no one dared to disclose.

Next he went to her bedroom. She was sleeping quietly as if she had no worries in the world. She had once more a pillow close by, but this time she had placed it between her legs. It was a cold night and she was probably feeling cold even under the blanket. Surely she must have been cold; otherwise, why would she throw also a wolf's fur over her body?

He took off his caftan, lifted the fur and slipped under the hairy hide. She didn't wait long to react by pressing her firm buttocks on his groin. She was still half-asleep and every move she made was half-instinctive half-conscious; but, that didn't mean she didn't know how to provide full pleasure openhandedly to her bold invader. If the pleasure she enjoyed was more or less intensive, it was very difficult still to discern. One critical issue was certain. It was not equal as equality is impossible in a universe that thrives on inequality.

"Suleiman!" she cried with the passion of an "Eureka" even though her eyes had not opened yet, and he considered her cry a call to intensify his efforts, because it was clear she could use more, much more of his love. Her flesh was like a sponge that absorbed every drop of moisture in the feverish action that seemed to transform magically heat into friction into waves of pleasure in a demonical circle that seemingly defied the most sacred laws of Mother Nature.

****

If this primordial dance of humans on top of a wild animal's fur was a religious ritual that summoned the forces of good and evil to fight for supremacy, it was very hard to say even for a man whose eyes were used to discern even black flesh in the darkness, the Kislar Aga. His main duty was to

265

provide more pleasure to his one and only master, the Sultan, utilizing the flesh of an odalisque. He had fulfilled this obligation in the best of his abilities that night, so his next concern was to pay a visit to the most frustrated odalisque or Kadin and sooth her passions to prevent an explosion of lust that could demolish the reigning peace inside the Eski Saray.

Now it was time for him to leave. He had done his duty to his master, as everyone knew that to start a good fire that could burn a log to ashes you had to use tinder. The Kislar Aga was the tinder of every imperial harem as he understood his duties since the days he was the Kislar Aga in the imperial majesty the Mameluke Sultan in the Citadel of Cairo, and later when Selim Khan took command of Egypt and the Middle East.

Perhaps he was not as bright as Ibrahim Pasha, but he was bright enough to choose what was best for the Empire's interests, and obeying a single master was safer than trying to serve many masters with conflicting interests. Tonight everything had gone well and in nine months his true master would have another baby to show and prove Hurrem's worth as well as he had proven his as a competent and discrete Aga.

Chapter 9
In the At Meidan

"And never marry an idol worshipper unless she worships Allah.
A faithful slave is better than an infidel who pleases you"
(Quran, Sura II, 221)

The date of Hatidge and Ibrahim's marriage quickly approached and the impatience in Constantinople grew quickly like a plague that started in the Seraglio and slowly spread from the wide avenues to the narrower streets all the way to the crooked "mahala" of the Vlaherna district and the Yedikule, until no resident of the Ottoman Metropolis was left immune.

Soon no one could find the patience to hear the guns on the Sea Walls thundering once more, announcing the time had come to start singing, eating, dancing or secretly drinking. The happiest of the entire lot of nations were the Greeks because they saw that within three generations a man who had Greek blood in his veins would become the bridegroom of the Sultan. They hoped that if one day Turkish and Greek blood mixed well enough, then the old prophesy for the resurrection of the marble king would be bloodlessly realized.

However, all these mad hopes and illusions were kept secretly, deep in their hearts, and not a single whisper escaped so that their divine plans would not be revealed.

The only Romans that kept their distances from these events were the Orthodox priests who most strongly despised the change of faith of the new Grand Vizier. They were afraid that perhaps this trend might spread wildly among their flock reducing their influence.

On the other hand, to balance the world also the cynic realists existed. They considered the price was a fair enough for a slave to achieve so rich rewards; so, they decided to keep a safe distance from these events and waited until an accurate assessment of the new conditions could be made. Anyway, after the Fall of Constantinople, the Greek Patriarch had the same rights over the remaining Romans as the Roman Emperor used to have long ago.

Of course, there were recently also few poisonous rumors the Sultan did not thoroughly approve of this union that would separate him from his favorite slave. Now Ibrahim Pasha would have to spend the nights with his bride. Nevertheless, the fact that Ibrahim Pasha's new palace was now being built across the At Meidan within walking distance from the Topkapi Seraglio appeared as a logically balanced choice.

The Grand Vizier should always reside close to his master to be available at first notice, but it was a decision that raised a few eyebrows. This new palace was closer to the Sultan's residence than the Eski Saray, an undeniable fact which meant the Sultan's ties with his Grand Vizier were stronger than with his Kadin and his sons, or even his mother Hafsa Sultan, the all-mighty Valide Sultan. She was the audacious woman who had stolen the title "Sultan" rather than the more common and modest "Hatun" the moment Selim Khan left his last breath possibly to revenge her long neglect.

For the Sultan this marriage had to be a very difficult choice as blood ties should be strong; but on the other hand, which subject would complain against a Sultan who gave the welfare of his empire higher priority than his own blood?

Sultan Suleiman was a fair sovereign and had shown the proper attention to the education of his firstborn son, Mustafa. He had subscribed him to the Janissary Corps and trained him in the Seraglio School as any other ordinary student to become as an accomplished military leader as all his ancestors. These were the critical decisions that characterized a mighty Sultan, not with which eunuch or attractive youngster he spent the nights.

Nevertheless, the general consensus was that as long as the welfare of the state was the Sultan's main occupation and not just lusty women and debauchery, the Ottoman Empire had nothing to fear.

Mustafa had soon proved he would become a great warrior. As he grew up, the blood of Selim was making its mark. The boy had the same fierce look in his eyes and showed the same dexterity in handling arms, the sword and the bow. He was also a capable horseman, a virtue that meant his mother's Tatar blood had been combined with the Turcoman to provide almost perfection. And there were many colts with the blood of Karabulut in the Sultan's stable for every grandson of Selim to choose from. After all, the Sultan had given only a mare to his bridegroom as a present, and that meant a lot to anyone who knew about men and horses. The very best stallions were reserved for the members of the imperial family, not a slave of dubious preferences.

This was probably the reason why there were rumors that claimed the

Sultan had tried to find another bridegroom for his sister. There was even a name that had leaked, Iskander Chelebi Pasha; however, these unsubstantiated rumors were quickly refuted. If the Sultan had chosen Ibrahim as his Grand Vizier, why would he rather give his sister as a bride to a minor Vizier good only in finances?

Suleiman's beloved daughter Mihrimah was just too young to be considered as a bride for Ibrahim Pasha. If she was ten years older maybe a marriage like this would make sense, but now it was simply inconceivable. The rumors that Hatidge Sultan was in love with Ibrahim and could not wait to become his bride made more sense than any other dubious rumor.

Ibrahim was the most handsome man in the Empire and anyone could see that now when his beard had grown, dispersing better than anything else the malicious rumor that Ibrahim was a eunuch. A eunuch was unquestionably the new Hasodabashi, Asphodel. It was an appointment that also made good sense. If a eunuch was good for the father's harem, why should be changed when the son became the Sultan?

Ibrahim had simply served as an Odabashi, when Suleiman was just a Prince Heir in Manisa and Sultan Selim was still alive. Now that Suleiman had become the Sultan and Selim's harem was dispersed or engulfed, it was natural for the Sultan to choose the same Hasodabashi in the same way the Kislar Aga of Selim who governed the Eski Saray had remained unchanged. This was what logic demanded. To avoid any complains there was no reason to change a hierarchy that had worked perfectly through many happy years.

As long as Piri Pasha was efficient in the siege of Belgrade and the city had fallen in record time, no one would ever think of changing him; but the siege of Rhodes had been unnecessary long and produced many casualties for minimum gains. Changing Piri Pasha with Ahmet Pasha had also not produced any fruits and the city had fallen through negotiations, which was a solution bad for the moral of the Janissaries. Thus, the leadership had to change to reflect the fact the Sultan was not very pleased with the outcome.

This had to be the message the Sultan was trying to give by posting Ahmet Pasha far away to govern Egypt. If a Pasha was not good in war, maybe his talent was peace and taxation.

There should always be a second choice for every man to prove his worth. From the moment Ibrahim Pasha was chosen to become Grand Vizier, having Ahmet Pasha in the Eternal City would create only difficulties. Till then, Ahmet was the next Pasha in line to become Grand Vizier and his ambitions had most justly been frustrated after his failure in Rhodes.

Now what was left to see was if Ahmet Pasha would succeed in Cairo and if Ibrahim was the best possible choice as a Grand Vizier in the Eternal City. This only time would show and the Sultan had shown he was a patient and wise young man. If he was also eager to conquer, his reign would do nothing but beneficial for the Ottomans.

****

One of the great harem mysteries for Suleiman Khan was how Hatidge Sultan had fallen in love with his favorite slave locked inside the Harem according to the old Muslim ethics. Hafsa Hatun had explained to him that Ibrahim was the best choice for a bridegroom, but this could not explain the strong emotional bond that was evident in this union. When he asked his mother for an explanation, all he got was the all familiar excuse that Eros was beyond ordinary logic and should remain so to add spice to our lives.

He had been obliged to refrain from this line of questioning, when his mother posed a similar question to him, namely, how did he ever choose Ibrahim and make him his best friend in Manisa? Ibrahim being an accomplished oud player didn't make much sense to her. With the same reasoning he should make his favorite poet the next Seih-ul-Islam or Kapudan Pasha to rule the waves.

He stopped immediately this discussion with hearty laughter for her joke, but offered no explanation, admitting there were few secrets that should not be revealed. However, he was still puzzled about his sister's romance. His next source was the Kislar Aga, but that occasion had been proven ill chosen. Hurrem was then present, and forcefully intervened with a general motto:

"My darling, our Kislar Aga doesn't know whatever happens in the Harem. He is just one man and there are at least one hundred rooms and closed doors. How would he become aware of every rumor spreading from room to room? Women in the Harem have so much time to spend, doing practically nothing but bathe, sit, smoke hashish and opium, and talk waiting for your invitation. Your noble princesses have even less to do than any of us in this damned Saray, because they expect no one to summon them to do their duty as women. Instead of complaining, you should be thankful that since the loss of her husband, she kept herself so seductive to attract the eyes of your most selective slave. The only explanation I can find is that she trusted blindly the opinion of her mother who undoubtedly searched extensively the virtues of your friend to make sure her son was keeping the right company, as any loving mother should. If your mother approved of Ibrahim, who in your Harem would dare to doubt her judgment? Isn't she who chose me as your best courtesan? Wasn't this the more successful match any Valide Sultan has ever made? You have to realize that your mother all these years she spent abandoned by your father in the Eski Saray did nothing but evaluate how much the constant expression of passions between a man and a woman is critical for their happiness. Unquestionably your father was a great warrior, but do you truly think he died a happy man? The rumor says that during his last days he spent in his tent surrounded by eunuchs, at last he was yearning for a woman."

"I've never heard of any such a rumor. Who told you this?"

"There is no way to find how a rumor starts and you should be aware this law. Rumors are like the Labyrinth. The only useful path one can try is to search if where there is a fire under the smoke he sees rising. As you know at the time Piri

Pasha was almost constantly with your father, so he can tell you better than anyone else, if this is true or not. All I know is hearsay among Black Eunuchs; but you know how unreliable men without balls can be. If they were reliable and trusty, why any wise Ottoman would say that trusty men have big balls?"

"I am a bit confused with your unusual logic. Are you suggesting I should go and ask Piri Pasha about my father's last days?"

"This is one handy man your father trusted blindly, but if you feel uncomfortable to make a similar inquiry, you can ask Ibrahim to ask it and then check Piri's balls too. From what I've heard your father trusted him blindly and made him his falconer too. You must definitely trust him too, because you made him your Grand Vizier. Ibrahim must be aware by now what happened in Chorlou, because he was very close with the two favorite eunuchs of your father, Menekse and Asphodel. Poor Menekse died in Chorlou, but his brother is your new Hasodabashi. It means your trusted Grand Vizier trusts him completely, so you should trust him too. However, a wise sovereign should not trust the words of a woman like me, because another motto says that only men are true to their word, and I am definitely a woman."

"You are right! Asphodel must be the only man who knows exactly how Selim Khan last behaved," Suleiman consented a bit confused by her arguments.

"Indeed this would also be a good test to prove the loyalty of your new Hasodabashi. If he confirms what I told you, then you need no other proof that sometimes even men with crushed balls maybe be as sincere as the woman of your heart."

"I'm somewhat confused with your line of reasoning today. Who do you suppose I should ask about the name of the woman my father called in his deathbed?"

"Look for a man who you can trust completely. He will tell you the truth."

"Do you know of such a man?"

"Of course I do, but it's just hearsay, so I will be the last woman who will poison your heart. I'd rather remain your best fuck. Anyway, whenever I see you, I simply cannot focus my attention on anything else but how to empty your full balls. Do you think that there is any truth to the rumor that men who empty their balls often are not as sincere as abstinent men who keep them full for the right woman?"

Suleiman could not abstain now from laughing his heart out. This woman knew a way to wipe all his worries away in a single stroke. His father was right. The best way for a man to trust a woman was to make her the mother of his children. Children shared the same blood with their mother, and watching a woman go through the toils of birth was the proof a man needed for her fidelity; so he tried a sweet tasting blackmail.

"Tell me where I can find such a skillful woman, and I will make the best present you can ever imagine."

"Is this what you promise to all your Kadin to make her fall at your feet and kiss the tip of your caftan?" she snapped back with a subtle allegory, kneeling also in front of his feet to prove her uninterrupted devotion to his magnificent authority.

"The name, please!" he insisted with determination, but his will to resist was no match for her relentless fortitude to please him.

****

Kissing the edge of his caftan could be just the start of an invasion. A caftan was no better protection than a woman's dress. It only hid the skin from eager eyes, but it was just a cover to hide strengths or weaknesses; however, skillful hands or hungry lips could turn any strength into a weakness. This was the will of Allah who constantly tested the will of women, Sultans or even Grand Viziers to find their true worth as His followers.

Women should be weaker than men as they could be raped if they dared to refuse to bear the sons of the faithful. This divine plan was sound; but a sound plan did not always succeed, and every citizen of the Eternal City knew that.

Agia Sophia was a divine temple built under divine instructions; however, the dome had collapsed few times. This didn't mean the divine plan was fallacious. It simply meant the builders were of lower stature than the task. If Allah made earthquakes and the domes fell, it was simply Allah's will to test the builders' skills. Thus, if a Sultan's caftan was shaped like a dome it was to make sure his subjects realized his authority was universal and only under it a slave could find happiness and prosperity.

****

Hurrem was aware of Suleiman's weaknesses and how to take advantage of them. The Kislar Aga had taught her that to test a man's worth she always had to put him under stress, and then see how he behaved; so, she lifted the corner of Suleiman's caftan and slipped quickly under it. It was a delicate moment and the Kislar Aga was discrete enough not to follow the developments, so he paid his respects and with a deep bow left the room in a hurry. This didn't mean he was not curious to check the performance of his best protégé. She had proven beyond the shadow of a doubt that she could easily extend successfully simply by instinct the limits of his instructions into unknown territories.

Nevertheless, if Hurrem's plan was to make the Sultan forget his initial inquiry about Ibrahim and Hatidge, the plan had failed because it was not a good idea to try to erase the suspicion of debauchery with more debauchery. On the contrary, it was the best way to amplify it. Even her insinuations about how a Sultan would test a man's sincerity may have sounded like a witty remark, but it was the first hint that White Eunuchs should not be trusted. Then, the next step would be that men who trusted eunuchs should also be regarded with suspicion; but the most elegant hit under the belt was her remark that the men with the empty testicles should be the next in line of suspicion.

She had lived under Selim's terror long enough to know that such a mentality would not disappear simply because the instigator had ceased to exist. Despite the demise of Menekse, the White Eunuchs were still a unit with powerful influence. Every potential usurper of Selim's authority had to put all eunuchs Black or White under his rule.

Ibrahim had already made the first move reinstating Asphodel in an influential post. It would very hard for a woman to challenge the hold a masculine man could exert on a feminine eunuch. It was much easier to try and eliminate him and her obvious ally in this challenging quest would be the Kislar Aga the Chief Black Eunuch. Despite the rumors for his dubious preferences, her instinct said from the first day she saw his eyes he was a man she could trust.

****

Suleiman didn't feel like inviting Piri Pasha from his Silivri retreat for such a trifle matter. Retiring him so suddenly was enough of an insult. Only if he couldn't find the truth among his immediate associates, he would resort to such a desperate measure. Anyway, posing questions to different people was a good way to test their sincerity; so with the occasion of giving him more detailed instruction, he summoned his new Hasodabashi, and after making sure he had grasped his instructions on how his harem should be run, the subject of discussion turned to Selim's last words. Asphodel's reply was surprising but seemed truthful enough.

"I wasn't present inside the tent, but a tent cannot muffle sounds as well as the thick walls of the Seraglio or an inn do. Selim Khan on his deathbed asked repeatedly for Mahidevran Sultan to come from Manisa. This was what my brother Menekse heard and later confirmed to me. Did he lie?"

"Isn't this demand a bit strange?" Suleiman rushed to ask hiding his astonishment for the revelation.

"Yes, it would be, if Selim Khan was healthy and sane on this occasion; but he was in a comma and anything was possible for a dying man in distress."

"Why was this order not carried out?" Suleiman asked.

"It was not because of Piri Pasha's decision. I assumed he considered it a command affected by the Sultan's state of profound comma. If I was not a White Eunuch but a Black one, I would often see Mahidevran Sultan in my dreams too. Dreams are induced by what we see more often. This is why recently I see Hurrem Sultan in my dreams more often than any other of your concubines."

Suleiman knew sometimes the White Eunuchs were too witty for their own good, but he realized better than anyone that a wise Sultan needed clever and trusted associates to remain in power. Asphodels logic was immaculate. Because of his choice he was also responsible for his eunuch's dreams.

"Do you know if Sultan Selim had ever sent a poisoned caftan to Manisa before he died?" he asked to change the sensitive subject of his Kadin.

"Yes, he did send a caftan and I was the one who carried to Manisa on horseback! Menekse gave to me one of Selim Khan's caftans, but a caftan is not poisonous unless it is immersed in the blood of a smallpox victim; otherwise it has no ill effects in case someone wears it. This is why we wash thoroughly in the Seraglio every garment or rug that comes to Your Majesty as presents from the East or the West and especially Venice and Persia," Asphodel replied confidently.

"Why would my father wish to send a poisoned kaftan to me in Manisa?"

"I wouldn't know for sure a gravely ill man's last wishes. I can only suspect with my devious mind that for some reason he wanted to eliminate a son he considered unworthy. Fortunately Allah opposed Selim Khan's last will and we should all pray for the safe delivery of Your Majesty. If Your Majesty had been eliminated only Allah knows who would now sit on the throne of Osman. All I know is that one night he invited Ibrahim for a while into his chambers."

"For how long did Ibrahim stay in there?" Suleiman asked with feverish curiosity.

"If I remember correctly, he came in a bit after Maghrib and left a bit before Isha'a prayers. Sultan Selim was very pious and kept faithfully all prayer times."

"Which day was that?" Suleiman asked with considerable interest for details.

"I remember that night as if it was tonight. It was the night Sultan Selim came back from Egypt."

"I wonder what they did back then."

"I know! They went to the hammam for the Sultan to get clean after such a long trip."

"Ibrahim was not his slave to clean him. He was my falconer!" Suleiman objected.

"I'm sure that after such a glorious expedition, Sultan Selim had many much graver sins to absolve than mistreat a slave. All I know for certain is that the Sultan has treated us most kindly, when he was still alive. Only after his death a Grand Vizier dared to lay a hand on my brother, Allah rests his soul."

"Do you mean to tell me you don't know anything else about what happened that night?" Suleiman asked in a state of growing rage.

"I don't know and I don't care to know what happened to a slave, when Selim Khan locked the door behind his back because I might get jealous. All I know is that anything the Shadow of Allah did was well made, and a slave is not responsible for anything he endures. However, if my Sultan wants to know what Sultan Selim has done to me every time I cleaned him in the hammam, he only has to ask me and I will show him how a eunuch can clean a man from all his sinful thoughts?"

Perhaps the face of Asphodel was fluent enough; but maybe it was a silly question what mature men did to attractive eunuchs employed in hammams in the Eternal City since the days of the Romans. What is true is that Suleiman Khan stopped asking question after question.

****

274

"My darling you are so naïve sometimes, I don't really believe you can be so wise all the other times," Hurrem remarked after listening to Suleiman's narration of Asphodel's confessions. "If you really want an answer, I will tell you because my mother told me that I should not keep secrets from my master. My father was a priest and had heard many confessions from the most evil men in Northern Ukraine, where we used to live many years ago, before I was capture by your friends the Tatars."

"No! I don't want you to tell me anything. I have a very good idea."

"A vague description is never good enough. You should order me to show you what Ibrahim has done to your father too, so there is no mistake and none of us commits a sin, according to your devious eunuch with crashed balls you seem to trust so much."

Suleiman couldn't stay stern any more. Hurrem for one more time had made him smile with her tricks. This woman knew how to manipulate his desires. His laughter was cut short as she started licking suggestively her fleshy lips. Only now he realized how many things Hurrem had in common with Ibrahim, so depending on his mood the one could easily replace the other.

Damned woman! Somehow she always knew how to get the best of him. Nevertheless, despite Hurrem's imaginative theatrics, Ibrahim was the only one who could provide a definite answer, and he had to do it before he became the bridegroom. The excuses were there. He had to know exactly what kind of man his sister would marry.

****

For their meeting he had chosen the Marble Kiosk by the sea. It was the kiosk his father had built and now after his death he had ordered to be locked. It was the kiosk they had both faced successfully his father for the first time, and laid down the foundation of their friendship that had evolved in the same night into a blazing love affair he had never experienced before with another man. If since then their feelings had considerably cooled off because of the appearance of a remarkable woman, it didn't mean the magic of that night had been completely extinguished. Their friendship and devotion to the common cause of conquering the world remained undeterred. Perhaps tonight was the right moment for Selim Khan's spirit to be exorcised from their lives.

If the weather played a part in his disposition, he couldn't complain. A soft northern breeze was blowing softly that had cleared away the usual haze that rose from the sea surface that time of day. Perhaps this cool breeze would clear away the clouds that darkened their relationship.

When Ibrahim arrived he was a bit worried about the probable cause of this meeting, as the Sultan purposely had not mentioned any particular reason besides the last details of the marriage ceremony. However, when the ordinary pleasantries had been completed with uncommon haste and anticipation, Suleiman felt an unexplained difficulty to pose the question he had in mind all along. He may be the Sultan, but he was embarrassed to ask what exactly had happened between Selim and his friend. He simply did not know where to start.

"Asphodel told me this morning that the last words my father said in his bed was to summon Mahidevran Sultan from Manisa. What do you think might have been the reason?"

Ibrahim could do anything but smile, hearing of his master's new insecurity crisis.

"Is that why you called me here?" he asked and his master flatly denied it, but gave no alternative cause besides his oncoming marriage.

"Well, I think it's fair for you to know, that besides your father, I have also seen Mahidevran in my dreams. This princess is the stuff any slave's dreams are made of. If I was in your shoes, I would have moved her permanently in the Hasodabashi's bedroom and dismiss all the other concubines and the Hasodabashi from my harem."

"You are not in my shoes and you have never made love to a princess like her. She is just too demanding. She thinks a man is made just to keep her content and does not care at all about this man pleasure. She would never be content living in such a small room for all her life. Hurrem is the exact opposite. All she thinks is how to make me feel content and the king of the entire world. This is the kind of woman I need to become truly the world's emperor, not a haughty Princess who makes me feel inadequate. However, I simply cannot dismiss any concubine of my harem yet without creating the wrong impression. The mob has already started claiming that Hurrem is a witch. Imagine what they will do, if I was to evacuate the Eski Saray. My Valide does not wish to hear of such a possibility."

"I am a bit luckier. I feel Hatidge is the one woman for me; but I am a slave and you are a Sultan. No one will think badly of me, if I have just one wife; but for a Sultan I can certainly see the problem that arises. Almost every Janissary has a couple of whores and few widows under his protection; thus, he wouldn't feel obedient to a leader who he thinks he is less of man than he is."

"My father didn't have such a problem, but he still had to change a decision several times because of these audacious rebels. I wish there was a good way to get rid of them," Suleiman said and sighed.

"Please don't even think about it. It's always better to manipulate such valiant rebels than exterminate them. Now that I have become a Janissary too, I will manage them to our advantage. Trust me!"

"I trust you. This is why I'm going to give you my sister and Selim's daughter. I remember how well you have manipulated my father in this very kiosk and left untouched that night. Did he ever try to invite you again in this kiosk? I still remember this was his solemn promise."

Ibrahim hesitated for a minute. Many times in the past he had thought this moment was bound to come someday when he had to face the truth or lie. Most of the time he had concluded that a lie was the best way out; but tonight in the eve of his marriage his moral was high and he didn't wish to lower it for any man or a woman."

"Yes, he did invite me, the same day he returned from the Egyptian campaign."

"Did you accept his invitation?"

"Your father is not a man who you can refuse anything. Don't you remember how he tried to seduce me in front of your eyes? If you were not there, naked as I was I wouldn't be able to resist him."

"So what happened when he invited you here?"

"I was alone, and I was a slave. When that night ended I was still a slave, but a falconer too. I believe it was a good bargain. If I had refused, in a few days I would become a eunuch like Sinan Pasha and your sister was going to marry another man. A marriage does not make sense when children cannot be born."

"What did my father did to you?" the Sultan insisted.

"I don't know, and this is not a lie or an excuse. He drugged me the same way you slept stiff with your dancing angel. Now, that Selim is dead I will never know what happened to satisfy your curiosity. I have stopped thinking about that night. What's done is done. A slave does not have many options, if his master commands. Have you ever considered the possibility what a frustrated widow may demand from a slave she just bought?"

"No, I haven't; but what is the meaning of this silly question?

"It's not silly. It's rhetorical, so I will answer it for you. I will do whatever your sister demands of me! If you wish me to have a choice, you have to make me a free man. There is no other way around it. And now tell me. Do you still want me as a brother-in-law?"

****

If this was a true question or a rhetorical one no one knows. The Sultan had the advantage not to answer questions he considered they had an obvious answer or if they were offensive. This time he remained silent and simply clapped his hands to signal the servants the time to serve dinner had come.

The sea under the northern breeze was calm and the galleys of the imperial navy stationed at docks of the Golden Horn hardly moved; but their number was constantly growing as the expedition against Rhodes had proved that a bigger fleet might be useful in few operations against Venice, Spain or Malta.

The sea-breeze was bringing in the luxurious hall the first gentle scents from the blooming redbuds, tamarisks and lilacs of the oncoming spring whetting their appetites. The Sultan had ordered for this occasion of the official reopening of the kiosk a sumptuous buffet with all sorts of game brought by the imperial hunters from the vast forest of the European peninsula by the Black Sea shore that now had been named "the Belgrade Forest" to remind the future generations of his first successful military expedition. Soon the tantalizing smells from the roasted lamb had covered every other delicate scent emitted from delicate flowers. It was as if on purpose male odors had to replace feminine aromas.

The servants came closer and offered them two golden goblets full of Thracian red wine, and Ibrahim raised his and made a toast to their everlasting friendship emptying the content to the last drop. He then asked the servant for a refill, saying:

"If I have to sin tonight, I must have at least a good excuse. Allah's Shadow has tempted me."

Suleiman didn't seem to have any objection and followed with a toast of his own.

"Let's drink to our many weaknesses that bind us together; but let's don't forget to leave some wine for the last toast, asking from Allah to forgive every sin of ours till now, so that we can make a clean start tomorrow morning."

The affluent and exquisitely cooked food was not the only surprise the Sultan had prepared to honor his brother-in-law. From the open garden windows the sound of drums playing a martial tune was heard. Then, four tall and slim dancers dressed in black entered suddenly the hall from the garden performing a series of magnificent jumps that gave the impression they were flying in midair. They had golden scarfs tied around their waists and a pair of Damascene swords in their hands. They quickly divided in two pairs and started impressive duels trying hard to hit their opponent while at the same time avoid his attacks.

It was an exhibition of martial arts that filled the hearts of every onlooker with the instinctive fear a strike might miss severing a human being's member. All the motions did not seem like fake and the male sweat running from the dancers' bodies testified to that effect; so when this thrilling dance finally ended, Ibrahim could not help but release a deep sigh of relief that no blood was shed or mortal wounds exchanged. This was not the rule however, because their naked upper bodies had distinct signs of long old scars.

The Sultan seemed very pleased by the martial skills of his soldiers, even though since the fall of the Eternal City the war had taken a new turn rewarding artillery and rifle marksmanship rather than swordsmanship.

As the sword dancers retired, a new group of four men appeared half naked in leather trousers. They were all very bulky, full of impressive muscles that practically dripped olive oil. Ibrahim had watched once before in a river island in Edirne similar wrestling matches and knew what to expect. At that time he was fascinated staring at muscles hardening and relaxing as they tried hard to slip behind their opponent's back or fall on top of him on the grass to secure victory.

Now after his struggle with Basmi, he had realized that when two opponents fought for supremacy, their victory should be only temporary, and soon after the roles should change, because it didn't really matter who was on top the reward being the struggle itself. Now this all-male wrestling match seem like a very simpleminded barbaric sport that had no relation to the sophisticated exchange of pleasures the Nubian had taught him.

"These were two of the most impressive shows that will occur after the marriage ceremony; however, I see that you are a bit bored. They may not fit your nonviolent mood, but I assure you the mob at the At Meidan will just love to see them at your wedding," Suleiman noted.

At Meidan was the location where the old Roman Hippodrome was built that now lay in ruins. Thousands of people had died on these grounds when the Roman Emperor Justinian had ordered the Hun mercenaries of the Roman army to slaughter the rebels during the infamous Nika Riot. Now wrestling matches and mock swordsmen duals seemed like a great improvement for mankind; thus, he didn't feel guilty for serving an Ottoman Sultan instead of a Roman Emperor. Despite his special moments, Suleiman was also a vast improvement over most of the Roman Emperors he could think of, making serving him a much easier task.

Suleiman now came closer and whispered in his ear:

"This next show I've chosen just for you. I'm sure it will tickle your interest."

He hadn't finished the introduction when several half-naked Nubian females appeared running around randomly in the center of the hall with the swiftness and grace of African gazelles. The only covers of their breasts were elaborate necklaces made of multicolor crystal beads that hid the top half of their breasts like intricate embroidery.

Around their waists from leather belts numerous chains of similar beads were hanging all the way to their thighs as if they were rosaries, while among their knitted hair black and white ostrich feather were fixed that winnowed as they moved around seemingly without purpose.

Lastly a very tall man with impressive physique entered the hall. He had his face and back covered with a lion skin, while between his legs he held a long drum he used to give the dancing beat of his female partners. As the female dancers with their seductive moves approached him one by one, he hit the drum rhythmically few times and then they retreated, demonstrating the urge of the female gender of an African tribe to try to take advantage of the periodic overflow of male potency during the rainy season or the inundation of the Nile River. This primordial custom was so well choreographed Ibrahim started wondering if it was possible the Sultan was trying to show him he was aware of his clandestine activities, or if this highly suggestive dance between a male and his mates was just another random coincidence. Was this the subtle message Suleiman wished to convey, or something less intricate?

"Among all these exotic dancers, did you see anyone you craved? I want to offer you a wedding present that will really please you, even though my sister might get jealous," the Sultan noted with an imperceptible smile while Ibrahim remained hesitant.

All these Nubian dancers were indeed admirable creatures with bodies as flexible as snakes and gracious movements reminiscent of black panthers and he wouldn't mind adding them to his collection of slaves. In fact, his palace was large enough to accommodate many more servants and pages Hatidge had, if he so desired. If Sultan Selim had collected all sorts of wild animals after his expedition in Africa to use as game inside the Gülhane Gardens, he felt he was entitled to keep as many remarkable creatures for his pleasure.

He was actually doing them a favor as in his palace the living conditions were infinitely better than in their native villages. The only troublesome thought that bothered him was that somehow the son resembled the mother, trying simpleminded tricks to find his true preferences the way Ulysses had tricked Achilles into abandoning his female disguise. This delayed reply allowed the Sultan to make his move.

"I see you are puzzled. Indeed these dancers were all so exquisitely coordinated I wouldn't also think of separating them. Thus, they are all yours. Your palace needs certainly a lot of servants. These Nubians slaves may be excellent dancers, but I bet with a little training they can satisfy many other uses. Hurrem told me Nubian slaves are in great demand since my father came back from Egypt. Would you ever imagine now they are more expensive than even the Circassians? Few merchants claim that with such high prices one can make a good profit by breeding them, but I cannot say one should be so optimistic. If they become too many, then their price will fall."

Instinctively Ibrahim saw the trap he was in, but now it was too late. He simply could not refuse a Sultan's present without offending him; but at the same time many of these servants may be spies the Sultan planted firmly in his new household.

"If I hesitated, it was simply because I didn't know, if I should make this leading dancer my Kislar Aga or my Odabashi," Ibrahim remarked looking for a good way out.

"This is indeed a serious dilemma you must solve with my sister," Suleiman replied revealing his plan.

Was it possible Suleiman had devised this scheme or was it someone else's devious suggestion?

"I am grateful my master is so generous and thoughtful. Dancing is one of the most respected arts for ancient Greeks, so I will cherish this gift until the day I die, because no harem can ever be happy without few black slaves," Ibrahim announced gracefully, treating this gesture as lightly as possible; but it didn't mean he was not greatly puzzled.

****

That night this curious event was quickly forgotten as no one wanted a dubious present to spoil a night that was so unusual. And it was unusual indeed since the moment Ibrahim got up to leave, the Sultan suggested that it was very late for him to leave. Thus, he should stay in the Marble Kiosk as a guest, while he retired to his Selamlik instead.

Ibrahim didn't feel comfortable to sleep in Selim's Kiosk, but he could find no good reason for him to refuse this gracious offer. Was this some kind of conspiracy to create an obstacle to his oncoming marriage? His mind simply could not devise a way how this union could be canceled or even delayed, so he graciously accepted this offer too.

He was already trying to sleep these puzzles off, when there was a slight knock on his bedroom door. Hesitantly he gave his permission for the visitor to enter and he was surprised to see Asphodel approaching.

"What kind of eunuch conspiracy are you up to this time?" he asked him trying to look as confident as possible.

"I thought you might wish to try tonight few of your new possessions," the Hasodabashi explained. "I wouldn't miss such a chance to celebrate the last few days of freedom."

"Is this the meaning of this gift?" Ibrahim inquired.

"It's very difficult to decipher what Allah or his Shadow has in mind; so, if I were you I wouldn't even try. I would simply enjoy his generous gifts."

"Is this the best advice you can give me? It might well be a trap."

"It might well be a trap indeed, but the Sultan is the Shadow of Allah and Allah is very benevolent. Why should such a close friend try to trap you?"

"I don't know exactly, but I can surely find a couple of reasons if I try hard."

"And I will be very glad to hear them and become wiser."

"Someone may alert my bride to be, and make her jealous."

The eunuch unexpectedly burst to a nervous laughter.

"No! Princess Hatidge is not the jealous type. After all she is a widow and knows men well. I'm not the Kislar Aga to know what happens in the Eski Saray, but if I was in her slippers now that you are so far away, I would invite my gorgeous slave Basmi and enjoy my last days of freedom too as much as my bridegroom or maybe even more."

"I don't believe she is as lusty as you," Ibrahim asserted regaining his good spirits. "Are you trying to make me angry and retaliate?"

"My duty is to make everyone I serve as happy as possible tonight. Just before coming to you I led Hurrem to my master's quarters. Spring is in the air. Can't you feel that? Actually, I could even bring you the Nubian drummer. He is not a eunuch, you know. It would be a pity Allah would not excuse, if he is castrated before someone trained enjoys his impressive masculinity."

"He is my slave now and I have no plans to castrate him. This madness has to stop."

"Keeping an uncut man among many female slaves is not something I would advise you. It's simply a matter of time before one of your women is tempted, and the rumor says your Princess is tempted by black skin. On the other hand, even if your women are not tempted, how can you be sure of yourself? The fewer temptations we have around us the better for our morality. This is the reason why saints and dervishes seek shelter in the wilderness," replied the eunuch with a suggestive smile.

"On the contrary the more temptations we have the greater is the trust we create following the honorable path. Now go and let me sleep."

The eunuch's mission had been a failure, and Ibrahim could discern what the plan behind this dubious gift had been. Now, he had to find out which was the devious mind that had conceive it and there was only one good way to achieve this goal, become devious too much more than the eunuch.

"Do I also have Aphrodite's dimples in my back like Hurrem?" he asked as innocently as his mood permitted, but the eunuch was equal to the task, and he was well acquainted with every carnal terminology.

"I don't know. I was never interested too much in your back. I'm more attracted by your firm abdomen, but I'm sure Menekse must have noticed such a detail," he snapped back indicating that he was well aware of his brother clandestine activities.

"Didn't you two ever talk about me? I don't believe you. You eunuchs are both observant and nosy. I have even noticed your dimples."

"Did you, really? Selim never told me anything," Asphodel wondered.

"Then, I must be more sensitive than Selim," Ibrahim asserted.

"Indeed you are! You are a great catch. Hatidge Sultan is very lucky to find a man like you. You are in love with love, and you are also so flexible. You can adjust and rise to every occasion. This was what Sultan Selim liked most about you."

"Do you really think so?"

"I know so. You are also a great actor. You can adapt to every role fantasy demands. I'm not as good as you are. I have a one track mind. Poor Menekse resembled me; but Selim demanded absolute obedience to all his demands."

"What do you mean?" Ibrahim asked trying to mine more information.

"You know very well what I mean. Only an idiot would miss my point, and you are not an idiot. I'm not going to tell you anything more. You will be soon a member of the House of Osman and you are bound to protect the name of your family, because rumors may spoil the image of your sons too as much as the Sultan's. The reputation of your offspring might suffer. Then, the mob may get ideas and revolt. Who knows what the future will bring? My brother was killed just to keep Selim's death in darkness. Imagine what they would do to keep people from knowing the Osmanli family is rotten to the bone?"

"Suleiman is a brave and fair sovereign," Ibrahim argued without much conviction.

Asphodel smiled ironically.

"Look carefully at yourself in the mirror. You will see you can play the role of the Sultan much better than he, unless you are blind."

Ibrahim didn't rush to reply. Instead he went to the mirror and took off all of his clothes.

"You may be right," he concluded without much conviction, "but do I have Aphrodite's dimples?"

"No, you don't, but you can play the role of a woman better than even me."

"What about Mahidevran? Selim asked for her rather than me."

"You are insane. No man can pretend he is as attractive as Aphrodite, the Goddess of Love, without becoming utterly ridiculous. She can tempt even me. She is the kind of woman who can turn any queer into a man. This is why she was chosen as a bride for Sehzade Suleiman. You are good just to make a fucking lesbian respectable," Asphodel snapped full of anger for Ibrahim's marriage.

"Why are you telling me all this crap, if you think I now belong to the Osmanli? Your life might be in danger," Ibrahim asked still staring at the mirror judging the image he projected.

"I don't really care what happens to me. My fate has been cast the day Selim died. I know too much. Sooner or later my mouth will be silenced; so be careful not to fall into the same trap. They don't need a poisoned caftan. Even **a cook can kill a Grand Vizier**."

****

The marriage celebrations of the Princess Hatidge and the Grand Vizier lasted for ten days, but the elaborate preparations started few months earlier. It was as if some kind of military expedition was prepared.

In the spacious At Meidan three magnificent tents were erected. The first one was a spoil of Sultan Mehmet from the battle at Otlukbeli against Sultan Uzun Hassan of the White Sheep Horde. The second tent a spoil of Sultan Selim from the battle of Chaldiran against the Shah Ismail of the Persians, and the last one the loot of the battle of Marj Dabiq against the Sultan Qansuh of the Mamelukes. Three potential rivals had been vanquished and their treasures had enriched the Ottoman throne.

Inside these luxurious tents sumptuous banquets had been prepared with all sorts of meats, game, and even fish. In these magnificent celebrations many guests were invited, among which the Seih-ul-Islam, all the Christian Patriarchs of the Empire, the various Beylerbeys, and every notable Pasha leader of the victorious Ottoman Armies were the most prominent.

Naturally, the foreign representatives and ambassadors had to come too, bringing precious gifts, as failing to show up to such a joyous occasion for the Grand Vizier would surely have an adverse effect to their diplomatic relations with the Sublime Gate, as the entrance to his foreign relation ministry next to the Gülhane Walls of the Seraglio was named.

To entertain the large crowds that had gathered to see the bridegroom, the bride, and the splendid gifts, there were many theatrical groups presenting a variety of performances ranging from comedies to romantic stories to fit the dominant mood of this happy occasion. There were also wrestling and fencing matches, weight lifting events, acrobats, singers, oriental and exotic dancers along with beast tamers and their wild beasts locked in their cages.

The occasion demanded from every citizen to make an appearance at the At Meidan wearing his best clothes and his most precious jewels, even if this was just a bracelet with the words of the Prophet, or the earing of a pirate. This opening ceremony lasted for two full days.

The third day at noon exactly after the second prayer, the long parade started in front of the stage where the Sultan's golden throne was posted surrounded by the numerous officials. At the head of the parade the immense float of the bridegroom was leading the parade drawn by twelve Arabian mares. It was a float surrounded by Greek ancient columns adorned with golden ornaments and fresh flowers. It even had fruit trees full of flowers and ripe fruits ready for picking. This particular float design was Ibrahim's inspiration, because he wished to underline his Greek lineage and fertility. Unfortunately, there had never been a way to please everybody in the Eternal City, and many fanatical Muslims from the Fatih district accused him of being a pagan.

Ibrahim had dismissed these charges with a smile, and this was most annoying for the Muslim fanatics eager to start a conflict. If ancient columns made a structure pagan, then all the imperial mosques in Constantinople, Edirne, and Bursa, or even Damascus should be considered pagan too, as they all had columns stolen from ancient temples of Olympian gods.

After the bridegroom's float another chariot followed with peacocks and other paradisiac birds. Then elephants, giraffes, zebras, and camels paraded tied with chains as well as ferocious lions, tigers, and panthers locked in cages driven on wheels. Then the right moment came for the trained light cavalry to enter the parade and they impressed everyone with their dexterity to hit targets with their arrows while galloping at full speed.

The slaves came next, carrying the Sultan's presents to his brother-in-law who was also the custodian of the bride. There were twenty half-naked black slaves dressed in luxurious trousers, carrying trunks full of golden home utensils or pulling the reins of sturdy horses and camels loaded with precious silken rugs, delicate fabrics, furs, embroideries, or precious caftans.

Finally, at the end of the column followed the Grand Vizier's personal guards armed with gold platted weapons, swords, axes, maces, bows and arrows, shields, armors, and helmets, seated on heavily ornamented saddles full of precious stones and golden inlays.

The celebrations went on and on for seven more days until the eve of the marriage. That day the bride's dowry parade moved from the Seraglio to the couple's new residence, Ibrahim's palace at the edge of the At Meidan. It was by far the richest dowry the Eternal City had ever witnessed since even the day the very first Roman Emperor moved to Byzantium from Rome. Every bit was part of Selim's booty from the Middle East. Tabriz, Aleppo, Damascus, Jerusalem, and Cairo had all unwillingly contributed to enrich the happy couple.

Many Christians said Ibrahim had become filthy rich in a single day, but the truth was different. The dowry always belonged to the bride. The bridegroom could only make use of the dowry for as long as the bride was pleased with him and not a single day more. Nevertheless, the bridegroom was not completely without rights. He could get a divorce simply by going to a Mufti and saying three times in a row, the magical words, "I divorce you", but it was bad luck even to think such glorious day of such a solemn development.

When the end of the parade passed before the Sultan, Ibrahim approached the Sultan and offered him an exquisite necklace with a huge diamond designed and bought for countless ducats from Venice, the luscious city where the best craftsmen from the City of Constantine had been relocated long before the Fatih's guns demolished the Great Walls.

At this thrilling moment, thousands after thousands fireworks were ignited that turned the night into midday, while all the guns on the Sea Walls and the Ottoman fleet went off, announcing the end of the long celebration for the ordinary folks. However, for the close relatives and all the members of the Ottoman aristocracy, the holidays lasted for few days more.

Ibrahim had a weakness for firework displays and he never bypassed a chance to use them. He thought they had something in common with the cycle of a human life. Initially the exhilarating explosion of the youth and the quick rise towards heaven came with a trajectory full of sparkles and blinding light, and then the brilliant explosion at the highest point of maturing and social recognition. Then, the descent of old age commenced, when the light emitted from every human being gradually vanished, leading the individual in the dark path to oblivion. He personally hated this prospect and hopped that when he reached the peak of recognition his life would end. No man had ever chosen his beginning. At least a man should be free to choose the way of his end.

****

The religious marriage ceremony was surprising simple. The bridegroom entered the Has Oda, approached the throne where the Sultan was siting and prostrated three times, as Suleiman was the legal guardian of the bride. Then, he paid his respects to the Seih-Ul-Islam who was sitting behind a pedestal with an open Quran.

The Grand Vizier was wearing over a white silken shirt adorned with floral designs embroidered with colorful threads a brocade caftan in deep blue color. Around his neck a golden chain hanged a pink sapphire cut in the shape of a droplet, another present of the Sultan. On his head he was wearing a large turban second in size only to the Sultan's and around his waist a golden girdle was tied where Selim's dagger was tucked in to remind him the Avret Bazaar, where the path of his unbelievable ascend had originated.

He sat down on the rug opposite the Sultan having the Seih-Ul-Islam at his right side. The religious meaning of this ceremony was that he was petitioning the bride from her guardian, and the Grand Mufti was there to witness and sanctified the transaction. Essentially, the entire ceremony was nothing more but the glorification of a slave purchase, with the basic difference that the slave was a Muslim and had all the rights this religion granted to a slave. This was at least how every bridegroom saw it, but only Time would tell what the true essence of every kind of human union was, as no one in his right mind should try to guess what the future would be.

****

Ibrahim raised his eyes and looked at the Sultan's face. It was solemn almost grim, an indication that he would rather this marriage had never happened; but in this world even the Sultan and the Shadow of Allah must realize that in this life all the wishes of a human being could not be fulfilled.

This special moment all the women of his life were against him and he had to capitulate. How this slave had managed to unite them was still a mystery; but Suleiman had to admit that his capitulation had been carried out in an almost perfect manner, as perfection was a non-existing concept in this world.

Suleiman had paid dearly for this ceremony, but he was the kind of man who didn't care about expenses. Money was just a tool for a man to achieve his greatest goals. This ceremony was unquestionably a defeat but not a rout. Ibrahim was still his slave and sooner or later he would feel that nothing had really changed between them.

With this ceremony Ibrahim had accepted the responsibility of making his sister happy. This was one of the basic arguments his mother had pointed out to win his consent. Hatidge was clearly unhappy in the Eski Saray and as a brother and guardian he had to do something about it, before another noble widow made a fool of herself purchasing a dozen of young slaves of all races and colors to show she was a benevolent ruler and not a racist.

The words of the Prophet were clear on this issue. A widow had to wait only for a few months after her husband's death and already more than a year had passed with Hatidge Sultan locked in his harem. Soon the Sultan would be obliged to build a "yali" for her on the Bosporus, and then every restrain would collapse and most rightly so. The Prophet's words were plain enough not to be misunderstood. The mistress should use her slaves as if they were members of her family, namely as husbands for instance.

Hatidge's preference for black skin was undeniable and that could only lead to the pollution of Osman's blood. How would an Ottoman Sultan feel if one day it became known that his sister had produced a black heir of the Ottoman throne?

From the moment Hatidge had met Ibrahim, and fell in love with him, there was nothing he could do to restrain their union. Marrying his sister with her lover was the best way out; otherwise, he would have to face the scandal when the rumor she had slept in the same room with Ibrahim behind closed doors leaked. No one except Allah knew what had happened back then and a black pagan slave like Basmi was not legally admissible as a reliable witness.

There was no way in this city for such a damaging secret to remain a secret for long. Someone was bound to notice a Grand Vizier visiting the residence of a Princess at night. And what if a child was borne from this union? How could this event be prevented for long, if his sister wished to have a child or maybe more than one? At least by building a palace at the At Meidan, he could keep an eye on this dangerous union, while Ibrahim Pasha became responsible against the law for any transgression.

In this respect the Valide Sultan's suggestion was I line with Hurrem's. By making presents he created obligations. Slaves were human beings and for as long they were alive they remembered who had benefited them. These dancers were the best wedding present for a young couple. Slaves had the tendency never to forget who freed them from the chains of the slave trader and offered them a hospitable home. In a palace full of black slaves, both Ibrahim and his bride would be under constant observation.

Hurrem had personally taken care of this present as now he was the Sultan and he had no time to waste in buying slaves. She even had explained to him the reasons why the black slaves should not to be castrated. Eunuchs were unquestionably more obedient, but they also kept a grudge that lasted a lifetime. Sooner or later they were bound to try to take revenge on the man or a woman responsible this grave wound. On the other hand, if they were whole they would always remember their benefactor and follow his orders.

Ibrahim had been the best example of this kind of fidelity. He had never forgotten who had saved him from Selim, and no matter what had happened this remarkable slave would support and serve him to the best of his abilities.

Of course, keeping a slave untouched had its drawbacks. If Ibrahim was a eunuch, his sister would never fall in love with him; but even this development was an advantage, as Hatidge marrying a Turk would be infinitely worse. Now any children born from this union would be his slaves too, not a potential usurper of his throne.

****

Now that the ceremony had ended, the Seih-Ul-Islam had to leave to attend his other duties. Suleiman had to visit his sister and announced his decision to offer her to the bridegroom. After this moment she belonged to the Grand Vizier and had to follow his orders as if she was part of his household. However, Hatidge was also the sister of the Sultan who was the master of the bridegroom, so she had certain rights of possession too, besides the divine rights for happiness a marriage bestowed on any Muslim wife.

The Sultan got up from his throne and led the way to his chambers where his sister was waiting to hear the happy news and Ibrahim followed. The Valide Sultan was already there as well as Hurrem who had insisted on being present. She was not an essential part of the ceremony, but who would dare to complain if the Sultan was followed by a certain slave? Slaves following a master always increased his prestige. After all, if the Grand Vizier had a beautiful woman at his side, why should the Sultan look inferior standing all alone?

Suleiman had to admit that Hurrem's arguments were for one more time very persuasive.

****

The moment the Sultan entered the hall all the women surrounding the bride sitting on sofas rose to their feet; but today he had eyes only for one, his sister; so, he approached her and saw her with great pleasure kneeling before his authority. Ibrahim had explained to him long ago that kneeling was a subtle way for a subject to lower itself to the level of his sovereign's genitals and show his submission and will to endure the worst punishment or disgrace. However, this was not Hatidge's intention that day as she raised her eyes to boldly look at his face almost simultaneously.

She was curious to measure the effect this ceremony had on his mood. Suleiman was sterner than he should be that day and this impression annoyed her. She still remembered the long smile on her father's face during her first marriage. Sultan Suleiman should be smiling now because he was rewarding a worthy official who had done much more than his duty.

The Sultan had spent a great deal of money in her second attempt to find happiness, but he didn't seem pleased enough to smile. What might happen if in the near future she was bearing a child?

On the contrary Hatidge had done her duty as a bride. She had attracted every pair of male eyes during the ceremony. She had covered her beauty under a veil as every bride should. Her veil covered with a thin fog her visible neckline, her bare shoulders and her slim waist, as every bride had the right to expose her femininity and fertility, so that no poisonous tongue could claim the bridegroom had married her just for her immense dowry and high social position.

The white dress she had ordered was very tight at her waist as the tradition demanded. Her legs were also covered down to the ankles, and only when she walked her toes would show painted a fiery red as her desire. Under the long veil she was also wearing a short "feredge" so even the Seih-Ul-Islam's strict advices were satisfied; but how could her eyes hide the passion for a man, a passion locked for more than a year behind the walls of the Eski Saray?

Her girlfriend Gülfem had often urged her to get out for few hours and visit her room at the inn, but Hafsa Sultan had never given Hatidge the permission to leave the Palace unescorted to roam the galleries of the Grand Bazaar, not even now when she was about to get married.

Ottoman men were great hypocrites. Everybody knew they were doing all sorts of despicable orgies with boys, but tried to keep women under lock and key. Thank Allah there were the eunuchs who sympathized with the young odalisques and tried their best to provide them inside the Harem with the illusion of a man, using all sorts of devious tricks only a eunuch could think of.

Almost all of them kept their missing parts stored in a jar full of vinegar. They claimed they did it, so when they died they could be buried as complete men. Then, in Paradise they could enjoy all the pleasures of the faithful. However, everyone knew they were among the worst kind of liars. The true reason for this charade was to impress a frustrated concubine with their lost splendor, so she would choose them as their favorite pages.

Thank Allah, when Gülfem Sultan found out what was going on, she informed the Valide Sultan. Hafsa decided to protect her daughter from every degenerate eunuch by offering her a very skilled slave, Basmi, who was trained in Cairo how to seduce a man or a woman.

Basmi claimed men were by far the easier of the two to seduce. To excite a man it was enough for a woman's beauty to be covered by a long dress, so only the man could uncover what lay hidden under it. It was all even an ugly woman had to do to have men go after her just to solve this trivial mystery. On the contrary, for a male to excite a female creature full disclosure was required as women were the more demanding critics of another female beauty.

Today Hatidge had followed her advice to the letter. Under the feredge only her eyes showed, but it was more than enough to create a favorable sensation. Her eyelashes were painted black to look longer, her eyelids dark blue to add mystic, and her eyebrows thinned to look as feminine as possible, so that her new husband could distinguish her eyes from her grim father's as much as possible.

The Princess didn't need any advice on this issue. She knew well enough her father's image was daunting, so she should look inviting. Her father had abandoned his harem, and she had no intention to allow this to happen with her man. So, under her dress she was naked, but nothing was visible under the delicate lace. Laces were like veils, but they didn't hide as much. They only confused a man's eyes with their intricacies so he could not aim accurately the arrow of Eros.

Hafsa didn't approve that the bride's back should be completely naked all the way to her waist, to show her dimples, but the argument that her hair was longer than her waist finally convinced her. As long as Hatidge Sultan was standing one her two feet nothing indecent would show. This was the final verdict and Hatidge Sultan had managed to impose her point of view over any other religious doctrine claiming that hair should be concealed under a scarf. This day belong to her and no one else. She was the daughter of Selim and she had to prove to this audacious slave that she would be forever victorious.

Her brother the All-Mighty Sultan was essentially an unimportant parameter this momentous day, just a ceremonial figure obliged to follow certain routines to satisfy the religious tradition for the crowds. He was a weak character Hurrem had mesmerized to think she was the woman of his life, simply because somehow she could turn him on more than any other odalisque.

This special day Suleiman Khan was wearing a colorful caftan embroidered with a hunting scene from the exploits of a Mogul Sultan with tigers, deer and wild boars. Around his neck a thick golden chain had a ruby the size of a walnut suspended, while every finger of his was adorned by the sparkle of at least one very elaborate ring. Even in his right hand thumb he was wearing a magnificent bowman's ring as if he was going to aim arrows against an enemy.

However everyone knew a Sultan was too precious to be left unprotected in the middle of a battlefield, an easy target for the enemy to shoot at.

The Sultan was in the rear waiting for the Janissaries and the Spahis led by his valiant Pashas to crush the opponent, so he could take the credit. All this gold platted weapons and armament was a pathetic, hypocritical show without substance as steel was harder than gold, silver or copper but gleamed a lot less.

****

The preliminaries soon were completed and the various guests had taken their proper place around separate round tables low enough for people to seat on pillows on the floor. The newlyweds were seated around the Sultan's table along with the Valide Sultana.

What was more surprising and unusual was Hurrem's presence in this distinguished group. It meant that the Sultan had placed her separately from any other woman in the Harem, and the reason was clearly the two children she had bear until this moment.

Tonight Hurrem was dressed with the dignity that characterized her elevated status. The dress was appropriate even for an older woman, and she wore over it a veil that allowed only her eyes to be visible by the distinguished guests as the Quran prescribed for every descent woman.

The Valide Sultana had advised her not to challenge the bride's beauty, and Hurrem had accepted her wise opinion in a gracious way, so that Hafsa agreed with her advice that the Sultan should be escorted by his two Kadin and only one of his concubines, so that the bridegroom would not be encouraged from the start to form his own harem.

However seated around the table, Hurrem couldn't resist the temptation to attract the bridegroom's eyes any other way she could, as for instance, by talking when men talked and she should remain silent.

During the dinner the atmosphere did not warm up reversing the Spartan climate of the religious ceremony despite the valiant efforts by few of the guests to generate hilarity with some rough and rude jokes that didn't manage to change the Sultan's solemn attitude.

In general from Selim's era it was well known that sometimes valiance was not justly rewarded. It was common knowledge that through the years, many friends were separated because of conniving women, while very few couples were dissolved because of a friendship. This was what the ancient poet Homer had described as Eros being undefeated in battle, and a single look at the bride was enough to explain Ibrahim's choice.

On the other hand, allowing a slave to be present among the guests, left a lot to be desired. Hurrem was an attractive specimen, but being a Christian slave, meant she had practically risen from the social gutter of the Ottoman Empire. If this comparison was the root of Sultan's distress no one knew, but no one was also bold enough to search and find out the true cause of his bad mood.

Poking at an open wound was bound to create painful reactions, so it was simply a matter of self-preservation not to interfere in a family dispute. It was much safer to say nothing and wait for the end of the dinner to depart safe and sound. This was probably the reason that a sigh of relieve slipped from everyone's lips, when they saw the Sultan rising from his seat to announce the end of the festivities and their ordeal.

Soon only the closest members of the Sultan's family would remain in the hall, but none of the guests tried to be excused and leave. Everyone was curious to find out how all the tension in the air would be relieved.

The Valide Sultan who was mostly responsible for this union tried to break the silence with some meaningless chatting about how well Hurrem's dressed fitted her slim figure, but Hurrem cut her off by revealing that she was bound to gain weight once again in the very near future. The Sultan didn't respond to this subtle invitation to praise her fertility in front of his two Kadin and this was the last offence of her status Hurrem was willing to take.

"My Master," she remarked removing her veil, "tonight I can feel your heart is heavy, but I cannot figure out the reason. Is the fact your sister is leaving your harem forever, or your intimate friend who has just married her does not care for your company as much as before?"

Her words sounded innocent enough, but a bit deeper a suspicious mind could discover traces of an insult. Was Ibrahim part of the Sultan's harem? Rising in such a short time from Pasha to Beylerbey and Grand Vizier was a remarkable achievement, but combining such high offices with the menial duties of a Hasodabashi was not easily explainable or digestible.

Her comment was a magnificent mixture of submission and rebellion and Ibrahim could do nothing but admire her wits. This woman had an unbending determination; but most of all she was a mysterious source of attraction he also felt almost as strong as the Sultan. She was like a modern version of an ancient hetaera perfectly capable of invading the heart of a conqueror by manipulating his mind. Ibrahim could not discern how deep the limits of her influence were, but it was fairly obvious Hurrem knew very well what to say without endangering her position. She was simply testing the Sultan's endurance, ready to retreat in case her words caused an explosion of anger.

Her calculation was accurate and the strong answer everyone was expecting was not heard. The Sultan remained indecisive as if he was waiting another more explicit insult to react.

The Ottoman Sultans were raised like lions and there was nothing more dangerous than to try to push a lion in a corner with your whip. Nevertheless, the last few years Hurrem had fed this lion with both her hands, and knew better than anyone how his mind worked.

From the moment she was the mother of his children, executing her was out of the question, while any other punishment seem like a pat on the back. What could Suleiman really do? Could he stop visiting her at night, return to his two Kadin or try another concubine? He definitely could, but did he wish to?

The Sultan was used only to the best, and she was the only one who knew how to raise his optimism to the heavens. Under the circumstances all Suleiman could expect was more abuse and Hurrem happily obliged.

"My lord, please tell me. What should your most favorite odalisque do to see you smiling? Should I entertain your magnificent guest with a dance of mine, or do you prefer your friend to play a love song with his organ he so skillfully uses for our pleasure?"

This time Suleiman's face turned red with anger, but it was also clear his anger could not find a suitable exhaust to explode. However, this time even Ibrahim Pasha, his counselor, was unable to offer him relief, because he had also been startled by this unexpected attack to the authority of the Grand Vizier's status. With one stroke Hurrem had debase the Sultan to the status of a pimp of a belly-dancer, and Ibrahim to the low level of a wandering troubadour.

Ibrahim could now feel nothing but respect for this woman who demanded her rights to get married to the father of her children. He had been in her shoes and knew how to respect such a desperate surge of courage.

Naturally, a Grand Vizier could not lower his status by playing love songs with his oud in public, and a Sultan's favorite courtesan could not start dancing in front of another man. This was at least a chance Suleiman could not take.

Hurrem's Muslim garment did not allow free movement, but who could exclude the possibility of her taking it off? Who could eliminate the chance she was wearing an oriental dancer costume under her dress, or even use just her long veil as cover? During her previous two dances she had not stop at anything to drive her point through in front of an audience.

Now that she had made a request, no one seemed willing to pick up her challenge and give her permission to realize her threat. Her words were a burning coal no one was willing to burn his fingers by touching it, so silence started to depress everyone much more than the lead roof over their heads. However, the well-justified reaction came from an unexpected corner.

Princess Hatidge got up and picked up Hurrem's challenge to her husband's status, while at the same time relieved her brother from the ordeal to find a proper answer.

"Hurrem was not born a Tatar and she is ignorant of our customs. In my marriage no slave will dance in my place to please the eyes of my man."

It was not a lie. In every Ottoman wedding the first dance belonged always to the bride and it was devoted to her husband. It was a dance that was meant to be like a public erotic foreplay and an appetizer for the night that would follow. A small music band was already waiting in case the Sultan allowed this audacious display of his sister's charms for the pleasure of the audience.

Suleiman was in no position to prohibit anything that would open a path out of an embarrassment, so he nodded gladly his approval with a long smile of relief. However, anger had painted red Hurrem's face as hearing the word "slave" she had to swallow the insult, as to reply to a Princess' abuse was inconceivable even for the most favorite concubine of her brother. Hurrem became so upset she didn't utter a single more word for the entire night.

In the meanwhile, Hatidge with the determination and speed of a Tatar warrior she disappeared in the next room to give instructions to the hidden orchestra. Few moments later the first notes from an oud were heard, and in the doorstep Hatidge's slim figure reappeared cradling her body according to the notes of the slow-beat tune.

She had her eyes closed and all her movements resembled that of a snake that wakes up in spring after the long hibernation of the winter months. With slow but deliberate step she approached her prey, Ibrahim Pasha, and like a snake that wants to seize a rodent, she quickly placed her hands around his waist touching his knees with her breasts.

The music well-directed and rehearsed, played repeatedly the same sensual motif as she moved her torso suggestively up and down his knees making her mother's face turn red with shame; however, Hatidge's intentions was considerably purer than projected. She imitated the movements a snake makes to remove its skin which in this case was simulated by her veil. Thus, as it retracted, it gradually revealed her toes, her ankles, and then her thighs and buttocks.

It was right then when everyone noticed that her dress among its numerous pleas had also two long cuts that went along her entire height up to her waist. It was a dress that permitted a woman to ride a horse like a man, and no Tatar rider would have any right to protest. After all she was a widow who didn't wish to delay the consumption of the marriage or use eunuch hands to take her complicated dress off, but her husband's. This was perhaps why her back was already exposed all the way to her waist so that the bridegroom could easily expose her breasts the moment he felt some degree of privacy or darkness was available.

However, this was not Ibrahim's intention just then. She was a Princess not an enslaved dancer and he knew well the limits of her authority and his audacity. He had been advised by the new Hasodabashi, Asphodel, that after the marriage ceremony he was allowed to remove in public only her veil, and so he did leaving her the freedom of choice for how long and how deeply the members of her family and guardians would feel the effects of her emancipation.

Hatidge seemed indeed frustrated by her fate and unconsciously blamed everyone for her bad luck to lose a husband. Human greed was an infectious disease and everyone could be held responsible. As her lips traveled freely on her husband's silken cloths all the way from his toes to his neck, she may appear she was teasing her husband, trying to arouse his desire, but in fact her every move was a demonstration that her slavery inside the Eski Saray had ended, and in one long jump she had landed in a Galata tavern to challenge Hurrem in the seduction trade.

To make absolutely sure she was not a naïve virgin but an experienced widow her lips made a brief stop at his waist and then rose higher through his open chest to his neck and finally his lips. This was the final aim of and snake and there she made use of the fangs to insert the fatal poison of everlasting love. By then her victim was totally mesmerized by the dark abyss of her eyes and offered no resistance. It was the moment when the urge of every snake to swallow its victim whole passed over her eyes, but she didn't advance a step further. Instead she decided she had to break first every bone in his body, so she embraced him tightly moving her hands all over his body while her lips tried to steal his breath. It was a passionate kiss that lasted for as long the music was playing to make everybody realize that from now on she would be the sole user of this slave and she was determined to utterly exhaust him to achieve this aim. For everyone else this was just the first course of a long banquet that would last till daybreak; but Ibrahim felt along with the warmth of her lips the hardness of her teeth as a solemn warning.

He didn't react as it was not clear how much of his past she knew and which of his many sins she might try to punish that night. It was a warning he should remember in the future; but now silence and calm prevailed, as the crisis had been averted thanks to his wife.

The Sultan got up with a long smile that showed his appreciation for his sister intervention and her determination to become a proper wife for his close friend. He knew better than anyone else that insatiable passion was the firmest foundation for a marriage. Thus, to express his gratitude, he took his necklace off, as Hatidge, realizing she was going to be the recipient, got up and approached him. She tried to kneel, but Suleiman had enough of similar gestures. Tonight he was among friends and members of his family and he was more relaxed, so he placed the necklace around her neck and kissed both her chicks. He had never valued riches more than feelings, and he felt her unreserved support tonight should be richly rewarded.

But now it was time for the bride to retire and with a firm grip she pulled Ibrahim up from the pillows on floor. They both greeted the Sultan, her mother and the Sultan's two Kadin and rushed to take the carriage and return to their new love nest. Her dance had triggered her long missed desires and she couldn't wait to feel a man inside her after so long. All this time, she had heard so much gossip about her husband, she felt he must have certain rare abilities and could not wait any longer to taste this juicy fruit her mother had chosen for her sake.

Hurrem simply did not deserve a friendly gesture.

****

Hurrem couldn't remain inactive any longer. She had played a dangerous game and she had lost. She didn't expect such an attack from the rear, but she should. Hatidge was a woman, but she was also the sister of the Sultan. She had taken command of the situation the moment she realized her brother was not up to the task. The House of Osman had to be protected at all cost.

Tonight the Sultan would be in the wrong mood. It was simply too early for reconciliation, but she was not going to ever repeat this mistake. Hatidge's reaction had to be analyzed too along with Ibrahim's. They were a married couple and they seemed ready to defend their common interests.

Tonight she couldn't predict how long it would take until she had found another opportunity like this to drive a wedge between Suleiman and his slave.

She only knew it was in her hand to make it happen. Now all she could see with the eyes of her mind was Hatidge's long last kiss.

Instinctively she had closed her eyes to stop the torture, but nothing happen. Instead she started seeing Ibrahim's passionate caresses. She knew exactly how passionate and imaginative he could be, if a woman could trigger his interest and challenged his ability to please her. Now she could also hear in her brain Hatidge's passionate sighs and pictured him trying his best to drown them. It was a vision she couldn't erase from her mind. She was not jealous of him. She was jealous of her. She had analyzed on many occasions her feelings. She simply couldn't love a Sultan since she was a slave. True love had to have the element of equality; otherwise, it turned gradually to exploitation, as the weaker one part was the more the other part instinctively tried to exploit it.

During this momentous day she had actually realized she had fallen in love with Ibrahim. She knew this love was difficult to enjoy, but she was willing to try. The Princess had all the rights of the world on her husband and today she had displayed her will to exert them.

The Sultan had also all the rights on her because he owned her, and he was going to make her pregnant again and again any chance he got. She didn't object this process. The moment she got pregnant, the Sultan was going to avoid her and spend his nights with his two Kadin according to the Ayin.

However, for as long as she was pregnant, she was a free woman. In fact, if Ibrahim gave her a child, it would be just the perfect punishment for all the disgraces and the offenses she had to endure in her life.

She must be going crazy with jealousy. She was now in her room and the wind blowing made the chimneys sound like a woman's passionate orgasm. Were all these chimneys built on the roof intentionally? Was their shape built like a fat penis as a deliberate choice as a minaret? Only an architect could explain to her what the true reason was, but she was afraid to ask.

The damned imperial architect who had built Ibrahim's Palace was a true Janissary, not a phony one like Ibrahim or the Sultan. From the first day she stepped into the Eternal City, a handsome masculine Janissary guard from the Imperial Guards, the famous Haseki, was her more desirable mate in all her dreams.

Tatars were short and slim, good only for horse riders. On the other hand, the Janissary Imperial Guards were handpicked between all the volunteers for their imposing stature and the special hats they were made them look even taller. Was she crazy from lust, or had the Janissaries and their vigor pushed her over the edge? For some mysterious reason men from the mountains attracted her. They were much more interesting than any short man riding horses on the steppes. Ibrahim was such a man. She could discern traces of his ancestors, in his long strides. He was walking more comfortably that he was riding a mare. If she didn't know his past, she would have assumed he was a Janissary rather than a Spahis, but she could never mistake him for a eunuch. Suleiman must have been a desperate fool to try to masquerade his presence in the Harem as a

Hasodabashi. Now he was trying to correct one mistake with another. Hatidge was not the kind of woman who could keep Ibrahim for long. He had to prove to himself over and over again that he was a true man, and any true man in the Orient had to pay a visit occasionally to a brothel.

****

Hurrem was not the only woman who had troubled sleeping. Hafsa Sultan also couldn't sleep because of what she saw and heard. Her surprise from her Russian slave's behavior was overwhelming. She could never believe Hurrem would try to humble her son, an Osmanli so much, even in a friendly circle.

Her disappointment went even further because of her son's failure to promptly react to the challenge. He behaved as if he was a waif, a sailboat without ballast or rudder trying to cross the dangerous currents of the Bogaz Straights. His military skill in riding horses or handling the sword was completely irrelevant for the struggles that lay ahead.

She had to admit that Ibrahim up to that moment had never tried to offend her son. On the contrary, he didn't miss a chance to support him or publically show his submission by very graphic and deep prostrations; so, she was perfectly justified to make him her favorite state official and have many long hours of consultations. How these meetings would end was her prerogative from now on. She could honor her daughter's marriage, or try her luck with few more tastes of debauchery. Allah had been at last kind with her. From now on Ibrahim was not her only choice after all. He had been only a new beginning, the second man who had ravaged her in her life. At last she had realized what true marriage meant for a woman, a social screen that allowed only a single man to use her divine gate to achieve immortality.

On the contrary Hurrem had broken every social rule. For the time being she had chosen not to embarrass her son by an intervention, but tomorrow morning she was going to show her what rights a rebellious slave had in her son's harem. Finally, Selim Khan was proven right. A son to become a Sultan he had to show he hadn't taken after his mother. Unfortunately, Allah had given her a son who had not only copied her delicate facial and bodily features, but he had also duplicated her submission to a stronger will. Her only hope now was that her son had also her patience, wisdom and perseverance to eventually prevail.

****

When everyone else retired, the Sultan tried to put his mind in order inside the empty hall. At last what he was afraid all along had been realized. Hurrem had erupted and shown her teeth. Within the same evening he had lost his favorite friend together with the woman of his life. He was now in a state of panic. He was a powerful Sultan, but he felt powerless, lonely and isolated. He needed Ibrahim's emotional support this night, but now the slave didn't really belong to him. From now on all his nights belonged to Hatidge, and she had every right to demand absolute loyalty.

On the other hand, this was the least he could do to show his gratitude for her brave support against Hurrem's onslaught. He hadn't expected his sister to have such an emotional strength, determination and respect for her family's dignity. Unquestionably, Selim's blood was running in her veins. Perhaps sons resembled their mothers and daughters took after their fathers and Ayin was not always correct about few critical matters.

In his mind the grim image of his father appeared looking sterner than ever. No concubine or Kadin had ever dared to behave like this without losing her life, while he felt incapable of raising his hand and give her a good thrashing for her deeds. Was he the beginning of the Osmanli family descent? Dynasties of Roman Emperors had gradually fallen into the spiral of decadence.

He called a servant and asked him to bring him a lighted nargileh. Tonight he needed to escape from himself and opium was the best way he knew to accomplish it. Tomorrow a new day would start and the sun was Allah's way to give people the hope that everything could change for the better. Along with the nargileh the Kislar Aga arrived ready to serve him.

He had to admit that only the color of his skin was unfamiliar to him. In every other respect he was as attractive as Ibrahim and maybe more; but he was a eunuch, one more dubious choice of his grim father after the Egyptian campaign. Was it fortuitous or intentional had always be his fundamental question related to all his father decisions. This time flooding the Grand Bazaar with black slaves had created a sensation.

The first black slaves according to the prevailing rumors had arrived when Mehmet Fatih had reached the Syrian borders where the Mameluke Sultan of Cairo reigned. He was the one who used black eunuchs as guards of his harem.

The rumor claimed Fatih had tried to imitate him and had bought very few Nubian eunuchs for his harem creating the Black Eunuch Corps, tradition followed also by his son, Bayezid. Then son after son, traditions propagated in time and expanded along with the borders of the Empire, but why Selim had brought so many Nubian slaves in the Seraglio it was not crystal clear. Unquestionably, they were rather rare and very expensive slaves and large slave numbers were a testimony of military power and magnificence.

Selim had used only White Eunuchs as his personal courtiers. Suleiman had seen one day a White Eunuch sneaking out of his father's bedroom when he visited him a bit too early. At the time he didn't pay any attention, but after Ibrahim he knew what a man sneaking out of a kiosk bedroom truly meant. Fortunately he had many more spies on his payroll, seeking the roots of all rumors than his father, and only Ibrahim and Iskander Pasha knew of their existence on the Sultan's personal payroll. Even for a Sultan it was impossible to have a secret from everyone, because each spy had to have a salary.

He could afford to pay few spies from his purse, but not all of them. Selim had found an economical way to stop gossips. He imposed terror; but he was not as cruel as his father. Ibrahim had convinced him there were many ways to achieve your aims without killing anyone.

He had chosen as Hasodabashi Asphodel, one of the two main White Eunuch favorites of his father following Ibrahim's suggestion. His reasoning was quite convincing. Asphodel should never be executed because he was so submissive. Submissive people should be rewarded rather than punished.

This eunuch should be used as an example for the mob. Only audacious, vindictive eunuchs like Menekse should lose their lives. It was a lesson for the entire White Eunuch corps. If they didn't learn how to behave, the Black Eunuchs would replace them. If they failed too, then a corps with virgin young men should be created that would replace both corps as his father wished.

A Sultan should not appear extremely violent. If a corps revolted, another corps should be created as a counterweight. Ibrahim had to be right. In his life Hurrem had balanced Mahidevran's aggression.

"Bring me Mahidevran Sultan," he ordered the sleek Kislar Aga.

"Excellent choice!" he instinctively replied.

If Mahidevran was not a Princess and the Kislar Aga a eunuch, he might start having suspicions. The Kislar Aga was a very attractive slave and the prevailing rumor claimed that recently wholesome Nubian slaves had been sold for exuberant prices, much higher than eunuchs black or white.

He was the Sultan and he couldn't show personal interest why this was so, or who of his Black Eunuchs were eunuchs or not. He had the Chief Eunuchs responsible for these menial morally degrading tasks. Perhaps, Ibrahim could be made responsible, but by now he was truly a member of the family.

****

Arriving at their palace the newlyweds were briefly separated. Hatidge retired to her chambers to get ready for the night and Ibrahim threatened that he could not wait much longer. Shyness had made her even more attractive than elaborate preparation. He gave her few moments more and pushed the door open. The bed was already prepared and the strong scent of the gardenias the servants had used to decorate the bed-posts, trying to turn it into a flower garden flooded his nose.

From the ceiling sheets of tulle were hanging to isolate the content of the bed from the eyes of any waiting lady. Next to this cataract of veils there was a second line of defense if need, a heavy velvet drapery adorned with paradisiac birds nested deep in a virgin tropical forest was capable of isolating any soft personal sound connected with lovemaking. Only stern commands could reach the ears of the most intimate courtier to come for assistance.

Ibrahim's first impression was that the bridal bed was a bit oversized occupying the better part of the bedroom, but he would be the last man to complain for a bit of excessive luxury. Left and right of the bed two magnificent lamps were posted made of Çeşm-i-Bülbül glass resembling the eye of an owl another product of Selim's plunder from Persia.

Inside the lamps incent oil was placed each day and a new wick was lighted after sunset to make sure the eyes of the bed's occupant could enjoy the charms of her approaching partner. As the light from the flame passed through the tinted glass it created red and blue spiral designs on everything that touched, adding a fairytale dimension to the surrounding space.

The room walls were covered with exquisite Iznik tiles depicting red tulips sprouting defiantly in a dense field of thorns, a subtle, but most fitted enactment of a marriage convention. Between them the carved doors glittered, inlaid with pieces of mother-of-pearl, leading to rooms full of the bride's dowry. One door was still open and inside he saw the Sultan's ruby casually thrown in an open jewelry box among many less precious pieces, but still good enough for an ordinary woman to kill for. Hatidge had an expensive taste. Perhaps he should seek few details about the fate of her departed husband.

In the background a mashrabiya screen concealed the passage to the bathroom and the chamekan of a hammam, while the floor was covered with a colorful nomad rug made of fluffy Ankara sheep wool. He had been told that the entire setting was the Princess choice and he should not interfere. Perhaps it was a bit too elaborate for his Roman background, but it fitted perfectly the dream atmosphere his wife tried to create for his pleasure.

Come to think of it, with this marriage he had entered the domain of oriental fairy tales, and now the time of a complete realization was approaching with tantalizing slow rhythms. He discarded every other thought and got prepared to enjoy the best life had in store for a man.

The room looked empty but on the floor lay Hatidge's wedding dress along with her undergarments. The Princess couldn't wait to feel a man again in her arms and become a woman for a second time. This rush was highly flattering, so he whispered her name first softly and hearing no response he called her louder and more demanding:

"Hatidge!"

From behind the velvet drapery around the bed a muffled laughter responded; so, he came closer and found a way through the velvet and tulle screen. In the middle of the bed the Princess rested with her back facing him. Her face was still hidden behind delicate veils and only her closed eyes were visible as if she was in a trance. Her entire body was now bare, eager to be examined and touched.

He didn't lay a finger on her, but let his sense of smell enjoy the familiar perfume of the spices from remote islands in the Indian Ocean mixed with the heavy opium scent. He took few deep breaths as he lay next to her.

In her scent the entire oriental magic was contained and materialized to mesmerize even the most selective occidental man. He felt as a crusader ready to liberate the Holy Lands from Muslim occupation and oppression.

He couldn't keep himself from smiling with this ludicrous thought. The Islam was still alive inside his wife. She was eager to offer him her entire self, but still denied him the pleasure of tasting her lips. He was not willing to take any more of this Muslim nonsense, so he threw away her veil and sucked her lips until they were bare of lipstick. Then, he whispered to her ear his request to tell him what she liked most and how he should proceed next, and he read in her eyes sincere surprise. Perhaps she was expecting him to rape her, but he had come all the way from the Ionian Sea where women were pampered and spoiled, and she should appreciate this courtesy.

She didn't say anything. She was simply too bashful to tell him what she desired most. She didn't have to say anything more. He knew women were made to bear children. Men were the explorers and exploiters. He entered her in haste and she immediately showed her total agreement by tying her legs around his waist. She wanted him so much that every move he made was followed by a deep sigh of relief. She had a lot of tension to relieve, while he was cool, patient and deliberate. He had already most gracefully decided the first night belonged to a bride who had been a widow for too long. Since she was the Sultan's sister, he fell she should also have all her desires satisfied to the full extent of his abilities. However, his attitude was not what she hoped for.

"Don't you like me?" she asked and her eyes revealed her despair.

"I adore you!" he reassured her and to prove his sincerity with a few strokes he exploded all his current passion; but it was not enough to convince her, and this might be the result of all the gossip that circulated in the harem about him. He had to do much more to convince her he belonged only to her.

****

It had been quite some time since the last time the Sultan had invited Mahidevran in his bedroom, perhaps much more than a year. It was unfortunate, but she had lost a son and she had to be punished for her negligence according to the rules of the Ayin. It was one rule that had to be changed. A woman who had just lost a child should be supported rather than punished. This had been Ibrahim's advice, but he couldn't apply it back then. Hurrem had been too overpowering. She used every trick in the miniature book to get pregnant once more, and she had accomplished it. Perhaps being pregnant gave her the illusion she could challenge his authority. This was at least the excuse the Kislar Aga had given him to reduce his anger for her audacious behavior.

Women were emotionally disturbed when they carried a baby in their wombs. Punishing a pregnant woman was unthinkable. It was twice as unthinkable if they were carrying a son the Kislar Aga advised him In Ibrahim's absence. Was this an attempt by the Nubian to replace his counselor?

Mahidevran was indeed the perfect choice or his present disposition. If she got pregnant too, then Gülfem's time might come. Allah's Shadow should try his best to bring order into his world that was disturbed by Hurrem's audacious behavior.

****

Allah knew that hope and unrestrained optimism were very seldom the world conqueror since the days of Alexander. Since then, every great man had taken precautions for a rainy day. The end of the Osmanli dynasty was not close, but the decline had already started after Selim's early demise.

Complicated systems could go astray for a number of reasons and there was no way to point out the critical one, because one calamity resulted in another, and sometimes the very first may not be a calamity at all. It may well be a victory, a miracle or a glorious conquest that raised optimism to unrealistic levels.

****

Mahidevran was about to leave Ibrahim's palace. As time went by, no eunuch had come to summoned her. She had promised Kislar Aga a rich reward if he was to inform the Sultan that her fertile days had arrived, but during these days of celebrations the Harem was in a state of total chaos.

Ibrahim had invited the entire Sultan's harem to stay in his new palace, so all the odalisques could watch the parades from the immense balcony behind a mashrabiya long enough to accommodate an even more populous harem than the Sultan's. Ibrahim had such a nerve, and audacity, it was very hard for anyone to deny him anything anymore.

Nevertheless, Ibrahim had been very courteous on that occasion. He had explained to the Sultan that despite his wishes, the Ayin did not allow the Sultan's women to appear in public or sit next to men on the official grandstand. The reason was fairly obvious, as he explained. No one would pay any attention to the Sultan, the groom, the officials or the parade.

Despite her sour mood, she couldn't resist rewarding his wit with a smile as every other concubine did. Ibrahim had a curious sense of humor other Ottomans lacked. He also knew what beautiful women in a harem needed to hear as often as possible elaborate flattery.

His suggestion the Sultan accepted was for the entire Harem to pay a visit to his palace and stay there until the parade ended. Then, while he and his bride retired in the Selamlik, the Harem could visit his harem accommodations and his new hammam Sinan had built following his suggestions. Having separate hammam for the harem and the Selamlik was an expensive waste of precious resources, like marble, granite or onyx. A palace build for a happy harem should be a common ground where both the master and slaves should unite as often as possible, as every union was blessed by Allah, even if it didn't produce fruits.

Mahidevran considered Ibrahim as a wise man, but if she was in his shoes, she would never abandon the post of the Sultan's Hasodabashi. He was the ideal man for this position. As the Sultan became gradually busier with military expeditions, his concubines became more and more frustrated, and a eunuch Hasodabashi was useless. Frustration levels rouse to the point of explosion, as month after month passed with the armies fighting abroad. Conceivably in a war any man could be killed or captured, even a Grand Vizier or a Sultan. Ibrahim was simply mad exchanging the Harem, a Sultan's paradise on Earth, for a hellish battlefield the place where Kismet reigned supreme.

But now the time had passed and it was time for the entire Harem to leave and return to the Eski Saray.

Unexpectedly the formidable Kislar Aga appeared and conveyed to her the Sultan's urgent invitation. She was to appear as soon as possible. This was the last she wished to do because under the warm sun she was feeling sweaty and dirty. Asphodel had appeared next from nowhere like a jinni with an optimum, as usual, solution. She was welcomed to use the palace's hammam, and become as clean and perfumed as a flower.

Hatidge Sultan wouldn't mind if she was to wear a dress of hers, because they had almost the same dimensions as far as he could discern after two pregnancies each. Even Hatidge's perfumes were at her disposals, if she didn't mind the change of scents. His logic was simply overwhelming and indeed the solution he offered the best under these conditions.

****

Hatidge despite her past experience, this time she was scared. Unconsciously many times she had feelings of guilt for what had happened to her first husband. It was true she had not been very happy with him. He was a rude Albanian good only for looting and stealing.

She had complained to her mother, but she advised her to be patient. Her argument was valid. Her father, Selim Khan, was also a violent man, but eventually he gave Hafsa all the children her heart desired.

Warriors had other priorities. They were not made to please women. It was the era of conquests. Killing and raping was the way empires were built. This was what the Tatar race had done and built an empire from China to the Balkans and from Siberia to Arabia. She considered herself lucky for attracting Selim and becoming eventually the most powerful Valide Sultana of all till then.

Her mother was a fool. She had sacrificed her youth to gain social status. How pathetic was for a woman sacrificing precious time for imperial pomp?

Was she insane too for marrying a Grand Vizier? No, she wasn't! She would never consider marrying Ibrahim, if he was not such an intriguing man. The way he had seduced her in a single night by raping Basmi so thoroughly was enough for her. Since then she had made sure she found out everything there was to know about him. The Kislar Aga had also informed her there were rumors he had several clandestine affairs going simultaneously, but as usual no one talked about them. In the Harem many lips were sealed. It meant many precious reputations were in peril.

As a widow she didn't care one bit about this man's past. All she cared about how Ibrahim would behave after their marriage. Now with her eyes closed she waited to be loved. For her the first time in bed with a man meant a lot.

She didn't wish to make the same mistake twice. Ibrahim was from Parga.

Everyone knew that in the Eternal City. Parga was a Venetian outpost, but it was close to Albania, and she had just about enough of men who used women only for their pleasure. She was a Princess not a whore. If her father used her mother just for reproduction, she was not willing to have a similar fate. The sins of the parents should not trouble the offspring. If they were bright enough, the sins of the parents became the most valuable lessons for their children.

****

Ibrahim wasn't sure about Hatidge's feelings. All he could discern was that she kept part of herself concealed. She probably didn't trust him completely. Perhaps in the back of her mind was the fear he had married her just for her social status. It was the other way around. They had made him Grand Vizier, so that a member of their illustrious family will not feel inferior marrying a commoner. Now all he had to do was to show her he simply desire her as a woman.

He stared at her lips for a while undecided. They were two pieces of flesh full of sap. They were tinted red like tulips from the highlands of Anatolia. A little higher Allah had placed her dark eyes, and she was imaginative enough to dye them emerald blue like the Iznik tiles on the wall to give them immense depth.

From the first moment he saw her, the pitch black color of her eyes had attracted his. They reminded him of the abysmal sea, sometimes deadly ready to devour him, while others playful like a spoiled child. He knew now he would never be able to fathom her heart, but that didn't mean he wouldn't even try.

He would try again and again until he could rise to the task no more. She was worth it. She tried to hold him back, but as her resistance increased, so did his passion. It was a struggle she couldn't win against a decisive man. She tried to push him away with her legs, but his lessons in wrestling with Janissaries were not wasted. He skillfully used her resistance to lead her to an unattainable position. It was really strange, but if in wrestling men the winner was the one who pinned his opponent back on the ground with a woman the conqueror was the one who pinned her face on the mattress. It had to be the mouth a man was most afraid of a woman.

Her back was simply immaculately white without a single mole, and his fingers could not stop touching her skin softer than the best Venetian velvet. Its only adornment was her twin dimples he couldn't resist their attraction. She couldn't do much as his weight pushed her deeper in the soft woolen mattress. Soon she was practically helpless, he could enjoy her anyway he wished; but this was not a worthy goal. It was far below him. All he wished from the beginning was to show her that there was no reason for her to resist him. She would be better off capitulating and let him use her assets for mutual pleasure.

If she was a man, he would try to talk him out of struggle. With a woman he had to use his tongue too, but utter not even a single word. Instead he let his tongue free to taste her skin, as snakes used their tongues to find their way even in total darkness. Part of him might well be a snake too. Her tastes were nothing he had ever tried before. They had none of the saltiness of a man. Her breasts were sweet like milk, while her back left behind the unmistakable scent of oriental spices.

All Turkmans, men and women, fell uncomfortable when someone sought to find their weaknesses. In their blood they always had the thirst for victory; so, when the time had come to face defeat, they tried to retain a piece of their dignity. Hatidge was no different; but in the end she simply could not silence her sighs that betrayed the spots of her greatest weaknesses.

She had no descent way now to hide the truth. He let his tongue free once more to seek for the weakest spot of her fortifications. Her taste was like Macedonian red wine with a dry, sour bouquet full of wild flower perfumes. He drank and drank time and time again until he lost his mind and forgot who he really was. Was he a Barbary pirate eager to plunder and rape? Was he Venetian Doge willing to demolish a city to make sure he had conquered it for eternity? No! Now he was Mehmet Fatih looking where to aim the immense cannon and then focus the spearhead of his Janissaries. He attacked time and time again her twin bastions, but they always bounced back more formidable than ever.

His attack had to be focused once more at the Kerkoporta and the depths of the Lycos Valley. And then, when her resistance collapsed, to gallop through the Edirne gate all the way to the temple of Agia Sophia and turn it into a temple of another god she would be willing to worship until they both died.

And then a miracle happened. He heard her moaning loud and clear. It sounded like a prayer to Allah, but since Eve was created by His wisdom to use few of Adam's ribs to combat male loneliness, all women sounded the same when they prayed to their only god for delivery, the only god who could perform the miracle of resurrection not only for the pure, but for the sinful too, not only for the rich and powerful, but also for the weak and poor, the slaves and the masters. Her sigh was unboundedly the sweetest song he had ever heard; but it was much more than a sound. It was a promise that whenever he came begging for shelter, her embrace would always be open like a friendly harbor.

He opened his eyes and saw Hatidge's face tense as if she was suffering. He whispered her name and she responded by opening her eyes too to see what were his intensions. She shouldn't have dared to do that. Her eyes brought back painful memories. It was as if Selim was resurrected threatening him.

He simply had too many grudges against her family. She had to pay the debt in pain. He struck her again and again, but he failed to achieve his cruel manly goal. Her mesmerizing flesh had devised miraculous ways to turn pain into pleasure, and he had nothing left but accept her superiority of purpose.

****

Seeing him surrendering his essence was the signal she needed to follow him into the Paradise of women the Last Prophet had said nothing about. He had tried everything to conquer her heart and he had finally succeeded.

The Bible was right in this respect. Women would bear children through pain; but with this man the pain would always be sweet. Her mother had guessed right. Ibrahim was the only man for her. He was very gentle and considerate at the beginning and only at the very end when she was hesitant and pensive whether he was equal to her nobility, he tried hard to hurt her to prove that men and women were equal under Allah; but by then the Gates of Paradise were wide open and his desperate efforts had only turned her first wedding night into an unforgettable orgy she had never before experienced in the arms of a man or a woman.

She could feel it was going to be just their first one. The sensation that the man of her life could turn her into his whore within few hours turned her on once more. It was a very logical development of feelings. If this was what he liked, then she may have lost all the advantages of an Osmanli Princess, but she had won all the special privileges of a Galata prostitute.

Seeing him lying on his back exhausted, she got up and run to the bathroom. The Kyra she had asked for instructions insisted that if love lasted for more than an hour, the die was cast. She had also clarified that if the man was on top of the woman, Allah would probably bless the marriage with a child after nine months. Allah didn't like rebellious women that treated a man as if he was their stallion. Now she could let Basmi wash her clean and spray some more perfume where Ibrahim's tongue may wander next, in other words, all over. The experienced courtier used only few moments to turn her again into a tasty dish.

****

He rolled over and came to rest on his back gazing at the ceiling. Hatidge coming out of the bathroom took advantage of this respite and hid behind the Mashrabiya screen without a word. He tried to get up, but her mesmerizing scent reached him and it was so enticing it had hypnotized and immobilized him. It was too tightly connected to her presence he could simply breathe, remember and hope for a repeat performance of her act.

She didn't wish him to forget a single moment, so she soon reappeared behind the screen, only this time she had nothing in common with the frighten girl in pain that few moments ago had left. In her eyes he could see now only insatiable lust. Pain was nothing but the threshold of creation, so as a woman she should learn to enjoy both. Just before his eyes a flower was turning into a juicy fruit eager to satisfy the hunger of all his senses. A man's body seemed now too bare, plain and arid compared to the divine affluent softness and fertility of a woman.

She read his thoughts in his eyes and decided it would be to her benefit if she tried to tease him, so she started once more her serpent dance allowing him to discern through the delicate like lace Mashrabiya design only tiny portions of her flesh and then connected them in his mind to form the inspiring splendor of the whole.

She had quickly realized that in his exposed position he revealed plainly how anything she did cradling her body gradually turned his weakness into hardness. She could even detect which part of hers he liked most and concentrate her efforts into exploiting his most intimate preferences. In the end what she appreciated most was the quickness of his recovery. She was not much younger than him and this small age difference was in her favor. Her dead husband was her first male back then, so she didn't have many means of comparison; but now her memories helped her decided that at least in that respect there was no comparison.

She suddenly fell she had been exceedingly greedy and a tease should not last too long becoming a torture. Excessive greed was not an ingredient of a successful marriage. Respect for the other's feelings was. He wanted her flesh once more and Allah had made clear that the male species should have the first word and the female the last. His body had slowly turned into a powerful attraction and every moment of delay was a moment of pleasure lost.

The Prophet had surely advised that wasting time was the greatest of sins. Perhaps this was the reason she rushed to mount him, but maybe she felt she needed to establish equality. Now that she was comfortably seated, she didn't need to rush. She clapped her hands and Basmi appeared carrying a nargileh with three mouthpieces. She offered her mistress one and then another to her master. He seemed a bit surprised for her presence, but Basmi had not said her last world. With a pleasant smile she put the third mouthpiece in her mouth proving her mistress' pleasure was directly connected to her presence.

Hatidge felt the need to explain.

"There is no way I would leave her alone in the Eski Saray. We should learn how to share our happiness, don't you think so?"

It was a very curious statement, but the opium in the smoke prevented him from realizing the implications. Basmi also attracted his attention as left briefly the room and came back carrying a tray with frozen sherbets and Turkish delights from the island of Chios. She then looked at him to see if she had forgotten to bring something important. He saw his gaze fixed on her body, and she felt ashamed she was still wearing clothes while her master and mistress were exposed. She smiled and left every piece of clothes she wore on the path leading to their side.

She had a very good idea where her services were needed and she made certain she was not going to disturb the present balance but enhance it. If women were to reign supreme there was no other choice but take advantage of his present inability to claim his independence. If total submission was his state of mind, a slave should not dispute her master's choices but confirm them, and her body was perfectly flexible to adapt to the existing restrictions.

Her mistress had taken control of Ibrahim's best asset, so her slave had to be content for the time being with what was left, his hands and his lips. There was just a single solution and she knew it. Ibrahim looked too overwhelmed to react to the ominous prospect of a second rider. She offered him her lips and he gladly accepted the switch from Turkish delight to suckling meat. The poor boy was still hungry for flesh. Now all she had to do was to take care of her mistress primal need to breastfeed a hungry child.

She had the same needs but she had to wait for her turn as mistress always had to be served first. She would certainly prefer a man of her race, but she had reached a certain age when for a slave it didn't pay great dividends to be over-selective or a damned racist.

****

His strategy for this crucial night had failed badly. He had opened two fronts, and become surrounded. Now he was being smothered just hoping the two maenads would be as merciful as Allah. His future looked grim. Hatidge's curious comment could only mean that she knew about his escapades as a Hasodabashi. His head was literarily in her hands.

As she exploited him thoroughly, Hatidge had revealed the reason for this entire debauchery. He was going to be taught a lesson for taking advantage of all these frustrated women in the Harem.

Osman's breed was truly remarkable and beyond the strict Muslim morality. Extreme pleasures were a way of life for them, and he had but a single life to experience it.

****

His fears were largely exaggerated. As he calmly inquired for the true reasons for this show of female aggression, Hatidge explained she was an intimate friend of Gülfem. It meant that besides the notorious eunuch conspiracy, women were also conspiring under certain conditions when the exploitation by men exceeded certain limits.

He had never dared to say no to a woman inside the Harem. His primal fear was that for a slave denying pleasure to any female inside this sacred domain where women ruled was a capital crime punished by castration.

****

He was never capable to estimate accurately the time that passed making love making, and Hatidge and Basmi combined influence had doubled his confusion. It was as if the moment he entered a woman time moved slower. To him many hours had passed, but the sound of the fireworks and cannons signified simply the end of the festivities.

If Allah was just, in nine months a new Osmanli would be born with his blood to wipe away every disgrace he had suffered as a man. However, he never felt shameful. If Selim and his son needed his flesh to be content, he could make the same claim. If someone should be ashamed it was not the sheath that dreaded blood, but the sword that had shed it.

He pushed gently Basmi inside Hatidge's embrace and hastened to the hammam to seek redemption in the regenerating action of the steam. In his memory he recognized this feeling well. It was not the first time he was overwhelmed be two wild riders. Only the genders and their faces were confused and unrecognizable for the time being. This much he could discern with some degree of confidence, as the kind and intensity of pleasure each rider excited in his flesh also varied considerably. Treating him simultaneously as a man and a woman in ecstasy could only add to his confusion on how to properly react or what to say. He could only recall that in the end he felt exhausted but fully content.

He pushed the door open of the chamekan open and was quickly lost in the clouds of his memories. It was there inside such an enchanting environment that the myth of the Olympian gods and goddesses was first created. If this was a Roman bath or the steam coming from a hot spring up in the mountains it was not important; what counted more the divine images that resided inside the clouds.

In his confused mind the two mesmerizing beings he thought he saw as he entered had to be Aphrodite and Hermes. Aphrodite was lying face down on the pedestal while Hermes was lying on her waist rubbing her back with a sponge full of suds.

Silently he came close enough to see why Aphrodite's back seemed so familiar. It didn't have only the twin dimples but every dark mole his memory could recall. As Hermes' back could also be identified with confidence, he simply could not deny his flesh the pleasure of administering justice or seek the fair revenge of an eye for an eye, the most archetypal human reply of all. A crest should be followed by a crest and a trough by a trough. This was how Mother Nature sought divine harmony and reached active equilibrium.

Without a word he pulled hard on the towel the goddess used to cover her nudity and having Hermes at her back there was not much she could do to avoid the inevitable. He took her right there, because he wouldn't have any hope to mate with a goddess under different conditions. It was a one in a lifetime opportunity he was not going to lose it. In this position she was totally exposed to determined attacks, so she wisely decided to make the best of this unusual encounter.

Hermes hardly complained but instead did he best to keep the goddess from screaming at the invisible assailant behind his back. He leaned over and murmured in her ear a few words and at once the raging goddess turned into an obedient mare eager to take both her riders to a heavenly ride. It was a ride that couldn't last long so the immense frustration had to be turned into a cataclysm of pleasure through intensity rather than duration.

Ibrahim was well prepared to for such a contingency as his previous brawl in Hatidge's bedroom had turned on not only his five senses, but also his sixth, imagination. It was part of the female conspiracy to offer him the mouthpiece of a nargileh with a bowl full of dreams. Somehow, once more he had the impression he had lived this scene before, but his memory was still too confused to recall every intimate detail. However, this was not the right time to go down on memory lane.

There was a woman under his spell eager to be impregnated and he would be a sinner to deny her this privilege. If Allah's Shadow had to be as benevolent as Allah, his Grand Vizier couldn't behave like a damned spoiler. He had to grant every logical favor one of his subjects requested, and he should have no guilt feelings for cheating his wife during their first wedding night.

It was not even a cheat. He had an enchanting dream for many years and suddenly he was faced with a divine miracle. A pagan mortal could never resist the will of a goddess and a Muslim faithful the power of Kismet.

Hatidge despite her imperial status she was as mortal as he was, and this was why their marriage was built in solid ground and it would last forever as long as they were willing to show some understanding for each other illusive dreams and mesmerizing infatuations. He had no objection of her pleasing her most intimate slave. In fact, he was truly delighted to let her mingle with Basmi as often as it was humanly possible.

Basmi was an unlucky enough creature to be stolen from her home country and carried in a foreign land where people didn't care much about her future, her precious offspring because she had black skin. In fact, he wouldn't mind giving her all the children Basmi cared to have with a white man to be fully content. Her beloved mistress was incapable of seeding, despite her unselfish love and unending desire, because Allah had imprisoned her in a different gender. Imprisoning her was perhaps an exaggeration. It was much more like a temporary detention; so, he couldn't object because he felt the same way many times and he would be a hypocrite. In a sense all people were prisoners of time and space.

Empires were an unconscious human attempt to erase fictitious lines on a map, or in other words their spatial bonds. The only way empires could expand would be if all people forgot their racial differences, petty grievances and status distinctions. Under this prism a bold mortal mating with a goddess was a patriotic act in true Roman or Ottoman spirit especially since the goddess approved wholeheartedly his sacrilegious act.

Now the only remaining moral doubt was if the Shadow of Allah would consider this event in a similar way, if he ever found out the truth. But this seemed such minute possibility that should be neglected, the same way no man takes seriously into account the remote possibility of a stroke during ejaculation.

****

"Where have you been?" Hatidge exclaimed noticing his unsuccessful attempt for a silent entrance.

"You know well where I have been," he snapped back. "I'm not as used as you smoking hash and I fell asleep. If Asphodel was not there to wake me up, I would be still sleeping. I actually saw the most magnificent dream in my life. I had just impregnated the goddess Aphrodite, when he woke me up. It may be difficult for a Muslim to imagine my delight, but impregnating two goddesses Aphrodite and Artemis in one night is a feat not even Hercules has achieved."

"There is only one God, Allah. Everything else you imagined is just an illusion. I only hope that damned eunuch didn't take advantage of you again," Hatidge noted with a pretentiously solemn look that sent chills down his spine.

Was it ever possible she knew everything about him? He simply had to prove he was innocent of any such crime. Women did not appreciate men who found pleasure with other men even if they were eunuchs. Hatidge Sultan must have been aware of her father's indiscretions. Even if she didn't know from personal experiences, she was too close to her mother for comfort.

"No, I swear on my life that he didn't. Our marriage has saved me from any such dubious temptations and your brother's Nubian gifts must be ample proof for my distaste for the male gender. However, you know well enough how attracted I am to black skin," he protested with his usual audacity.

"Then prove it, and we will believe you!" she demanded, but he didn't mind seducing the goddess Isis too. The image he had the chance to admire as he sneaked in was simply too inspiring for his fertile imagination. While he was away, Basmi had turned his beloved bride to an obedient slave of her desire to be devoured, and he simply had to retaliate to bring the world of Allah again into divine equilibrium. Was this an omen he was destined to bring Africa under his spell?

****

Suleiman had to accept that being separated from Ibrahim would not be as easy as he had hoped. Through all these years and the times they had spent together he had become an integral part of his existence.

He had chosen him, following the instructions of the Persian Book on the proper choices for the friends of a prince. With these instructions in the back of his he looked for a proper friend, but his mind was sidetracked when he saw Ibrahim naked in the Avret Bazaar. The book talked about handsome friends and the Quran used the same term too; but there was no way one could be handsome without being sexually attractive one way or another. A human body could be admired or desired from different angles, and he had to admit Ibrahim was a magnificent species every way he looked at him. Was beauty a more subtle word for sexual attraction? If Ibrahim was here, he could ask him; but now he was alone and he had to ask himself and be perfectly sincere too.

Perhaps it was his father he wished to imitate; but it might well be an even older trend. Mehmet Fatih was the first Sultan who had divided in his residence the Harem from the Selamlik so drastically. Perhaps Hurrem was right to ask for a reunion. Now he wouldn't have to wait so long for Mahidevran to arrive. She certainly took her time to get dressed to perfection. What a waste of time! The moment she came in, he would rip her clothes off. Then, he would rape her to give her another son, as it was customary. Then, they would both go to the hammam to get cleaned from their sins, but in there even more sinful thoughts might be generated, as usual. This was the case where a woman like Mahidevran or Hurrem could prove to a man like him how inadequate he really was despite his military power or his awesome life or death authority.

He had to admit that this was never the case with Ibrahim. He was also a man and their passion ended practically together. Was this one of the reasons they were practically inseparable? With all his odalisques he had to go to sleep to recover and wait relaxed for the sun to rise. What happened to his female guests after such a passionate union had never become a problem. The Kislar Aga would carry them back locked inside a closed carriage to the Eski Saray.

What happened back there if the odalisque was not pleased with the Sultan's performance was anyone's guess, but certainly not Kislar Aga's. He knew by force all the Harem secrets. The only concern of Ayin was to keep Osman's blood pure from any drop of slave blood. It was an immense illusion. Ibrahim Pasha the slave tonight was mixing most thoroughly his blood with that of Selim Khan and he was unable to do anything about it.

A knock was heard on the door and he gave permission the visitor to enter. The Kislar Aga appeared and he guided Mahidevran Sultan in. She was as beautiful as ever before, and in simpler terms this meant he desired her. She had a smile in her lips and this meant she was eager to please him. Her long smile was a gift he didn't expect. He was expecting to hear all sorts of grumbles and he would become desperate to find reasonable excuses for his offensive attitude of allowing Hurrem to become the new member of his imperial family.

However, his worries proved unfounded. Mahidevran behaved as if nothing important had happened, and by the time she reached his bed she had left all her clothes on the Persian rug, displaying an unusual urge to be used. He was still waiting to hear her arguments, but all he heard were the whispering of two words that sounded like a command or a request depending on his disposition:

"Come here."

The picture she presented was too inviting to be denied. He could already smell her perfume filling the room, and from the red color of her skin it was clear she had spent at least one hour preparing her flesh for this union.

"Have you changed your perfume?" he asked just to show her he stilled remembered few intimate details of her.

"Of course, I have. Don't you like it?"

"Yes, I do like it. It is spicy. It reminds me of Hatidge."

"It is Hatidge's! Women like to use all the ingredients of a winning recipe!"

There have been almost ten years since the moment he had lay his eyes on her young flesh, and there were very few signs of change. In fact, she had become even more attractive as her pelvis had expanded, making her waist line look even thinner. Her breasts since then had also grown from lemons to juicy oranges. He rested next to her, but she showed him the distance was not to her liking. She put her arms around him and pulled him on top of her to show him he had to behave like her master that night. It was a welcomed change of attitude as most of the time she was riding him to exhaustion.

This was not going to be one of these occasions. His desire was stronger than ever, and he was sincere enough to accept the true reason behind this uncommon passion. It was her perfume. With his eyes closed, she had triggered a most powerful illusion, the illusion of the prohibited incest.

Hatidge Sultan was partially responsible for the emotional mess he was in stealing his favorite male lover, and she had to be punished. For a true man the proper way to punish a woman was to rape her and hopefully get her pregnant. It was a primitive feeling his father had explained him after his circumcision. Circumcision was the proper way for a marauding male to rape virgins with impunity. It was unquestionably a painful operation, but it occurred once in a man's lifetime.

As he mounted her, he heard someone coughing behind his back and opened his eyes. With this unexpected run of events he had forgotten completely to dismiss the Kislar Aga. Now, under the candle light with his glittering skin he looked even more handsome than Ibrahim. Did it mean an Osmanli Sultan yearned for the flesh of a Nubian slave as much as the degenerate Mameluke Sultan his father had hanged from the Cairo main gate?

Ibrahim had graciously accepted his generous present. Had he fallen in the same trap Hurrem had set for his favorite companion to prove Ibrahim was not man enough to be feared?

Ibrahim was right. There were many answers even to the simplest question. The Kislar Aga had waited for too long to announce his presence. He had not only seen Mahidevran getting naked but him too. Should he ask for his head for this gross indiscretion?

Sultan Selim would never think twice about such an obvious answer, but Selim didn't make Ibrahim his Hasodabashi and Grand Vizier.

He was much more sophisticated than his grim father, and Ibrahim and their long discussions were responsible for all these cultural exchanges. In this chaotic universe to every phenomenon there were at least three explanations or possibly even more. The Aga had waited to stare at Mahidevran's divine body was the most obvious one, but this answer did not match the preferences all spies reported. He had waited to see him naked! And why did he cough? He was too tempted or too disgusted from the spectacle of him on top his Kadin?

He was about to send the Kislar Aga away, when he heard Mahidevran's voice dispatching the same order with a much more courteous way than he would under the circumstances. He had to admit that women had a much better way to command men inside the Seraglio. Maybe it would be dangerous to have women as officers in a field of battle, but in peacetime women were more convincing and effective. Even an order like "fuck me" sounded much better when a woman like Mahidevran gave it than a fearsome Janissary.

He laughed at the ideas that came down to his mind at this late hour, but laughter was not what Mahidevran was expecting to hear; so, in a magical way she repeated the order he had in mind, and there was no way in the world he could deny her solemn request.

****

The months of honey and wine passed quickly as terrible news arrived from Egypt by land. The second in line Vizier, Ahmet Pasha, had been extremely sour for the unusual promotion of Ibrahim. He considered his transfer to distant Egypt a great chance to start his own dynasty; so, he kept for himself the collected taxes and started collecting mercenary troops to secure his status, hoping that Suleiman's hand will not reach that far.

As it usually happened in cases like this, the Sultan's first reaction was to send the closest faithful Vizier with an army to set matters straight. This time it was Çoban Mustafa Pasha, a very loyal and able Vizier from Albania, who was employed first by Selim in the Egypt expedition and later distinguished himself in the Belgrade and Rhodes campaign. He had become by then Beylerbey of Syria.

Çoban Pasha crushed the rebellion and sent Ahmet's head in brine to the Topkapi Saray. However, his military efficiency was not enough to calm down the Egyptian revolt; so another less harsh and more diplomatic man should be tried. It was a task that fitted best Ibrahim, who despite his recent marriage was the best available choice.

For his followers it was a great opportunity to prove his worth as a diplomat. For his opponents Egypt was also a good test of his loyalty. For Ibrahim it was a test of his intelligence. After Ahmet's prompt demise, only a madman would try to establish a Sultanate in Egypt, when he had everything he desired already in his palace on the At Meidan.

Suleiman's only concern was his health condition. Somehow his health was betraying him, and this was probably why Ahmet had tried his luck for establishing another empire. Thank Allah, Mahidevran was pregnant once again and her birth would even up the score in the Harem.

Egypt, on the other hand, was the richest of all Suleiman's possessions, but for Ibrahim Hatidge was now the greatest treasure. It was practically impossible to find such a considerate wife willing to overlook his promiscuity. Nevertheless, every departure from Constantinople was a test of nerves, as the enemies who stayed behind had every chance to start their unrestricted conspiracies. Everything was possible now, because of the Sultan's sickness. It was simply a question who the conspirators thought was the easiest target.

The Sultan's instructions were straight forward. He had to extinguish any rebellions, organize Egypt, and win the trust of the Egyptians. He had to show them the Ottoman rule would be beneficial and Ahmet's rebellion was just a sorry exception and a personal failure. Ottomans were there to stay and with cooperation the trade would flourish and past splendors would return now that Mameluke power had ebbed. To signify the urgency of the reforms, the trip to

Egypt would proceed by sea and Sinan would be his most immediate associate.

Ibrahim didn't mind his presence. This Janissary had proven his worth in both the Belgrade and Rhodes sieges undermining the fortifications, and shown his skills as a master builder, designing his magnificent At Meidan palace that had mesmerized all visitors. Unfortunately, Hatidge seemed reluctant to follow him in such a dangerous trip. This was also Valide Sultan's suggestion, and he had no reason to challenge it. He had to admit that she had handled Hurrem in the best possible way after the events during their marriage. Hurrem would have to learn how to behave, if she wished her children to survive.

Asphodel had been very reassuring in this respect. Hurrem had turned to be a very devoted mother and an accomplished Harem politician. She had taken advantage of Suleiman's sickness and Mahidevran's pregnancy to prove her worth once more. Unfortunately, there was every indication she was pregnant too; but, in a harem every pregnancy was a blessing for all women. It was an opportunity for other odalisques to get pregnant too. He was doing his best to promote next Gülfem, according to Ibrahim's instructions, but this was something only Allah or Kismet could accomplish.

****

The last evening before the fleet's departure Ibrahim chose to spend with his wife. It was a gentle autumn evening and the eastern wind known in Venetian as "levanter" carried to the City from the East the heat of the Anatolian highlands. It was the special wind that made women's blood run faster in their veins. The servants had spread rich "kilims" and fluffy pillows on the garden grass, for their masters to eat and drink, while the cooks sent constantly new trays full of appetizers according to the princess' instructions for a light dinner.

Hatidge looked rather excited affected by the eastern wind and hardly touched any dish. Instead she preferred to cool her lips with the frozen sherbet. Her gaze seemed lost inside the labyrinth of thoughts, but her lips were betraying what kind of thoughts dominated her mind. She was uncomfortably filled with desires; otherwise she wouldn't try to exhaust in one night the precious provision of ice that came down from the Olympus peaks by mule caravans every day.

Nearby, Ibrahim could not take his eyes away from her lips as each time she took a sip, her tongue would come out to sweep away the white foam of sherbet resting on her fleshy upper lip shaped like a slim mustache. Was she thinking what he was thinking? Was it a coincidence she had chosen the sour lemon sherbet instead of the strawberry or cherry he normally preferred?

Coincidences like this often betrayed secret thoughts. Since their marriage Hatidge had completely dominated his existence, and every day he couldn't wait for the evening to arrive, drink some wine, smoke a nargileh and then retire. He didn't believe the amount of desire this seasoned woman could create by a few suggestive glances or by the captivating dresses she chose to wear. Many of them were his choice, bought from Venice where women were more liberated, revealing rather than hiding under delicate lace their most attractive feminine feature, their breasts. It was the prevailing fashion in the West the East had to follow even though there was never a birth deficit in the Orient.

For the Orient superiority in numbers meant they would be the invaders, not the Romans or the damned Christian Crusaders. This was the unconscious reason the Last Prophet had allowed four legal wives for every man. Promiscuity was the best oriental defense, and enemies never fought to extinction, but would rather surrender to live and fight another day.

****

Ibrahim had to admit she had gladly accepted his suggestions as they were more in line with her new disposition. She was fed up with the local hypocrisy that Muslim widow had to look as sad and unattractive as possible to satisfy the spirit of her deceased husband rather than the direct command of Allah for more warriors.

The truth was the exact opposite. Her husband's spirit would be more pleased if Hatidge Sultan was treated disrespectfully by her new husband. Her mother had explained this was a common complain of all the women in the Empire. Their husbands were treating them like whores. It was not entirely their mistake, but staying for many months away from home, it was natural they would get used to the alluring ways of the slaves they captured that would do anything to please their masters, or the caravans of whores that followed the troops wherever they went. Then, when they came back home, their women would look boring and timid compared to the wild women they associated during the expeditions.

Now that this marriage had been consumed, Hatidge saw her first marriage under a different prism. If a woman felt humiliated, it was not the act by itself that counted most, but the intentions of the man who did it. Even the worst treatment performed gently by the right man could be turned into profound satisfaction. In fact, she was especially open to suggestions when Ibrahim tenderly proposed and Basmi enthusiastically accepted his pagan suggestions. Then, it was practically impossible not to feel the inescapable urge to try them first. She couldn't say if Ibrahim was such a great diplomat as her brother said; but, undeniably he had a practical way to make her inhibitions disappear, namely the threat to try his paganism first on Basmi.

Her petty urges could well be the result of envy, as Basmi suggested, or her tendency to impose her superior social status, as Ibrahim asserted; but deep inside she knew it was nothing but a combination of human greed and Allah's will. He had made the universe this way and she didn't know exactly when she was going to die. She had lost too many years of her youth involved with her previous marriage; thus, she had to soak her flesh somehow with every new kind of pleasure Ibrahim's mind was capable of conceiving.

****

The fatal attraction her black eyes exerted on him was overwhelming. Every time her eyelids closed he pictured her as she exploded her passion like a dormant volcano in bed. Every time Hatidge licked her lips, he couldn't but think his ecstatic raptures. He wished he could delay the fleet departure for a few days; but the lively levanter blowing was the ideal wind for a trip to the South. If only the weather could last for a week.

Thank Allah; he had at least an entire night devoted just for her. She had realized the extent of his passion and she had already sent Basmi to sleep all alone. Hurrem's behavior at the wedding had underlined her instinct that her audacity was triggered by jealousy for her success. Within few months she had achieve what Hurrem had not, namely a sumptuous marriage, despite her consecutive pregnancies and successful deliveries.

The vicious Harem rumors that had lately reached her ears, claiming Hurrem was much more for Ibrahim than the favorite courtesan of his master, but possibly the father of her next child, were so outrageous it could conceivably have a grain of truth; but tonight Ibrahim desired only her and to communicate his intentions he took a ripe fig, split it open and sank his teeth in its flesh, igniting her daydreaming.

She opened her lips and let the tip of her tongue slip through to challenge him. Ibrahim felt it was the right time to break the silence and start the foreplay.

"What kind of present would you like me to bring you from Egypt, perhaps few more Nubian slaves?"

It was not an entirely innocent tease, and he saw in her eyes her jealousy exploding; but, she seemed confident enough to treat his offer as a joke and retaliated.

"Yes, that would be a nice gesture, but only if you wish to make Basmi even happier than she is now."

"Then tell me what else you would fancy, even if that means I must share you with someone else."

"We still have the four Nubian slaves my brother has given you, if I ever feel our passion declining; but for the time being the best gift you can offer me is the precious moment, when I make you close your eyes," she said and she was perfectly serious.

Ibrahim felt a bit uncomfortably hearing her severe tone, so he tried to excuse himself.

"Your Sultan brother should not see me coming back with empty hands. He might think I don't value his sister as much as I should."

"I'm fed up with all these dubious presents with devious motives. The best gift I ever had from him was his most beloved slave. Now all that I'm missing is more time to enjoy him."

316

"If you don't tell me what present you want, then I might waste this entire night trying to guess it," he teasingly threatened her.

However, Hatidge was not to be threatened.

"My darling, whatever offers you have in mind have ceased to excite me for a while. Now my greater concern is what is growing inside me, and I will do whatever I can not to disturb its sleep."

Ibrahim could not retain his excitement, and tears watered his eyes. He was going to be a father too. Somehow Allah had given him a child with the blood of Selim's in its veins. His race had finally taken revenge for the fall of the Eternal City.

He gazed at her dark eyes that sometimes could be so forbidding and threatening almost as much as Selim the Grim. He smiled because he knew that inside the walls of her heart there was now a traitor that would open the gates the moment he appeared in all his glory. Her lips were already trembling from the desire to please him despite her feeble threat. She was as lusty and as noble as he. She was also as wise to know that the greatest part of pleasure was in expectation. This was the reason why even dying people left this world with open eyes.

****

There was an old Roman myth that promised the defeated Romans that one day a new Roman Emperor named also Constantine was destined to conquer Constantinople and enter through the Golden Gate. This myth was so popular among the Greeks that Mehmet Fatih was so terrified with the prospect of such an invasion that he closed with a wall the most magnificent gate at the southern end of the land walls.

It was a pathetic attempt to avoid the inevitable for such an innovative besieger. If with his artillery Mehmet Faith had brought down the mighty Great Walls of Theodosius, what kind of luck the feeble Ottoman stone barricade would have after many centuries faced with modern cannons?

These thoughts circled Ibrahim's mind when he went into his room to get prepared for the incoming midnight feast of Osmanli flesh. It sounded absurd and extremely greedy, but from the moment he found out the Princess was pregnant he couldn't have enough of her.

She had disappeared first as was her habit, but she didn't hide behind the veils of her sumptuous bed. She was lying naked on his bed in his selamlik waiting for his arrival, eager to taste his passion as soon as possible.

Was she informed about his special weakness of dimples and wished to show him under the chandelier that hers were as adorable as Mahidevran's?

Conceivably Asphodel might have revealed one of his secrets to gain her trust. He was too insecure about his future especially now that Ibrahim was about to depart for Egypt; but he simply knew too much and his fate was to learn even more if he kept popping where he was not invited. Now even Mahidevran may wish him dead; but now Hatidge looked so inviting he didn't feel like losing his point of focus with random thoughts.

Lying flat on his bed pillows Hatidge Sultan looked like Constantinople spread over seven hills. In this position she seemed she was trying to defend only one of her gates leaving the rest of her charms entirely at his disposal. However, the thought she was carrying in her womb possibly his son turned all his violent passion at once into tenderness. Now every thought of piercing or hurting her was magically transformed to a powerful yearning to kiss, suckle or caress her as if she had turned into a defenseless baby.

Somehow she guessed what kind of tender feelings possessed his mind and gladly concurred to all his bold explorations revealing all the emotions his touch triggered and what he should do to help her reach her peaks.

Motherhood had made her extremely sensuous and selfish, but this was simply half the truth. The moment he distinguished her passion like an obedient, docile courtesan, she abandoned the role of a master and assumed the duties of a slave eager to please. It was a miracle of true love that as long it was alive it had the power to turn proud nobles into humble servants.

****

This trip to Egypt was the second time the master would be separated from his slave and this thought brought back painful memories from their first long separation. As the fleet squadron hoisted sails from the Golden Horn, the Sultan couldn't stand the pressure of and embarked in a galley following his slave all the way to the most remote of the so called "Prince Islands".

Arriving there, he didn't hesitate for a single moment and embraced warmly his slave as if he was his brother. Ibrahim was in fact much more than a close relative. Above all he was his friend and Allah had made the world so you could not choose your brothers, but only your friends. Now his fogged glance had nothing to do with that of a Ruler of the Universe.

"Do not forget me!" he said trying hard to make it sound like an order, but his whisper revealed his weakness. It was so faint one may have thought he was heard to hear his own voice. The words might sound familiar, but the slave couldn't remember who uttered them and on which occasion.

"Do not worry about me. In few months, Allah willing, we will be together again drinking wine in my garden," he promised, but to prophesize about the future was always a challenge for any mortal. Ibrahim's soothing words did not have a lasting effect and soon his mood turned sour once more. This marriage had created deep suspicions the slave was seeking a way to regain his freedom. Even his promise they would drink wine in his garden was a subtle refusal of an invitation to the Marble kiosk.

"What makes you think you will ever yearn to return back to the Eternal City? Is it just two black eyes or something more?" Suleiman asked.

Ibrahim was now the Grand Vizier and together with this immense power came the will to exert it. He simply could not pretend total obedience anymore.

"Maybe besides a pair of black eyes there is also a pair of gray," he uttered, but his tone of voice was not very convincing.

"You are lying to me!" the Sultan said with a solemn tone as if he was diagnosing a deadly disease. "No slave can serve two masters."

Ibrahim seemed amused by this assertion as the Sultan was the first to try this difficult balancing act.

"A loyal slave can learn every new lesson his master is willing to teach him," he teased him, and for one more time Suleiman was unable to argue effectively, and Ibrahim took advantage of his powerlessness.

"There is wise scientist in Italy who teaches that the sun, the moon and all the stars do not rotate around our Earth but the sun. He claims that there are mysterious forces that govern the orbits of every star, and consequently that there might be more than one explanations to each phenomenon. Maybe our belief that everything must comply with our needs is erroneous too, because the sun does not circle the Earth. I don't know how you feel, but recently I found out that my singular path needs more than one source of attraction to be stable. If there is only one attraction sooner or later there will be a collision. As any other human being, I must decide what I should leave behind when I die. However, the fact that I have chosen to marry your sister is a telltale sign that the same blood keeps exerting both the attractions I now feel."

"I know how you feel, because sometimes I feel the same way," the Sultan admitted. "What can we do to find our balance once more?" he asked quite confused by Ibrahim's idea.

The moment Suleiman decided he should be true to himself realizing he was not the center of the universe, Ibrahim agreed to open his heart too. The very first day he became a slave, he had learned that he should not fight against the forces of Nature, but try to use them to his advantage. He hadn't resist the will of the pirates back then; otherwise, he would be dead by now in the bottom of the Aegean Sea. The captain had been his first teacher. He had taught him that if a master wished him to sit on his lap, it made no sense to deny him this pleasure. This was how he had next become a falconer, occupying his first official post in his illustrious career. A small concession had been enough to set his life in the right track the same way a snowflake had the power to start a mighty avalanche, when the conditions were right.

Then, to reside permanently in a room next to Suleiman, his master had made him his Odabashi. If this was a mistake of his master he couldn't yet decide, because for him was a blessing. Soon he came for the first time in contact with women and their divine power to attract and transform a male.

Eventually even Suleiman had benefited from the slave's experience on how to seduce women. After a long siege a violent assault may fail sometimes. If he had not helped his master to solve the riddle of Rhodes, he wouldn't be now his Damat and Grand Vizier ready to seduce the Egyptian rebels too into submission. Slowly Ibrahim had been transformed into a legend in the Ottoman Empire how submission to Suleiman's will was enough for a slave to achieve immense power and riches. Now he felt so confident, he was not complaining that his life had become so complicated that he couldn't find enough time to spend with Suleiman and his sister. On the contrary, he was blessing Allah for making his life so full of a variety of pleasures and exciting adventures.

"Do you promise me you will come back to me?" the Sultan asked.

"Yes, there is no way I can ever escape the attraction of the Eternal City," the slave promised without hesitation and he was perfectly sincere; he simply did not wish to explain in more detail all the centers of attractions that were pulling him back.

Hafsa Sultan had advised him that with the House of Osman he had to be sincere, but few harem secrets should never be told. Truth sometimes could become more dangerous than a thousand lies. Thus, hiding the truth was less dangerous than either a lie or a truth.

****

Allah the Great had made the world in such a way that all the great problems were solved according to His will, while the Devil could influence only minor details. This was why He was so great and the Devil so small compared to him that most people didn't even feel Devil's existence.

****

As the Sultan's galley slow retreated in depths of the horizon, Ibrahim could not sweep away from his mind Suleiman's wet eyes. They were nothing he ever had to face before. Gone was the optimism, the tenderness or the passion he had to deal with few years back. Now only profound melancholy was to be seen and a sense of helplessness.

It was a pity they had not met all this time. Since the day of his marriage announcement he could not remember a single day when they had been all alone. He always was so busy enjoying his marriage he had not suspected something was going wrong to try to fix it. For days he didn't even have to time to get out of his palace. Now, he was on the way to Egypt leaving everything he loved behind. Only Allah knew how life would be in the City when he came back.

Chapter 10
In the Pyramids of Egypt

**"Try the taste of all your passions and put yourself in shame "
(Rumi)**

Ibrahim's expedition to Egypt was the chance Hurrem waited to regain her status and to achieve this goal she wrote a letter. She preferred this solution because words had wings, while letters could be read again and again multiplying their effect on a man's mind. Face to face confrontations were also more risky. You could guess your opponent's intentions, but at the same time he could guess yours too. Letters had also the ability to hide between the lines your intentions, while eyes could not lie as easily as ink and pen.

Now that she had to explain her acts writing was the best way to do it. In the past she never wrote letters, even though she could ask the Kislar Aga to write her what she wished to say. The Kislar Aga had been more than helpful, but in the Seraglio she could not trust even herself. Few times, especially when Suleiman was gone, or when he was sick in bed and indisposed, she could not contain her frustration. Nevertheless, now that she had learned the Ottoman language, she could even write love poems, if her emotions were inspiring enough; so, she did not have to use her body to make a subtle point clearer. She could simply write down what was in her mind. It was a profound transformation that turned her from a dumb whore to a sophisticated lady of the court.

Now that Ibrahim was away, she had an open field. She simply had to wait just few more days, so that the Sultan realized the void of his absence. Then she had to wait few more hours so that the sun had set.

When the sun died and darkness crept through the windows, then a human soul troubled by illness was more sensitive to the greatest insecurity of all, his death. When a person fell lonely and unprotected he became vulnerable against the most dangerous predators of all, the ones that lurked in the most remote corners of its own mind. This was the best time for her assault, as it would be foolish to attack when there were chances she might lose.

The letter wrote:

To my beloved Sultan, Ruler of the Universe and my heart. Our children are growing day by day and they are very healthy; but they miss you terribly. Every night they have trouble sleeping and often see terrible nightmares. When they open their eyes, the first thing they do is look around them, expecting to see their father; but recently they never do and they become very disappointed. If you can steal few moments and visit us in the Eski Saray, it would mean a lot to them. If you don't wish to see your slave, I could have them sent to you in a carriage. If you have forgiven your slave, she would be happy to accompany them to your apartment, but since she is expecting she cannot do much to please you.

She is very sorry for her unacceptable behavior and she didn't wish to embarrass you; but, she felt very badly when she saw a slave of yours being able to marry your sister, the most distinguished Princess of all, and mix his blood with yours, while you, a glorious Sultan, cannot marry the mother of two healthy children. I'm not aware of your plans, and you may have in mind to marry me, if my next child is a boy, but I'm afraid for the worst. People say that you invite almost every night the one after the other your two Kadin. If your heart belongs to someone else, please do not write me anything, because such sad news may kill our coming third child.

My dearest, if you so wish, you can keep your children in the Seraglio and offer this foolish slave as one more present to your close friend Ibrahim. She wouldn't mind this torture provided you do not harm her most precious offspring. For her feelings worry not, because from the moment you stopped wanting her, her life has ended.

Your eternal slave, the one who used to make you smile

****

When Suleiman received Hurrem's letter it was already dark. He had just come back from a lonely stroll in the Gülhane Garden under the moonlight. Mahidevran was not available. She was moody, because of her suspected pregnancy and Gülfem was keeping company to Valide Sultana. Anyway he was too tense already for any woman to do him good. Ibrahim's absence since the days of his marriage had started affecting his health by increasing his depression. One month had passed and he still hadn't received any letter from him.

When he was alone, he always felt insecure. Perhaps this was the reason Hurrem's letter touched him so deeply that he started crying. If it wasn't so late, he might have gone to Valide's apartment seeking her advice. At this hour his only refuge was Hurrem's embrace. She was nothing more than a slave, but one look into her eyes was enough to turn every humble request of hers into a firm command. He had tried many times to resist her attraction, but he had always failed. She was simply too canning for him and knew better than any other woman how to excite his fantasy with very simple gestures, like licking her lips, or putting her thumb in her mouth like a suckling baby; but her greatest trick was when she turned her back at him full of grit and stubbornness, whenever he considered refusing a wish. With her female intuition she had discovered one after the other all his weaknesses, and they were too many.

Reading her letter, he had to agree his children were the ones who were suffering most during their separation. It was indeed very inconsiderate of him not to visit them; but on the other hand if he wanted to see them and she was there, he knew she could easily manipulate him into forgiving her.

He was almost certain she would be waiting wearing one of her most revealing dancing costumes, claiming she was practicing dancing to keep her body fit. Then, she would promptly proceed to show him how flexible she really was despite her pregnancies mimicking all these obscene poses she copied from the book of the Forbidden Pleasures.

"The Forbidden Pleasures", the book he was raised with she had ridiculed repeatedly. She had practically turned into the "Daily Pleasures", with her insatiable lust. Her ferocity was another mystery for him. Every time they met she was like a blazing furnace of desire looking for him to quench it. After his recent sickness and his swollen toes, he felt too exhausted to meet her in person, so he decided to write her a short note announcing he didn't feel he should meet her just yet, but she should sent him his children with a carriage.

He was about to finish his reply to every valid point she made, when he noticed the last few sentences. Superficially she claimed that becoming Ibrahim's slave was the worst punishment for her. It may well be a sentence meant to despise Hatidge, a quite understandable reaction, considering his sister's support to a hesitant brother. However, the expression she used for this dubious kind of punishment meant she had at least once considered the possibility of becoming Ibrahim's slave and compared it to other alternatives she considered worse.

He then remembered once one of Ibrahim's more audacious comments about the possibility of sharing few of his concubines with him. Was this an example of how the members of his harem thought? Were they comparing him a Sultan with Ibrahim a slave?

From the moment Ibrahim's palace was built, people in the Eternal City had started wandering whose palace was more luxurious or higher. Ibrahim who followed closely the City's gossip had explained to him that these were the plans of Sinan and he had nothing to do with them. He also noted that Topkapi Saray was built on much higher grounds, so his residence was undoubtedly higher; but this comparison was very annoying. Ibrahim was healthier or at least he looked so. Whether Ibrahim was more attractive than him or not, he was not the proper judge. Only women were made to judge the true worth of a man. Unquestionably, there were many women in his harem that would kill to sleep with his slave; but this was simply the result of their frustration for his inferior vigor due to his illness. They would even fall in love with a Janissary guard, if the Black Eunuchs allowed them to roam in the Seraglio Gardens at night.

How did her mind arrive to such an eventuality? Perhaps it was a mistake offering this Nubian dancing group to his brother-in-law. It was just an impulsive thought because he read in Ibrahim's eyes the lust for the drummer. Impulsive thoughts were the most sincere ones after all, because the mind didn't have time to connive.

There were just too many conspiracies in the Harem with all these promiscuous women waiting idly for an invitation. Even his mother had conspired against him. He had forced Ibrahim to admit that she had also invited him in the Harem, where he met Hurrem for the first time.

Making Ibrahim his Hasodabashi was also the result of a conspiracy, as well as Ibrahim becoming Selim's falconer. Was he becoming insane imagining that even his father and mother were conspiring against him?

No, he wasn't! His father had tried to send him a poisoned caftan, and his mother gave away Hatidge as his wife behind his back. Perhaps all these were not conspiracies after all. Perhaps they were just the way everyone behaved, when he tried to achieve a goal in the expense of someone else's. If this was so, then he should also be justified to take advantage of everyone else too. This was what being a Sultan meant.

****

When Hurrem saw Asphodel in her door opening, asking her to get dressed and follow him, she was terrified. She was afraid the Sultan had decided to punish her, in which case her children would be doomed.

Ibrahim's marriage had been a disaster for her, as suddenly even the

Valide Sultan despised her. Thank Allah, she was just three month pregnant and her constant dancing exercises had kept her fit.

She asked the servant to wait and went in to get dressed accordingly. She had prepared this dress for such an occasion. If Suleiman had a crush for obedient slaves, she would most certainly adjust to his preferences.

****

Seeing Hurrem wearing a man's caftan was an unexpected surprise and he couldn't resist smiling. It was not the first time Hurrem was dressed in strange costumes. Besides belly dancing suits she had used in the past also Black and White Eunuch's uniforms. Now that Ibrahim was gone, she appeared dressed like him. Was she trying to comfort him or ridicule his fixation?

Following the protocol, she kneeled before him and kissed the corner of his caftan. Tonight he was not in his better moods and to cut her visit short he allowed her to get up with the magic word "peki". She didn't get up, but completed her act with the typical Grand Vizier oral salutation.

"I greet the most magnificent Sultan Suleiman Khan, the Shadow of Allah, Lord of the age and the entire world, protector of Islam, Guardian of Mecca and Medina, Master of Damascus and Jerusalem, Caliph of the High Threshold, and Keeper of the House of Pleiades."

She had used the same words and she was certain he would notice the perfect coincidence. He did and he responded to her challenge with one of his.

"I'm glad to meet Ibrahim's new slave," he noted; but sometimes it would be better to leave the best for the end.

"I hope my master was not upset reading my suggestion. Everyone in the Harem knows the Sultan shares or exchanges everything he likes with his Grand Vizier, his clothes, his jewels, his mares, even his authority. A concubine costs fewer ducats than his best Arabian mare."

The Sultan now discovered he was in a defending position and had to find excuses.

"A mare has no great value for me. I can have hundreds if I want to. I never left anything of a true value to slip through my fingers," he claimed but Hurrem had an answer to this claim.

"I always thought that a priceless jewel is worthless, if you don't wear it; also, a mare you don't ride will grow fat and useless. I have almost forgotten the last time I relieved you."

"I don't like to use items that have hurt me once. If a mare throws me off her back, I might even decide to slaughter her."

"And I know that the truth cuts like a knife and Allah's will is only they who love you to speak the truth. I was speaking the truth and that's why even your friend did not utter a word that day to defend you."

Suleiman suddenly turned thoughtful. Hurrem had been very pointed that day, but she didn't lie. She read his heart and simply expressed openly his feelings. Ibrahim who was always so talkative had remained silent. However, few truths should never be revealed. Even the Prophet Mohamed had not revealed everything, but left many issues for the people to decide how they should be resolved. Perhaps now it was the right time to find out if Hurrem was always truthful with him.

"If you are so truthful then tell me, have you ever made love with another man?"

It was a foolish question she always knew how to answer.

"Do you really want to know? Don't you know your mother bought me from a slave trader? You are a slave master too. Do you let your slaves defy your commands without punishment? Are you so naïve you don't know Allah had made women in such a way they can please a thousand men and still be untouched? Do you believe in Allah or in Virgin Mary?"

The Sultan was not ready to cope with so many issues, so he tried to find a way out.

"I don't care if you served other men before you entered my harem. All slaves have to follow orders."

"If the truth is what you are seeking, please tell me. Do you remember the world before you were born?"

"That's a stupid question. Of course I don't. No one does."

"Then, are you sure Sultan Selim was the father of all his children? A father does not kill his children. Would you ever decide to kill our children too?"

Suddenly her tongue cut deeper than a Damascene sword.

He didn't know if she knew Selim had tried to send him a poisonous caftan. The excuse Ibrahim had offered him was that his father was delirious and he tried to kill him any way he could, when he realized that he was his only heir and the Mute Executioners could not pass through his personal guards and strangle him inside the Manisa Palace. At the time he believed this explanation, but now Hurrem was scratching open that painful old wound.

Hurrem realized the state of turmoil he was in, and felt it would be to her advantage to offer him a good way out.

"If you think I am a whore, fuck me any way you like and don't care if I lose my baby; but if you think the child I'm carrying is yours, let me chose the way I will clear your mind tonight from all the truths and lies that have tortured you needlessly for so many years."

In his mind too many doubts were lingering now about what to do next, while she moved closer to kiss the corner of his caftan. He was still hesitant about an answer, when he felt her left hand unfastening his silken belt. Then he noticed her right hand was equally busy unbuttoning her caftan.

She was as usual nude to save time. She was offering a treat for any man hard to resist; so, he left his self in her hands, as he wasn't ready to murder an innocent unborn child just to feel like a conqueror.

****

When the last trace of desire had been extinguished, in his eyes a new doubt appeared. He knew that any postponement of making a decision was a weakness, but tonight he had realized that if one day these azure eyes of hers closed, he would be completely alone into the immense world the House of Osman had conquered. She was the only being who made him feel like a man, she and Ibrahim.

****

Ibrahim's trip to Alexandria went smoothly through the Aegean, but bypassing Cyprus, the weather changed for the worse reaching gale force from the north. The crews were experienced and decided that it would be much safer to reach Gaza, and then travel the rest of the way by land rather than attempt to enter the harbor of Alexandria on a lee shore.

Since the Ottomans captured Rhodes, the trip from Constantinople to Alexandria had generally become much safer, but still the weather remained a problem. However, as the Ottoman fleet grew stronger and stronger, fewer Christian ships from the West reached the Holy Land harbors in Eastern Mediterranean and the Aegean, and this meant more riches for the Ottoman pirates that roamed the Aegean.

Selim was the first Sultan who foresaw that a great Empire should also have a powerful fleet to protect its shores from invasion. In this respect Venice was the most dangerous enemy, as it was the nation that few centuries ago ruled the Mediterranean waves, and had managed to conquer Constantinople by sea using effectively ships as siege machines. Suleiman followed his father's wise decision and as the Empire became richer, so did the fleet become stronger.

An able family of Ottoman admirals had already been born in the island of Lesvos, the Barbarossas. They had a proven ability in pirate raids practically in the entire Mediterranean, turning all the Northern Africa harbors into safe shelters and every Berber nation into Suleiman vassals. Having a strong fleet and using it to transfer troops and cut supplies, gradually one by one almost all the Aegean Islands had to capitulate and become allies of the Ottomans instead of the Christians.

If Constantinople was the gate to the Black Sea, Alexandria and Egypt were the gates to the Indian Ocean, because Ottoman ships could be transferred by land into the Red Sea and then travel to the Indian Ocean following with relative safety the shoreline.

****

When Ibrahim reached Cairo, his first duty was to show how pious and faithful he was; thus, he went to all the great Cairo mosques and prayed for the success of his mission. Religion was the key to the heart of all the Egyptians who through the years had changed so many faiths. When Alexander the Great had conquered Egypt, he had respected and worshiped their gods claiming that

Amun and Jupiter was the same god under different name and so did Ibrahim.

When many centuries later the Christians came and made the great mistake to destroy the ancient Egyptian temples and all the pagan symbols. The Egyptians never forgave this great sacrilege, and when the Arabs invaded, they turned Muslims in short order.

Ibrahim was not willing to repeat such a mistake. First he visited the Mosque of Al Azhar, then the Mosque of Sultan Hassan, and finally the Ibn Tulun Mosque with its immense court that could fit all his Ottoman troops for the Friday prayer. He wished to show to all the Muslims he was honoring the first Egyptian Sultans, but not the Mamelukes who dared to stage war against Selim Khan.

Then, he asked the people's representatives to come and express their complaints against the previous Ottoman rulers. They claimed that the governors were interested only in collecting taxes and didn't do public works; so many mosques were damaged from the earthquakes, while few of the water barriers of the Nile remained damaged since the days of the Crusades.

Ibrahim promised that a capable Ottoman engineer in river projects, Sinan, would soon fix all the existing problems. It was a duty Sinan accepted gladly because he was curious to find out how the Egyptians made buildings that could stand up to earthquakes for hundreds of years. There were many new dams and bridges that had to be built on the Nile and its tributaries, and many similar projects had to be carried out through the Empire now that finally peace in the Holy Lands had been established.

Ibrahim then called the representatives of all religions. He explained that now when they were Ottomans there was no reason for envy between then, as everyone had the same rights and obligations to the Sultan. The Sultan would take care of all the citizens and resolve all their fair complains. He was as mighty, just and benevolent as Allah. No peace-loving citizen had anything to be afraid of in the new order. They would all enjoy peace and security, as no one dared to challenge Sultan's power and invade his lands. With peace and the support of all the programmed public works, commerce would flourish now that all the highways and routes on land and sea were secured. The invasions, destructions and pillages that had plagued these lands during the Byzantines, the Christian Crusaders, the Mongols and the Mamelukes belonged to the past, as Egypt was now under the direct supervision of the Sultan who had sent the next most powerful man, his friend and brother-in-law to solve all the existing problems.

Suleiman Khan had greatly appreciated the wise stance of most Egyptians who had not supported the rebel Ahmet Pasha. His prompt capture and execution was a telltale sign of how swift and severe was the punishment of every man who disrespected his authority. Now the road to prosperity was wide open and it was up to each subject to apply his skills to good use and become rich.

"Look at me," he urged them, "ten years ago I was a naked slave freezing in a slave bazaar of Constantinople, and now I'm the Grand Vizier, the brother-in-law of the Sultan and the next most powerful man of the Empire. I have gained all these privileges, because **I am a slave who never thinks just what he can achieve for himself, but only what he can do to serve his master**. Every able and trustworthy citizen sooner or later will be rewarded justly by our wise Sultan for all his services according to their worth. However, if he dares to betray his trust, he will be severely punished and perhaps lose his head, because the Sultan's hand can extend very far, crossing stormy seas and endless deserts."

At last, to underline what would be the sorry end of everyone who had betrayed the Sultan, he hung from every gate of Cairo all the Mameluke rebels who had supported the traitor Ahmet. His words, but mainly his example impressed favorably his Egyptian subjects, Muslims, Jews, Christian Orthodox or Copts alike. All these indigenous sects had been born in this ancient land many centuries ago, but through the years they had fought violently against each other suffering from the greed of crooked state officials. However, now every indication suggested that better days were on the way, as all nations under the rule of the Ottomans were progressing. This was indeed the central point of Ibrahim's talk.

"What good is for a nation to be led by one of its members if he is unworthy and degenerate, incapable of caring for his own people? Everyone who trusts that all men are equal, children of the same god, should not complain if a capable leader belongs to another race. Remember what happened to Constantinople that gradually from being the first city in the world, year after year became a poor and dilapidated village, a village that had to pay foreign warriors to defend it, as its citizens were not willing to fight for leaders that brought nothing but poverty, misery, wars and plagues to the Roman Empire."

He took a deep breath and continued.

"Now, in this same dilapidate city, new houses, hospitals, palaces, public baths, and magnificent Muslim temples have been erected, and the population is constantly on the rise. Now, the Sultan has so much power, that all our old enemies have capitulated and begged for our friendship. Never again in its history Constantinople had so many riches as now, even during the era of Justinian and Heraclius and this is the only truth as I see it, the Grand Vizier of the Ottoman Empire and the right hand of Suleiman Khan. And I hope to die, if I'm lying."

Finally, staring at his audience Ibrahim reached the focus point of his speech.

"I know well that it doesn't matter if your master belongs to another race, if he speaks a different language, or if he worships another god. What really counts is that he is capable of great deeds, if he cares for his slaves as much as they care for him; so, come and joint our family of nations known as the Ottomans. Let us all become brothers and children of the same god few of us call Allah, while others God or Jehovah. Then, the benevolent Shadow of Allah will let all his believers enter Paradise on Earth alive, as Allah does for His believers up in heavens when they die."

The Egyptian representatives had never heard anyone use such conciliatory words since the days the armies of the Prophet Mohamed had reached their land and made them change their faith from Christians to Muslims.

They immediately fell on their knees and paid tribute to the Ottoman Grand Vizier Pargali Ibrahim and when they left his palace on the Mokattam Hills, they transmitted his benevolent message from the richest merchants of Alexandria to the poorest Delta fellahs.

Soon the beneficial results of Ibrahim's leadership and Sinan's building projects became apparent, and the river of rebellion that had overflowed in the Ahmet era returned to its banks without any further bloodshed.

****

When his heavy obligations for a quick recovery were carried out, Ibrahim felt this trip was a unique opportunity for him to visit the great monuments of the ancient Egyptians around Cairo. He had felt great despair when he learned that as the Colossus of Rhodes had disappeared, so had the Pharos of Alexandria collapsed in a great earthquake, so, now nothing could be seen of these magnificent monuments. The remaining monoliths had been used to build the fortress of Mameluke Sultan Qaitbay guarding then the Alexandria harbor.

However, the worst piece of news was that many eons ago the tomb of Alexander the Great had disappeared, a monument that was for him well worth the torturing journey to come to Egypt and organize the Ottoman state. Now the only monuments left to see close to Cairo were the Pyramids of Giza and the Sphinx that had magnetized the imagination of millions of visitors from Herodotus to Caesar and from Octavian to Adrian.

****

Ibrahim and Sinan started one day the journey towards Giza using camels because none of them had the opportunity before to ride on top of this remarkable animal. They were followed by few Spahis of Ibrahim's personal guards of horseback. These troubled years it was dangerous for anyone to wander in the desert unescorted as tribal bandits raided to steal or take hostages. Their guide on foot was an old man, a Copt who knew Greek.

After a long ride among palm trees and clover fields, they finally arrived at the ancient necropolis, and the Copt started his lecture on top of a demolished building full of drifting sand, smashed wooden coffins and bones wrapped in bandages.

"These are the remains of pagan rituals meant to help the ignorant natives to achieve immortality. What an illusion!" he remarked full of scorn for his pagan ancestors.

Ibrahim dismounted his camel, and reached to pick up a scull half covered with dried-up skin.

"He seems very old and sad," he noticed. "I wonder if his hopes for afterlife were frustrated after his death or if his dreams while alive were denied. I really wish to know if a Grand Vizier or a Sultan of the present age will be remembered by a single soul after few thousand years," he wondered, but no one dared to provide an answer for such distinguished rulers. Perhaps the fact the Sphinx loomed so close in the background affected the prevailing mood.

Ibrahim remembered Oedipus myth and asked loudly the statue for an oracle, but the guide expressed his contempt for his ancestors' pagan beliefs.

"The Ancient statues and the dead cannot provide us with answers. We have to have faith to the words of the prophets!" he asserted, but Ibrahim had always reservations about any kind of blind unsubstantiated belief.

"Indeed they can't, but sometimes they can secretly entice the living to provide reasonable answers. I'm sure by sunset I will have my answer."

Perhaps the Copt would like to make a critical comment, as Ibrahim's words sounded too pagan for his comfort; but he wisely decided that challenging further a Grand Vizier may be proven unwise.

Next they arrived under the Great Pyramid of Cheops. According to the Herodotus' testimony this project had lasted for twenty years and thousands lives of workers were wasted for this mountain of stones to be completed.

Supposedly it was a huge tomb with many secrets; but it was now wide open, as many of its monoliths had been removed and used by the Mamelukes to build mosques and palaces in Cairo. As the old man informed them, first an Arab Caliph had entered hoping to find a treasure; but he had found nothing worth his effort and expense.

"Let's go in," Ibrahim suggested full of hope. "We might be luckier than a Caliph."

Nevertheless, their visit didn't last long. The ascent proved to be very tiresome, and when they finally arrived at the Cheops' tomb, they found only an empty broken sarcophagus as time had erased every trace of the mighty Pharaoh. Soon the atmosphere inside the tomb became stuffy and presented no interest to anyone but Sinan, as all walls were bare of any hieroglyphs or other inscriptions. He could only examine the way the tomb was built and check the spaces between the monoliths with his knife.

The Copt was last to arrive and the first to leave the tomb and took the only torch with him, leaving the tomb in total darkness. As complete darkness suddenly fell, Ibrahim felt the panic growing and tried to seek the exit in all fours; however, wherever his hands reached they touched only smooth, immovable granite. He screamed in terror and deep inside the pyramid Copt's reply sounded as if it was coming from a distant universe far beyond; but soon a ray of light illuminated the threshold, showing the proper way out as the Copt realizing his mistake, had returned.

Like thieves, they quickly descended the downward slippery passage, and when they were again under the sunlight, Ibrahim let a sigh of relief. It was the first time he had been inside a grave lost in darkness and separated from the world he knew by an immovable mountain of stones. Perhaps the tomb was the solemn answer of the Sphinx to his question.

Sinan read his thoughts and remarked:

"This is how death must feel, an impenetrable eternal darkness hiding every exit," he asserted.

"No, of course not, if you believe in God, Paradise awaits you," the old man asserted with conviction; but Ibrahim had not become Grand Vizier by believing illogical religious teachings.

"Blind faith is the most popular refuge of people with limited intelligence, incapable of searching for the truth," he replied and his answer expressed the frustration he felt for this meaningless conversation.

"In which god the ancient Egyptians believed?" Sinan intervened.

He was well aware of the old men's habit to talk forever, displaying their importance and wisdom.

"Many centuries before Christ or Mohamed, my ancestors believed in two great gods, Osiris who was the god of pleasure, good living and resurrection, like the Dionysus of the Greeks, and Seth who was the god of hate, chaos and destruction like Mars. Seth trapped Osiris and killed him. He then cut him into little pieces and threw them all over Egypt; however, Osiris' faithful wife Isis found Osiris' penis and used it to get pregnant. Thus, Horus the falcon was born. The evil Seth seduced the young Horus, but the wise youngster didn't allow Seth's sperm inside him to poison his mind. Thus, in the end Horus fought against Seth, beat and pursued him in the desert, away from the river Nile," the Copt claimed.

It was now plain enough the old man had an insatiable urge to talk, but Ibrahim who was bored with Islam and Christianity before, suddenly got very interested to participate in the discussion now developing about the ancient Egyptian gods.

"This myth sounds like a much more imaginative variation of the Jewish myth about god and devil. Myths like this are useful tests greedy priests use to distinguish among their listeners the people of low intelligence that they can scam and earn plenty of cash," Ibrahim claimed derogatorily, but Sinan who knew him better realized the myth had seduced his imagination.

The old man looked at him with anger for his remark, but continued his narration undeterred.

"Gradually the ancient Egyptians added more gods with animal heads in their pantheon; but all this nonsense was nothing more than tricks of the priests who wished to multiply their profits, suggesting that ordinary animals had common character trends with humans. For instance, we still say proud as a horse, tricky as a fox, faithful as a dog, headstrong as a mule, valiant as a lion, etc. Thus, a man by worshiping such a god can benefit, improving his virtues."

"When gods multiply it's a sign they are inadequate to satisfy the needs of the developing human intelligence. Please tell me what kind of animal was the god of love?" Ibrahim inquired now eager to learn.

"They say that the goddess of love and motherhood was Hathor the sacred cow," the Copt informed him.

"Hathor sounds a lot like Hurrem. Any difference is negligible after all the years that had passed since then," Ibrahim remarked winking at Sinan. "Only recently Mother Earth became round rather than flat, but humans have not created an original feeling other animals do not share. What a waste of time and effort for humanity worshiping animals!"

"Yes indeed! Now all these phony gods are dead and their temples have turned into piles of stones," the aged Copt concurred. "Now, only one god exists, the god of the Christians, the Muslims and the Jews which is one and the same."

"Do you wise Copts believe there is life after death too?" Ibrahim asked.

The old man bent and grasped a handful of sand.

"Our belief in life after death has been instilled in this very sand, many thousands of years before Moses, Christ or Mohamed were born," he announced with pride. "This has been the very essence of our firm belief, and for this reason it has been very easy for us Egyptians to change our religions twice within the last five centuries!"

Ibrahim could not resist now the temptation of irony.

"Then, I have outsmarted you! I have changed twice my religion within ten years!" Ibrahim snapped back.

The old man now seemed a bit annoyed. He considered Ibrahim's claim as a mockery of his beliefs; so, hesitantly and with the courtesy an ordinary man pays to a powerful official he asked the Grand Vizier of the Ottoman Empire:

"If I may ask, in which god now Your Magnificence believes in?"

"As a wise friend of mine once said, I should trust that in this universe everything is in a state of constant evolution that oscillates between creation and destruction, and I believe his words. This is why I also firmly believe that this evolution does not start and stop with humans but extends also to the gods human beings invent with their fertile imagination. No god is eternal. He only lives as long naïve men honor him by building mosques and temples in his name. Who remembers now Osiris, Seth and Isis the Pharaohs trusted, or Zeus and Hera, Alexander the Great or Caesar worshiped piously on this same sands we are now walking? For me Christ died and Allah was born in a single night when my father told me the myth how Constantinople was conquered. If this event had not happened, perhaps Osman and his breed, even Allah might be one more myth lost in the desert sands. However, when this critical moment came about, the god of the Christians and all his saints didn't move a finger to save his holiest of all cities. Only a dying god would let the infidels enter the sanctuary of his most magnificent temple, Agia Sophia, and loot it bare like a raped woman."

Now the old man felt the need to defend his god.

"God is all-wise, all-powerful and perfectly fair; but no one knows what He is thinking when He lets the sacrileges of his temples to happen."

The words of the Copt had now acquired the persistence of a fanatic; however, Ibrahim had a much clearer view of his reasoning and had no difficulty in versing a devastating answer.

"Your god is so wise, benevolent and fair that he doesn't lift a finger to save the life of a newborn child. By avoiding action he is favoring the maggots rather than his believers, spoiling universal order. Allah now reigns supreme in the Holy Virgin city; but, no one knows who is going to be the god of my grandchildren, not even I know, the Grand Vizier of the Shadow of Allah the All-Wise. The only fact I know is that as the generations pass, people multiply while the trust in gods decline, as human knowledge increase teaching people how to solve their problems without divine help. Thus, if we must worry that someone might become useless in the future; these must be the eternal gods, not the mortal humans. Humans have found the path to immortality through their children, which is the only way to preserve a trace of our souls that comes closer to death and extinction with every passing day."

"And which is your second change of faith?" Sinan inquired intervening to change the subject that was gradually leading to a religious confrontation.

"My dear friend, this happened in a Galata tekke the day I dreamed of my death. Right then all gods died inside me and their entire universe with them."

"That's true!" Sinan exclaimed. "Death is the moment when man is united again with god and the universe and returns to the state he was before birth. It is the moment when our being explodes in tiny pieces that travel into the infinity of space and time never to be reunited until the end of time."

"My world was born with me and it will die the moment of my death. This is my truth," Ibrahim proclaimed decisively. "However, after my death my children will try to put some order in the chaos your gods have created in six days and left behind unfinished."

The Copt crossed himself scared of the consequences of all these sacrilegious words, but didn't dare to protest. He thought this distinguished Ottoman official was a great sinner who sooner or later he would be punished by God as severely as the Lord saw fit. However, Sinan the Janissary was not scared to express his opinion openly.

"The world we all live in is just a stage setting of a theatrical performance with us as actors. This setting is just one in an infinite series of settings extending towards the eternity and Allah. Wise is the man whose thoughts can penetrate their opacity that makes God invisible to the eyes of the common people. This is the only way a man can reach his final goal, the union with Allah the Great."

Ibrahim remained thoughtful for a while, and then asked Sinan in what kind of God he believed. Sinan replied without delay as if he was a child reciting a poem he knew by heart.

"I believe in a single God, and in his angels, and in the Holy Books, and in the prophets the heralds of Allah, and in the Day of Resurrection, and in the force of destiny, and that everything good or evil comes from Allah, and that there is another life after the one we live now."

The Copt nodded affirmatively. The difference between his beliefs and Sinan's were too insignificant to mention them and lose an ally in such a crucial argument.

"What are your objections?" Sinan inquired, and Ibrahim replied without animosity.

"I wouldn't like to spoil any further our day with meaningless quarrels between three faithful who even though they agree in the essence they slaughter each other sharing the world. To me God and Devil are nothing but two imaginary boundaries man has built with this simpleminded mind to limit the excesses of his unstable behavior; but as the years pass these two limits get further and further away. Soon they will be so far away, no one would know if they really exist or if they are creatures of his imagination. However, my god raises no barriers and he does not offend my human intelligence claiming that a single book may contain all the truths. My Allah has shown me Mother Earth and Father Sky and ordered me: This is the universe I made just for you! Try to find me wherever you can; but if the god you trust can seed life with one hand and mow it with the other, then I, Grand Vizier Ibrahim who represents His authority because I am the Shadow of the Shadow of Allah, have also the right to do the same."

These grave words were heard more threatening that he wished to and put a sudden end to the discussion. Before anything else he was indeed the Grand Vizier and no one dared to doubt his words without punishment.

Ibrahim mounted his camel and hit it on the neck with the whip. The wise animal realized which were his wishes and raised his back legs first, pushing him forward like a horse that had stumbled on an obstacle.

Ibrahim leaned backwards and soon enough the camel stepped next on its front legs recovering its balance. It also left a strange cry that sounded like a complaint to Allah of a lazy creature forced to carry more load, and slowly moved forward, making Ibrahim very proud of his accomplishment.

He glanced backward to see if Sinan was equally successful, and saw the Copt by Sinan's side supporting him to regain his balance.

Arabs and Copts were very similar creatures, he thought, but he didn't mind cooperating with anyone too to achieve his goal. He was alone in Egypt away from Suleiman and Hatidge, but Sinan was a good substitute of both. He was bright and persistent in his beliefs. He was also a handsome man and the way he looked at him had always been honorable. It had the lucidness of glass and the hardness of rock. Sinan was a rare jewel he didn't wish to lose. Anytime he looked at his eyes trying to search his mind, he never saw the glitter he found in the eyes of the greedy Osman breed.

Sinan was under his command, but he would never order him to do something that might offend his manliness to prove his loyalty. He was not plagued by the Sultan's insecurity to impose his authority on all his subjects. Sinan would always be his loyal, fearless friend he could trust with his life.

Back in the Giza just before they said goodbye to the aged Copt, the old man approached with respect and asked Ibrahim with a voice full of agony:

"You, who everyone says are so wise and knowledgeable, please tell me.

335

Do you really believe there is a God?"

Ibrahim looked at him from the height of his camel and instead of answering, he replied with a question.

"My wise aged Copt, please tell me: Do you believe Alexander the Great is still alive?"

In the eyes of the old man Ibrahim saw the reflection of the terror of death, as his fears had been confirmed. Then, the old man turned away speechless and without looking back even for a moment he disappeared into the night. The Sphinx had spoken to him too that night.

****

Returning to the palace Ibrahim found a letter from Hatidge with all the latest news. Hurrem had reconciled completely with Suleiman the moment a new son was born. His name was Selim. Mahidevran had also born a child almost simultaneously, but it was a girl and her name was Raziye. Hatidge's pregnancy was also approaching smoothly its conclusion. The midwives that looked after her everyday were claiming she was getting more beautiful. It was a sign she was going to bear a daughter. Basmi was always by her side, but she was not pregnant, and neither was Gülfem. They were both unhappy.

Were all these references a coincidence, or did they contained a subtle hint?

The plain truth was that too many women had taken control of his life, so he didn't have much free time for him to enjoy their favors. He felt like a slave taking orders, and this letter was a subtle command that he had to reply. He asked his page to call the scriber.

The scriber was a slim young man dressed in a white gallabiyah with intricate golden thread embroidery around the collar. His clothes were simple but elegant, and his entrance filled the room with the scent of lavender. His skin was darker than his, revealing his native roots; however, his hair was chestnut brown with blond highlights and his eyes dark green as if they were drenched in Nile water. He was definitely not an Arab or a Berber.

He seemed a bit scared of his mission at first and Ibrahim tried to win his trust by trying to make him feel relaxed. He asked him about his lineage. He was the son of a Greek merchant, while his mother was from Lebanon. His name was Antonio, and he knew how to write in practical every language spoken in the Near East, Arabic, Ottoman, Persian, Jewish, Greek and Venetian.

Ibrahim had to test next his skills by dictating few letters. Hatidge was his first obligation. He asked her about Hurrem's novel behavior. Finally, at the very end he reassured her that he had missed her and couldn't wait to come back as soon as possible and spend all his nights into her embrace.

The scriber's writing was clear and formed an orderly line of calligraphic letters as if they were verses of the Quran; so he asked him if he was really a Christian and the young man replied he was still too young to decide which god he should trust. It was an unexpected surprise; but they still had some more work to do.

He next started dictating the letter to Sultan Suleiman. It started with good wishes for the newborn son by Hurrem, and then asked about the health of his other children, Mahidevran Sultan, his new daughter and his mother. Then he started explaining what he was doing in Egypt and the prospects this country had in the Ottoman Empire. The letter ended with wishes of health and a personal touch that he was missing his company especially during the night.

The youngster smiled listening to the content of the last line. Ibrahim noticed it, and asked for an explanation, but the scriber became upset and with red chicks he failed to utter anything.

Ibrahim reassured him that the he was very pleased with his performance and he was going to keep him in this position provided he was sincere and gave straight answers, so he could trust him completely with the state secrets.

The young man still scared replied that he found this familiarity with the Sultan a bit unusual and too similar with the last line of his wife's letter.

"Your inquiry is correct, but this is exactly how I feel about it. Marriage and slavery raise few common demands on familiarity," Ibrahim replied but the young man's replied was reassuring.

"There is no conflict between a master and a slave's wishes, if the desire is mutual," the young man replied with a friendly smile; nevertheless, Hatidge's image was too strong and dissolved any other sinful aspiration.

******

Few months passed of fervent activity and frequent trips to Alexandria.

This particular day, after the daily round of inspections of the various projects around Cairo, Ibrahim invited Sinan to his palace. Sinan was a most valuable assistant during the day and a safe shelter after sunset among many native flatterers doing their best to promote their personal interests.

He enjoyed talking to this man Allah had sent to serve and protect him from harm, as with time their friendship flourished. Sinan many years ago had been admitted to the Janissary Corps and became separated from his family in Cappadocia as he was forced to move to Constantinople.

The Janissary Corps was always a center of constant agitation with religious overtones. Most of its members belonged to the Ali Bektash Order. According to the principles of this sect, all the gods were just one, and all the world's prophets from Moses and Abraham to Plato and from Buda and Christ to Mohamed were equally valid. This freedom of thought was a virtue Ibrahim appreciated, because it went much further than the usual religious restrictions. It was a belief that united and fortified the faithful to face the common destiny of all humans, death.

For Ibrahim all religions had failed to achieve their common target. Instead of uniting the people into loving and caring for each other, they had become the cause of countless wars and senseless slaughters, adding one more serious obstacle for peace among humans besides race, language, custom and gender, namely shedding each other's blood for obscure imaginary concepts.

From the first words he heard coming out of Sinan's mouth, he had realized he was a human being worthy of much better position than just becoming an officer of the Janissary Corps in charge of building bridges and mining under enemy fortifications.

His first civilian commission he had offered to him was his palace, and soon many others would follow as newly enriched people didn't have deep cultural roots and needed a Grand Vizier to show them the proper way to obtain nobility via knowledge rather than riches.

For a while many noblemen were jealous of his success and tried to excite the envy of the Sultan for his palace; but to no avail. If the Sultan was envious of his palace, he should build an even better one for himself using Sinan's talents for innovations. One should try to follow progressive trends rather than envy them, was his suggestion, and Suleiman soon commissioned a new Has Oda to Sinan's hands to impress the foreign ambassadors with its majesty.

With the frequent earthquakes in the Eternal City, even Agia Sophia the Great Mosque was in great need of extensive repairs. Since it was an imperial mosque, it also needed as addition of three more minarets besides the one built by Fatih to reach true imperial status.

Sinan was a very observant engineer and had noticed the way the buildings that withstood earthquakes were built, analyzed the methods and copied the procedures, adding time-tested building improvements based on his knowledge from ancient structures.

"I want you to become the Empire's architect, and I will do whatever it's in my power for you to take this novel position. I want the Eternal City to become as majestic as it was long time ago. It must rival Venice. If they are content living in swamps and lagoons, we have the Seven Hills, the magnificent Golden Horn and the intricate Bosporus Straights that outshine Venice assets. However, we are still in Cairo and we have plenty more to see and there is plenty of sunlight still left in the day. Let's use the sun's light to become a little wiser for the sake of the Ottomans."

****

Since the distance was greater this time they rode Arabic horses and took the road to the south towards Memphis the ancient metropolis of Egypt. Galloping they passed swiftly the Giza plateau, and as all the pyramids they encountered looked ruined and dilapidated, they didn't stopped until they reached the village of Dahshur.

Egypt had enchanted them both. It was a giant stage where History had remained active for thousands of years and one could find traces from practically every great man from Moses, to Darius, from Alexander to Caesar, and from

338

Jesus to Mohamed. Now the Grand Vizier of the Ottoman Empire was retracing the steps of mighty pharaohs, great kings and world conquerors. There had to be a mysterious force that attracted great men to the Nile River, and whoever was not able to feel it should not bother come and step on its sands.

****

To rest their almost exhausted horses they sat at a small inn by the village's square. Close to this village there was another great Pyramid built of red rock and next to it a smaller one with an unusual shape, built as if the architect had changed his mind in the middle of the project and made its peak less acute.

Ibrahim was very puzzled noticing this drastic change.

"I wonder who built such a singular pyramid so different than any other. It looks as if the builders suddenly changed their minds and decided they couldn't wait any longer for the Pharaoh's tomb to be completed, or if their lord died halfway through and his widows decided they shouldn't waste so much effort and expenses."

Sinan had an even sharper explanation.

"And I suspect this Pharaoh was a wild man like you in love with innovations and wild ideas entering his mind from nowhere, frustrating the architect and the builders with his suggestions."

Ibrahim applauded hearing this sharp remark. It was a welcomed change of climate under the hot afternoon sun.

"You are right! My life would become unbearable, if I was ever refused the right on variety and the freedom of choice," he noted. "My wish to try before I choose is practical an instinctive need instilled in me by Mother Earth. What many other people praise as virtues, loyalty, consistency, or stability are for me signs of stagnation, decay, or even boredom. Perhaps this is why I became an Ottoman, and changed my life half a way through like this strange pyramid."

Behind him in the distance a giant red pyramid looked in the afternoon sunlight like raging volcano spitting lava, while far to the left in the direction of the sun a shapeless mass of black bricks seemed completely out of place among the strict geometrical constructions of more able builders. It was another pyramid that had collapsed under the weight and wear of the centuries.

"It is strange how in life what few people build stay erect for many centuries, while others cannot stand the tests of time," Ibrahim asserted.

"Only what follows the words of Allah may hope to last for an eternity," Sinan asserted.

"If Allah had revealed the proof of the Pythagoras' theorem to Moses or Mohamed, perhaps I would become the most loyal follower of the Quran," Ibrahim replied in good spirits.

"My master, the prophets wrote down only the more intricate laws that must govern live men, not the laws for the inanimate rocks. This is the trivial duty of a humble architect like me."

"Do not underestimate the wisdom of your buildings. As long as they remain erect, they fill the heart of every human who admires them that man can also build something as eternal as a mountain. However, everything around us that looks strong, firm and eternal right now is just an illusion. It might collapse the next moment simply because of a gentle breath of wind or a monstrous earthquake. Everything around us is temporary and fluid, free of the bonds of human laws that try to prove we are the sons of God and we will inherit forever whatever He has built to use as it pleases us. If you as an architect admire the pyramids that still stand, my thought belongs to the one that has collapsed unable to resist the toils of Time. Time is for me the most powerful god, because with every day that passes he becomes bigger and stronger. Men can waste their lives building pyramids and gods or dream of stars and galaxies, but Time simply waits patiently for its turn. In the end Time will make you and me and our gods dust. Then you and your Allah will be united and turned into dust too."

****

This trip to Dahshur was the longest they had ever attempted. If they had more time, Ibrahim would rather stay much longer in Egypt. He yearned to travel all the way to Thebes, to the end of the Roman world, to see the giant temples of Luxor and the Colossae of Memnon Herodotus had described.

He even wished to go even further than Alexander or Caesar, to the source of the Nile that no one had ever seen; however, he was not a free man to do as he pleased. He had obligations to the Osman family that pressured him.

One month after the first later another one arrived from Suleiman. He ordered him to come back by land as soon as possible and organize all the providences he found on his way in the Middle East, because there were many grievances against the ruling Ottoman officials. The entire East had to remain peaceful for the next few years. It meant Suleiman was about to embark to an expedition in the west, against the Hungarians that ruled the heart of Europe.

Nevertheless, that evening in Dahshur the European war was still away and he could watch the sun go down deep in the Western Desert, the domain of the dead with his mind full of thoughts and desires, waiting eagerly for the next morning when the sun would rise again brand new from the Arabian Desert, the domain of the living. Perhaps in Egypt his life could one day find its lost balance.

The sunset was a magical moment for all men. It was the moment when darkness swiftly came along with all the dangers lurking at night, when man had to remain as inconspicuous as possible, waiting for the hours of darkness to pass until he could see again the path he should follow.

In Africa where all these carnivorous beasts roamed at night these worries grew stronger as well as the relief at daybreak.

With the sunrise, man could bake bricks from the Nile mud and built his house and his future, putting order to the chaos of the creeping desert and the overflowing river. There was not much for the Ancient Egyptians to live for in this world, and that was why they had built in their minds the illusive prospect of a second life, when everything would be just perfect and complete.

However, all their magnificent tombs were now open and empty from all the treasures and offerings, as if the occupants had risen from the grave and moved somewhere else to live their second life. Here in the fringe of the desert all the essential elements of human life were present for any man to judge their worth, the sun, the sand, the water, the mud, the birth, the death, the sunrise and the sunset. This was the reason why their gods were so many and so simple.

For Ibrahim Egypt had been a very educational lesson in simplicity after the complexity of living in Constantinople. He was born in the Balkans between East and West, where men had to steal the women of their neighbors, if they wished to build an empire like the Romans. In the Eternal City life was not simple, sun or darkness. It had many shades, so gods became complicated too.

Ibrahim suddenly felt terribly alone. He drank one more sip of a bitter sweet juice the locals called coffee, and felt his mind rising from the swamp of continuous repetitions of the same worries on how to hide his inner thoughts from everyone else. After all he was still alive, wandering on the sand dunes on his horse, while Alexander's tomb was lost.

He sipped a large draught of smoke of hashish and his mind transcended once more. His death was once more lurking behind his back counting his days and hours.

"Sinan, please tell me my wise friend! Should I also pay you a huge commission to build me a pyramid, when I feel that I'm about to die?"

"You most certainly could, but it will cost you much more than you can save in your entire life. I believe there are better ways for a man to waste his money these days, so people remember him. As we both saw, after a while all tombs are demolished for the people to build more useful buildings with their stones. Building a palace your offspring will use to live in, seems to me like a better idea, if you wish your children and grandchildren to remember you. If you wish common people to remember you for all times, then build a temple."

"No! If my children feel the need to remember me, they simply have to look at the mirror. There they will discover how I looked; if they wish to look deeper into their souls, they might also find my strengths and my weaknesses. Building magnificent tombs is a waste of time, since Alexander's grave is lost. The only hope for a man to be remembered is to bear many children. Even writing a book with my thoughts is dangerous, because it may turn like the Bible or the Quran, a lurking trap for my children's minds leading to stagnation. So let's go! The sun is setting, but we must go back to Cairo, because another sunrise is bound to come, and we have only a night to find a safe path from our past to our future."

Indeed the sun quickly disappeared and with it the pyramids that stood there since the beginning of time vanished into the darkness that swallowed everything in its path.

And then Ibrahim understood who the true god in the minds of men was.

It was the unknown lurking in the darkness. It was ignorance that threatened their lives. This was the reason why all temples were dark and mysterious.

The monument the Athenians had built to the "unknown god" was in fact a subtle ancient identity. The unknown was the god of all the wise men, and each time men learned something new, this god became just a bit weaker like the eternal struggle between Zeus and Prometheus.

This was also the reason the Christian priests preached "Believe and do not doubt." They sought to keep their financial benefactor intact; but their fears were unwarranted, because all men had limitations and no matter what they accomplished during each day there would be still unsolved mysteries the next morning.

God had never been the light of the world, but always the darkness. Man's mind was from the very beginning the light that fought to diminish the darkness of ignorance as man was the only being that tried to put the chaos God had left behind into his divine order. Jesus when he claimed he was the light, he didn't mean he was God. He was simply a man who sought for the truth inside his soul. However the ignorant people of his era didn't wish to risk their present for an unsafe future, and this was why they crucified him.

Was he following the steps of every prophet? Even Mohamed had been chased out of Mecca in the very beginning of his career.

He turned to Sinan and noted:

"The darkness always scared me since I was a boy. It's the beginning and the end of every man's life. Birth and resurrection happens in the same moment. A woman's scent will never be free to linger inside a religious temple; so don't expect me to pay you to build any temples. In a temple only the sweet smell of frankincense exists to cover the horrible scent of death."

On his way back, he felt freer. Getting in touch with death in Dahshur, he had been freed from all his past restrains. He had one life to live and he should live it the way he felt proper without the obligation to follow the commands of an invisible master. He was not the slave of Allah, but only of his Shadow, who was also a man and had similar weaknesses like him.

After his marriage, he had also Hafsa and Hatidge Sultan by his side; but tonight his master was far away unable to utter a single command. After all these years of being a slave tonight he was free at last of all the nightmares of the past and he had every right to celebrate his elusive, temporary freedom.

****

Early this morning in the Eternal City nothing revealed what was about to happen. It was one day like any other, with working people waking up early up to go to work on time and be spared of their bosses' reproaches.

The builders were already mixing the mud, while the masons had started cutting the stones to the right shape and size. The bakers had already started pulling out of the ovens the first loaves of bread for the people's breakfast. It was part of their daily routine to leave empty space in the stoves for the roasts that soon would arrive prepared by the most industrious housekeepers.

The many gardeners were already crying loud for the housewives to hear that they had plenty fresh vegetables and fruits for them to choose, if they hurried. There were many empty fields still available among the Roman ruins for anyone to grow food within the Great Walls and save some food money. Only the laziest people were still in bed, but the city criers would soon make sure that everyone would become useful.

The revolt started as a soft murmur at the At Meidan, and no one paid any attention the same way every summer tempests start with a soft breeze that hardly has the strength to shiver the leaves of a poplar tree. This immense square on the First Hill was bounded in the direction of the Sea Walls by the ruins of the Roman Hippodrome now used as a quarry. It stood there since the days of the harsh Roman Emperor from Africa, Septimius Severus and it was later enlarged by Constantine the Great. Traditionally it was the point of focus of every rebellion, as if the ground was still cursed.

In the old days, responsible for the riots were the Greens and the Blues fractions, and later the icon lovers and the icon haters; but on this particular day, responsible for the rebellion were the Janissaries, and their thunderbolt exploded unexpectedly, even though it was brewing for many years, since the day Suleiman had become Sultan and failed to start the war against the infidels the very next day. After the fall of Belgrade, this anger had receded; but when they came back from Rhodes empty-handed it became a volcano waiting for the right moment to blow its top. And the right moment arrived when the Sultan instead of marching against the Hungarians as he promised, he had gone hunting in the Belgrade Forest, while his Grand Vizier was even more isolated in Egypt and the mighty Ottoman Empire was headless for a few critical hours.

Since Ibrahim's marriage the complaints had recently reached new peaks. The expenses for such an elaborate celebration had been immense, and Ibrahim's palace was constantly there at the At Meidan to remind the Janissaries how well provided were few Janissaries. The Sultan should have saved all this money and make more guns, or spend them to reward all these brave men who put their lives at risk for his sake instead of a lover of dubious morality.

As usual the original flame was ignited inside the taverns around the Bayezid square close to the barracks at mid-day. Later the riots extended into the barracks, and as more and more Janissaries participated in the rebellion, they overturned the cauldrons and started hitting them with their ladles creating hellish noise. Soon after they marched from the barracks and the Et Meidan to the At Meidan like raindrops that first formed brooks and then torrents and rivers until they reached the sea.

When they reached their goal, they split and many of them went up hill towards the Topkapi Saray, while others concentrated in front of Ibrahim's Palace trying to break the gate.

On the way along the Divan Avenue, every store or house they found open they plundered it and then set it on fire, as if it belonged to an enemy; but, they didn't stop there. Every woman, maiden or boy the meanest Janissaries found that resembled an infidel they raped inside the deserted houses, while others less excited showed their preference to goods and merchandise they could resell. Even men were not left unharmed. Everyone that didn't look pious enough they beat him up, tortured or circumcised him in public to prove he had changed his faith.

Janissaries were not the only ones who took advantage of the revolt but the anonymous mob too, and soon in all the streets around the Bayezid mosque one could see people carrying rugs, furniture, fabrics, clothes, even golden household items and utensils, while others set the looted houses in flames as if the Eternal City had fallen once more.

The smoke was the first sign that something was wrong and immediately a detail of Spahis left to warn the Sultan; but it took them several hours to reach him in the hunting grounds. When Suleiman heard the news he rushed back to the Seraglio, and sent a message to his trusted Vizier Mustafa Çoban to concentrate every available trooper and come to meet him at the Imperial Gate.

Ibrahim's absence was evident, as many of the officials were still sour at the Sultan's choice of Grand Vizier and looked for excuses for their negligence or hesitation to support the Sultan or for taking the side of the rebels.

In the meantime the most violent of all the rebels had concentrated in front of Ibrahim's Palace trying hard to break in and loot its treasures. However, the palace was built like a fortress and had a main ironclad gate made of oak, armed with steel nails. Inside the palace there were also the personal guards, the servants and the black eunuchs defending the Sultan's sister with their lives.

Arriving at Seraglio after a rampageous gallop through the Eternal City, Suleiman was aware of the extent of the riot. The rebels had pierced the second gate, the Orta Kapi, and reached the Gate of Salutations; but there they stopped as no one dared to break inside the Sultan's residence.

The moment the rebels noticed his arrival, they surrounded him and with a cataract of curses and abuses they asked him to start immediately the war against the Christian Emperor in Rome.

Suleiman recognized most of them. They were brave officers that still fought in the name of Osman since the Chaldiran saga. However, among them were also several shabby characters from the City's underworld he knew nothing about. One of these scoundrels was so audacious that he dared to take hold of his horse's reins, trying to throw him off the saddle. Suleiman realized that if he didn't react as violently, he, his children and the Empire could be lost.

He pulled his damascene sword off its sheath and struck hard at this rebel holding the reins, severing the head from the torso with one stroke. Then, as two more audacious rebels pushed his horse from behind to throw him down on the grass, he stroke again and again with as devastating effect. The blood from the open wounds splashed on his clothes and face, as their headless bodies still writhed, painting the grass red.

This courage saved the Osman dynasty right then and there, because even though the other Janissary could easily pull him down and cut his head off too in revenge, they were convinced by his warlike appearance much better than any other argument that this man could lead them into victory. The presence of death so close diminished the effects of every other raging feeling.

The Sultan realized that for the time being prudence had extinguished religious frenzy, and from then on diplomacy would yield the best crops.

"What just favors do you wish from me and you have plundered the entire city in my absence?" he asked them with the stern look of a father who chastised his naughty children.

One of the rebels moved forward and replied courageously:

"We just want to fight the infidels. Too many months had passed since we captured Rhodes, and we are getting rusty in our barracks."

"Well said! I have also grown rusty inside the Seraglio, keeping company to eunuchs and women, not true men."

His tone was now mellow and listening to his words everyone released his tension too with hearty laughter.

"Tonight I invite every "jorbadgi" (officer) to come and meet me here in a banquet, so we can all decide when it will be most advantageous for us to start our march towards the Red Apple."

These were the words every Janissary wished to hear to go back to his barrack in peace.

The Sultan was not a slave of the Gate as they were. He was born free, but his name was written too in the official lists of the Janissary corps. The Sultan was certainly not the son of a slave woman like them. He was born free and the son of a Princess; however, his name was recorded as Suleiman the son of a slave, and he was paid the same salary of the common soldier like everyone else.

Naturally, this feeble amount was a trifle compared to the one fifth of the entire loot the Sultan kept after each battle as their leader. However, this small amount had a psychological significance, because it made them feel he was one of them. Preserving discipline before the war against Hungary finally cost him 200000 golden ducats, an amount the Sultan most gladly paid to save the Empire. This amount was negligible compared to the expenses of Ibrahim's wedding. Only the golden saddle made in Venice he offered to the groom as a present had cost a similar amount.

Nevertheless, his brother-in-law was certainly worth every present, as the Egyptian taxes his Grand Vizier had secured with his trip were more than 1200000 ducats. Perhaps the only issue the Janissaries justly complained was the way the riches of the empire were distributed.

****

Coming back from Dahshur the trail led them through the town of Imbaba. This wretched settlement at the outskirts of Cairo had been for centuries the end and the beginning of the caravan trail to the Sahara and the quickest way to Sudan and the Africa Continent by land. It was the road the slave traders took carrying camels, animal hides, ebony and ivory.

During the day Imbaba was a giant stinking bazaar where men, women, animal dung and oriental perfumes were mixed exquisitely; however, after sunset, when the sun went to sleep, the northern wind tried to do its best to remove the awful stench and if possible the human greed.

It was also the time when men tried to spend any extra coins they had secured through the day by advertising their merchandise and haggling prices to make their lives worth living.

Going through the narrow streets of Imbaba, the shrilling notes of Egyptian tunes reached their ears. Full of curiosity soon they found themselves in front of a rather miserably looking "locanda", the Egyptian made combination of an inn and a tavern.

Ibrahim insisted they should take a peek no matter what. The place looked rather shabby and perilous, but Sinan presence by his side was enough of insurance. Ibrahim still had in front of his eyes the dramatic events of the Avret Bazaar, and he was certain that after all these years the terrifying Janissary could still reappear like magic and replace the sensitive architect, if he ever needed protection.

His curiosity was well founded. Logic said that it was not easy for a nation to live by the desert where the sun and the heat could dry it out in few hours, if there was no other spring of energy besides the River Nile. Through the years of his studies in the Seraglio School, he had realized that Eros was the source from where a man's mind could derive the energy to build and create something original like a unique civilization. When this spring was exhausted then man was ready to die.

Nevertheless, that very moment death seemed far away, left behind in Dahshur. The enticing music that reached their ears could not have any other purpose but waking up their tired bodies.

Entering the humble hall, the heavy scent of hashish mixed with frankincense to keep away the mosquitoes invaded their noses, displacing any other perfume they had used to cover the scent of the sweat.

The walls of the brick-made locanda were covered with plaster painted with ochre. They were illustrated with fictitious scenes from imaginary trips in magical places around the world, where various predatory animals were hunting their prey inside forest of palm trees, and sailing boats were traveling in uncharted oceans full of strange monsters.

The floor was covered with colorful kilims made of camel wool where many groups of dark skinned men dressed in dark colored gallabiyah and colorful turbans were sited around round low tables. In front of them large trays were placed full of tea pots, sweets and smoking water pipes expelling thick clouds of smoke.

Nobody had noticed their entrance as every customer was focused his attention towards the center of the hall, where under a bronze lamp with seven candles in the midst of numerous azure glass pieces, two young men were dancing dressed in almost transparent clothes covering the essentials as if they were female belly dancers.

This spectacle was not what they had hoped for, but now it looked rather logical, as caravan crews were always comprised by men who had to travel for months back and forth from Cairo to Timbuktu, Ethiopia or Sudan. One dancer was a mixed breed Arab with skin in the color of light tea, while the other was an ebony-colored Nubian. Their gestures were audaciously explicit and their disposition highly erotic, as they danced touching each other's body in a most promiscuous way that would put even seasoned prostitutes to shame.

The locanda clients were staring tensely at the spectacle, and constantly threw silver coins at the dancers' feet asking the youngsters to remove few more clothes. The youngsters followed reluctantly these request continuing this Salome dance parody, but only when they considered the collected coins sufficient. This lucrative tease didn't stop when they were bare naked, as they still kept on dancing and filling their purses with more coins, by making more alluring promises in Arabic to the highly excited crowd of male admirers.

Ibrahim followed rather detached the developing spectacle, considering that if he had not attracted Suleiman's attention, he would have probably ended in a Galata tavern in a similar position. He couldn't help but feel compassion for these two unfortunate youngsters. On the contrary Sinan seemed insensitive to this kind of spectacle and started laughing with the dancers indecent tricks.

It was the kind of reaction the rest of the customers did not approve and gawked at him with anger as his laughter spoiled the still lingering seductive atmosphere.

The tavern keeper, very experienced with brawls, tried to change the mood by announcing an auction. The youngsters were his slaves and he was willing to rent his property to the highest bidder for the entire night.

The bidding started right away and the amounts were practically negligible compared to the Galata market offering similar entertainments. Soon enough the two youngsters didn't fail to notice the two well-dressed strangers and tried to invite their participation in the auction by rubbing their thighs on their legs, disappointing every other customer. However, Sinan had enough of this audacious demonstration and looked at Ibrahim who seemed mesmerized by the spectacle.

Sinan tried to get up, but Ibrahim decisively held him back and turning his attention to the tavern keeper, he made a generous offer for both boys doubling the amount offered by the local camel sellers till then.

He saw the slave owner's eyes glittering with greed, but the rest of the audience were very reluctant to accept the fact these two promiscuous youngsters would slip away so easily from their hands. Few of them got up and approached Ibrahim with threatening gestures holding aggressively the grips of their curved daggers. However, their aggression was immediately put at bay as

Sinan got up and uncovered his heavy yatagan sword under his luxurious caftan.

Now it had become clear from their clothes they were not of native stock but Ottomans. The threatening gestures turned at once to submissiveness, as their sharp knives were toys compared to the fighting capabilities of the heavy battle-tested weapon in the hands of a seasoned Janissary. No one would have any chance of survival coming to a sword battle armed only with a feeble knife. After all they were all merchants and caravan travelers, with hardly any experience in man-to-man combat; so, they all decided to return to their seats and the tavern keeper decided it was safe for him to announce that Ibrahim was the highest bidder.

The two youngsters immediately showed their delight for the outcome and rushed to kiss the hands of their new customers. Then they promptly asked permission to leave for a while to get dressed and pack too eager to follow their new masters for the rest of the night. Sinan paid the fee as soon as they had reappeared dressed in rather flashy clothes.

They went all out and the cool air of the desert helped Ibrahim's mind to assess the situation better. The tavern keeper had followed them offering his hospitality in case they decided to rest for the next few hours and use the two slaves for their pleasure; but this was not what Ibrahim had in mind and instead asked the keeper how much money he asked to give him full possession of the youngsters.

It was then that the two youngsters decided to intervene and explained with dignity that it was all a misunderstanding. They were not slaves to be bought or sold. They were free to go whenever they pleased already.

The tavern keeper was simply their employer who kept a portion from their earnings for his expenses and gracious hospitality. They were not obliged to do anything. It was just their pleasure and the way of life they had chosen following one of the oldest and most benevolent professions they knew. They were offering a taste of Paradise to every hard tested man who reached Imbaba after a long and hazardous trip through the Sahara desert.

Their previous experiences with Ottoman Pashas were quite different than the present one. They have exploited their entire menu and graciously offered them a generous bonus at the end. The clothes Ibrahim and Sinan wore were much more elaborate and expensive that meant they were of even higher status and cultivated taste.

Sinan's patience was finally exhausted, and he took command of the situation explaining sharply that their services were not needed. It was clearly an answer the youngsters took as an insult, and started making derogatory remarks about their preferences, claiming they could do much more than any whore in Cairo could accomplish, but to no avail.

Ibrahim and Sinan walked away, forcing them to go back inside the tavern where all their admirers welcomed them warmly happy that their lives had recovered their balance and purpose.

Now Ibrahim and Sinan could not restrict their laughter. It lasted until they had reached the Nile River. Faced with the acute problem of survival, every man chose a different path to complete his unique orbit from birth till death.

****

When they finally reached the governor's palace, Ibrahim decided he would rather be alone to digest better the lessons of this trip. The Janissary was a noble man ready to fight to protect him from any harm. He had proved Ibrahim could depend on him even in cases where he was outnumbered.

The plain truth was that this quick trip to Dahshur had been very tiresome. It was late at night past midnight and he felt exhausted. It was not so much the event at Imbaba. Much more responsible for his depression was the trip to the necropolises of Saqqara and Dahshur.

Ibrahim felt completely drained from any trace of hope. In the Egyptian deserts Death was present by your side in every step. There were indeed a thousand ways for any careless man to die besides the lack of water and food wandering at night in a desert full of spiders, scorpions, cobras and vipers lurking for victims in total darkness. It was exactly the same as inside the Seraglio.

There were all these eunuchs white or black that could be also conniving against him. Who could safely protect his life from a madman who would decide his life was worthless compared to the riches his family would receive, if he managed to exterminate a Grand Vizier and open this lucrative position to another man of influence. Sinan couldn't simply follow him everywhere.

Thank Allah he had been very wise to behave compliantly to every white eunuch's demand; but unfortunately black eunuchs were also slowly gaining power, as concubines claimed gradually more rights from the Sultan.

To change the theme of his depression and regain his confidence he recalled the night events in Imbaba. The similarity of these two youths with his life story was still puzzling him. He had been extremely lucky to meet Suleiman. This was all he could say right now. The attention of a single powerful man was enough to turn his life upside or downside.

Up to now he had almost convinced himself slavery was the reason that was enough to explain all his acts till then. Tonight two youngsters had proven that there could be other reasons too and slavery was just an excuse to submit willfully to the demands of a man. If this was so, then now that he was in Egypt he could easily escape from any obligation to his powerful patron.

It would be extremely easy to take with him all the gold he could carry and take the next camel caravan to Sudan. There with such a fortune he could live happily ever after in the arms of Nubian slaves. The arm of the Ottoman Sultan could not reach that far. It would be an easy task to get aboard a Portuguese vessel and reach India or Portugal free from all his past.

Even such a thought was enough to depress him. Over there he would be just a rich man. As an Ottoman he was the second man in power not only in the Ottoman Empire, but in the entire world. His wife was the Sultan's sister, and she was expecting his child. He even had a lusty black slave that would never say no to any suggestion. He had also a Janissary friend willing to die for his sake. There was nothing missing from his life anyway he looked at it.

He had to accept that even if Suleiman had not been in the Avret Bazaar, and he had passed in the arms of that repulsive fat man, he still had hopes of adjusting to life's oppressing realities. It was clearly impossible for any man to be absolutely free the moment he decided to abandon the desert and seek the company of his fellow men. Every man was destined to become the master of many men and obey few to survive within the pyramid of human authority.

As long as every year he managed to rise by one step, a man could remain an optimistic master even if he had not reached the very top. As a Grand Vizier he was one step under the peak, so it would be simply insane to quit the struggle and lose all his earnings till then voiding all his investments in disgraces.

These two youngsters seemed perfectly happy to please a bunch of camel sellers every night. This meant that happiness had nothing to do with how far a man had risen in the pyramid of the human authority. Happiness had more to do with whether your function in human society was in agreement with your personal dreams of what was your existence worth, a very subjective and vague assertion indeed.

Even the Sultan was under this unwritten law no matter what illusions he entertained about himself. The fact he was sending him letters urging him to return was a sign of weakness. Every letter he received from his wife the Princess showed that now that he was still in Egypt, Hurrem had gradually started dominating again his intimate friend. She had moved in the Seraglio sleeping almost each night in the Sultan's bed. Only after his return, life in the Seraglio might become normal again, but even this development was not a certainty.

The need he felt to belong somewhere was too strong a motive for a swift return. It was a clear sign he was a slave of at least all the human creatures involved that considered his presence an essential ingredient of their happiness.

He was sure Hafsa Sultan would also be glad to see him kneeling in front of her ready to obey her commands. Even Hurrem might seek his company occasionally, even though he was sure she would never admit it in public.

She was simply too liberated and conscious to write a letter acknowledging her weakness. Sooner or later, if he was ever again sleeping in the Sultan's Hasodabashi room, she would suddenly appear like an assassin to startle and overpower him. As a man he was capable to repulse her advances if he so willed, but it was practically impossible to find the will to refute such a mesmerizing proposition. She had become one more of the Sultan's caftanshe felt so good wearing too. In fact, since she was such a dominiaring factor in the Sultan's existence, it felt very enjoyable fighting out with her to determine who was in command.

Was he a weak character? Tonight Sinan had showed him the proper way to react to any dubious offer. If Sinan was not at his side he was certain he would not have denied the charms of these two youngsters. They were both good looking and perfectly capable in satisfying all his desires for the night much more than Selim's twin eunuchs.

Adopting Sinan's manly ways he had simply wasted his coins and degraded the image of the Ottomans in the eyes of several drunken Arabs and a deeply puzzled tavern keeper. If he wished to find more excuses he could rather easily, as any other man that at a certain point of his life had to make a decision, any decision. The best any man could hope in such a case would be the majority of humans would agree with his choice and cheer for him.

Nevertheless, fortunately or unfortunately, everything in life was not decided by the rule of the majority. There were cases when a single man's opinion could make all the difference in another man's life.

Sultan Selim was such a case. That night he could easily have him castrated, if he kept on denying him and it wouldn't make any difference, if the entire humanity was in favor of retaining his honor as a man. A few more objections and delaying tactics, and he were going to lose his manhood forever.

The trick was not if he was capable to find the right answer to a certain question, but to avoid questions all together. He had to be wise enough to guess what another human being had in mind and provide it, before the master was bored playing a losing game of wits.

He took a look outside his window to the Nile River that was flowing almost with imperceptibly speed his waters that no one knew where they came from. Going upstream was the obvious choice, but the river was so long, no one really cared to lose many months or possibly years of his life to answer such an uninteresting question. For all the Egyptians it was enough that enough water was available to turn an arid piece of desert into the Garden of Eden.

Perhaps one day if he ever was free from all his weaknesses he would try to go upstream and search for the spring of the Nile River. For the time being he was soon to travel downstream to Alexandria. Going downstream was always easier even though it meant that his trip would be short and he might reach the sea of nonexistence where the river's water would mix with the ocean and lose its dubious identity. Perhaps this was what Sinan meant in that humble mosque by becoming one with his creator. Sinan must have been very naïve back then. Death was another way to name the union with your creator. Why should anyone wish to rush his last moment?

He took his clothes off and looked at the mirror. His flesh was still full of life. He was not hallucinating. He was young and his well-shaped muscles could attract any woman or man into his embrace. This carnal attraction was a mystic force that gave him enough of optimism to look forward. As long as women desired him, the gates of immortality would be open for him. He only needed to be very careful what to do with the men intimately involved his life.

He decided that he had to dictate an urgent letter to his master assuring him that he was coming back soon and serve him. He was the Grand Vizier and he had to simply give an order for the scriber to appear, but he couldn't utter any demand as long as he was naked. He had to get dressed and regain his dignity in front of a servant. Was he even weaker than a humble servant?

****

Soon Antonio had appeared before him with all the equipment of his trade. His gestures were timid and relaxed indicating he was still sleeping when he was summoned. When the courtier had left, he asked Antonio to sit on the edge of the bed next to him. He simple had to test his theory about human characters. Was Sinan an exception or the rule? He had to know if the power of authority on human beings was sufficient to make them twist their morality.

He started his dictation of the letter to Sultan Suleiman Khan. Only with the sound of his name Antonio's hands started trembling. It was a good sign for what he had in mind.

The letter was initially formal explaining to his master briefly his most recent activities. Gradually it became friendlier inquiring about the Sultan's and his sons' health as well as his relationships with his wives and odalisques and Antonio's hand regained its stability. Antonio was now ready for the final stage of the entire pretense. Ibrahim started now being more romantically inclined, describing their first kiss and caress, and how excited he was when they were united. It was all mostly fictional but it worked and Antonio's trembling hand made a mess of the letter, as he went ahead and described several of the Persian miniatures about the forbidden pleasures with him and the Sultan as heroes.

He decided it was enough of an ordeal for poor Antonio and he had no reason to prolong it. He pulled the letter out of his hands and placed it on the flame of the candle. When it had turned into a feeble piece of ash, he left it in a flower pot. Then he sat once more on the bed and pulled Antonio to come closer. One kiss was enough to convince Antonio for his benevolent nature. This night he had to find out with what kind of pleasures Mother Nature rewarded a man when he succeeded in conquering another man to make it worthwhile.

****

In the morning when he woke up he realized he was alone. Nothing around him revealed what the previous night had happened. Only his memory and the bed had traces of Antonio's visit as his scent was still traceable by his sensitive nose. Soon an industrious servant would come and change the linen. All the servants by now would know what had happened. It was simply impossible for anyone to come and visit him without triggering a security alert. Then, this piece of valuable information would slip away possibly even beyond the walls of the Governor's Palace. He didn't mind. In the Orient such rumors acted in his favor. In Egypt the phenomenon of the pyramid of command was most plainly exemplified by the pyramids of Giza.

Was it a coincidence a pyramid had four sides as the number of women prescribed by the Prophet Mohamed as ideal? No one could tell. He didn't have four wives yet, but now he had a slave of his own to order him around.

352

The stern image of Sinan went through his mind. Why had he chosen Antonio rather than Sinan? Was he afraid of a stern denial, or was he repulsed by male virtue? He could only be certain of only one fact. Sinan would never act as Antonio. He was also too noble to participate in any pretense that put his commander in the position of Antonio. In Sinan's mind Grand Vizier Ibrahim had to be impeccable, otherwise he would never consider putting his life in danger for his sake.

A Grand Vizier needed devoted men like Sinan much more than submissive scribers like Antonio. By now he was old enough to realize that manliness was a superficial sensation that was created by the illusion you were capable to impose your will and have other men follow your commands.

It was an illusion because in reality what counted most was the final result. If by appearing for a while as weak as a woman, but in the end you had everything to gain by forcing your opponent's unconditional surrender, it was indeed a fair strategy for domination. Males sometimes behaved as recklessly as bulls. Whenever they saw a red flag they attacked. Romans as well as Ottomans used red banners in battles, but he was much more sophisticated than that. He would never attack a red flag because behind it the knife of a butcher may lurk.

Weakness had the ability to cause aggression and many times this was intentional as a show of power was what a weakness desired to become content. The spring was not responsible for a brook's choice of paths. Responsible was the ground slope. By pretending he was weak he had triggered both Selim's and his son's aggression. It was the way he had achieved his present post, while Antonio was just a scriber. Antonio didn't even have a wife to grow sons in her womb for his sake.

He could now see more clearly what Antonio's crucial mistake had been. He was simply too accommodating raising no demands. Raising demands after the conquest was a feat very few Greeks had achieved after the Ottoman conquest. He felt now proud for his achievements. Perhaps, there was nothing truly wrong with slavery. The mistake was caused by the slave.

Inside all the holy books a lot of wisdom was available provided one was capable of reading between the lines. The Christian command to love each other was so vague it allowed for many interpretations. The most obvious one was that now that he had become intimately connected with Antonio, he would be very reluctant to intentionally harm him. Love between males curbed male aggression. Retreating was a good way to exhaust your opponent and make him believe his victory and domination was a done deal.

Here in Egypt life had a different quality and possibly the River Nile, this mysterious god was responsible for this evolution. He was a good provider and people had very little work to produce to satisfy their hunger. This lack of pressure made them calm and content. If this was the result of their belief that sooner or later everything was going to be all right, may have been the answer. If there were nations of conquers and slaves, the Egyptians were undoubtedly the mythic Lotus-Eaters. They were happy to know they would be alive to see the sun tomorrow morning.

If he had the blood of a slave in his veins, what were the chances his children would live free? Their only chance was they would have some of Selim's bloods in their veins. Perhaps this was the instinctive attraction of Hatidge on his flesh. He wished she was here, but princesses never followed their husbands to their dangerous missions. A Pasha was expendable the daughter of a Sultan was not. If she was here, he would never start an affair with a commoner. Anyway, he didn't feel any regrets for any relation with a man. Hatidge was a woman and quite incapable to offer him a man-to-man experience in the same way he was unqualified to play the role of a woman in a woman-to-woman experience. He was simply unable to offer her the tenderness she deserved. Basmi was clearly more than eager and able to carry out this task.

His wild confused thoughts were interrupted by a hard knock on is door. A slave was carrying an urgent message from the Sultan and had arrived by land. It was a sealed message only his eyes should see, as the messenger explained.

The news about the Janissary revolt was the last Ibrahim expected. He quickly run through the words and only when he arrived at the last line his heart stopped pumping. His family was safe even though outside the Seraglio Walls his was the only palace they had tried to storm, but failed. Sinan's construction had withstood the bold assault.

It was clear now that his days in Egypt were numbered. Ulysses had to leave behind the shores of the Lotus Eaters along with as many of the doubts of his youth he could keep alive in his memory. Since the day the pirates had captured him, he had never been sorry on the eve of his departures; however, now an unexplained sadness had slipped into his heart. He remembered the words of the old Copt about the water of the Nile being cursed and whoever drinks it he can never be happy again until his return. Something was telling him he was destined to see the pyramids never again.

Departing, he didn't fail to say good bye to Antonio, leaving behind few caftans and jewels as presents for his services and his devotion. He had feelings of guilt. He had started feeling and behaving like a Sultan. The young man seemed desperate and was begging to take him as a slave to Constantinople. This was quite impossible. His life was already complicated enough, even though he was not fully responsible for this Gordian Knot. The only thing he could now say to limit the pain was that with the first chance he got, he would be back. It was the only way for Antonio to let him go.

"Don't forget me!" he begged profoundly moved and their similarities took metaphysical dimensions. Finally, everything in this world was nothing but brief unrelated in time or in space episodes that kept reoccurring time and time again with minute differences. No doubt Allah was by now too bored to act and change something significant. Everything was old under the sun and especially in Egypt this motto was depressingly valid. His life had started completing one of its cycles, and now he was mature enough to realize that the era of his innocence had ended without him realizing it.

****

The return trip from Cairo to Istanbul lasted the better part of two months. Ibrahim and Sinan had too many things to do and too many issues to attend to. They passed through Jerusalem and Damascus and they found the walls had to be repaired and modernized; so at least Sinan had to come back. Also the tax collection system had to be improved because there were many complaints for injustices. Suleiman and Ibrahim had agreed that Ottoman success was based on law, a multiple of public works, and lower taxes. If the people were happy with the government, they would never risk a rebellion against such a powerful army Sultan Selim had organized; on the contrary they would have no objection to enlist in this army, as the rewards for bravery and devotions were tempting. Ibrahim was the best example of such a man.

Finally, this tiresome trip ended too and Ibrahim reaching Üsküdar discerned in the distance Agia Sophia's dome and the tower of Galata. He was home at last and soon he would be in his palace in the arms of Hatidge and her slave Basmi. He was feeling content with his accomplishments and this tranquility was a feeling he had never experienced before. Under tension he was at his best, and if his stress was diminishing, in the past he would try to raise its level. It was the only explanation he could find for his various escapades within the Harem.

Of course, he was not the only daring one. Most harem women were literally bored to death, and sought adventures at every opportunity. There were too many excuses for a woman to start a clandestine affair, and now he was wise enough to know a woman's motives. They just couldn't spend an entire life waiting for a Sultan's invitation, and they had every right to conspire against this unnatural male monopoly.

At the beginning, conquering a dashing woman had been very exciting; but soon after his marriage he started feeling he was not made to be just a stallion harem mares used to break out of the stable monotony. Perhaps, having a Princess as his wife had made most other women appear inferior. Perhaps this was the reason he was behaving now exceedingly greedy by hopping to add and few men into his menu for a change.

He had no complains with his new office. His power had multiplied; his days were full and his nights also. What was most worrisome though was this feeling of content that slowly crept into his mind. Was it a sign his hunger for life was becoming saturated that after a while nothing was truly original, but simply a rerun of an older story with new heroes?

The ancient Greeks were wise enough to realize that what remained eternal as long as human beings were alive were their steady character trades, like being a father, a mother, their lust, their trend to try to cheat or make material gains, to be industrious and productive, but most of all to fight for supremacy.

Nevertheless, when the time came to realize that there was nothing truly new under the sun, perhaps this was the sign that youth was coming to an end, and from then on he was going to be condemned with enjoying the various subtle shades of life that distinguished a new cycle from the past ones, so that he would be willing to open his eyes every morning and have courage to get out of bed and start working.

****

His first mission as soon as he stepped on the Golden Horn wharf was to inform the Sultan for his arrival and he was at his disposal along with twenty mules load with gold from the taxes he had collected during his trip from Cairo to the Eternal City that fulfilled his obligations.

Then, he went straight to his palace to take care of his other domestic priorities. His servants were waiting for him at the entrance with a long smile, and he assured them that he was going to reward them handsomely for the brave defense of his household they put on during the Janissary rebellion; but he had to see first his wife.

He went up the stairs and entered her bedroom. A big surprise was waiting for him. His wife was nursing a child, while Basmi was assisting in performing her duties. His wife did not stop her effort, but just smiled to show her pleasure for seeing him. It was apparent she had been informed of his homecoming spoiling his surprise entrance. On the other hand, he had no idea she had a child.

"How do you like your daughter?" she asked him when she was finished, and he found no good reason to complain for her silence.

Having a child was one of his dreams all along. Now all his expensive presents for his wife seemed unworthy even to mention. He was a father and that was enough to extinguish all his previous worries of boredom. Life was exciting once more.

He approached her with almost religious piety. She was a true picture of Madonna nursing the Holy Child and that made him the Creator. At last he had accomplished creating something truly unique in his life.

He took his daughter in his hands and looked at her face. She had the dark eyes of his mother, and her snow white skin. He felt that now he was closer to true happiness than ever before. Whatever was going to happen from then on his happiness could never reach a higher point. He was as happy as Ulysses when he saw in the distance the mountains of Ithaca. Now his only concern was whether he would also be able to reach the end of his journeys.

****

The return of the Grand Vizier to the capital of the Empire put again the state machine to work with a faster pace. Now the Sultan was not alone addressing every problem. He had Ibrahim as his right hand to monitor closely the preparations for the next military campaign.

The Janissary rebellion had sent a message that was well received by the leadership of the state. The army should not remain idle for a long time, because then the discipline was lost and the Janissaries turned their aggression against the citizens. Nobody knew whether this trend was the result of a religious fanaticism, or simply the mutiny started each time the money they had acquired from their last sack had been exhausted. However, there was many times that first to rebel were the dervishes from the Bektash religious order. Fortunately, in this order Sinan belonged too, who was keeping Ibrahim always updated to the trends prevailing in the main body of the dervishes. His absence to Egypt was possibly one of the reasons for the Sultan to be taken by surprise.

Ibrahim's reunion with Suleiman was exceptionally heartily. They had many months to get together and there were many issues to be resolved. The most important was the Janissary rebellion, and its significance became more apparent when Suleiman revealed all the details about their attack on his palace. This type on incidences should never be repeated.

For Ibrahim the personal bravery Suleiman had demonstrated was a pleasant surprise. The last few years Suleiman had showed unusual timidity against Hurrem. In her case he didn't have to draw his sword and shed her blood. It was more than enough to strike the floor with his boot like his father Selim to put everyone's life around him in order; but Selim Khan was unique and unrepeatable.

When the Sultan completed all he had to say, Ibrahim started his narration:

"In Egypt long time ago there were Emperors like you called Pharaohs. They were generals, high priests and ultimate judges like you too. When the river Nile flooded and their fields were covered with water and mud the people didn't have anything to do, so the wise Pharaoh ordered them to build mountains of stone called pyramids during their free time to avoid rebellions for his glory.

The people are the base and you are the peak. The people have a duty to make the highest pyramid and put you on the top. This is the secret meaning of the Egyptian pyramids. The Egyptian people were happy only as long as they managed to build a bigger pyramid during their generation than all the other pyramids existing before them. Eventually, they failed in this task, became disappointed and stopped building pyramids all together. Then Egypt fell into decline, and was conquered by the Persians, the Greeks, the Romans, the Arabs and now the Ottomans."

Ibrahim stopped for a moment his narration and then continued with his final conclusion.

"People are happy only when they feel that tomorrow will be better than yesterday, and a wise Emperor's duty is to make sure this belief is strong.

The Janissary rebellion came about because your army stayed inactive for too long. The same could easily happen with your people when this flock feels you are not taking good care of his needs, or tax them too heavily for your own sake. However, when they feel they serve the most glorious sovereign they will be as obedient as bees that look after their queen.

When there is war, you should lead them into victories, and when there is peace you should try to make their lives majestic, as your glory reflects magnificence on their life. Great leader is the one who can dream and inspire his people to share the same dreams.

Everything in this universe goes through a process of continuous creation and destruction. Your army should become the instrument of destruction of your enemies, while your people the instrument of creation of a new order with you at the top. In every beehive there can be only one queen, so in your Seraglio you should be the one and only Sultan.

You should never forget that your mighty father made you the Shadow of Allah, so you become the intermediate between Allah and your flock. Your decisions are faultless and Allah's Law should be interpreted and spoken by your tongue through your lips."

Suleiman didn't have anything more to add and as usual shook his head in agreement. He drew a long draught from his nargileh amber mouthpiece, and for a while he appeared lost in his thoughts. He knew his slave was right, but it was not always easy to achieve perfection even for a mighty Sultan. He knew well that even his mighty father was not perfect. He had his weaknesses and his weakness for eunuchs was one of them. He had no similar weaknesses, but the truth was that women were his weakness. Only Allah was perfect.

Ibrahim's suggestion that the Quran had to be explained by him had merits. The power of the clergy and the dervishes had to be reduced; but to achieve it he had to start a new even more ambitious war to prove that his dreams were even more glorious than what a mufti could ever suggest. It was the only way he could be accepted as the true law giver of his empire. Now he was ready to utter his decision.

"Suleiman Khan the Son of Selim Khan forever victorious had decided to make you Serasker of the Ottoman Empire as a just tribute for your wisdom and everything you have contributed to the glory and prosperity of the House of Osman."

****

The very next day Ibrahim's new appointment had been posted. The firman with all the elaboration and magnificent decorations appropriate for such an office very eloquently described his new powers:

"I command Ibrahim Pasha Grand Vizier to become my Serasker on all my dominions. All my Viziers, Beylerbeys, Judges, Sheiks, Bey, Pashas of my victorious Spahis, and Janissaries, all my high and lower state officials, all my subjects, rich or poor, free or slaves, will obey him as Grand Vizier and Serasker and will accept whatever he believes and will do what he commands as if it was coming from my mouth like a rain of pearls. Everyone will accept his suggestions and will omit none. He will have the right to choose everyone he

considers fit for every official post from Beylerbey to the most insignificant according to his balanced judgment and his shrill intellect. Whenever the conditions demand for my armed forces to intervene, the Serasker will be the only commander, and no one should dare to disobey his commands. And if few slaves choose to resist any command of my Grand Vizier and Serasker or dare to repress my faithful subjects contrary to my high wishes, Allah forbid, whoever and how many they are, they will submit to the just punishment their offense demands."

****

The concentration of all the power in the hands of Ibrahim had the advantage that from now on the Sultan would invest less time to govern the Empire. Even the Sultan's presence in the Divan was superfluous as even in the past all decisions were following closely Ibrahim's suggestions.

When Hurrem asked him what was the true reason for this new even higher appointment, Suleiman had prepared a logical answer. Now he had all the time in the world to spend with her and his children, whereas Ibrahim's day would be full of worries.

Ibrahim's first decree as a Grand Vizier at the Divan was to announce the new policies. It was a session that was to be different than any other.

"From now on my Sultan's slaves will not be divided to faithful or infidel or even heretic, but will only be distinguished into those who serve their Lord the Sultan, and to the rebels who disobey the laws of the Shadow of Allah. The first can expect prosperity while the second will expect a severe punishment from His hand. He is our All-Wise and powerful Sultan, Padisah and Islam's Caliph and only He knows what is good for the faith and his subjects in total agreement with the word of the Holy Quran."

With this simple order the Sultan put an end to the quarrels and the discrepancies of the existing legislation and gave equal rights to every Ottoman citizen independently to his religion, race, color or language.

However, this change went against the authority of the Muslim clergy that judged complaints and always gave right or believed the excuses of Muslims against all other religions. Now every attempt to counter Sultan's decisions could be considered as a conspiracy to topple the House of Osman and a sacrilege against Allah. It was one more very shrewd move of Pargali Ibrahim to make sure his main concern was how to bolster the Sultanic authority. It was a necessary precaution against any attempt to challenge Suleiman's commands while they would be both far away from the Eternal City fighting the sworn enemies of Ottoman State, the Hungarians.

No one dared to openly say his objections, but many had long conversations in private quarters as far away as possible from the Sultan's spies. Nevertheless, privately or in public no objection carried any weight any longer. As long as the war was going on and the armies were victorious no one could challenge Ibrahim's authority.

Gradually, the results became apparent to all concerned. The severe punishments prescribed by the Islamic Law were rare and typical sentences like floggings, amputations or even executions were replaced by light or heavy fines that improved the empire's finances. Now even the senseless lashing of animals was reduced.

Another welcomed measure was the reduction of loan interests, while the land properties of the rich were also reduced and the confiscated properties were distributed to poor and hardworking farmers. Increased import tariffs were imposed to protect the native industry and all the revenues were used for public works, new roads, bridges, hospitals, schools and libraries. It was not a strange phenomenon to see many Hungarians burn their homes and farms and cross the borders of the Ottoman Empire to start a better life. Similar were the choices of many citizens of Peloponnesus who abandoned their Venetian highly taxing overlords to move to Ottoman villages.

In the eve of the Hungary invasion, Europe had plenty to fear and envy too.

End of Second Volume

References

Including references in a novel is an unusual choice; however, in the case of historic novels it is a prerequisite, as it is a common phenomenon many facts to be twisted according to national aspirations and petty racial jealousies.

1. "Ibrahim Pasha, Grand Vizier of Suleiman the Magnificent," Hester Donaldson Jenkins, Columbia University, Longman, 1911.
2. "Suleiman the Magnificent and His Age," Metin Kunt, Christine Woodhead, Longman, 1955.
3. "Suleiman the Magnificent 1520-1566," Roger B. Merriman, Harvard University Press, 1944.
4. "Suleiman the Magnificent, Sultan of the East," Harold Lamb, Doubleday & Company Inc., 1951.
5. "Suleiman the Magnificent," J. M. Rogers and R. M. Ward, British Museum Pubs, 1988.
6. "Dawn of the Beloved," Louis Gardel, The French Millennium Library, 2003.
7. "The Ottoman Empire 1700-1922," Donald Quataert, Cambridge Univ. Press, 2000.
8. "Sinan," Arthur Stratton, Charles Scribner's Sons, 1972.
9. "The Essential Rumi," Coleman Barks, Castle Books, 1997.
10. "Sufism," James Fadiman and Robert Frager, Castle Books, 1997.
11. "The Qur'an" Translation by M.H. Shahir, Tahrike Tarsile Qur'an Inc., 2001.
12. "Inside the Seraglio," John Freely, Penguin Books, 1999.
13. "The Ottoman Centuries," Lord Kinross, Morrow Quill Paperbacks, 1977.
14. "The Decline and Fall of the Roman Empire," Edward Gibbon, Wordsworth, 1998
15. "Constantinople," Philip Mansel, Penguin Books, 1995.
16. "Istanbul, the Imperial City," John Freely, Penguin Books, 1998.
17. "Imperial Istanbul," Jane Taylor, I. B. Tauris, 1998.
18. "Lords of the Horizon," John Goodwin, Vintage, 1998.
19. http://en.wikipedia.org/wiki/Grand_Bazaar,_Istanbul
20. http://en.wikipedia.org/wiki/Spice_Bazaar,_Istanbul
21. http://en.wikipedia.org/wiki/Tughra
22. http://en.wikipedia.org/wiki/Assassins
23. http://en.wikipedia.org/wiki/Bayezid_I
24. http://en.wikipedia.org/wiki/Selim_I
25. http://en.wikipedia.org/wiki/Suleiman_the_Magnificent
26. http://en.wikipedia.org/wiki/Church_of_the_Holy_Apostles
27. http://en.wikipedia.org/wiki/Hagia_Sophia
28. http://en.wikipedia.org/wiki/Cilician_Gates
29. http://en.wikipedia.org/wiki/Skanderbeg
30. http://en.wikipedia.org/wiki/Pargali_Ibrahim_Pasha
31. http://en.wikipedia.org/wiki/Selamlik

32. http://en.wikipedia.org/wiki/Roxelana
33. http://en.wikipedia.org/wiki/Ayşe_Hafsa_Sultan
34. http://en.wikipedia.org/wiki/Mimar_Sinan
35. http://en.wikipedia.org/wiki/Mahidevran
36. https://en.wikipedia.org/wiki/List_of_Ottoman_Grand_Viziers

A final author's note

A reliable historian must rely on hard historical data; otherwise his writings would not be taken seriously by academic historians. Pargali Ibrahim's existing biographies are undoubtedly short and puzzling, almost as short, puzzling and vague as the historic portraits of the legal wives of Ottoman Sultans of noble or not so noble lineage.

Erasing or distorting the existing data for the virtues or faults of political figures or national figures by various temporary or subsequent historians has been a common practice through the centuries that continues today in the form of falsified or censored news. It is also certain that it will continue in the future despite the greater security and reliability of the presently available storage media, while in the past even the entire existence or deeds of a Pharaoh like Tutankhamen could be erased or usurped by simply chiseling out few hieroglyphics. If today anyone can take a high definition digital picture or video clip of a celebrity, unfortunately or fortunately during the Suleiman era similar capabilities were unimaginable.

In the case of Ibrahim, his intimate relationship with Suleiman Khan is for many historians a sensitive subject or even a taboo. However, a modern novel writer's imagination is not limited by such a professional code of ethics; so, conceivably a novel can contain imaginary character trends of the heroes or the villains.

Editing the present novel several times before publication, the author was obliged to emphasize the role of few eunuch slave heroes, especially when after reading several books, he became aware of the existence of Sinan Hadim Pasha, one of the several Grand Viziers that served under Selim the Grim, as well as two eunuch personal servants of that formidable Sultan.

The role of eunuchs in the actual historic events and their personal relationships behind closed doors with the Sultans and the concubines of a Sultan's harem is another taboo for ordinary historians. Since this novel tries to illuminate hidden details of the heroes' characters, the author felt obliged to utilize all the existing indications from the past and present as well as his "common" logic. Of course, his common logic may be quite different than the one in Suleiman's era.

For instance, not many people consider these days the option of buying slaves white or colored to serve their needs, and colored people are not castrated to preserve the decency of white men and women residing in the same space.

This was not the case in Suleiman's era, and the following old Ottoman miniature depicting the interior of Ibrahim's Palace is very illuminating of the existing trends of the extremely rich of that era employing Nubian slaves.

In the last miniature the public spaces in the interior of the Topkapi Seraglio in Suleiman's era is depicted, where another artist chose to eliminate entirely all color servants, even the highest official, the Chief Black Eunuch, preferring to include several White Eunuchs present in the depicted ceremonies, as it is also the case in the miniature at the beginning of Chapter 6.

Printed in Great Britain
by Amazon

26631626R00209